SWEPT BY THE TIDE

She stared blankly at him for a moment, then exhaled a long, tortured sigh as if he had brought up all the world's ills. "I'm not married because I don't want to be." She spoke proudly, then paused. "Marriage isn't what it's cracked up to be."

"Is that so?" Obviously, Miss Emily Morgan hadn't found the right man. Darian smiled and rode on ahead, feeling comfortable. "Marriage isn't to be entered into lightly, that is true." He glanced back to see her reaction, but her expression was veiled, and seemed more sorrowful than he expected. "I came close to matrimony myself once, but the arrangement ended before it could be transacted."

She eyed him doubtfully. "'Transacted?' How romantic!"

"You may be right. I was not romantic enough to enter into a sacred union, so it is best not to have undertaken the adventure."

Emily frowned, but she didn't look at him again. "Romance, Captain, is an illusion, and it's the last thing you should count on when choosing someone to wed."

Darian stopped his horse and waited for her to catch up. "But what better way than to follow your heart, to be swept up in its most passionate currents?"

She rolled her eyes and snorted. "The only thing those 'passionate currents' will get you is solitude."

BLUE-EYED BANDIT

STOBIE PIEL

LOVE SPELL BOOKS NEW YORK CITY

*To two wonderful friends who have believed in me
and supported me, Chris Keeslar and Tim DeYoung.
Thank you for making Dorchester such a special
home for my books and for me.*

A LOVE SPELL BOOK®

August 2000

Published by

Dorchester Publishing Co., Inc.
276 Fifth Avenue
New York, NY 10001

ISBN 0-505-52394-9

BLUE-EYED BANDIT

Prologue

" *'Captain Darian Woodward, the Civil War hero known for terrorizing the Southwest under the alias of the Blue-eyed Bandit, was hanged for treason on May twenty-first 1870, restoring order under the command of the renowned General Clement Davis.'* "

Emily Morgan made a wide berth around the paperback romance section of her store—avoiding that section had become ritual to her, but the muffled voices from the back room attracted her attention. A tall dark man read the solemn words to his extremely pregnant wife, then paused as if it had been his father's obituary.

She shouldn't be listening—as the bookshop owner, she should have directed her strange customers to the "rare and used" section and left them in peace. But they

9

were so odd. Odd and beautiful. The husband was Native American, with long black hair, a beaded earring, and the best body she'd ever seen. His looks alone were worth spying on. His wife had pale blond hair tied up in an off-center bun. When the two entered Emily's shop, the woman's pretty face had been knit in a worried expression as if a close relative lay on death's door.

Emily felt sure the wife was crying now, as if the words read about a long-dead outlaw were spoken about her brother. She heard a muffled sob, followed by soft words from the husband.

"It can't be true." The woman sniffed. "Hanged. Adrian, he can't be hanged. He's so young." Young? Weren't they reading about a man who had died soon after the Civil War ended? And why did she speak of him in the present tense?

A romantic woman, obviously. As Emily herself had been, years ago. The woman looked about Emily's age— it seemed romantic ideals hadn't been driven out of her yet. Maybe, for some women luckier than Emily, those romantic dreams didn't fade.

Emily tiptoed back, seized her small stepladder, and inched her way up, then peered through her selection of children's books into the "rare historical works" section. *Maya the Bee* was a large book, and got in her way. She edged it gently aside to get a better look at the couple. The husband had his arm wrapped around his wife's shoulder. She was crying. Pregnant women can be emotionally overwrought, true, but the husband himself appeared devastated by the passage they'd read.

They were grief-stricken about a desperado with blue eyes who had terrorized Tucson over a hundred years ago. And not very well, either, or Emily would have heard of him—certainly, a movie would have been made.

"It's over now, Cora. Captain Woodward has been dead for over a hundred and thirty years."

The wife, Cora, dried her eyes, but more tears came. "I encouraged him to mutiny. If not for us, he would have stayed what he was before. . . ."

Adrian shook his head and frowned. "An uptight, Victorian yuppie. At least he died a man." Cora sputtered as if this logic wasn't enough by a long stretch.

Emily took another step to the top rung. Mutiny? She furrowed her brow tight. Somehow, she'd misunderstood what they were reading. Maybe it was all caused by the heat—her air-conditioning unit had been unreliable lately, leaving her with only a fan in 98-degree heat.

Cora maneuvered her round body back and forth between the Tucson history section and Emily's collection of antique maps. She folded her hands on her stomach. By the look of her, her child's due date had to be in days. "I cannot believe that General Davis is considered a hero. That man had no scruples. I am sure he was behind that evil gunfighter Tradman's actions. . . . And he wanted to hang you, too."

Adrian stood motionless, watching his wife pace. His dark face formed an even darker glower. "Recorded history doesn't appear to be terribly accurate."

Emily listened in disbelief. They spoke in low voices, so she doubted they were sent to her as a joke. And there was no doubting the authenticity of their emotions—which meant they were both crazy. Emily eyed Cora's round stomach. This didn't bode well for their unborn child's future.

Cora and Adrian fell silent. Cora rested her head on Adrian's shoulder as he stroked her hair. Emily watched them, and a deep longing rose in her heart. To feel loved, protected, by a man who shared her dreams, her heart. . . . Of course, Cora appeared to be a romantic woman, able to touch a man's heart, and hold it. Though Emily had once believed that she, too, was capable of inspiring love, she had learned—or been taught—that it wasn't so.

Maybe Cora had found the secret, after all—find a man as crazy as you are.

There is no point in wanting what you can't have. Emily wasn't a romantic woman, but she was bright and inquisitive, and Cora's bizarre claims interested her. She leaned closer.

Cora drew back and looked at her husband. Her face twisted to one side as if she were scheming. The look on Adrian's face indicated he recognized the expression, and feared it.

"Cora. . . ."

"We have to do something. We owe that to Captain Woodward. If not for him, we'd be—heaven knows where. You'd be dead, your people would have been massacred, and I would be lost in time without you."

"What we do in the past might alter the future."

"Nothing happened because of our trip, Adrian."

He hesitated. "That was us, Cora. We're sane, normal people. Darian Woodward is another matter entirely."

Emily's skin felt suddenly cold. There was something innately terrifying about eavesdropping on crazy people. She started to ease back, but the ladder creaked, and she held herself motionless. *Maya the Bee* slipped to one side, and she caught it before it could fall to the floor.

Cora stood up, closed the book, and looked her nervous husband straight in the eye. "We have to go back and save him."

Adrian clasped her shoulders, "Cora, we barely escaped the past with our lives. You are not going back, not when you carry our child inside you." He kissed her forehead, and from her slumped shoulders, Emily knew Cora had conceded.

Adrian closed his eyes and drew a deep breath. "The

captain's fate is my doing—I will go back and set it right."

"Not without me, you won't! Adrian. . . ." True fear resonated in Cora's voice and she clasped his arm. "They wanted to kill you. They will kill you. Your father said so. You'll end up in this book right beside Darian."

Darian. They spoke the desperado's name with love. Why, Emily couldn't imagine. If he had been a bandit, his real goal must have been money, and engrandizing his own ego. Not a very romantic motivation.

Cora nestled into her husband's arms, protected and loved. Seeing them, Emily realized how truly alone she was, how much her heart had dreamed of loving this way, and how empty it had been as those dreams drifted from her grasp. She closed her eyes and saw herself, standing alone at the door of her first apartment, waiting for a man who would never return. She remembered opening an attorney's letter and reading formal words— the exact moment when she realized she had been a fool, that she never would be truly lovable, truly loved. . . .

"There has to be another way." Cora sniffed, brushing away tears. "If you can't go back, and I can't . . . we'll just have to find someone else to do it instead."

Adrian didn't appear hopeful, and Emily could see why. "That won't be easy, Cora. Who would we ask?"

"My friend Jenny? She's adventurous."

"And she just got engaged to Davis Sprague, in case you've forgotten. I don't think that stuffed-shirt account- ant would look too favorably on his fiancée trekking back in time."

"I suppose they wouldn't believe us."

"There is that little problem, too."

Emily closed her eyes. They were planning to talk someone into going back in time! Yes, there might be a bit of difficulty finding someone crazy enough to take them up on *that* offer.

Cora tapped her lip thoughtfully. "It would have to be someone very brave, someone who knows history enough to fit in."

Adrian's brow angled. "Someone with a damned good imagination."

Cora ran her fingers idly along the spine of the antique books. "It's so unfair. Darian Woodward was the kindest man I've ever known. This book has to be wrong. I can't imagine him terrorizing Tucson."

Adrian chuckled. "I can imagine him lecturing the inhabitants until they turned blue and died of boredom, but not terrorizing, no."

"He was such a good man—handsome, and brave, and so noble. I just can't believe he could have met such a bitter ending."

Handsome, brave. Noble. Emily sighed, too. No, they don't make men like that anymore. She thought of Ian, her first and only lover. She had believed in him utterly—but she had been so young, and so trusting. She hadn't been able to see beyond his handsome face and his boyish charm. There had to be more in a man than sweet words and a pretty face.

Darian Woodward sounded noble—not a man likely to pretend to love a woman, share deepest secrets, then abandon her without a trace. Emily caught herself. *I have to stop comparing every man, even long-dead ones, to Ian Hallowell.* He was gone, and she would never see him again. She had trusted him with everything.

She would never trust anyone that way again.

Cora picked up the history book and read it quietly again. She closed her eyes as if in prayer, and tears dripped to her cheeks. "Darian saw so much pain during the war, he had lost so much. He was so young. He hadn't *lived.*"

Emily's heart moved at Cora's description. It was touching, fiction or not. A brave, young soldier, noble and strong. . . . Emily clamped her hand to her forehead—this strange couple must be the two most talented actors that ever lived. She was listening to their story as if it was fact, not the fiction she knew it was. Maybe they were authors working out a plot. How they would laugh if they knew she overheard them, and absorbed their emotions as her own!

Adrian took the book and set it aside. "I hope he wasn't still a virgin when they hanged him."

Noble, brave, and . . . *a virgin*? The ladder toppled back, then forward. Emily braced herself on the bookcase. It crashed. She crashed, too, facedown at Cora and Adrian's feet. She peeked up. "He was a virgin?"

They both nodded, eyebrows tilted in equal surprise. Neither spoke. Emily cleared her throat, adjusted her long braid back over her shoulder, then sat up. "I'm sorry—I didn't mean to eavesdrop. . . ." Her face warmed—it was so obvious that she had been eavesdropping in the worst way.

Cora and Adrian looked at each other. An eager smile formed on Cora's lips. Adrian reached for Emily's hand and helped her up. "You're the owner of this shop, aren't you?"

Emily tried to regain her poise, and felt foolish. "I'm Emily Morgan, yes." She looked around at the scattered books. "I've worked hard to build this place up. I have the best collection of children's books in Tucson, and the local history section is the finest in Arizona."

Cora moved to her side and touched her arm. She seemed eager. "We know—that's why we came here. We live in Scottsdale, you see, and we've been trying to find out what happened to some. . . ." She eyed her husband.

Adrian hesitated, then shrugged. "Old friends."

Emily looked between them. "I thought I must have misunderstood. . . ."

Cora seized Emily's arm and helped her from the pile of books. She glanced hopefully at Adrian. "What do you think? Would she work?"

Emily shook her head violently. "No. No, I would not 'work.' Don't even *think* it!"

Adrian hesitated, assessing her with a critical eye. "Ever done any adventure training?"

Emily bit her lip. She felt as if she were being tested, with a poor likelihood of passing the exam. "Not exactly. But I was born in Arizona. I know my way around."

"Mountain climbing?"

"No. . . . I've hiked."

Adrian looked disapproving. Emily hated the sense of failure, the feeling she didn't quite measure up in some way. She'd felt that way for years, but for these two crazy people to judge her. . . . "I know martial arts!"

He appeared even more dubious as he assessed her. "You're kidding?"

Emily frowned. "Look, I might not exactly be tall or big-boned, but neither was Bruce Lee!"

His dark brow arched. "What form of martial arts did you study?"

She hesitated, not remembering the exact term. She'd only taken a few lessons and flubbed rather badly in a very short time. "It was kind of . . . kickboxing."

"Ah. What belt were you?"

She closed her eyes. "Yellow."

Adrian repressed a smile and Cora offered a commiserating sigh. "Adrian is a black belt, in several forms. He tried to teach me, but I didn't do it very well. I admire you for trying."

Emily decided she liked Cora, who seemed to believe in her abilities despite any actual evidence of prowess.

Adrian, however, didn't appear convinced. "Can you ride?"

"Yes." She hesitated, struggling with her conscience.

"You know, more or less. I've been on a horse before."

Cora smiled as if this were proof enough, but Adrian remained dubious. "You look kind of . . . delicate."

Emily's pride soared, flying miles above her reason. She attempted to stand straighter than usual, in an effort to look taller. "I am not delicate." She fumed at the suggestion of any fragility. "There's nothing I can't do if I put my mind to it."

A slow smile grew on Adrian's face. "Is that so?"

"Yes, it is. I've lived on my own for years now. I put myself through college. I took over this shop when my grandmother died, and it's very successful." *What am I saying?*

Adrian's smile widened. "I'm not sure how running a bookshop will help you get along in the past, but I suppose Cora and I weren't any better prepared." Emily gaped in horror. *Dear God! He thinks I've agreed to this mad scheme!* "We'll fill you in on what you'll need to know, tell you about the people you'll most likely meet. You'll have no trouble."

Cora touched Emily lightly on the arm. "You have no reason to trust us, I know, but you might be just the person to help. Fate has brought us together."

Trust was a dangerous thing. She'd learned that the hard way. In any case, she could do better than trusting two people who believed they knew a man who had died a hundred and thirty years ago.

Adrian put his arm around Emily's shoulders. She tensed, distrusting whatever insane plan he had in mind for her. "Let me explain . . ." He paused. "No, that would take days. I'll sum up. I was born in the past, in the late 1800s. Using a sacred whirlwind known only to my people, my father sent me forward in time during a famine, and I grew up in this time period, where I met Cora, and we fell in love. She dumped me"—the man gave his wife an amused look—"and after a few years

17

apart, the whirlwind caught us while we were skydiving and sent us back to the past together."

Adrian paused for a breath, and Cora wrapped her arm around Emily's other shoulder. "It's a little hard to believe, I know."

Emily glared. "A little?"

Cora seemed to sense Emily's rising anxiety—and her sudden impulse to bolt for the door. "It's simple, really. When we were in the past, we met Adrian's father, Adrian got into trouble with the U.S. Cavalry, and Captain Woodward came to our aid. He stopped his commander, a pompous, evil man named Clement Davis, from annihilating Adrian's people, and then Darian mutinied. Because of his connection to us, it appears he was executed. Adrian didn't really belong in the past, even if he was born there, so we came back here. But we can't leave the captain in the past to suffer for something we did. Darian never believed our story, but he's a good man. Maybe he'll listen to you."

Emily shook her head, trying to block the strange lure of their words. "Why me?"

Cora patted her shoulder fondly. "I think you're the perfect person."

"Why?"

Cora glanced at Adrian, who looked uncomfortable. "Well, all things happen for a reason. There must be one why you were here, eavesdropping on us. . . ."

Adrian's logic seemed to need support from Cora. "Don't worry. I didn't think I could do it, either, but it all turned out fine. We'll just pack you a few necessities, a dress suitable for the time period, that sort of thing . . ."

Emily began to tremble—she wasn't sure which of her many, conflicting emotions caused the response. "I do not believe in time travel."

Adrian smiled, and his dark eyes sparkled with mystic power. "You will."

Chapter One

Emily sat in Adrian de Vargas's small plane, crouched low in the open door. Time travel couldn't be easy—a snap of the fingers, a step through a mirror, a bump on the head. . . . No. It had to be . . . awful. It had to be . . . *skydiving*.

She had jumped seven times in seven days. She had practiced, first attached to Adrian, then on a bungee cord, then by herself. Each time was worst than the last. Why she ever agreed to their bizarre proposition, Emily didn't know. Maybe it was best not to know—not to plumb the depths of her troubled subconscious, nor to learn the true source of her pathetic need to trust someone.

She had spent three weeks living in Adrian and Cora's Paradise Valley home. She had been at the hospital when Cora gave birth to a boy, and they had treated her like a sister. All the while, Cora cheerfully filled her head with crazy stories about the heroic Darian Woodward.

Innocent. Trusting. Noble. A virgin. Darian Woodward was a true gentleman who kissed a lady's hand, and would give his life to save her. A man who would never desert a woman who had given him her heart. A man who needed her.

Emily had closed her shop for the month of April—her air-conditioning unit had failed, and she needed a break. She didn't truly believe Cora and Adrian's story of time travel, but in the weeks since they came to her shop, she'd found herself embroiled in their lives, and whether it was true or not didn't matter. She liked pretending it was true—it gave her empty life meaning and excitement. Most of all, she liked having friends who cared about her.

Her new friends now prepared to drop her out of a plane. Cora sat on the far bench, an encouraging look on her face. She nodded helpfully as Adrian adjusted Emily's parachute.

Emily's teeth chattered—more now than the first time. Maybe because this time Adrian was "summoning" mystic whirlwinds that, he claimed, would spin her back into the past.

"I've changed my mind!"

The whirlwind scrambled Emily's desperate voice, and her call went unheard. Dust and small pebbles battered her skydiving goggles, spinning her in a dark, chaotic cloud above the desert.

"What was I thinking?" She clung to her parachute, but it availed nothing. She was skydiving into the past to rescue a Civil War hero turned desperado from a hanging he probably deserved.

I wanted so desperately to believe in someone that I let two crazy people talk me into . . . this! I am such a fool! "Help!" Emily closed her eyes tight. *When will I ever learn to think first, act second?*

But Emily had never thought first—she felt first. Her heart chose what goals she wanted, and then her brain kicked in to find the best way of accomplishing those goals.

She was falling out of the sky because her heart was touched by the story of a hero who died young, and wrongly. She'd forgotten to count . . . twenty seconds, and she was supposed to pull the chute, to end the "free fall." Her hands shook, but she found the cord and pulled it. The parachute popped out and up. Never once had she had any faith that the parachute would come out, but every time, it did.

It rose above her like a sail, blue and gold. The wind stilled and for a moment, all was peaceful. Perfect.

It should have been comforting, but it wasn't. Each time before, she'd fallen with relative speed, then come to a safe landing. This time, the wind rose beneath her. The whirlwind was really coming for her. She hadn't believed it, but it was true.

Dust whirled around her, roaring like the ocean in a storm. Emily cranked her neck up and tried to see through the flurry of dust. She'd lost sight of the plane that dropped her. Cora and Adrian were gone. She couldn't see anything. She was alone. More alone than she'd ever been in her life.

The whirlwind spun faster and faster. It seemed to lift Emily and her parachute rather than drop her as she expected. Small rocks pelted her cheeks and her eyes watered from the wind's sharp sting. Her arms ached from clinging to the parachute. Her legs twisted as the whirlwind jerked her first one way, then the other.

Adrian had explained the procedure as if it happened every day. *Just stay calm, wait until the whirlwind pitches you free, then flare the chute and go in for the landing. No problem.*

She longed to be brave. Instead, hot tears stung her eyes. It was easy for Adrian because he'd skydived several times a week for years. When he took Emily for their first run, he'd talked casually throughout the landing, never missing a beat when they hit ground.

She forced her eyes open. The wind spun around her, and for a moment, she felt motionless. Then the whirlwind edged her to its outer shell. Its howling reached a pinnacle, then quieted. She snapped forward as if someone had punched her in the back.

She burst from the whirlwind into the glaring Arizona sunlight, only a few feet from the red-gold desert. "Help!" She began running before she hit the ground. Accomplished skydivers didn't miss a step when they landed. She'd practiced every day. She'd rehearsed it every night in her mind. She'd dreamt about it. It should be easy. Second nature.

Emily fell flat on her face, and the parachute crumpled on top of her. She didn't get up. She just lay facedown in the dry grass. Her heart throbbed. She felt cold and hot at once. Seven times a charm—and this was her worst landing yet.

Emily eased back a corner of the parachute and peeked out. Nothing. No sound but the wind, and that was fading as the whirlwind dissipated, dissolving away from her. She looked left, then right. Nothing.

She was totally, utterly alone.

She saw Camelback's distinctive hump, so she was still in Arizona. But when? She wanted to stand up and investigate, but her muscles refused to obey. She listened for a moment. Insects chirped, which sounded familiar. She listened a moment longer, half expecting to hear the giant footfalls of a *Tyrannosaurus rex* coming toward her.

Nothing.

"I am the most gullible woman who ever lived."

Emily shoved her diving goggles up to the top of her head and studied the landscape. The sun was hot and cast shadows on every nook of Camelback's giant boulders. She shaded her eyes against the sun and studied the landscape from beneath her parachute. No houses dotted the mountain's side. No roads sliced along its slopes.

She waited awhile longer, not sure how long she lay beneath the parachute, but it was starting to get hot. If she hadn't traveled back in time, it would be obvious soon. If she had. . . . Her stomach churned with sudden nausea. Then what?

She had a job to do. Get up! Her body refused to move. She tried to remember the purpose of her adventure. Cora's description of the blue-eyed, idealistic Darian Woodward had tugged at Emily's sympathies. A man who believed he could change the world, and right all wrongs in the process.

Ha! The world wound on, fueled by greed, indifferent to the pain of its inhabitants, always operating on the lowest common denominator.

But Darian Woodward needed her. She had a clear image of him. A cherubic face, with wide, innocent blue eyes and a bewildered expression. Not perfect and god-like as Ian had been, but earnest and true, almost child-like in his sweetness.

Emily's lip was bleeding from her crash into the past. Her knees were scraped and burned from skidding over the dry earth. Her flight suit was torn. "I know where I am. In hell!"

"What have we here, lads? An angel?"

Emily froze at the gruff voice. A voice of the past. She fought panic, gathered her courage, then flipped herself onto her back. She tangled her arms in the parachute, then kicked it aside with her legs.

Seven dark figures formed silhouettes against the morning sun. They stood in wedge formation, with the tallest in the center. The two on the ends had their hands on their hips. Four others held rifles. The man in the center held a revolver aimed at her heart.

She was in the past. Adrian and Cora hadn't lied. For a sick instant, she wished they had.

She drew a tight breath and tried to smile. "Hi." She paused. "I'm just. . . ." She bit back the word, "Help," then froze into terrified silence.

The leader tilted his head toward his men, but he kept his gaze on Emily's prone form. "Not an angel, gentlemen. What we have here is something else. Something else entirely."

She felt foolish lying on her back in the midst of her tangled parachute. She had to talk to them, calmly, showing no fear. "You're probably wondering what I'm doing here. It's simple, really. . . ." She fought for a logical reason for her presence, but her mind went blank. "It's sort of an experiment. They do that back . . . now, right?"

Perfect. She was babbling. She expected to meet people from the past. Cora had warned her that reactions could be hasty. For one thing, men of the past might find her skydiving suit irregular. "What I'm wearing is part of the experiment. And this. . . ." She fumbled with the parachute. "It's a . . . kite."

"Indeed?" The leader sounded skeptical. "Where did you come from?"

"Oh . . . around here. Not far, exactly." This response wouldn't do. Her voice betrayed a quaver of fear—the last thing she wanted to convey. Worse still, her teeth were chattering, something she felt sure the bandits would notice. "Um. . . . Just out of curiosity. . . . Are you going to shoot me?"

"Certainly not!" The bandit leader sounded offended. "Why would you think these gentlemen and myself pose any danger to you, a young woman alone?"

"Well. . . . You're pointing guns at my head."

"Gentlemen, lower your weapons." In unison, the men put away their rifles, and the leader stuffed his revolver into a holster.

They weren't going to kill her. Something in the bandit leader's voice eased her fear, and she felt like herself again. She puffed a breath of relief. "Thank you."

Emily sat up and the man came into focus. His face was shadowed with an unkempt blond beard and his hair fell below his shoulders. He wore what looked like an old uniform jacket with golden epaulets on the shoulders. A scruffier, more disgusting man, she'd never seen.

"You look like Custer!" A bandit, if ever there was one. Emily scrambled to her feet and backed away. She'd been dropped into an outlaw gang. *Thank you, Adrian.*

"General George Custer?" The bandit seemed flattered. "An honorable soldier. Thank you."

Emily rolled her eyes. "Oh, please! He was a murderer who tried to wipe out a Native American village. I cannot believe how history makes heroes of that kind of murderous rogue."

The bandit's blue eyes lit with indignation, and Emily cringed at her impulsive reaction. "Then again, I'm sure he was a very nice man."

His full lips curled beneath his ratty blond beard. "General Custer fought with honor at Gettysburg. . . . Who are you?"

She held out her hand, but he eyed her suspiciously and didn't take it. "Emily Morgan." Emily tried to appear casual. "I'm looking for a man."

The bandit grinned. "You've found one. Seven, in fact."

It sounded like a threat, and her fear returned. She shouldn't have relaxed just because he sounded polite. "The man I'm looking for is noble and brave, and you would be in serious trouble if you hurt me." Her voice came high and rushed, a clear indication of budding terror. The more she fought displaying her insecurity, the more it flamed around her.

The bandit chuckled, and glanced around at his men, who laughed, too. Emily fought dislike. The way he tilted his arrogant head to one side in particular infuriated her. "And who is this esteemed gentleman who is so willing to be my lady's guardian?"

Emily grit her teeth. Fear couldn't outweigh the irritation this man provided. "Captain Darian Woodward. He's supposed to be somewhere around Fort McDowell."

The other bandits closed in around their leader. A heavyset older man fingered his musket. "Captain Woodward is hell and gone from Camp McDowell, girl. What do you want with him, anyway?"

Emily eyed them doubtfully. "I've got a message for him."

The men exchanged glances, but the leader fixed his cold gaze on Emily. "This message, would it come from Clement Davis, by chance?"

"Who? No. It's from Adrian de Vargas."

The blond man caught his breath, and the others murmured in astonishment. "The Indian left this place months ago." He pinned her with an icy stare. He was

26

a fiendish looking man, dangerous and wily. "What do you know of him?"

"He's a friend of mine." She paused and cast an accusatory glance toward the sky. "Or I thought so an hour ago."

"What is the message?"

"Nothing I care to tell you! I was instructed to tell only Captain Woodward." She looked the bandit up and down, and affected a disgusted sneer. That should set him aback a bit. "Not some creepy desperado like you."

He grinned, and his blue eyes twinkled. *Blue eyes.* A grim sense of doom swarmed Emily's senses. She shook her head. "No. . . ."

The bandit bowed. "It seems fortune plays into your hands, and mine, Miss Morgan. If you are searching for Darian Woodward, you need look no farther. You have found him."

Emily stared at the object of her rescue. "You are nothing, *nothing* like Cora described."

Darian Woodward's expression changed from smug self-assurance to ripe concern. "Miss Talmadge? Have you seen her? Is she well?"

"She is until I get back home." How could they do this to her? One glance told her that the worst of Darian's reputation was deserved. He wouldn't have to do much to terrorize Tucson—just walk through with that mocking smile on his face, with his renegade followers at his side.

"If you know Miss Talmadge, I demand to hear of her welfare."

Emily wiped her fist across her sore lip. Yes, it was bleeding. Not that the honorable Captain Woodward would bother to offer her a handkerchief. If she were a more romantic woman, like the delicate, sensitive Cora, maybe he would offer a hand. But, no. She was the kind of woman left by the man she had loved most in the world. . . . The kind of woman who went back in time to save a hero, and found . . . this, instead. "Cora is fine. She and Adrian sent me to look for you."

Darian looked proud. "I am important to them." His expression altered again. "Your words indicate they're still together."

"They're married. They just had a son. I have some pictures that you're supposed to show Adrian's father when we find him."

Darian eyed her doubtfully. "Pictures?"

"They're in my backpack. I'll show you later."

"I am pleased he took steps to salvage her reputation, at least."

"I can't believe they did this to me." Emily studied Darian's unkempt, dangerous appearance. His tangled blond hair fell to his shoulders, dirt stained his cheeks. "I cannot believe Adrian called you adorable."

"Did he?" Darian appeared pleased. "Imagine that." He paused. "What do you want with me, Miss Morgan?"

She glanced at his men and hesitated. "Look, can I talk in front of them? I'm assuming you know where Adrian and Cora came from. . . ."

His cold blue eyes narrowed to slits. "The Indian made outlandish claims of having come from the future."

"He is from the future, and so am I."

Darian drew a long breath. "I did not believe him, and I do not believe you." He studied her face, his blue eyes intent and piercing. He was sizing her up—as a woman. Emily blushed. Virgin, indeed! She began to feel nervous. What if Adrian and Cora had been really wrong about this man? And she was alone, with him and men that looked to have no scruples at all.

"You may speak in front of these men, Miss Morgan.

They are all soldiers formerly of the Union army, and loyal to both justice and myself."

"They look like bandits. Like you."

His bearded chin elevated and his full lips curled in disdain. "We are men of honor, men betrayed by a treacherous officer who does not deserve the title 'gentleman.' "

"If that officer's name is 'Davis,' you'd best stay away from him." Emily gulped. He was still looking at her in that slow, thoughtful way, with those eyes so bright that she almost felt scalded. "That's why I'm here." Her voice betrayed her nervousness. "When Cora and Adrian went back to the future, they found out what happened to you."

She didn't want to frighten him. Cora had told her to break the news gently, with sensitivity and tact. As a romantic, sensitive woman would no doubt do. Well, she wasn't a romantic, sensitive woman, and after the pain her old dreams had caused her, she wasn't going to start now. "You were hanged as a desperado in Tucson."

Darian's brow elevated, but he appeared both doubtful and unconcerned. The burly sergeant tapped Darian's shoulder. "Girl's crazy, Captain. Not surprised she was hooked up with that Indian and his woman."

"It's true! I'm from the year 2001, and that's where Adrian and Cora are now. You must have seen me land. The whirlwind brought me."

Darian glanced at her parachute. "We saw a whirlwind appear out of nowhere. In its wake, we found you." His gaze moved from the top of her head to her feet. "What are those shoes? Not lady's proper slippers."

"They're Timberlands. Hiking boots. I figured I'd have to do some walking. I guess Adrian is more powerful than he realized, because he dumped me right at your feet."

Darian ignored her as he turned to his men. "It is possible that Davis learned the Indian claimed to be from the future. Perhaps Davis is attempting to use you to dissuade me from my quest." Emily started to object, but Darian cut her off. "Yet his methods in the past have lacked imagination and subtlety. . . ."

The sergeant snorted. "That's the truth, sir, and no mistake. Last time, he sent a half-drunk gunfighter after you."

Emily looked between them. "He sent a gunfighter after you?"

The sergeant whipped off his cap as if he'd forgotten to do so earlier, yet considered it of gravest importance. "Yes, ma'am, he did. Called himself a Texas Ranger, but he weren't no more than a hired gun."

"What happened to him?"

The sergeant nodded proudly at Darian, who gazed out across the desert like a legend. "Captain Woodward here took care of him. Fellow who comes creeping up behind this man's got a surprise coming."

Darian appeared impossibly smug, so Emily affected a disinterested demeanor. "I take it you're a good shot."

His lip curled upward at one side. "During my service in the Civil War, I became proficient with the revolver." He was pretending to be modest, knowing his success spoke for itself.

"So, you're a gunfighter, on top of all your other crimes."

Never had a man looked so indignant and yet so proud at once. "I have committed no 'crimes,' madam. I have done only what is right, in the honorable pursuit of justice."

No doubt, he'd deluded Cora and Adrian, but she knew his type and she wouldn't be fooled as they had. *I was such an idiot to believe a man like that existed anywhere, let alone in the lawless Old West.*

"Well? What are you going to do about the future? Are you going to pay attention to Adrian's message, or not?"

Darian rubbed his bearded chin thoughtfully. "It is remotely possible you are telling the truth, but not a likelihood. If so, Miss Talmadge would seek to warn me because of her generous, tender heart."

"Cora obviously didn't know you as well as she thought. But if you hunt down this General Davis person, you'll get yourself killed. So give it up, and find something more your speed to do." She should flatter his pride. A romantic woman would take that tack. She had done the same for Ian many times. "Head back east and become a grocer, maybe."

Darian Woodward's blond brow arched, those expressive lips curled into utter disdain and untarnished arrogance. "Miss . . . ?"

"Morgan. You can call me Emily."

"Miss Morgan. . . . I take Miss Talmadge's message, and thank you for delivering it. You have warned me that my quest is dangerous. I will consider my methods more carefully. But my honor is at stake, and I will not turn back upon my righteous quest." He paused and his lips formed a sneer. "Grocer, indeed." He shook his head. "A few months ago, General Clement Davis deceived our commanders, and convinced them I both mutinied against him—which I did for good reason—and am a traitor to the United States Cavalry. That will not stand, not in the eyes of God, nor in my own conscience."

"You are such a lunatic. If you go on with your 'quest,' you'll die. That's all I came to say. If you don't want to listen, fine. I'll just be going now." She shouldn't have come to the past. Darian Woodward

31

wasn't innocent and idealistic. He was an arrogant gunslinger, a bandit, and he didn't want to be saved, anyway. Fine.

Darian eyed her suspiciously. "Where are you going?"

Emily gathered up her parachute and tried to fold it according to Adrian's instructions. She'd brought along a hiking backpack with supplies, but the day was hotter than usual for April, and she wished she could leave the chute behind.

"I'm supposed to find Adrian's father, an Apache man named Tiotonawen. He'll send me back home. So, where do I find him?"

"Tiotonawen has moved his village south to the Catalina Mountains."

"Great! Now what?"

"As it happens, Miss Morgan, my men and I are on our way to Tucson, a small town nestled in the shadows of the Catalina Mountains. If you wish to find Tiotonawen, your journey lies alongside mine."

"Perfect! That's where you die, you nitwit! Do *not* go to Tucson!"

"General Davis has been in Abilene, Texas, where he savaged my name. He is currently on his way to Fort Lowell in Tucson, where he has ingratiated himself with the renowned commander, General Forbes. He will arrive there in days, and I will meet him for a final confrontation."

"Well, enjoy your hanging, pal."

"As for yourself. . . ." Darian paused, considering. "You might prove useful, if your story is true. You will accompany us to Tucson."

Emily glared. Just as she'd guessed, Darian was willing to use her for his own ends, just as Ian had done. The only difference between the two men was that Ian had been clean-cut, handsome, and Darian was a fright to look upon.

"I'm not going anywhere with you. I can find my way to Tucson on my own, thank you."

Darian moved toward her. Despite his contrived graciousness, he moved like a lion. "You will not travel alone. You will come with us."

"You're going to take me against my will?"

His blush soaked from his neck to his hairline, but his bandit cohorts chuckled. Emily frowned in disgust. "Oh, get your minds out of the gutter! I didn't mean that!" She paused to huff. "I studied Tae Kwon Do for two years." After Ian deserted her, when she tried to prove to herself she was a strong woman. . . . True, she'd never gotten it right, and finally attempted yoga instead, but Darian Woodward and his gang didn't need to know that. "You'd be sorry if you tried anything."

Darian hesitated. "What's Ti. . . . what's that?"

Emily angled her brow and affected a dangerous leer. "Practical feminism."

Chapter Two

If Miss Emily Morgan represented women of the future, Darian was determined not to procreate. The girl was mannerless, rude, and smug. She dressed like a man, and not even a gentleman.

She might be considered a beautiful woman, with her long, dark braid, and the soft curls that fell around her forehead and grazed her cheeks. She was delicate in appearance, if not in manner. Yes, she might pass for a lady, in other circumstances. If not for the peculiar, snug blue suit encasing her slender body. If not for the "Timberlands."

Her face formed a pleasing oval with high cheekbones and a small, straight nose. Those features were more than adequate for beauty and remained untarnished by her pugnacious manner. Her green eyes were bright, tilted at the corners and fringed with black lashes so long they curled upward at the tips.

She seemed self-assured despite her diminutive height, but beneath her direct manner, Darian sensed a guarded heart. A fragile heart. This was not a woman who would trust easily. And he needed her trust, lest she escape and warn his enemy of his intentions.

He wasn't sure why she had come to him, but though it seemed unlikely that Davis had sent her, neither did he believe Adrian would have chosen this method, either. "Before I allow you to accompany us, posing a threat to the welfare of my men. . . ." Emily interrupted with a groan, and he noted that she clenched her fist into a tight ball. "What proof have you that the Indian sent you?"

She stared hard at him, then rummaged through her blue pack. It appeared made of a strange, shiny material, but it looked sturdy. Better than his own. She withdrew an envelope, which she opened, and withdrew small sheets of paper.

Darian took the paper and studied the image. For the first time, he considered that her story might be true. He had seen daguerreotypes, photographs, but nothing like this. Cora Talmadge beamed out at him, her image small but exactly as he remembered her. In her arms, she held a black-haired baby with a feather tied to its hair.

"It is Miss Talmadge."

"And here they are at their wedding." Emily gave him another image, and as she said, Adrian de Vargas's strong, self-assured face smiled out at him, as he stood posed with Cora. She wore a white lace gown, which though ladylike, seemed too scant for decency. Darian stared a long while, shocked.

Emily seized the photographs. "These aren't for you. They're for Adrian's father."

Darian looked at her, wonder filling his soul. He lived each day as it came, holding to what he believed true.

Could there be another world, so different, out there, yet within reach? And what would it mean to live in that world? "How is it that you came to know Cora Talmadge and her husband?"

"They befriended me when I overheard them talking about you." Emily looked disappointed as she gazed into his face. Darian wondered what she expected when she came to look for him. "They came to my shop to research your fate. And they found it."

Darien didn't want to hear about his "fate." "What wares do you offer at your 'shop'?"

"Books. Rare and used. I took over when my grandmother died, and now the children's section is one of the best in Tucson. The romance novels sell the most, though." She paused. "Although I don't read fantasy myself." Darian wondered why she considered romance "fantasy" and why she was so quick to distance herself from the notion. "I keep a good section of new titles, too."

After he wore out the classic literature, he had spent a great deal of time reading dime novels during the war, and he found them boring, but he had needed escape, after all. "It has been long since I held the wealth of fiction in my hands, and allowed it to balm my soul in the realms of sweet imagination."

She shifted her weight from foot to foot. "Huh?"

He smiled, reluctantly. "I miss reading."

"I suppose you like heroic tales of tragedy."

His smile deepened. "As it happens, Miss Morgan, I like comedy." He also liked the more romantic, chivalrous tales, but decided not to mention that, since it seemed unmanly.

She studied him intently. He wondered if she was impressed with what she saw. "Well, you're not what I expected, and I don't trust you. You look worse than a

36

bandit, and I have no doubt that you earned the title fair and square." Darian was too offended to argue. "But I've decided that I will go with you to Tucson. I don't have much choice, really. Once we get there, I'll hunt up Adrian's father, and you. . . ." She stopped and her expression softened. "Maybe by then you'll have wised up."

Darian ignored her intimation of doom, then turned to his soldiers. "You have conceded to obey me. Wise." He paused, liking the brief "huff" from her lips. "Allow me to introduce the gentlemen in my association."

"You mean your gang?"

He decided to ignore that comment, too. "Sergeant MacLeod has served with me since the battle of Antietam Creek in Maryland. We came west together at the war's end."

Emily smiled at MacLeod. She was pretty when she smiled, sweet and somehow—tentative, as if she was never quite sure how people would respond to her. That, Darian understood—she was certainly different, and it must have caused her any amount of grief.

She held out her hand and MacLeod took it uncertainly. Before he could kiss her hand, she shook his, then let go. MacLeod eyed his hand in confusion, then shrugged.

"Sergeant MacLeod, I am pleased to meet you."

"And you, miss."

Darian turned to the other men. "Here are soldiers Wetherspoon, Ping, Herring, Bonner, and Clyde."

"The magnificent seven. Hi."

She seemed to find his men amusing. He had no idea why. "My men are the bravest and most honorable in the Arizona territory."

"No doubt." She covered her mouth and coughed, but he felt certain she battled laughter. True, Ping in particùlar didn't appear entirely formidable, but he was loyal to Darian, and that's what mattered. "So. . . ." She looked around as if trying to distract herself. "How do you get around? Do you have horses or coaches or something? I guess it's too early for trains."

"We travel by train in the East, of course. Here . . . we walk."

"Walk? Are you kidding? You must have a horse!"

Darian smiled, pleased with himself. "What kind of cavalry officer would I be without a horse?"

"You were . . . joking?" She spoke as if the impossible occurred.

"We have seven horses and a pack mule concealed in a nearby hideout. You may ride the mule."

"Oh, can I? Gee, thanks." She rolled her eyes. "What are you going to do with the packed stuff?"

"We don't have that much. You can squeeze in around our gear."

She sighed, but she didn't argue. "It figures. Cora stole a horse and got to ride around with Adrian. I get a mule, and have to hang out with . . . you."

Before Darian could stop her, she peeled her blue suit apart, exposing a white, sleeveless shirt more sheer than a chemise. Wetherspoon choked back a cough, Daniel Ping gasped, and MacLeod chuckled as Emily Morgan climbed out of her already inadequate garment and exposed more womanly flesh than Darian had ever seen in his life.

She didn't notice his shocked attention as she squashed the blue suit into a ball and assembled it into her kite pack. The white, sleeveless shirt was tucked into cutoff trousers that resembled drawers, but shorter. She wore a belt for uncertain purposes, and he noticed a pearl drop necklace hanging in her . . . décolletage.

She snapped off the luminous spectacles that were

perched on her head, and added them to her pack, then took out smaller spectacles with round black lenses and put them on instead. She adjusted her long, dark braid so that it fell behind her back, then seized a clear water bottle and drank.

As Darian and his men watched spellbound and horrified, she squirted her face with the water, then drank, letting the droplets run down over her chin and along her neck. She rubbed the moisture into her skin and sighed.

For a brief, horrifying flash, Darian imagined licking the droplets off her neck and tasting her warm skin. She hooked the bottle onto her belt, put the pack on her back, dusted off her hands, then turned to Darian.

She must have noticed his abject horror, because her brow furrowed in confusion. "What on earth is the matter with you? Why are you looking at me that way?"

"I. . . . You. . . ."

"Cut it out!" She glanced down at her attire. Perhaps she hadn't noticed that she was wearing . . . nothing. She rolled her eyes, groaned, then made a fist. "This time period is so . . . nuts. Cora made me pack a suitable dress, but I'm not wearing it unless I have to. Understood? I'm not the dress type." She paused, as if daring him to defy her. Why did she deny her femininity, when it was so blatantly obvious? "If you don't like what I'm wearing. . . . Deal with it!"

Before Darian could issue a single objection, she started off in the direction of his horses. He stood speechless with his men, aghast beyond any argument.

After a moment, Sergeant MacLeod slapped Darian's shoulder in a familiar gesture, then headed after her. "I'd say you'd better get used to female flesh, Captain. . . . At a good, safe distance."

Darian smacked his lips thoughtfully. "There's only

one way to deal with Miss Emily Morgan. I shall ignore her outrageous behavior and treat her as I would any other lady. With respect and honor."

Ping cast a doubtful glance his way, then headed eagerly after Emily. "Good luck, Captain. It ain't gonna be easy."

Darian gathered his ravaged senses together, then followed his men to the hideout. Emily was already inspecting the horses and the mule when he caught up with them. He'd never seen a woman's legs this way. Naked. He'd imagined them to be plumper, but Emily's were slender and looked strong. Her ankles appeared trim where they disappeared beneath her heavy boots.

She hesitated before mounting the mule. "Um. . . . When do we have lunch?"

"We dine at sunset."

"On what?" She spoke with grave misgivings and Darian repressed a grin.

"Rattlesnakes, grub . . . whatever we can dig up." Good. He'd never seen a more appalled expression. "We are soldiers, Miss Morgan. Expert huntsmen. You can expect hare, and perhaps venison on occasion, well-cooked by Herring, who has become an admirable chef."

"If you don't eat until night. . . ." She fished in her pack and drew forth a flat item wrapped in paper. She tore off the paper, which she jammed into her tight pocket, then stuffed a dark brown bar into her mouth. "Chocolate. . . . Sorry. . . . Did you want some?"

She spoke with her mouth full, which didn't surprise him. What did surprise him was his reaction to seeing her eat. She licked her lips with glee, then her fingers. His body assumed a masculine response that added fierce heat to his face. "You will put on a dress as soon as we can locate one."

She looked confused, and one of his men chuckled.

40

He suspected it was Ping. He expected a sarcastic response, but instead, a faint blush touched her cheeks as if she hadn't truly been aware of her nudity until now. She folded her arms nervously in front of her body, then tugged the hem of her blue denim drawers lower. "These are shorts. Not even short shorts. Everyone wears them in the future."

Darian held up his hand. "Say no more. I don't want to know. And I will thank you to refrain from referring to the future. It sounds a wretched world without morals or substantial character."

"That about sums it up." She shook her head as if she hadn't meant to agree. "But I'm wearing what I'm wearing, and you'd better get used to it!"

"Your attire is of no present concern, Miss Morgan." He paused, taking note of her well-formed knees. "But finding you a suitable gown will be of utmost importance."

MacLeod unhitched Darian's gray horse and passed him the reins. "I thought you were going to 'ignore' the lady."

"I am."

MacLeod's grin deepened, but Darian cast him a dark, warning glance, and the sergeant eased back. Darian mounted and waited for the others. Before anyone could help her, Emily led the mule beside a rock and scrambled onto its back.

Darian turned in his saddle to address his men. "Gentlemen, we ride for Tucson. It is a journey of many days, but if we ride swift and straight, we will arrive in time to deliver justice at last to the treacherous General Davis."

Emily snorted derisively, then urged her mule forward in front of Darian's horse. "Yep, we'd better hurry. Don't want to be late for your hanging."

41

Darian started after her, directing his horse in front of the mule. He didn't look at her as he passed, but it wasn't easy to remain indifferent.

Hanging. He didn't expect to be hanged. Hanging was reserved for the worst kind of criminals. It sounded humiliating. His death would be a public spectacle. Then again, he could issue a moving speech first, sure to bring tears to the crowd. He could condemn Davis with his last words.

Darian glanced back. Emily rode behind him on the mule, looking delicate and peculiar. A strand of dark hair had broken free from her braid and hung down along her face, curling over her shoulder. "Are you certain General Davis is recorded in heroic proportions?"

"Well, I've never heard of him, but that's what Cora said."

Darian pondered this awhile while Emily pushed the mule into a jig to catch up. "Was there any mention of my final words?"

"No."

He puckered his brow until it ached, then glanced upward at the morning sun. He adjusted his captain's hat for better shade, then scratched beneath the rim. It had been months since he'd enjoyed adequate bathing arrangements. Months since he'd shaved or visited the fort barber. He couldn't help noticing that Miss Emily Morgan looked at him as if he'd crawled from beneath a rock.

"I know a lot about Arizona history, but I've never heard of either you or this general person. Adrian found it in an old book, out of print for about ninety years."

He didn't like talk of time—of a future he wouldn't know. Now is what mattered. No matter where Miss Morgan came from, she was now in his care, and he would treat her as such. To that end, it was important that he assess her character. "How old are you?" Darian winced at the ungentlemanly question, but Miss Morgan didn't seem to mind.

"I turn twenty-nine in July."

Darian's eyes widened. She looked much younger. At her age, she should be married with many children, not roaming the desert alone. "Twenty-nine?"

"I know—in your time, I'd be a grandmother. How old are you?"

He hesitated. He was younger than she was, which gave her an edge against him. "In my mid-twenties."

"Cora said you were twenty-five."

"I will turn twenty-six in October."

"Pup."

Clearly, Miss Morgan felt no need to spare his gentlemanly pride. "You refer to your 'shop.' Why are you not married and tending your husband and children, rather than practicing a career in this manner?"

She stared blankly at him for a moment, then exhaled a long, torturous sigh as if he had brought up all the world's ills. "I'm not married because I don't want to be." She spoke proudly, then paused, alerting Darian to a dual nature in her words. "Marriage isn't what it's cracked up to be."

"Is that so?" Obviously, Miss Emily Morgan hadn't found the right man. Darian smiled and rode on ahead, feeling comfortable. "Marriage isn't to be entered into lightly, that is true." He glanced back to see her reaction, but her expression was veiled, and seemed more sorrowful than he expected. "I came close to matrimony myself once, but the arrangement ended before it could be transacted."

She eyed him doubtfully. " 'Transacted?' How romantic!"

"You may be right. I was not romantic enough to

enter into a sacred union, so it is best not to have undertaken the adventure."

Emily frowned, but she didn't look at him again. "Romance, Captain, is an illusion, and it's the last thing you should count on when planning a marriage."

Odd, coming from a young woman. Darian stopped his horse and waited for her to catch up. "What better way than to follow your heart, to be swept up in its most passionate currents?"

She rolled her eyes and snorted. "The only place those 'passionate currents' will take you is . . . alone."

Emily rode on, but Darian held his horse back to watch her. Her shoulders were slumped, but determined. Something had happened to darken her natural feminine dreams. She reminded him of himself. He had entered war with all hope and ideals, then come out knowing those ideals were illusion. Emily spoke of love, of romantic love, in the same way he spoke of war.

The Sonoran Desert was greener in the past than in Emily's own time, but after a full day of riding, it looked bleaker than Death Valley. "This is so boring. How much farther?"

Darian was talking to Sergeant MacLeod but he heard her and stopped immediately. "You are an impatient woman. We will ride until nightfall, then make camp for the night. We will reach Tucson in five days."

"Five days! In the future, it takes two hours." She slumped on her mule, who plodded on at the same methodical gait as it had begun the journey. Darian seemed unimpressed by her tales of the future. Perhaps he didn't believe her. "You don't believe me, do you?"

"I accept the possibility of time travel. Though Miss Talmadge had the grace and civility to come from this age, you and that Indian clearly do not."

"I came here to save you, not blend in with your repressed culture." She paused. "What are you going to do when you reach Tucson?"

Darian didn't answer at once, indicating he had no idea. "I will consider that when the time comes. I have learned General Davis's whereabouts. It is my intention to confront him."

"How did you learn his whereabouts? Telegraphs or something?"

Darian appeared uncomfortable, but the smallest soldier, Ping, trotted up beside her. Ping rode a stout pinto gelding, which always seemed to be jigging in an effort to catch up with Darian's long-legged gray. "The captain held up a stagecoach and rifled through letters. Got kind of a reputation after that."

"You held up a stagecoach? No wonder you're known as a desperado!"

Darian glared at Ping, who beamed with innocent pride and admiration. "I did not 'hold up' a stagecoach. I stopped it."

"At gunpoint, or did you just flag it down?"

His face tensed. "I requested that the coachman stop."

Ping nodded vigorously. "And when the fool tried to run, the captain shot the reins out of his hand. Lord, Captain Woodward sure can shoot!"

Emily diverted a pertinent gaze to Darian, who squirmed in his saddle. "At gunpoint. Go on."

"I inspected the contents of his coach, which contained postal cartons."

"Meaning, you held up a mail truck. Well, well. Get any good loot?"

He twitched. "My purpose wasn't robbery, woman. True, there's been a rash of bandit attacks recently, and money intended for army salaries has been stolen, but I had nothing to do with those incidents."

45

Emily looked him up and down. "No, probably not. If you'd gotten away with anything, you'd be dressed better." She paused, liking the flush of indignation on Darian's dark golden skin. "What did you make off with instead?"

"I intercepted several items destined for General Davis, and learned his whereabouts as well as his future plans."

Sergeant MacLeod cleared his throat. "And we made off with the old goat's paycheck, too. Had cash sent, the fool."

Emily gasped loudly. "Not . . . robbery?"

"It was a justified expense diverted rightfully to myself. The funds were aimed at Davis as a reward for capturing me."

"Capturing you? He didn't do that very well, it seems."

"After my mutiny failed, I was held in brief captivity. My men assisted my escape. . . ."

"Busted you out. . . ."

"And we formulated a plan to secure justice."

"By holding up and robbing stagecoaches. I see."

"You misunderstand completely."

Ping looked thoughtful. "If it had only been the one. . . ."

"Ping. . . ." Darian's warning voice stopped Ping's disclosure, but Emily had heard enough. She turned her most knowing gaze at Darian.

"There was more than one?"

Ping looked pained as if he longed to recite Darian's glory, yet feared his commander's icy wrath. Emily shook her head and sighed. "I know. Once you embark on a life of crime, it's hard to stop."

His eyes formed slits, and his full lips pressed into a tight line. "It was an accident. I stopped a coach I believed transported one of Davis's associates, but I was mistaken."

"Who did you hold up instead?"

MacLeod coughed to hide laughter, and Ping winced. Darian's eyes turned to frost. "A minister and his wife." He paused. "I apologized profusely."

"Then took them for all they were worth."

"Certainly not! Madam, I am not a common criminal."

"I didn't say you were common. An uncommon criminal perhaps. The outlaw Darian Woodward—blue-eyed bandit. Has a certain ring to it."

He stiffened into regal disapproval, turned to face the front and rode on without speaking. Getting under his skin gave Emily a pleasure she hadn't known in years. He seemed so sure of himself, so determined. She wondered if he'd always been this way, what he was like when he was young. Had he marched off to war expecting to change the world?

"Things never turn out the way you expect, do they?" She spoke quietly, to herself, but Darian heard. He stopped his horse and waited until her mule rode up beside him.

A faint smile curved his lips beneath his scruffy beard and mustache. "That, Miss Morgan, is a certainty." He paused, watching her face as they rode along side by side, she on her brown mule, he on his magnificent gray thoroughbred. "I assume Miss Talmadge convinced you I was a man worth saving?"

She glanced up at him. Her shoulder came to the level of his knee. He wore high black riding boots, supple and well-worn. He had long, powerful legs. "Cora really liked you a lot. She said you were really cute."

"You utilize the word 'really' too much."

"Oh, do I?"

"Yes."

Darian Woodward was infuriating. "At least, I don't say 'ya know,' and 'like this and like that' all the time."

He seemed baffled by her comment. Annoying that he had any impact on her at all. Why did she care what he thought of her speech, anyway? She didn't care if he liked her. She wasn't overly fond of him, either.

"As I was saying, Cora thought really. . . ." Oh! It was the power of suggestion! She coughed. "She thought highly of you. Adrian did, too."

"Yes, I know. You said he called me 'adorable.' "

"If you ever see him again, don't tell him I told you. He'd kill me."

"Since you say he is one hundred and some odd years in the future, I doubt I'll get the chance. Though it might be enjoyable to taunt him."

An unexpected sadness descended over Emily's heart. In her time, Darian was dead, whatever the reason. He was older than her great-grandfather. He looked so young. So sure he was right, and that the world worked to some perfect, righteous order, if only he could find it.

"Cora and Adrian feel responsible for what happened to you, Captain. You wouldn't have mutinied if not for them. You might have lived a long, happy life."

"Perhaps. Yet a man is defined by his reactions to circumstance. I would have learned of General Davis's unscrupulous activities in some other fashion. I would have defied him, sooner or later. There were tensions before the Indian and Miss Talmadge arrived. My end might not have been hanging. Maybe I would be shot in the back. Maybe I would have won. Might-have-beens aren't important, Miss Morgan. What is important is doing what's right and honorable."

"I used to think that. But how do you know what's right?"

He didn't answer for a moment. He just looked at her. "If you trust your heart, you'll know."

Emily looked down at the mule's neck. "I trusted my heart once, and I was wrong."

Chapter Three

They rode for three days, making even better time than Darian had hoped. Emily Morgan complained often, but she kept up a steady pace on her mule, and proved helpful making camp at night. By the third day, the men stopped noticing her exposed woman's body, and began treating her like a member of the group.

Darian woke early on the morning of their fourth day. He sat watching the sun rise over the eastern mountains. To everyone but Darian, Miss Morgan was an agreeable person. Ping was already devoted to her, and MacLeod treated her like a daughter. Herring cooked her special selections of hare and quail, even adding a sprig of sage on the side of her plate as decoration.

Despite her haphazard appearance, she kept herself scrupulously clean. She bathed at every stream they crossed, and had brought a strange, green toothbrush with a tube of paste to cleanse her teeth. The idea appealed to him, but it seemed ungentlemanly to ask to share her small brush. He had lost his wooden toothbrush months ago, and subsequently resorted to yucca leaves for this purpose.

Every morning, she took a bottle of lotion from her pack and applied it lavishly over her bare skin. She called it "sunscreen." The act seemed practical, but Darian couldn't help imagining his own hands at that task, rubbing the lotion in slow circles over her warm flesh. . . .

He caught himself and forbade further imagination. The other men seemed used to her presence and her near-nudity. Darian tried not to notice, to act as casually around her as they did. But instead of growing accustomed to the sight of a woman wearing a snug white top, he'd found his attention fixed on her figure.

Worse still, the sight of her provoked a masculine desire he found harder and harder to conceal. The first night was tolerable. She was exhausted, and had wrapped herself in her strange kite, then fallen promptly asleep.

The second night proved more difficult to endure. She devoured Herring's lavish meal, then chattered happily with his men. When she spoke, she gestured with excitement, her face animated and beautiful. The girl sparkled with an enthusiastic radiance Darian couldn't ignore.

He'd never seen anyone more comfortable with themself, except perhaps Adrian de Vargas, who had been too confident. He remembered a word Cora used to describe her lover. "Sexy." It aptly described Emily Morgan. She inspired illicit thoughts. What made it worse was that Darian knew it wasn't her intention.

She stretched her well-formed legs because they were

stiff. She licked her lips to taste. She splashed herself with water because she was hot.

Every action she took compounded his lust. He wasn't a lustful man. He was a gentleman. He was more a gentleman than anyone he knew. He had no doubt that marital bliss was achieved only through the most tender emotions. A wife should be treated with delicacy and sensitivity.

Yet Adrian de Vargas had picked the dear, sensitive Cora up off her feet, carried her to a bedroom, and done what Darian suspected were unspeakable things to her body.

The next morning, she had gazed up at him as though he were a god.

Something wasn't right.

He wondered exactly what Adrian had done to make Cora look at him that way, then told himself it was best not to know.

His thoughts were interrupted as Emily woke beneath her blue and gold covering, then struggled to get up. Darian swallowed and pretended not to notice. She had entangled herself again. Her feet were caught. Darian fought the urge to help her loose herself. With an annoyed grunt, she broke free of her contraption, then stood.

She was a delicate woman, but she didn't act delicate. Still, he considered her feminine. She would hate that term. He decided to use it at the first opportunity. Irking Miss Morgan had its joys.

She yawned and stretched, affording Darian a profile of her body. Her breasts were firm and round, supported by something he guessed was a partial corset beneath her white top. She bent and touched her fingers to her toes, then leaned her body left, then right.

A woman's bottom looked so much more appealing than a man's. A soft flare at the hips, yet firm. His body assumed an infuriating state of arousal, the same arousal that had woken him from sleep before dawn.

She combed out her tangled hair with her fingers. It fell in loose dark brown waves, sparkling with auburn highlights in the morning sun. It seemed to choose its own direction no matter what she did. Her hair would feel soft to his touch, soft and alive. Sexy.

Darian repressed a groan, then averted his misdirected gaze back to the mountains.

"Good morning, Captain. You're up early."

He glanced at her, pretending he hadn't noticed her waking. Or stretching. Or fingering her hair. "Miss Morgan, good morning."

He felt tense. Nervous. His men still slept, so he was virtually alone with her. They hadn't been alone together, and he didn't know what to say. She rubbed her hands over her arms as if they were cold. She looked around at nothing.

Emily Morgan was nervous, too.

Darian stared at her in disbelief, but the signs were clear. She drew short, uneven breaths and tried not to look at him. She fidgeted, then adjusted her hair. "Another day to go?"

Yes, she was trying to make conversation.

"We'll reach Tucson by tomorrow evening."

"Do you think they're expecting you?"

"No."

"Good." She cleared her throat. Maybe she knew what he'd been thinking about her and felt uncomfortable in his presence. "I'll just go for a walk now. There's a stream around here somewhere, right?"

Darian nodded south. "Two hundred yards, behind those boulders."

She forced a quick, polite smile. "Thank you." She picked her way between the creosote bushes, between

53

low, spiny cactus plants, and around a three-armed saguaro. As they traveled south, the desert had became more sparse, but the giant saguaros were more plentiful near Tucson.

From his few visits there, Darian preferred Tucson to the northern portion of the desert. He'd hoped to be stationed at the Tucson fort, but instead, had been placed as second-in-command of Camp McDowell beneath Clement Davis. The post should have been a substantial turn upward for his career.

Instead, it had led to the end of everything.

Emily disappeared behind the boulders, and Darian relaxed. She formed a strange quandary of characteristics. She flung herself forward with a determined, self-assured manner, yet he knew she was frightened. Of herself. And of him.

Emily tried to prove she wasn't afraid because she was terrified. She tried to prove she wasn't romantic . . . because she was too romantic, perhaps. Like himself. Despite himself, Darian's sympathy rose on her behalf. A woman who needed protection, yet denied the need—it had a peculiar effect on him.

She charged back over the boulders toward him. She tripped on a prickly pear cactus, but stifled her scream. Blood trickled down her leg from its spines. Darian rose to his feet as she stumbled forward.

Her face was white, her green eyes wide. "Darian!" She hissed his name as if fearing to be heard.

"Your leg. . . ."

"Never mind that! We have to get out of here. I saw men . . . Maybe ten or more."

"Indians?"

"No . . ." She paused to catch her breath. "These men look like soldiers. I heard them say your name. Sort of."

"What did they say?"

54

Emily bit her lip. " 'That Woodward bastard.' "

"That would indicate an unfavorable pursuit."

"I tend to think so."

Darian's men rose simultaneously, and silently gathered their gear. "The horses are already well hidden. Take position, gentlemen."

Emily looked frantically around. "What do you mean, 'take position'? Where? What are you going to do?"

He met her frightened gaze and he smiled. "We're going to defend ourselves. What else?"

Emily had never been more terrified in her life. Every Western movie she'd ever seen, even in snippet form, crashed through her brain as Darian directed his soldiers behind boulders.

Her heart beat so hard that she trembled. Darian touched her arm, and their eyes met. He looked so calm. Fearless. "Come with me, and keep low. Whatever you do, don't let them see you."

"What? Why?" Her voice shook, and she couldn't stop it.

Wetherspoon returned from scouting the approaching men. "They're Rangers, Captain. Ten of 'em, got carbines. They're out for us, all right."

Darian's blue eyes glittered. "They may wish they hadn't found us." His lips curved into a dangerous smile, and Emily's skin turned cold.

"Ten is too many! Can't we please run away?"

Darian looked at her, and he seemed more powerful than any man she'd ever seen. "When battle comes, Miss Morgan, face it. If you run, it runs after you, and it chooses its own terms."

His words chilled her because she didn't understand. He had seen so much she couldn't imagine. He'd seen war and death, he'd been betrayed. And he wasn't afraid. "What do I do?"

"Whatever I tell you, Miss Morgan."

Hoofbeats clattered on the rocks beyond the stream where Emily had bathed. Darian seized her arm and pulled her behind a large, split boulder, then checked his Colt revolver. It appeared fully loaded, so Emily guessed his procedure was ritual, something he'd learned after years of bloody war.

He kept his sharp gaze on the southern rocks, but his expression betrayed no fear, just the tension of impending battle.

"If we fail, keep yourself hidden until they leave. Then head south for Tucson." He spoke calmly, giving practical directions that Emily was too frightened to hear. "You'll need to locate a guide who can take you to Tiotonawen's village. Fort Lowell has many Indian guides. One of them should be able to help you, for a fee." Darian stuffed his hand in his pocket and passed her a felt bag. "This should be enough gold to secure you a trustworthy guide."

Tears filled her eyes. She was shaking, and she couldn't stop. "Please don't leave me."

He tore his gaze from the southern rocks and smiled. "That isn't my intention. But nothing in life is sure. If I should fall, you must follow the wisest course."

Horsemen thundered into Darian's campsite, dust flying from beneath their horses' hooves. Emily hid behind the boulder. Her heart slammed beneath her breast. She felt Darian close beside her. She wanted to touch him, to hold tight to him, but she was too terrified to move.

She wanted to close her eyes. Instead, she watched him because he was the only thing that seemed sure. He waited for the Rangers to slow, then nodded to Mac-

Leod. His men communicated silently, in signals Emily couldn't read.

MacLeod crept from one boulder to another, then signaled Ping and Wetherspoon.

She couldn't stand not knowing what their assailants were doing. She peeked from behind the boulder. The Rangers were rummaging through Darian's gear. Darian yanked her back down, but a Ranger shouted. "There!"

Darian cursed, then aimed his revolver. He fired and a Ranger fell. Gunshots erupted everywhere, echoing and blasting amidst a rain of dust and chaos. Bullets cracked rocks. Horses screamed—a sound so chilling it tore through Emily's soul.

The Rangers fired south of Darian's position, directing their fire at Ping and Wetherspoon. "Ping. . . . Why always Ping?" Darian groaned and rolled his eyes as if faced with an irritating problem at his day job. He laid his hand on Emily's shoulder while reloading one-handed. "Stay here."

Darian rose, crouched low, then sprang toward Ping's position. He fired as he ran, then dove behind another rock. The pale morning sun glinted on his hair as if seeking out the only beauty in catastrophe.

The Rangers shrieked when they saw him. A new round of fire opened up, so loud that Emily's ears hurt. Boulders shattered, spraying chunks of rock everywhere. She covered her head, but pebbles stung the backs of her hands.

A loose horse galloped by, his reins dangling. Emily fought a mad urge to run after the animal, sharing its wide-eyed panic. Darian had told her to stay put. She had to obey.

The smoke of musket fire covered everything. Men bellowed, and she couldn't tell the Rangers from Darian's men. The ground shook beneath the tumult of battle.

Another horse bounded past Emily's hiding place. The rider reined it back and it reared. Emily closed her eyes tight. If he saw her. . . . She had to run. Darian couldn't expect her to stay still when the battle took place right over her head.

She gathered her shaking nerves, then bolted from her rock. Something struck her thigh so hard that her legs jerked beneath her and she fell forward. A piece of boulder must have hit her. . . . Blood gushed from an open wound. Her brain lapsed into a surreal slow motion.

She looked down at her thigh. A round metal object protruded from her torn flesh and she screamed, horrified.

She tried to get up, but a horse spun to a halt. A man leapt toward her and grabbed her by her hair, then whooped. He yanked her to her feet, then jerked her back against his chest. He stank. In the dim blur of her horror, she realized that no matter how filthy he was, Darian Woodward smelled clean.

"Woodward, throw down your gun, or I'll kill your whore!" Emily's captor spit, but his whole body shook from aggression, bloodlust, and fear. He uttered a grunting laugh, then spat again. "Caught you with your pants down, eh, boy? Got your girl in her skivvies."

The thought of Darian Woodward, of all people, treated this way infuriated Emily beyond fear. She set her jaw, then slammed her elbow into her captor's gut. He grunted but he didn't let her go. If only she'd done better in her self-defense course! But nothing could have prepared her for this. . . .

Through her misty vision, she saw Darian Woodward appear out of a cloud of smoke. The sun glinted his golden hair as if heaven was seeking a young god to crown. He walked out from behind a boulder, tall and straight and confident. He smiled like a prince, lifted his arm, and aimed his revolver.

The shot hurtled Emily's captor backwards before she realized Darian had fired. Darian ran toward her, picked her up, and scooted them behind a boulder. He lowered her gently, then turned back to the fight. His back pressed against the red rock, and he fired again.

Another man fell, and the other Rangers whirled their horses around, then galloped away. Darian's men emerged like ghosts through the fog, then searched the area like hunters. In the midst of the skirmish field, Darian met MacLeod and the two men clasped hands.

They said nothing. Not a word. Shaking, Emily found herself looking for Darian's men. Bonner and Clyde gathered fallen muskets. Wetherspoon caught a horse, calmed it with a gentle touch to its damp neck, then tied it with the others. Herring checked their gear. Darian looked around for his seventh soldier. "Ping!"

Ping came running up the path, from the direction the Rangers had fled. "Four of 'em got away, Captain. I fired a shot after 'em, but they'll be hell and gone by tonight." Ping tossed his musket in the air, caught it, then laughed. "You showed 'em but good, sir! Whew!"

Even Ping wasn't afraid. Emily sank to the ground and leaned against the rock. The past was supposed to be fun. Cora made it sound wonderful. Never . . . this. Hot tears sprang from her eyes and trickled down her cheeks. Her breath came in small, rasping breaths.

Darian knelt beside her. "Look at me." He touched her face and wiped the moisture away with his thumb. She turned her head away. "Look at me, girl."

She did. She'd never seen eyes so gentle.

"You're hit, but it's not bad. Do you understand? It's over now."

She nodded.

"I've got to take care of this. You've got a bullet in you, and getting it out is going to hurt. Can you take that?"

"Yes." She was terrified she couldn't. Her tears came harder, but she bit her lip hard to stifle a sob.

He took out a knife and placed his hand on her thigh. His touch was gentle and warm. Though she was shaking, terrified, she realized that she had never been touched that way before. There was nothing ambiguous or noncommittal in Darian Woodward's touch, there was certainty and strength, and for the first time in her life, she felt protected.

He looked into her eyes, offering reassurance. He even smiled. "You look at me, not at what I'm doing."

Emily fixed her vision on his face and he turned attention to her wound. His hands worked quickly. The knife flicked, and the bullet popped out, followed by a gush of warm blood.

He cleaned the wound with a torn cloth, then bound it in white strips of gauze. She watched him in wonder. "Where did you get bandages?"

"I am always prepared for every possible occurrence."

In the aftermath of shock, Emily felt oddly numb. Dazed. Darian tied her bandage into a neat, secure knot, then sat back. She was still staring at his face. Her hand moved slowly as if on its own, and she touched his beard. "Thank you."

He looked shy, a striking contrast to his heroic confidence. "Can you stand, Miss Morgan?"

"I think so." She would stand if it killed her. He took her hand, and she forced herself up. "It's not so bad."

She swayed, then braced herself by gripping his shoulder. Darian Woodward had powerful shoulders, and his flesh even beneath his uniform jacket felt hard and strong. He put his arm around her, then picked her up. "You're too weak to walk. You'll ride with me."

She gazed up dreamily into his face. "Okay." His blond hair fell forward over one eye, giving him a boyish appearance despite the beard and grime. "Do you know no matter how dirty you are, you smell good?"

His eyes wandered to the side. "Thank you."

Sergeant MacLeod chuckled, but Emily couldn't tear her gaze from Darian's face. "You have pretty eyes."

"Thank you." He hesitated. "So do you."

The scenario of his rescue replayed in her mind. Slower, so she realized exactly what he'd done. . . . "What if you'd missed?"

He grinned, and even through his beard, she knew he had dimples. "Miss Morgan, I never miss."

Emily sat in front of Darian, quiet but pale. She leaned against his chest, but she seemed tense. She didn't say a word as they rode down from the ravaged campsite. She didn't complain when his horse stumbled over rocks, though the jarring must have caused her pain.

If Emily Morgan wasn't talking, her pain had to be intense.

"Miss Morgan. . . . If your leg is causing you a great deal of pain, we can stop and allow you to rest."

"You can't stop. Some of those men got away, and they might come back looking for you. Don't worry about me. I'm fine." She spoke through clenched teeth, and Darian's heart moved. She was a stubborn girl, but brave.

The sun grew hot, radiating upon the desert. The birds stilled and sought out shade, though an occasional hare hopped lazily across their path. Darian was used to the heat, and Emily hadn't mentioned it, but in her injured condition, it must be excruciating.

She adjusted her round, black spectacles and drew a tight breath. "I'm running out of water, though. If we pass a stream, would you please refill my bottle?"

"Of course."

Ping trotted up beside Darian, leading the mule behind. "Stream up ahead, sir, off to the left. Could fill up all our canteens. Just take a minute. Didn't get a chance this morning."

"Speak in full sentences, Ping."

Ping nodded dutifully, then resumed position behind Darian. Emily cranked her head around and looked at Darian. "You are so bossy."

"I am an officer. It is my place to lead the men in my command in all manner of behavior."

"Tyrant."

"Not at all." He paused, wondering why he felt hurt. "Only a short while ago, you considered me heroic." He paused again. "And you said I have pretty eyes."

"You do. Tyrannically beautiful eyes."

Insulting him seemed to bolster her spirits, but her color didn't improve. Emily's opinion of his looks didn't equal her appreciation of his heroism. And heroism, he had learned, came to a man who has seen so much, endured so much, that he has nothing left to lose. He would rather be admired for his looks.

Darian fingered his beard. He wasn't looking his best, perhaps. He favored a well-trimmed mustache over a beard, but he suspected he looked manly and virile in this unshaven state.

"You don't have lice in that, do you?"

Darian twitched, but MacLeod laughed. "Them critters ain't a problem out here, Miss. But they sure was hell to pay in Virginia. Weren't they, Captain?"

Darian straightened to a regal posture. "I have never had 'critters,' neither during the War, nor after."

Emily nodded at MacLeod. "The fleas kept them away."

She chuckled, but a spasm of pain twisted her face, and she fell silent again. Mercifully. Fleas, indeed.

"There are mesquite and creosote trees growing denser up ahead. We'll stop there and rest through the high sun, then ride on. Ping may gather water. When I was held captive by the Tonto Apache, I learned much of their food-gathering techniques. You will find prickly pear cactus, yucca, and roots that we can add to our larder."

Emily adjusted her position on his lap to alleviate pressure on her wounded leg. "Cora said they had fun dances, too."

"Their dances were obscene." Darian paused. "Not their ritual dances, but those which involved Miss Talmadge's Indian were unnecessarily provocative."

"Adrian? Why don't you use his name? Indian is so . . . politically incorrect. 'Native American' is better, although to be really correct, you should refer to the tribe name."

"Really?"

She caught his reminder and growled. "Okay, maybe I use that word too much. Anyway, by 'unnecessarily provocative,' I take it you mean sexy?"

"That word isn't used in my time."

"It is in mine. It refers to a quality about a person that makes you think of sex. It can be anything, really—what they're wearing, their voice, the way their hair falls over their eyes, the way they look at you. . . ." She peeked at him, her brow knit in confusion. "You can find the weirdest, most unexpected things sexy."

They stared at each other, blushed in unison, then looked quickly away. Darian's face felt hot, but he couldn't resist. . . . "I know."

*   *   *

Darian Woodward was an odd mixture of desperado and prude. Emily had never imagined that a real-life gunfighter could be sexy, but when he'd stepped out of the gunsmoke and saved her life, his image imprinted on her memory forever. He was magnificent. Bold and heroic and powerful.

She almost believed in a hero, in a man who upheld all he valued. Vague disquiet lingered in her heart. Darian wasn't taking her to Tucson for her good, but for his own. He needed her because she had information about the future. Maybe he had already realized that her knowledge could profit him.

She was already liking him, and admiring him. She couldn't deny a certain attraction, despite his unkempt appearance. Maybe he wasn't good-looking, not the way Ian was, but he was masculine in a Victorian way. Thank goodness. She didn't want a man who'd coasted through life by virtue of good looks and charm. There was something she didn't have to worry about with Darian Woodward.

Sex, on the other hand, might prove a dangerous temptation. . . . Maybe she wasn't the most romantic woman, but perhaps she could be physical. If she could only keep her heart out of it! Since Ian left her, she hadn't been tempted, and neither had she believed she could have an affair without hoping for it to turn romantic. But with Darian, it might be a possibility.

They reached a grove of mesquite and creosote, and Darian helped her from his horse's back. He set her down beneath the shade of a paloverde tree, then seated himself beside her. He tipped his wide-brimmed captain's hat forward over his eyes and fell promptly asleep.

Emily shook her head, then tried to make herself comfortable, too. Her leg throbbed, not just around her wound, but from her hip down to her ankle.

Darian's gang seated themselves like javalina beneath various bushes, resting, each man with his own thoughts. An odd bunch, they were. Herring was shaped like a tree trunk, with no curves or roundness, but solid. Bonner and Clyde looked like criminals, rarely spoke, and played cards whenever they stopped. Wetherspoon was thin and devoted to Darian. Ping had to have been a shop clerk before heading west.

MacLeod was heavy, with a red beard, and his voice carried the faint trace of a Scottish accent. He treated Darian both as a son and a hero. They all admired their mutinous young captain, and after his display of courage, she could see why. If he felt fear at all, he didn't show it, and that confidence had to rub off on his men.

Emotion seemed buried deep in Darian Woodward. She wondered if he ever cried, or laughed uncontrollably the way she did. She found herself studying his sleeping face, wondering what he looked like beneath the beard.

He had the most aristocratic, well-formed nose she'd ever seen, narrow and straight, in perfect proportion to the rest of his face. So he wasn't homely, just unconcerned with appearance. Her gaze wandered from his face to his body. He was tall and lean, with broad shoulders and slender hips. Her gaze stopped at his groin, and hot embarrassment flooded through her.

His erection was well-defined beneath his dusty uniform trousers. She'd seen naked men before, in pictures. She had a vague memory of Ian, but their youthful encounters had been rushed by circumstances, and he had been too shy to lie naked beside her.

She'd never been more embarrassed in her life. Who would have thought Darian Woodward would be . . . this way?

She fixed her vision upward to the blue sky, but her

cheeks flamed with embarrassment. She shouldn't have noticed. She never should have looked at his groin. The man was sleeping. Obviously dreaming.

She had invaded his private space. It wouldn't happen again.

She peered casually down at her hands, then fiddled with her bandage ties. Her vision seized its own will and skipped back to Darian's groin. For a brief, horrifying flash, she imagined making love to him. She would wake him with an erotic touch, then slip her hand beneath his trousers. She would kiss him and feel his desire, and. . . .

"Help me up!"

He startled and jumped up, blue eyes wide and innocent. Innocent! Of all things. "What . . . ? Are you all right?"

"I . . . I have to pee!"

This day couldn't get worse. Emily wanted the world to open and swallow her whole. She clasped her hands over her face. *Good cover. That's so much better than letting him know you're lusting after him.*

He held out his hand. She took it, and he helped her to her feet. She forced a pained smile, groaned, then hobbled away. *Maybe I'll just keep limping on, and never turn back.*

She hadn't had enough water to make her request necessary, but she had to get away from him. She took a brief, limping walk, waited a moment, then headed back. Darian was standing beneath the paloverde tree waiting for her. He looked concerned. Maybe he didn't know what "pee" meant. She could only hope.

She smiled formally when she returned, then drank as much water as she could hold. "I don't want to get dehydrated."

"It's time to go, Miss Morgan."

Did he have any idea how . . . exposed he had been?

Probably not. He probably didn't even remember what he was dreaming. He wouldn't have a clue that her mind had flooded with erotic images at the sight of him.

It was best forgotten. Her wound was causing her to think peculiar things. "Maybe I should ride the mule now. I'm a lot better."

"You look pale." He hesitated. "But if that is what you wish. . . ."

"I think it's for the best."

"Then it will be done. Ping, bring the mule."

Chapter Four

Darian Woodward, blue-eyed bandit, had become the image of sex personified. Emily rode behind him, her mind filled with erotic scenes. As one began, she snapped it off like an unwelcome television show, but another rose to take its place.

Darian, a medieval knight, lying on his back, naked, summoning her to his bed. Darian, a blond-haired Viking, sweeping her off her feet and ravaging her. Darian as a pirate. . . . She could imagine him in any role, but the dreams faded when she tried to picture herself that way. She couldn't see herself as the romantic figure in any dream, not when it had been proven so conclusively that she wasn't the type.

She tried to picture herself as another woman, perhaps blond like Cora. . . . No joy came in the image. She wanted Darian to look at *her* that way, no one else.

"This is pathetic."

He snapped around in his saddle and looked back. "Are you all right, Miss Morgan? You appear increasingly white."

She'd almost forgotten her leg. Lustful thoughts had the power to obliterate pain. "I think I'm delirious."

It was too soon for an infection, but she might have a fever. That could explain her thought pattern. She'd probably hallucinated Darian's erection.

Yes.

He slowed his mount and allowed her to catch up. She kept her line of vision away from his groin.

"The jostling of your ride may aggravate your injury." Darian tipped his hat against the afternoon sun. "If only we had another means of transportation."

"Well, like you said, the trains are back east, and I don't think there's a helicopter nearby to whisk me to a hospital. I'll be fine, Captain. Really."

"You're in pain. *Really*."

Sometimes, that teasing half-smile could be brutally sexy. Emily repressed a groan. "I'm just a little weak." *So weak I'm thinking of ripping your clothes off. . . .*

He noticed her expression and his eyes narrowed. "I believe you are indeed approaching delirium. If I could get you to Tucson, we can make suitable arrangements with the fort doctor."

"What? You're just going to ride into town? Won't they recognize you?"

"I am not well known in Tucson. The fort is ill-manned at this time, and until I confront General Davis, we will go unnoticed."

"It's only another day's ride." Emily's voice sank toward despair. Every stride the mule took antagonized her open wound. She'd been distracted by lustful thoughts, but the pain was growing. "Maybe after a good sleep." Which she wasn't likely to get wrapped in a parachute.

Ping cleared his throat as if for a speech, then edged up beside Emily. "The stagecoach will be passing by this way, Captain. I know you was planning to avoid it, but. . . ."

Emily's stomach tightened. "No. . . ."

Darian rubbed his chin thoughtfully. "If the coachman would allow us use of his vehicle, we could pay for his interrupted route."

"You are not stealing a stagecoach. Forget it. I'm fine."

His blond brow angled to a posture of superiority. "I have no intentions of 'stealing,' Miss Morgan. We will *borrow* it. I will explain the necessity to the driver, and he will understand."

"What about his passengers?"

"The northbound coach isn't likely to carry passengers. It's headed for Camp McDowell, where it will transport fort soldiers back to Tucson on leave."

Emily bowed her head. "Please, don't."

Darian didn't seem to hear her. He stopped, then turned to his men. "Ping, ride on ahead and scout for the coach. When you spot it, report back. Gentlemen, we don't want to alarm the coachman. Polite manners are to be remembered at all times."

Ping galloped on ahead, his tattered blue jacket flapping in the wind. He left a cloud of dust in his wake. Darian's outlaws loaded their muskets, and Darian checked his revolver.

They looked anything but polite.

"I cannot believe you're holding up a stagecoach. You really are a bandit, after all. History was right!"

Emily sat shivering on her mule, but Darian paid no attention to her as he ordered his men into position along a dusty path. Ping had reported back, and as the sun set over the Sonoran desert, the gang of outlaws prepared to attack. Politely.

"We aren't 'holding up a stagecoach,' Miss Morgan. We're preparing to make a request."

"If you're not holding it up, why are you all hiding?"

The magnificent seven took position in the shadows, behind rocks, near trees. Every one of them held a gun. Darian eyed her with a condescending frown. "The coachman might misunderstand our approach. We don't want to give him time to react unfavorably."

"Don't do this. I don't want to ride in a coach. Look, my leg is all better. I'm fine."

"You are pale, you're shivering, and the blood has soaked through your bandage. Riding has kept the wound open."

"I don't care!"

"A leg wound is grave, Miss Morgan. If it turned gangrenous. . . ." His voice trailed, but his expression hardened as he turned his attention back to the stage-coach pass. "We will prevent that possibility."

A whistle from Ping alerted them to the approaching stagecoach. Darian checked his revolver again. Ritual. The men moved slowly, in silence. An aura of confidence and rugged individualism surrounded them. They knew what they were doing.

From his horse, Darian hitched Emily's mule to a tree. "This time, Miss Morgan, you stay out of trouble. When we've garnered the coachman's cooperation, I will return to fetch you. Stay put. Do you hear?"

"Yes."

"Good."

She glared at him. He smiled. *You are so sexy.*

Darian turned his horse and cantered back to his position. He rode as if he'd been born in the saddle, with such expert grace that he was an art form to watch. *He's about to rob a stagecoach, and you're admiring him. Get a grip!*

Eccentricity appealed to her. Darian was nothing if not eccentric.

Emily's mule chewed thoughtfully on a juniper bush while Emily watched the gang prepare to "garner co-operation." The coach came into view, and her pulse raced. Darian nodded his silent signals, and his men responded.

They charged into open view and surrounded the coach. Ping and Wetherspoon grabbed the lead horses of the team, and they stopped amid frantic neighs. A man shouted. A shot fired, and Emily's blood ran cold. It wasn't answered, so she guessed it came from the terrified coachman.

"I ain't got nothing worth taking! Just a few empty trunks bound up for McDowell. Nothing!"

Darian issued calm orders as if directing seating at a church gathering. "Wetherspoon, if you would please check the interior for passengers. Sergeant MacLeod, relieve this gentleman of his gun."

Emily rolled her eyes. He was certainly polite. Crazy, but polite.

"Please don't be alarmed by the abruptness of our arrival. We mean you no harm. A manner of necessity has arisen, and. . . ."

"You're. . . . You're that outlaw Woodward, ain't ye?" The coachman stammered with fear, and scrambled to the far side of his seat. Darian tipped his wide-brimmed hat and nodded.

"Don't be alarmed, sir. As I said, we mean no harm. We have need of your vehicle, and since you have no passengers. . . ."

"Take it! Take everything. Just don't . . . shoot!"

"I have no intention of shooting."

"I've heard of you. . . . Just . . . let me go. . . . Please."

"There's no need for you to 'go' anywhere. We simply need use of this coach, and when we've. . . ."

"God help me!" The coachman leapt down from his seat and ran wildly out toward the open desert. Darian stared after him, aghast. His gang watched the coachman, confused, then turned in unison to Darian.

MacLeod shoved his hat back and scratched his head. "What's he about, Captain?"

Darian issued an impatient, annoyed huff. "I have no idea. Perhaps he fears retribution if his route is delayed. Be that as it may, we will borrow this coach for our journey, then have it returned to him once we arrive. Ping, leave a canteen of water for the gentleman. That sounds fair."

The men nodded, but Emily slumped on her mule. "He's done it. He's stolen a coach. Fair!"

Darian cantered back to her, brought his horse to an effortless, smooth halt, then unhitched her mule. He looked proud. "An unforeseen action has occurred, in that the coachman has abruptly departed, but as you can see, there were no injuries, nor any general unpleasantness."

"Oh, what a relief!"

"You and I will ride in the coach, so that I can keep an eye on your condition." Darian turned in his saddle to address his men. "Bonner and Clyde will take shifts driving the coach, and the others will ride in varying degrees of lookout. The moon is high until midnight. I have decided that we'll ride until it sets, so be sure to switch horses, men. When we reach Tucson, we'll have the coach returned, and the gentleman can continue about his business."

"You . . . are nuts."

His brow puckered. "What troubles you, Miss Morgan?"

"You stole a coach! That guy thinks you're a bandit. I'm not sure he's wrong, but do you know what you're doing to your reputation? Even if you could prove you were right to mutiny, how are you going to explain all this?"

His bewilderment intensified. "I have done nothing out of order."

"You're too 'out of order' to notice!"

He reached down from his high posture on the gray steed and patted her shoulder. "We'll be just fine. Don't worry." He spoke in a soothing voice, but Emily recognized an unyielding mood.

"Captain, I've seen a lot of crazy men in my life. But nothing, no one compares to you. I hope you know what you're doing."

"Miss Morgan, I always do."

Apprehending the coach had been good luck. Darian stretched his legs, crossed comfortably at the ankles. The coachman's hasty departure had been unfortunate, but perhaps for the best.

The full moon filtered light through the coach window, casting a blue glow over Emily Morgan's sleeping face. She lay opposite from him, curled up on the hard bench seat, her head resting on her folded arm. An uncomfortable position. She'd tried using her pack as a pillow, then abandoned it to the coach floor.

The coach wheels caught on a rock, then jerked. The motion knocked Emily off-balance and she pitched forward. Darian sprang forward and caught her before she could fall. She grabbed his arms to steady herself, then uttered a miserable sigh before resuming her position.

If he held her head in his lap. . . . The thought was

excruciating, and a sore temptation. It would be innocent. In such circumstances, a gentleman would be right
to do whatever he could to provide comfort.

Darian took a deep breath, then moved to her seat.
She opened one eye and looked at him suspiciously.
"What are you doing?"

He smiled. The effort felt strained. "Put your head on
my lap."

Her other eye opened, too. "I beg your pardon?"

"Give me your head."

"I don't think so!" She reacted as if he'd offended
her. Darian hesitated, baffled by her response.

"It is for your own good that I make this offer."

"Look, I don't even know how, okay? I mean, I think
you really have to trust someone first. It's not just . . .
recreational."

Darian placed his hand on her forehead. She felt cool
enough. His nose wrinkled as he tried to decipher her
meaning.

"Have I offended you in some manner?"

She propped herself up on one arm and looked at him.
Her jaw shifted to one side as she chewed the inside of
her lip. "You're not asking for . . . um . . . what I thought
you were asking for, are you?"

"I am not asking anything. I am offering my lap for
your comfort. Also, I might prevent your fall if Bonner
and Clyde should lapse from the straight path again."

Her lips formed an 'O' and she puffed an uncertain
breath of air. "I knew that." She eyed his lap. Even in
the moonlight, he knew she blushed.

She was a maiden, unmarried. Yet maidens of the future seemed more aware of masculine secrets than those
of his own time. It was possible, however shocking, that
she knew this area of his body posed a certain bestial
threat to her person.

"I am a gentleman, in all senses of that word. You have nothing to fear from me, Miss Morgan."

She smiled and her eyelids drifted sensually low. She leaned closer to him, then kissed his cheek. "I know."

Before he could respond or question her cryptic remark, she maneuvered herself down, then cradled her head on his lap. She placed one hand on his thigh, and tucked the other near her chin.

Of all the mindless, ill-planned, wretched mistakes of his life, this was the worst. He had no idea where to put his hands. His left hand could rest at his side, but his right remained a problem. He fingered his beard, then adjusted his hat, then scratched his left shoulder.

"Stop squirming."

He glared down at her. "I'm . . . I'm uncertain where to position my right hand."

She peeked up at him, then seemed to guess his dilemma. "How about on my shoulder?"

"Very well." He did as she suggested. She relaxed and closed her eyes. Her shoulder felt delicate and small. He moved his hand lower to her arm. She was a fit woman with firm, taut flesh. He struggled against the desire to caress her, to pat her gently as he might a kitten.

"I had a kitten once."

Her eyes snapped open. "Thanks for sharing, Darian." A smile played on her lips. She rolled over onto her back and gazed up at him. He adjusted his coat to cover her bare legs. "I've always loved cats. I've got three now. Cora is keeping them while I'm gone. What was your kitten's name?"

Her wavy brown hair fell around her face like a teasing curtain. He wanted to touch her. "Delilah."

"That's ironic. My fuzziest one is named Samson. The other two are Scarlett and Rhett. I'm surprised you like cats. I'd figured you for a hunting-dog-type guy."

"I like soft things." He couldn't help himself. His fingers slipped to her hair and he followed a thick curl. She caught her lip between her teeth. She looked young and uncertain. Shy. "Go to sleep, Miss Morgan. You're safe now."

She watched him for a moment, then offered a tiny smile. "Yes, Captain. I believe I am."

She was safe, but he was in agony. He stroked her soft hair, sifting it through his fingers. She seemed to like it, and reacted much as a kitten would to his touch. She almost purred with contentment. A faint, satisfied smile curved her lips.

His pulse grew stronger with every touch. It fueled his loins with a desire he'd never known. His entire masculine area was tight and hard. It ached almost to pain. A young, wounded woman trusted his honor enough to rest her weary head on his lap, and he was near contorted with lust.

She wasn't touching anything . . . significant. But she was so close. He'd held women before, when dancing. He'd kissed his former fiancée on the cheek, and once on the lips. A drunken woman had kissed him at a ball after the war, and stuck her tongue in his mouth. She'd tasted like bourbon, and he was disgusted.

Soon after he'd arrived in Arizona, an officer's wife had seized him, yanked him behind a cabin, and kissed him violently. Her kiss had been more interesting. His life and honor had been more important, so he avoided her afterwards. When her husband left the fort, leaving Darian in command, he'd found her in his bed, but he'd pretended she'd lost her way, and hidden himself in the soldiers' barracks until the colonel returned.

Those women had intended to provoke his manly, earthly desires. Emily Morgan didn't. She liked to tease him, to insult him, and she loved to chat. She never employed feminine wiles to seize his attention. But his attention fixed on her, anyway.

Darian tried to sleep, but images of kissing her flooded his mind. He saw himself lying beside her, touching her. Cora and Adrian had slept side by side, they'd cuddled, they'd held hands. He hadn't understood before, but it made sense now, this longing to be as close as you can get.

The moon faded, and the coach crossed over a shallow stream. Emily didn't wake, but her fingers curved, gripping his leg as if in sleep she sought his protection. Darian drifted in and out of sleep, never settling deep, kept tense by his arousal.

The moon sank, and darkness covered the desert. The men stopped to rest. Darian heard Wetherspoon snoring near the coach. He tried to sleep, too, but it wasn't easy. When morning came, his eyelids felt heavy from weariness. They started off again at the first light of dawn, but Emily slept soundly, still comfortable on his lap.

He tried to sleep again, but galloping hoofbeats startled him to wakefulness. He drew his Colt revolver on instinct, then eased himself from beneath Emily's head. She woke, and opened her bleary eyes. "What's the matter?"

"An interesting development. Keep low."

Darian opened the door, then swung out. MacLeod was ready. "We heard 'em, Captain. We're set."

"Out of sight. Wait until they're on us, then you know what to do. I'll handle them from inside."

"Yes, sir!"

MacLeod galloped off, and the other men hid themselves. Clyde jumped down from the driver's seat, tied the horses to a bush and took position behind a boulder, leaving the coach standing alone as if deserted. The coach horses seemed glad for the rest.

Darian eased himself back into the coach and waited. Emily sat up. "What's going on?"

"Hush, and keep low. It's nothing to worry about."

"What?"

"We're under attack. By bandits, I assume." She started to squeal, but he shook his head. "Sssh. Don't worry."

She tipped her head back and groaned. "Why would I worry?"

The horsemen galloped up and stopped. Already rattled. Darian smiled and shook his head.

"This is the one the head man told us to bring down. . . ." Darian listened with interest. Apparently, these bandits worked for someone, probably the person responsible for the recent robberies that had left many soldiers and officers without funds during the winter months.

Here was a chance to act on behalf of his country, even without orders. He would prevent the robbery, then find out who instigated these well-timed holdups.

"Where the hell is the driver?" Yes, the bandit sounded confused. Good.

"Must have seen us and run off." The other man chuckled. "This is the one. Get the trunk, and we'll get it out of here."

Emily cast a quick glance at Darian. "Trunk?" She whispered. "What trunk?"

Darian shrugged, then positioned his gun. He heard a rifle blast, and someone yelped in surprise, then swore.

"Figure you boys have gone far enough. Hands to the sky, and drop them guns." MacLeod sounded paternal. Darian nodded his approval, waited for the sound of dropping guns, then stuck his head out the door.

"You gentlemen seem to be on the wrong path this morning."

A squat, bearded man spotted Darian and his eyes rounded like saucers. "You're. . . . Why, hell and damnation! You're that outlaw soldier! Woodward, ain't it?"

Darian's brow puckered. "You gentlemen are mistaken. I was condemned unfairly. I've done absolutely nothing to warrant the title 'outlaw.' "

The bandit cackled as if Darian had pulled off a good joke. "Is that a fact? What you doing with that there coach?"

"I am transporting a young lady to Tucson."

The bandits howled with laughter, and MacLeod cast a doubtful glance Darian's way. Darian shrugged. "I suggest you men find a different source of employment. Holding up stagecoaches is illegal and dangerous."

"Whew! You're a whip, Woodward! Smooth as silk." He shook his head, still laughing. " 'Transporting a lady.' That's a good one. You've stolen enough gold stashed in them trunks to buy you five hundred 'ladies.' "

Darian's mouth dropped open. "Gold?"

The bandit hooted. "Just as if he don't know! Them trunks were being sent to the new general at Camp McDowell. Ripe filled with gold. I thought we were the only ones who knew about it. But the head man didn't count on you!"

Darian's eyes narrowed. "The head man? And who would that be?"

The leader laughed. "I ain't fool enough to be telling you that, Woodward! Let's just say we've had the 'inside track,' until now. There ain't a better outlaw than one who started on the side of the law. But you know that better than anyone."

The bandit turned to his two cohorts and shook his head. "Lads, we've been bested. We'll get on back to

Texas and hold up a bank. We ain't got nothing on this fellow!"

In unison, the three men whirled their horses and galloped away. MacLeod aimed his rifle, but his gaze shifted back to the coach. Ping looked at Wetherspoon. Bonner and Clyde climbed onto the roof and opened the trunk. Pale moonlight glinted on gold.

Darian held up his hand to stop all possible comments. The men resumed their places, all looking strained and embarrassed. Ping whistled in a high, uncertain tone as he rode forward with Wetherspoon. MacLeod glanced heavenward as if in prayer, and Herring wiped his brow with a handkerchief. Bonner and Clyde took the driver's seat as if nothing had happened.

Darian sank back into the coach.

"Well, well, well. Gold." Emily Morgan radiated more amused pleasure than anyone he'd ever seen in his life. "The blue-eyed bandit strikes again."

"So, let's see. You've been in a gunfight, held up any number of stagecoaches, and now you've stolen another one filled with gold. You're admired by renegades everywhere, a legend in your own time, and your name is on every wanted poster in the land." Emily sat back comfortably on the coach bench as it proceeded forward. "So . . . how goes the quest for 'justice,' Captain?"

Darian looked out the window, his expression dark. Emily peered over her shoulder and recognized the landscape just north of Tucson.

"The path to justice is often uncertain, Miss Morgan, but it is always true."

"If you change your name, and get out of Arizona now, you might be able to resume a normal life. Maybe you can run away to Mexico."

He turned to look at her, and she knew he would never run. "I will do no such thing. My honor has been maligned, and wrong prevails. I will not stop until I have altered this travesty of justice."

"How is marching straight to your hanging 'justice?' "

"No fate is certain." He didn't sound convinced, but his eyes narrowed as he watched her. "From what I have learned from you, I should be able to alter its course."

"I don't know much about your fate, Captain. Only that you were hanged in Tucson, and are remembered as a villain."

Darian rubbed his chin thoughtfully. Perhaps he wasn't used to a beard. Emily wondered what he looked like without it. "If I am remembered as villainous, then I must take steps to alter that reputation now."

"How? By stealing coaches filled with gold?"

"That was done for your benefit. In the other version of 'my past,' I wouldn't have taken this action."

"No. You would have held it up for some other reason."

"I would not."

"You are a stubborn man, Captain."

He smiled. "I am."

Emily sat back in her seat, shaking her head. She watched him a while. He met her gaze briefly, then turned his piercing attention to the landscape. He was such a scruffy-looking man, yet his posture was always straight, even rigid.

"You need to relax."

He glanced over his shoulder. He scanned her face, then allowed his vision to move lower. He shook his head as if his mind had traveled somewhere he had forbidden, then looked away. "Relaxing, Miss Morgan, is the last thing I need to do."

She tried to look out the other window, but found herself watching Darian again. She was smitten. Nothing serious, but definitely smitten. Probably because he seemed the antithesis of Ian Hallowell, strong and confident, brazen in his disregard of danger. Ian had been filled with self-doubt, with a tendency to feel guilty for things he had no control over. Nothing like Darian.

Darian Woodward held up a stagecoach, stole a fortune in gold, and saw nothing "out of order." Ian had come from an intensely conservative, old-fashioned family. He had deferred to them in everything—except in his relationship with Emily. At least, until he disappeared.

"What's your family like?"

Darian didn't answer at once, and he didn't look away from the window. "My family lives in upstate New York."

Emily drew a patient breath. "I mean, do you have sisters and brothers?"

"I have—had—three sisters. One of them died in childbirth during the war. My father died when I was twelve." He paused, and though his voice remained steady, Emily sensed a source of pain.

"Were you close to your dad?"

"My father was an honorable, good man. He raised his sons to follow in his footsteps."

"So he held up coaches, too?" She was trying to tease him, but he didn't react. "What do you mean, 'sons'? You said you have sisters."

Again, he paused before answering. "I had a brother. He died at Gettysburg." This time, Darian's voice came low, tight with restraint.

"Was he older than you?"

He paused for a very long time, and from his profile, she saw that he closed his eyes. "Barely. We were twins."

A chill coursed through Emily's veins. She touched his arm, then his shoulder. "I am so sorry." She didn't know what to say. What would it mean to lose your brother in a war? How could she offer help when she had lived a life of gentle ease? She felt sure Darian didn't want to talk about his brother's death, but the need to know him, to be closer to him, swelled inside her. She fidgeted, cleared her throat, but could think of no easy way to ask.

Darian sighed audibly, then turned in his seat to face her. His expression appeared blank, unemotional, yet his blue eyes cooled to a pale shade of gray, as if even his soul distanced itself from pain. "My brother and I had fought side by side from the time we joined the Union Army. We were given the rank of captain at the same time, and led our respective commands in unison. We operated with such precision, skill, and foresight that our commander saw fit to send us into the field together."

He sounded proud, but distant. Emily wondered what it would take to open Darian's heart, to see his heart in his eyes. "Was he a good shot, too?"

He smiled, still distant. "My brother had a slight edge over me in strategy, but I held the advantage in marksmanship." His gaze wandered back to the window, and again, she saw his eyes close. No tears. Never tears.

"How did he die?" She didn't want to ask, but still, she wanted him to trust her.

Nothing changed in Darian's demeanor, but she felt him as he turned inward. "We led our divisions into the field during the charge of General George Pickett. My division was first, and was gravely threatened. My brother led his own forward, because I was surrounded, and he drove them back." His voice never missed a beat, it betrayed no emotion. "My brother was shot in the leg, and when the battle was over, I carried him off the field."

"Did he die of the wound?"

"Eventually."

She hesitated, moving closer to him. He didn't notice. "I suppose the medical care was . . . primitive."

Darian tipped his head back and leaned against the seat. The morning sun on his wide forehead shone pale gold. "There were thousands of wounded, Miss Morgan. Each one's care took time, and many died. By the time they reached my brother, his leg had turned gangrenous. The surgeon considered any attempt futile, so went on to the next, who had more hope of survival."

"Do you mean they didn't even try?" How barbaric was the past, to let a man die without trying?

But Darian remained unmoved, unemotional. "The surgeon did what he thought was right. He was not unkind."

"I can't believe that surgeon wouldn't even try." Anger swelled in her chest, to think of Darian sitting with his dying brother, no one to help. "I would have tried."

He opened his eyes and looked at her thoughtfully. "I tried." His voice was soft and low, as if he hadn't meant to speak.

"You tried?"

"I took the saw and I cut off my brother's leg. He thanked me, and then he died."

Emily's heart quailed. Her eyes filled with tears. She wanted to speak, but no words came. Her tears obscured her vision, then fell to her cheeks. Darian stared at her, his expression blank, like a mirror. He watched her cry and sat immobile, as if her reaction paralyzed him.

As she cried, she realized Darian Woodward couldn't cry anymore. His courage came from his heart; he had seen so much that nothing frightened him at all. He reached for her hesitantly, then drew her into his arms. She looked up at him, into blue eyes filled with wonder, and the distance in those eyes faded.

"Your brother must have been very brave. Almost as brave as you."

His eyes glittered, but she knew the tears there would remain unshed. "He would have done the same for me."

She reached to touch his face. She had no words to comfort him. She had only herself. For a long while, they stared at each other, her hand against his cheek, his arms around her. Then slowly, without words, he bent to kiss her.

His mouth met hers with infinite tenderness, a soft exploration. She parted her lips and played gently against the corner of his mouth. His breath quickened, his shoulders tensed. Passion surged unexpectedly, and his kiss intensified. Emily gripped his shoulders to hold him closer. He tasted her, and she met the touch of his tongue with her own. His whole body tightened and a low moan grew in his throat.

Aroused, Darian Woodward became another man. Less a gentleman. His hands trembled as he felt the contours of her back, his breath came swift with desire. Emily was lost in their kiss, held close by a man so strong that she thought she might never feel alone again. She slipped her hands beneath his uniform to feel the taut, muscled flesh of his chest, then down. He kissed her with surging passion, abandoning her lips to kiss her face, her temples, her forehead.

"Captain!" Ping's cheerful voice jolted them both from their passion. Darian snapped to the opposite seat. Emily just stared, aghast.

Darian swallowed hard, trying to compose himself. "Ping. What is it?"

Ping swung open the coach door, still on his horse. He offered a bright smile and nodded at Emily. "Mornin', Miss."

"Good morning, Ping." Her voice quavered, but Ping must have attributed that to her injury.

"You're looking fine, this morning, Miss. Pink cheeks." His eyes narrowed. "Very pink cheeks. You fevered, Miss?"

She fanned herself with the edge of her parachute. "No—it's just a bit warm in here."

Ping eyed Darian. "Captain's flushed, too."

Darian's blush deepened as Ping studied him suspiciously. "As Miss Morgan said, it is warm inside the coach."

Emily tried to think of a way to extract them from the embarrassment of their situation. "Water. We need water. Ping, could you refill my water bottle?"

"Can do better than that!" Ping whipped his canteen from his saddle and tossed it in the door at Emily. She caught it, but Darian growled.

"Ping, you do not pitch articles at a lady."

Emily fought a smile. "I caught it, didn't I?"

He avoided looking at her and nodded. Emily drank as Ping rode on ahead. She still felt hot. She hesitated, then splashed a little water on her neck. Darian watched as if transfixed, then held out his hand.

"If you would. . . ."

She passed him the canteen. Darian took a long draught, paused as if assessing its effects, then glanced at her damp chest. He shrugged, then emptied it all over his face and neck.

Warmth filled Emily's heart. Not desire, but the deep, tender warmth of caring. "Captain Woodward, you learn fast."

He set the canteen aside and smiled. "Miss Morgan, I certainly do."

Chapter Five

They rode into Tucson, the coach left hidden in the Catalina hills, lest their possession of the gold be "misunderstood." So Darian on his gray, Emily on her mule, and the gang of outlaws emerged from the shadows of the hills—like an unexpected storm.

The whole thing felt ominous. Emily wished she had a magnificent horse to ride, too, and peered down at her mule's thin neck with misgivings. Her leg felt much better, but despite her doubts about Darian's plan, sleeping in a bed in a pleasant, old-fashioned inn sounded promising.

They stopped at the edge of town, and Emily looked around. "This is nothing like I expected."

Darian glanced at her. "You said that about me."

"I did." Emily paused to groan. "This can't be a good sign. Where is everyone?"

Darian shaded his eyes against the morning sun. "I'm

not sure. Tucson, though smaller by far than the grand cities and villages of the East, which is also a more civilized world by all accounts, is generally a bustling, albeit lawless hamlet."

Emily shook her head and sighed. "They weren't kidding about Victorians being long-winded."

Darian didn't seem to notice her comment, but his lips curled slightly as if he resisted her provocation. She felt strange with him after their kiss. As if she should know him better, as if she should understand what motivated him. But Darian Woodward operated to his own inner drummer, to a tune no one else could hear. And whatever that was now drove him downward upon the unsuspecting inhabitants of Tucson.

Emily assessed the small new town. Tucson looked more like an old stage set than she expected. A straight road through town, with a few short side streets. Shop fronts looked familiar, because she had seen them in movies. She even spotted a saloon, "The Gaudy Dove," farther down the main street.

Metal banged against metal. From movies, not from memory, Emily recognized the sounds of a blacksmith at work. "Sometimes, I think I must be dreaming."

Darian leaned down and eyed his horse's hooves. "It is time to have our mounts reshod. Let us approach the blacksmith first and make arrangements." He guided his horse toward the smithy, but a black-bearded man with a leather apron peered out of the shed, spotted Darian, then bellowed as if startled by a grizzly bear.

"Saints preserve us! No!" For such a large man, his voice came oddly high.

Darian's brow furrowed, but he offered a polite nod. "Good morning, sir. We require a moment of your time. . . ." He edged his horse toward the blacksmith, but the man choked back another cry, then burst from the shed, his apron flapping as he bolted down the street, then crashed into the saloon.

Silence followed, broken only by the creaking of the saloon doors as they swung.

Darian stared after the terrified blacksmith. He shook his head, then turned back to his men. "That was peculiar in the extreme. What provoked the gentleman to such odd action?"

Darian's men all appeared perplexed, but Emily groaned. She urged her mule forward, then turned it to face the others. " *'What provoked him?'* What do you think provoked him? *You* provoked him!"

Darian's brow furrowed tighter still. "I did nothing but issue a simple, polite request."

She tipped her head back and exhaled slowly. "Darian, I think these people have heard of you."

He brightened immediately, then nodded. "Good. Then we are in fine stead to proceed." He didn't wait for her argument. He motioned to his men, and they rode on into town, all proud and sure of themselves.

Emily and her mule held back as the magnificent seven went on ahead. Darian rode at the center, a little before the others. Dust coiled around their horses' feet, and a dry wind meandered down the street.

Something that resembled, yes, a tumbleweed rolled across the road at the far end of town, then disappeared behind the last building on the left. Emily stared. "It can't be. . . ."

In the silence of old Tucson, the wind made an odd sound. A sound she had heard before. A soft whistle, haunting, as if in a far-off echo accompanying the wind, accompanying the outlaw Darian Woodward, blue-eyed bandit, as he rode into town. . . .

* * *

Darian had been to Tucson before, and liked its simplicity. True, the citizens tended to be unkempt, and he had avoided the revelry of the saloon, but with work, it could prove a pleasant abode. He remembered it, however, as livelier, with ladies in bright dresses being escorted by their husbands to the various shops, people talking in the streets.

Perhaps this day was the Sabbath—he had lost track of time since hiding out in the desert. Darian considered this, then nodded to MacLeod. "All becomes clear, Sergeant."

MacLeod eyed him doubtfully, then scratched his forehead. "Does it, Captain?"

"Of course. Today is most likely the Sabbath, and the townsfolk are all in a place of worship. This would explain the blacksmith's reaction—he was embarrassed to be caught at work when he should have been at prayer."

"Not the Sabbath today, Captain. It's a Tuesday."

Darian shrugged. They stopped outside the saloon, and Darian dismounted, then hitched his horse to the rail. His men did likewise. "Then perhaps another holiday." He glanced back for Emily. She sat on her mule, still at the edge of town. He wondered why she hesitated. He motioned to her. "Miss Morgan, your presence is required."

He saw her glance heavenward, her shoulders slump. She looked dejected and resigned as she urged her sluggish mule forward and rode to his side. She stopped beside him, peered at him miserably and sighed. "I fully expect to be shot."

The woman had no faith in his abilities. "You will not be shot."

"Not shot *again,* you mean."

Darian frowned, then reached to help her from her mule. She sank down into his arms. He liked the feeling, too much. If he hadn't been thinking so much of her kiss, he might have planned his entry into Tucson with more care, but their passion filled his thoughts.

He had to get her into a dress at once, so that his desire could be tempered by the image of her as a lady. "Maybe you should put on the dress you said you packed."

Emily groaned, fished around in her pack and pulled out a thin gown that looked more like a lady's chemise than a day gown. Darian frowned. "That won't do at all." He could picture her in this garment, soft and clinging to her womanly curves. Darian cleared his throat, sensing that his face flushed. "Once we have made the acquaintance of the pertinent craftsmen in town, we will arrange for a suitable garment for you, Miss Morgan."

"If we live that long."

Her doubt grated. Darian's frown deepened until his face ached. He opened his mouth to argue the point, but something crashed from within the saloon, distracting him. He heard the discordant sounds of a piano, as if the keys had been roughly jarred. Another crash followed, as if a table had overturned.

Darian released Emily and motioned to his men. "Take your places, gentlemen. It appears that the saloon patrons are brawling, as is typical of their kind. We may be required to break up a fight."

As one, the men drew their guns. Darian enjoyed the moment. He liked helping people. He liked restoring order out of chaos. He prepared to enter the saloon, then noticed Emily. She clamped her hands over her face and sank down, groaning against the wall outside the saloon. He lowered his gun.

"Are you faint, Miss Morgan?"

She peeked out between her fingers, looking at him

as if he were some unimagined oddity. "You just don't get it, do you?"

Questioning his abilities—it had gone too far. "Miss Morgan, I will thank you to refrain from comments detrimental to the matter at hand."

Long-winded, indeed! Her comment had grated since they rode into town. He was a clear-thinking man, an orderly man. Succinct in all ways. He kept his goal—which was justice—in sight at all times, and he took in stride those slight obstacles arising against that goal. How could she question him, when his purpose was so obvious?

Darian forced Miss Emily Morgan from his consideration, turned to MacLeod, and nodded once. MacLeod inched forward, pushed the saloon door inward, and as expected, a shot rang out, whistling over their heads. Darian smiled, then shoved the doors inward. He dove for the nearest cover behind a long wooden bar, and took position. Shots rang wild, coming from odd corners. Only one came near the end of the bar, and that seemed to come from the staircase above.

Darian seized a quick glance, and saw a buxom female in red aiming a gun. He rolled his eyes, annoyed. Sad that the best shot of the group was a bar wench. Darian aimed, someone screamed, and he shot the gun out of her hands. The woman squealed, then dropped for cover, and Darian turned his attention to the other patrons.

A quick scan told him his other opponents posed less threat than the woman. He spotted the blacksmith under a table—not much protection. A reed-thin man cowered beneath a piano stool, and a ratty trio of men hid behind an overturned table. Another man crawled toward a back wall window and tried to climb out.

For an instant, he wondered if the townsfolk were

afraid of him. There seemed to be an unsubstantiated rumor circulating, known even to the local bandits, that Darian and his men posed some sort of danger. Another man crawled toward a back wall window and tried to climb out. The desire toward flight indicated guilt. Here was the most likely cause of the saloon patrons fear, not Darian.

Darian stood up and aimed his gun.

"Stop right there, my friend." The man froze, one knee elevated as he attempted to scale the wall. His hands went up. The other patrons held their position as if in terror, too. "Turn slowly." The man obeyed, his face white.

Yes, clearly this was the perpetrator of whatever brawl had preceded Darian's arrival. Darian glanced at the cowering patrons. He had apprehended the villain. There was no need for their fear.

"You may all relax now." No one responded. One of the trio was shaking so much that the table barricade rattled. Darian drew an impatient breath. "All of you, out from hiding and stand up!"

They responded, moving slowly as if their limbs were numbed by fear. What that villain had done to instill such fear seemed unimaginable. "You there, by the window—come here."

The man by the window shuddered, then approached Darian. His face was parchment white, his eyes bloodshot from too much liquor. Darian waited. The man came close, wobbled slightly, his eyes rolled back in his head, and he fell backward at Darian's feet.

There was a five-pointed star on his chest.

A sheriff's badge.

Apparently, MacLeod noticed the same thing, because he swore and called upon the Lord's assistance. Darian wasn't convinced. He eyed the piano player, most likely to know the town's arrangements.

"Who is this man who has fallen in a drunken stupor at my feet?"

The piano player closed his eyes as if in prayer. "It's . . . that there's the sheriff . . . sir. . . ."

The sheriff. Clearly, a poor choice for leadership, since the man had been the first to attempt escape. "His actions appeared suspicious . . . and he reeks of liquor."

This surprised no one, so apparently the "sheriff" was known for a fondness for drink. Darian considered the matter. "This is not acceptable behavior for an officer of the law. MacLeod, take this man to whatever jailhouse is nearby, and lock him up in a cell until he has recovered from this bout with shame."

MacLeod seized the sheriff by the feet and dragged him out of the saloon. Ping, Wetherspoon, and Herring entered the saloon, eyed MacLeod's unconscious charge in confusion, then took their places at Darian's side. Wetherspoon took a quick look around, then tapped Darian's shoulder. "Figured I'd get the horses set up for the night, Captain. They could use a good rest."

Wetherspoon always thought of the horses first, as a good soldier should. Darian nodded. "Well done, Lieutenant. See to it." Wetherspoon left to gather the horses, and Ping stepped forward, uttering a long, piercing whistle.

"Whew! You done it again, Captain! Lord, you sure can shoot! Popped that gun right out of that lady's hand, you did!"

"Lady" seemed a questionable term, but Darian liked the praise. "You, Ping, were supposed to be under cover outside."

"Had to peek in, sir. It's a thing of wonder to see you shoot."

Yes, Ping had a way with compliments. Darian glanced toward the door, wondering if Emily had noticed his skill. Probably not.

The woman in red at the top of the stairs bent to pick up her gun. She attempted to be sly, but her oversized red bustle caught on the banister. Darian watched as she picked up the gun, found it shattered, then hurled it angrily aside. "You can't waltz in here and take over like this, you outlaw! The sheriff will have your hide!"

Darian eyed the woman with disgust. She appeared sweaty and unwashed. *Washing.* An appealing notion. "I am an officer in the United States Cavalry, madam, and it is my duty to uphold the law—in any way I see fit." He added that last part himself, but since he had realized that the law wasn't always just, Darian had decided that his own judgment must reign superior.

Someone laughed, a nervous laugh. Someone he hadn't seen. He eyed the bar, then approached it. "A drink, please."

A trembling, pudgy hand reached up, seized a bottle of amber liquid and a short glass that clattered against the bottle. Darian heard liquid poured, and the glass emerged filled to the brim with bourbon. Darian grimaced. "I would have preferred water." Still, he was thirsty. He took a drink, found the bourbon fairly weak, then set it aside.

The woman in red sauntered down the stairway and approached Darian. She smelled strongly of perfume and her cheeks appeared inordinately red, as if embellished by some loathsome concoction. Despite her tartlike appearance, her gown appeared well made, and the jewelry she wore looked expensive.

Even in short trousers and a white shirt, Emily Morgan had a quiet dignity and ladylike grace compared to this woman.

"Who are you, madam?"

"I am the proprietress of this saloon."

"Very well." Darian sighed. He'd rather have dealt with the drunken sheriff. "My men and I require facilities, bathing arrangements. And. . . ." He eyed the door. "Miss Morgan, if you would come in here, please."

He heard a long, drawn-out sigh followed by indiscriminate muttering. After a moment, Emily limped through the swinging doors. She stood silhouetted in the doorway, her long legs close together, one wrapped in a bandage, her hair unraveling over her shoulder.

She looked beautiful, delicate, and young. Uniformly, the saloon patrons gasped and whispered. Darian's eyes formed slits. "Not a word, any of you. This is Miss Emily Morgan, a young lady in my care. She has been . . . bereft of her clothing, and has been wounded." Someone chuckled. Darian didn't see who it was, but it seemed to come from behind the bar.

The crude woman in red snickered rudely. "Lady? Ha! Outlaw keeps his whore in her drawers—makes a quick time of his rutting."

Icy fury flared in Darian's chest. "If any of you dare speak a disparaging word about my woman. . . ." He stopped and endured the awful sensation that he was blushing. "This woman in my care, who is accompanying us on her way to. . . ." He couldn't think of anything, and besides, it was none of their business why Miss Morgan was with him. "She will be treated with utmost respect, or you will have me to deal with."

Darian spun his revolver around his finger, and stuffed it back in its holster. Emily gaped at him, her eyes wide, her lips parted. She mouthed the words, "Your woman?" and his face flushed warmer still.

"For your protection." He hadn't meant to speak aloud, but everyone in the room seemed too terrified to defy him, anyway. So much the better. In fact, he liked their reaction. He liked the power that would make the eventual outcome of his quest that much easier.

He turned to the proprietress. "Miss . . . ?"

"Belle. Miss Belle." She spoke in a gravelly, hoarse voice, but her name seemed vaguely familiar, though Darian couldn't place the connection.

"Miss Belle, we require rooms in your upstairs facility, for which we will pay you handsomely."

She sneered. "In gold, no doubt?"

The woman must have heard about his supposed robbery. "In U.S. bills, from my own salary." He decided not to mention the gold just yet. "Is there a bank I might deal with in this town?"

Someone squealed. One of the trio behind the upturned table shuffled his feet and looked uncomfortable. Belle snorted. "That there's our banker, Charlton Parks."

Darian smiled at the man, who seemed the most upright of the lot. "Mr. Parks, I will confer with you later on a matter of utmost importance."

Parks began shaking, his face grew whiter and whiter. Red and yellow poker chips lay strewn around the table amidst scattered playing cards. A gambling banker. Darian's trust faded, and he gave the matter a moment's further consideration. Perhaps this man couldn't be trusted with a coach filled with gold. Best to leave the matter in more trustworthy hands.

"Bonner and Clyde will assist you with your banking duties during our stay in Tucson. I do not want it said that anything was handled unfavorably."

Satisfied with this arrangement, Darian looked around the bar. His gaze fixed on a painting next to the gold-framed bar mirror. The mirror was in bad enough taste, but the painting was atrocious—a scantily clad female draped over a sofa, her plump legs apart, exposing portions of her stockings and even one red garter belt.

"That. . . ." Darian's voice came low. "Must go."

Emily followed his gaze and laughed. "It's no Van Gogh, that's for sure." She limped to his side. "Good call, leaving Bonner and Clyde in control of the bank. Perfect choice."

He had no idea why humor infected Emily's voice this time, but the entire atmosphere of the saloon left much to be desired. Work was to be done.

Darian motioned to Herring. "Herring, remove that portrait, and. . . ." The bartender still hadn't emerged, but the bottle of bourbon became steadily emptied. Wonderful. "Replace the bartender with your own skills, and prepare us decent drinks as well as a meal. Thank you, Herring."

Herring took his place behind the bar, motioned the bartender aside, and proceed to polish the wood surface lovingly. Another matter handled well.

Darian turned to Emily. She was smiling at him as if he entertained her. He liked her smile, but somehow, he wanted more. "There is the matter of Miss Morgan's wardrobe. You, Miss Belle, are too plump to offer her attire, nor does your color choice suit her skin coloring at all. Is there another woman available who might loan, for a fair price, this young lady a gown?"

Belle nodded toward a closed door. "Girls! You can come out now."

Slowly, one by one, three young women emerged from a back room. Each appeared scantily clad, in colors chosen more for shock than beauty. The first girl, with red hair done in an impressive swirl, winked at Darian and licked her lips. To his great pleasure, Emily Morgan glared at her and moved slightly closer to Darian.

The second girl was dark and appeared Spanish. Despite a certain hesitant fear, she appeared enthusiastic and cheerful. The third girl was smaller than the rest, less buxom, and appeared shy. Her blond hair was done carefully, but she seemed painfully out of place in the bawdy saloon. Unfortunately, she was too small to share clothing with Emily.

Emily's expression altered. "She is too young to be in a place like this."

Darian waved the girl forward. "Young lady, what is your name?"

The girl looked at Darian with a mixture of fear and admiration. "I am called Penelope." Her voice was tiny, that of a waif.

Emily appeared concerned, too. Darian recognized her attitude—that of a strong, confident person ready to care for another. An attitude that reflected his own. Yes, he had been right. They were much alike inside.

Emily touched the girl's arm gently. "What are you doing here?

Penelope seemed confused by Emily, probably because of her peculiar dress in contrast to her refined manner. "I was left here when my parents died—they were on their way to California."

A strange, quivering moan emanated from Ping. "She is the most beautiful girl I have ever seen."

Darian cast a reproachful glance Ping's way. "Not now, Ping. The girl needs our care, not a suitor."

Ping blushed furiously and bowed his head in shame, but a tiny blush colored Penelope's cheeks. Ping didn't seem the romantic figure, but maybe the girl thought otherwise. What would Emily Morgan find romantic? Despite his better judgment, Darian hoped his own actions seemed heroic to her, and suspected that she wasn't as impressed as he hoped.

A bath. And perhaps shaving was in order. New clothing. . . .

The red-haired girl sauntered to Darian. "And where will you be sleeping, 'Captain?' Not with that skinny, half-naked girl, I trust."

Darian tried to meet the woman's eyes, and failed. All he saw were her breasts. Two immense, white mounds of flesh protruded from her low-slung bodice, straining almost to her collarbone. She arched her back to increase the effect. He opened his mouth to speak, but no words came.

Words faltered, but action, as always, came easily. "Ping, your handkerchief, please."

Ping asked no questions, but his round eyes also had found the same extravagant target. Ping passed Darian the handkerchief, and Darian refolded it, triangulating it to resemble a child's bib. The woman sucked in air through fleshy lips as if hoping for some sexual entanglement. Careful not to touch her abundant flesh, he tied it around her neck, then backed away.

Ping looked a little disappointed, but the woman's breasts were now adequately covered. The woman pouted, but Darian gave her no further heed.

"Now then. . . ." He motioned to Belle. "You, madam, will provide for these gentlemen and myself proper attire, which we will pay for in U.S. bills, not gold. And I require the use of your bathing bucket, as well as proper shaving gear. A new dress for Miss Morgan is also in order, provided by. . . ." Darian assessed the barmaids. He paused over the red-haired girl, wondering what Emily would look like clothed that way. He banished the notion, and selected the black-haired Spanish girl instead. "Provided by this woman—please deliver only her Sunday best, and not the more lewd articles. . . ."

The black-haired girl smiled at Emily. "We'll get you fixed up pretty in no time." She sounded pleasant, so

101

Darian relaxed. Emily hesitated, then went with the young women to the stairs. She moved gingerly, but with determination, as always. Her wound wouldn't slow her down. Nothing would. As he watched her, she was already chatting with the girls.

Marita and Penelope proved to be charming, delightful young women, and Emily liked them at once. Both had been orphaned early in their teens, and had no other option available beyond working for Belle, but neither had succumbed to the lures of prostitution.

The red-haired girl, Agatha, could teach Belle herself new tricks. Within five minutes, Emily had learned that Agatha used her wiles, which generally focused on the size of her breasts, to gain influence with local men, married or not. Since Marita and Penelope had learned to ignore Agatha, Emily tried her best, but it wasn't easy.

She entangled herself in the elaborate Victorian undergarments, putting her drawers on over her petticoat, though it should have been obvious that drawers came first. She pulled them off again, standing miserably wearing a light chemise. "I'm not very good at this."

Marita patted her shoulder. "You've been through a lot, Miss Morgan."

"Please call me Emily. 'Miss Morgan' sounds weird."

Marita helped Emily into the corset, and Penelope laced it. Tight. Emily was about to complain, then noticed that it did indeed push up her breasts, giving her a figure she hadn't known she possessed. "Well, well. This should surprise the captain."

Marita glanced at Penelope, girlishly eager. "Tell us, what's he like?"

"What's who like?"

Marita lowered her voice and looked around as if

someone might overhear. Someone dangerous. *"Him.* The outlaw, Darian Woodward."

Emily fought a smile. *His name precedes him.* "I hate to disappoint you, but Darian is really a very nice man. Sweet, even."

Agatha snorted. "We ain't talking about his taste, *'Miss'* Morgan."

Emily ignored her sarcasm and directed her comments at Marita. "I know, he's done a few things to ... well, tarnish his reputation, but I'm sure he'll set it all straight."

Agatha reclined on a large pink chair, and tossed her red hair back over her shoulder. "A *few* things? He's robbed a mail truck, held up a preacher and his wife, shot a gunfighter, then taken a coach filled with gold."

Emily couldn't argue, since she'd made the same point to Darian herself. "Well, there is that."

Agatha snorted. "Everyone knows he's behind the recent robberies of fort money. Half the officers at Fort Lowell went without pay this winter because the bandits made off with it. The Easter Ball over at the fort had to be canceled because of the situation."

Emily frowned. "I don't think Darian was responsible for those robberies."

"Who else? Fortunately, General Davis was able to fund a wonderful gathering here in Tucson, and we more than made up for the trouble your outlaw caused."

Emily turned to Marita. "Was Darian really blamed for that, too?"

Marita was gazing out the window, a soft, wistful expression on her face. "It was a wonderful night. I danced and danced. . . ."

Agatha rolled her eyes. "And you haven't seen him since, have you? Maybe if you knew how to pleasure a man, rather than clinging to romantic dreams. . . ."

Marita's attention flashed from the window to Agatha. "You mean, if I'd lured him to my bed? I don't think so, Agatha. That would dishonor both myself and him. I want more from a man than desire."

"Well, enjoy the wait. In the meantime, I think I may bed your handsome, shy beau myself."

Marita's fists clenched. "He's too honorable to be tempted by a shallow, greedy woman like you!"

Agatha tossed her red hair and leaned back in the chair. "Underneath, every man wants what I have."

Penelope maneuvered herself between Marita and Agatha. "Marita met a very nice young officer at the Spring Ball. All the girls wanted to dance with him— including Agatha—but he only had eyes for Marita."

Emily smiled. It had been a long time since she'd enjoyed the camaraderie of women friends. It felt like college, staying up late in the dorm, telling her roommate about her first date with Ian Hallowell. "What's he like, Marita?"

"Well, actually, he reminds me of Captain Woodward, only he's clean-shaven and, of course, he's not a criminal."

"Darian is not a criminal." She had no idea what Darian looked like without his unkempt beard. Probably not handsome, but she would like to see more of his face, anyway. After Ian's startling good looks, a plainer face would be welcome.

Marita's eyes glowed and she leaned toward Emily in excitement. "Tell us, what's he really like? Alone, I mean." She stopped and shuddered with glee. "Those icy blue eyes, that golden hair, those broad shoulders. . . . What's it like to be his woman?"

Emily didn't answer at once. The girls admired him, outlaw or not. Agatha pretended disinterest, but she waited motionless for Emily's disclosure. Intending to say, "he's a gentleman," Emily opened her mouth. "He's a lion. In every way."

What am I saying? Agatha responded with a husky breath. Emily looked at the three women. Different clothing, different hairstyles, but underneath, women hadn't changed in a hundred-odd years. Sweet and shy Penelope, thinking of others; exuberant Marita, who could brighten any day; and Agatha, for whom the source of her self-importance was capturing the most powerful man.

And that, despite his beard and unkempt appearance, was Darian Woodward. *I should tell them he's a prudish Victorian yuppie.* But she remembered Darian in the gunfight, Darian holding up the coach, Darian riding into town and taking over the saloon. She remembered the passion of his kiss. No, lion was more accurate, after all. "He's a lion. . . . But he speaks like a gentleman."

Penelope nodded appreciatively. "I noticed that. His associate, the slightly smaller man, appeared a gentleman also."

Slightly smaller? Ping was a full head shorter than Darian, and barely stood as tall as Emily herself. "Mr. Ping is every bit a gentleman. And an able gunfighter himself." Penelope's eyes glowed. "You should see him in battle. Completely fearless. Darian couldn't do without him."

Agatha rose from the chair and sashayed to the door. "It may be that I should get to know Captain Woodward better, after all."

She left before Emily could comment, but Penelope patted her shoulder. "I wouldn't worry about Agatha. He wouldn't have her on a platter. No, it's obvious—the captain only has eyes for you."

Marita helped her into a dress, the most beautiful dress Emily had ever seen. It had a dark green bodice with a narrow waist, then flared into a burgundy velvet skirt. Emily loved it. "Thank you, Marita. It's a beautiful dress."

Marita beamed. "I made it myself."

"Did you? You must be a talented seamstress."

Penelope adjusted Emily's sash. "She is. She made my dress, too."

"You should be designing clothing, Marita." Obviously, women of the past needed a little boost to regain control of their lives. Emily felt a new strength of conviction growing. "You could make a lot of money, and get out of this dismal place."

Marita sighed. "Who would I make the dresses for? And Belle says I owe her another year of my service."

"She doesn't own you." Emily tried on a pair of shoes, found them too constricting, and replaced them with her hiking boots. Penelope eyed the boots doubtfully, but said nothing. "Belle is obviously a rigid, controlling old hag. Darian will take care of her."

"She has influence at the fort, Emily." Penelope spoke quietly, without Marita's enthusiasm. Penelope was an observer, quiet and thoughtful. If she felt Belle was a threat, she probably was.

"I'll keep an eye on her, then."

From downstairs, something crashed and the three women went to the door. Belle was shouting at Darian, who answered her complaints in a calm, patient voice as always. "Madam, I have every right to keep the people of this town from leaving, as it serves the ultimate purpose of justice. To that end, my soldier Wetherspoon has gathered and secured all your horses, disabled your carriages, and I have also put a watch on the fort road. No one will leave until I deem it safe to do so."

"You devil! You've got something coming when Clem gets hold of you!"

Clem? Just as Emily suspected, Belle was somehow in league with Darian's enemy, Clement Davis. Probably lovers. *No, not lovers.* Sex partners. Emily wondered if Darian was too innocent to pick up on the connection. He sounded unmoved by the threat.

"It is my intention, madam, to confront General Davis, and I will do so—in my own good time. Now then—I require shaving gear and warmed water." He didn't wait for an answer. "See that it is sent to my room, which will be the last on the left upstairs. I understand that is reserved for your best customers."

Emily heard Darian walk toward the stairs, then stop. She peeked out the door and saw him cast a deliberate, knowing glance at Belle. His slow, dangerous smile sent shivers to her fingertips. "The general himself spent a great deal of time there, I understand."

He knew. Despite his innocence, he always seemed to know the general's more decadent habits. Emily watched him come upstairs. He doffed his cap to her, but said nothing. In his blue eyes, she saw pleasure at having bested Belle, and the glitter of expectation. She wondered what he expected, and the tingle in her fingers grew stronger. Darian Woodward expected *her*.

Chapter Six

Darian stood before the oval wall mirror and stared. He'd forgotten what he looked like without a beard or a mustache. He'd been reluctant to relinquish the mustache—it had made him look older, more commanding, but months without shaving had dampened his skill, and he had overshot the left side.

He ran his fingers on one side of his face, then the other. He looked older than the last time he'd seen himself barefaced, but then, he had been only seventeen. Age had delivered with it a new power, a masculinity that he had sorely lacked at seventeen. His twin brother had been larger-boned, and often teased Darian for his "pretty face" when they were growing up.

No more. The face in the mirror reflected wisdom and strength, fleshed out into the power of a seasoned man. A handsome man. He picked up a hand mirror, turned his face to one side, and took note of his profile. Strong, clean-cut.

Miss Emily Morgan would be impressed. He couldn't wait to greet her. He imagined her reaction. A gasp of delighted shock. A shy smile. Compliments, certainly. He would pretend not to know the source of her surprise, thereby forcing her to tell him that his looks far surpassed her expectations.

Darian dressed hurriedly, and put a black linen jacket over a new white shirt, careful to fasten the narrow tie in a neat knot. He went to the door, then went to the first landing, looking down over the banister. Emily was seated at a table with two girls, chatting as always.

He smiled to himself, then walked slowly, purposefully down the stairs.

Herring noticed him first. The chef's eyes widened, and then he shook his head. The red-haired wench's mouth opened, and stayed open. Belle also stood frozen watching him, as if his new image provided some threat worse than she'd feared.

The two girls saw him before Emily. One of them, the dark-haired one, squealed in appreciation. Emily turned, still talking, smiling.

She stopped in midsentence. Her smile faded to shock. Even more shock than he'd anticipated. Her green eyes widened, her lips parted, and she rose from her seat.

Darian stood, feeling tall and powerful as she walked slowly toward him. She wore a real dress of green and burgundy. She was more elegant and lovely than he'd dared imagine. She never took her beautiful eyes from his face. But as she drew near, he saw that the color of those eyes had paled, and crackled with something that he didn't understand. He had never seen her look this way, never imagined that she could.

The passion in her face stirred his own, as if he had seen her this way before and knew the depth of her feeling.

She stood before him, trembling, unable to speak. His heart thudded in response to the wild emotion he saw in her. Her eyes glittered with unshed tears, her chin quivered. Very slowly, as if her arm bore a great weight, she drew her hand back. Then, with a force he never dreamed she possessed, Emily Morgan slapped his face.

"Why did you hit me?" Darian stood outside her bedroom door, knocking again when she didn't answer. He had asked the question three times already, but Emily couldn't answer.

His image emblazoned on her mind. That face. That perfect, sensual, glorious face. . . . She closed her eyes to blot it out, but she saw him anyway. *Darian.*

But not Darian. *Ian.*

True, Darian was older, taller, more sure of himself. But there was no doubting the likeness. Darian Woodward was Ian Hallowell. She had been thrown back in time to some earlier version of the one man she had loved, the one man she had trusted. The man who broke her heart and made her a fool.

He knocked again. *How do I explain?* She couldn't blame him, and yet, she did. It was the same man. No wonder she had been drawn to him!

"Miss Morgan, I give you until the count of twelve to open this door. At that point, I shall be forced to relieve the door of its hinges. . . ." He paused, the anger in his voice warring with his need to give a detailed account of his plans. "I trust you will stand back from the door, if that occasion should arise, lest you be injured when I burst inward."

110

A moment of silence followed. Emily stared at the door.

Another moment passed.

"Twelve, eleven, ten. . . ." He dragged out "ten," and she sensed it would be a long countdown to "zero." *Why "twelve?"* She closed her eyes.

"Nine, eight, seven, six." He stopped and cleared his throat.

Why did he have to be so charming? So exact, in even his most ludicrous attempts? *Damn you!*

She heard an impatient huff. "Five, four, three, two. . . ." Emily fought tears as he prolonged "two" to its utmost, but she wasn't sure why she was crying. "Miss Morgan, I remind you that I am a man of my word."

Emily went to the door and opened it, just as Darian said, "One."

She smiled through her tears. "I know."

He shifted his weight from foot to foot. "May we speak in private, please?"

Emily stood back to let him in. "Come in."

Darian entered and stood uncomfortably straight in the middle of her room. He cleared his throat, twice.

Emily sat on the bed, her shoulders slumped. "I suppose you want an explanation."

"Yes."

She gazed up at him. She couldn't look away. He looked so confused, yet so sincere. Innocent. Emily rose again and went to him. She touched his face and felt the warm power beneath his skin. "You are the most beautiful man I have ever seen."

His blue eyes narrowed. "That would certainly explain why you struck me, unprovoked. And hard."

She sank back onto the bed again. "This is not the first time I've seen your face, Darian Woodward."

His eyes shifted to one side. "I have not been clean-shaven since I was a lad of seventeen."

"You may not understand this, but I knew you another way."

He looked like he didn't want to hear, but had no choice because he wanted to understand her actions. "What way?"

"As another man, sort of. Your name was Ian Hallowell. I met you in college, where your father was the head of the history department." She paused and sighed. "You were my husband."

Darian gulped, obviously shocked at her confession. She almost never spoke of Ian. Few of her friends even knew she had been married. Darian shook his head. "That is impossible."

She hadn't expected him to understand. She didn't understand fully herself. "Your parents said we were too young, so we had blood tests done in secret, and then we eloped."

Beneath Darian's shock, Emily saw something else— he looked almost hurt. "You're . . . married?"

"Not anymore."

He appeared relieved, but still suspicious. "Did your husband pass on?"

"In a way." She frowned. "We were married one week, exactly." She closed her eyes, not wanting to remember, but remembering anyway. "It was the most beautiful, blissful week of my life. Every night was magic. In that week, we planned out our whole lives, where we would live, how many children we would have, how we would raise them. . . . Everything." Tears burned in her eyes, but she refused to cry. "On our first week anniversary, I made a special dinner. You. . . . Ian was gone, he had an appointment or something. I was so excited. I had candles lit, I put on a pretty negligee.

I have never, never in my life, felt so feminine or so romantic."

Her throat tightened. She would never allow herself to feel that way again. Emily swallowed to contain emotion. "I waited, and you were late. I waited until the candles burned low and went out. I waited all night, but you never came back."

"Not *me*. What do you mean, 'never came back'? Perhaps some ill befell your husband."

"I thought so at the time. I panicked. I called the police. I called his parents, and they told me he was safe, but they refused to say where he was. I had no idea what happened, but I couldn't believe he would desert me that way. So I waited, for days, and then weeks."

Darian's mouth remained parted with horror at her tale. "What reason did he give? What happened?"

She gazed up at him, remembering the sleepless nights, the endless tears. "I don't know. I tried desperately to reach him. After a month or so had passed, he wrote me a cold, formal letter saying he had made a mistake. Then, a few weeks after that, I received papers demanding a divorce."

"He . . . *divorced* you?"

"Divorce is common in my time. It's nothing unusual. No big deal."

Darian seated himself beside her and took her hand. "It broke your heart."

Emily's tears refused to relent and she nodded. "I signed the papers. I couldn't fight him when he didn't want to be with me. I never saw him—you—again. You never told me why."

Darian squeezed her hand. "That should prove to you that this man and I are not the same. Do you truly believe I would treat you with that disrespect?"

"You're making me ride a mule."

"It's a sturdy beast. Miss Morgan, do you not know me better than that? Will you hold me responsible for another's actions?"

She looked into his blue eyes for a long while. She saw Ian, but there was something in Darian that had been missing in his counterpart. Depth of feeling, perhaps. Confidence, certainly. And yet, it seemed, Darian and Ian were one and the same, and Ian was a "later version" of the same model.

She wanted to trust, and she had trusted Darian. As if he understood her thoughts, Darian drew her hand to his lips and kissed her fingers. His skin felt warm, strong. There was nothing ambiguous in his touch. He flung the full force of his personality into whatever he did, with single-minded dedication, and emerged stronger than ever.

But if he failed, if he truly failed, what would he become? Emily closed her eyes. He would become Ian Hallowell.

"Darian, I believe you are a good man, but every choice you're making is leading you to . . . hanging. I used to think that was the worst thing that could happen to you, but now I know it isn't. You will go on, because souls never die, but you will have lost something of yourself."

He released her hand and sat back, assessing her. "I must follow my own heart. I must do what I know is right." He paused, then took her hand again. "Do not compare me to some other man, Emily. Perhaps he resembled me in some way. . . ."

"He looked exactly like you in all ways."

Darian ignored her interruption. "In some ways, as you remember him, but I am, first and foremost, a man of honor. I would not desert my wife for any reason."

"You ditched your former fiancée."

His mouth twitched impatiently. A beautiful mouth, full and firm, quick with expression. "I didn't 'ditch' her. I asked her to come west with me, knowing she wouldn't, and then, with utmost graciousness, severed our engagement."

"Well, at least you told her. That's something." Emily paused. "Did you love her?"

"When I was seventeen, I thought I did." Darian sighed, as if many more years than seven had passed since then. And in his eyes, Emily saw that it was true. "But war changes a man, Miss Morgan. It takes from him what he can't get back. I have seen life at its most desperate, at its fullest measure. You have no idea what it is to experience that fury, that passion, and then return to the pleasant drawing rooms of childhood. My fiancée had not changed. I had."

"I have always wondered why Ian left me that way. He seemed to love me."

"I am sure he did. What man would not? Especially after. . . ." Darian caught himself and blushed furiously, then fiddled with her eyelet bedspread. "Perhaps he had a reason he couldn't divulge."

"Like another woman?"

"You attribute his actions to self-interest?"

"Well . . . *yeah.*"

"This man, you say, resembled myself?"

"Exactly."

Darian patted her hand, then stood up looking down at her, sure and confident. "Then I can say with certainty that the reason this man left you was for you."

He hadn't expected her to hit him. Worse still, he hadn't expected her to cry. And most irritating of all was to learn that Emily Morgan had loved another man—her

115

husband—and now she held Darian responsible for this man's actions.

Darian sat at the bar while Herring cleaned glasses. Darian eyed one and picked it up. "Herring, you missed a spot." He passed it to the soldier, and Herring polished it again with a towel. Darian drummed his fingers on the bar. "She compares me to this other man—for what? A slight resemblance? Why can she not see me for myself?"

Herring said nothing, just listened.

"I do not compare her to my former sweetheart."

Herring's brow arched slightly, and Darian's cheeks warmed. This did sound, somewhat, as if Emily could be considered his current sweetheart. Fortunately, MacLeod entered the saloon and sat down beside Darian. A welcome distraction, lest Herring gain the impression that Darian was thinking overmuch of Emily.

"What state did you leave the sheriff in, Sergeant?"

MacLeod drew a long, disgusted breath. "Soused to the gills, Captain. Had Ping help me, and we dunked him in the water trough—didn't do much good."

"At least, he'll be cleaner. The man hadn't washed in years."

MacLeod sighed. "Or ever." He shook his head. "Fellow like that can't defend a town against a meadow mouse, let alone the kind of gunmen and renegades old Davis has up his sleeve."

"I am aware of that, Sergeant." Darian considered the matter. "Take his badge and keep him locked up. Shirking his duties, imbibing liquor while on duty—in my mind, that's enough to warrant a severe incarceration."

He felt a soft touch on his shoulder, and he knew who it was. Emily. His muscles tightened and his pulse moved faster. Did she have any idea what her presence did to him? Would she care? He tried to contain his reaction and turned to her. MacLeod was smiling.

"Miss Morgan. . . ." He glanced at her face and saw that she had done her hair up, apparently in an attempt to resemble the local women. Soft, wavy tendrils fell along her cheeks and around her forehead. *You are so beautiful. . . .* He stopped himself before he spoke aloud, but it wasn't easy.

She looked cheerful, as if she was about to tease him again. He found, despite himself, that he welcomed her mood. "So, what's this I hear?" she said, "Taking the law into our own hands, are we?"

"I am an officer in the United States Cavalry, and it is my duty to uphold the law."

She snickered and one eyebrow angled. "Then maybe you should slap yourself in jail, since the law is after *you* most of all."

She wasn't likely to flatter him in the near future, that much was certain. But he wanted more than flattery. He wanted to know she admired him, and something deeper—he wanted her to see good in him, to trust him. "The law is in error, and it is also my duty to correct its wrong."

Emily sat down beside him, her expression more serious. "Darian, it's not going the way you want. You're holding a town hostage. It looks . . . *bad.*"

"I'm not 'holding them hostage.' "

"You told your men to prevent anyone from leaving."

"I can't have anyone at the fort alerted to my presence just yet."

"You put Bonner and Clyde in charge of a *bank.*"

This wasn't the first time she had spoken of Bonner and Clyde as if they were something other than stoic soldiers. Darian considered them respectable, anyway. They were loyal to him, good shots. Perfectly reliable and capable of taking charge of a bank. "And your point would be . . . what?"

Emily bowed her head and placed her slender hands on the bar. "I could use a drink."

"Herring, make a punch suitable for a lady."

She frowned. "I was thinking . . . bourbon."

Ladies of the future couldn't have changed that much. Darian eyed his own drink, then passed it to her. Emily looked surprised, but then she shrugged and tasted it. Her eyes widened, she gasped, shuddered, then wiped her lips on her sleeve.

Their eyes met and a slow, sweet smile formed on her soft lips. "I was thinking . . . punch."

Herring slapped a glass in front of her. "You two can think 'punch' all you want, but you're getting water. This ain't an Eastern ballroom."

Emily sipped her water, but she seemed distracted. She chewed her lip, then turned to Darian. "Captain, I apologize for my actions earlier. For hitting you. I was wrong. You are not to blame for my ex-husband's actions."

She was trying to be formal, and Darian wanted her closer. He had become accustomed to her informal, natural demeanor, and he liked it. "You were wrong." Yes, annoyance flickered in her eyes, but she repressed it with an even more formal smile. "I have long realized that you are a delicate, tender woman with those strange attributes befitting high-strung, fragile constitutions. . . ."

"I am not fragile! I jumped out of a plane seven times!" She groaned. "It was a hideous mistake, but I did it. I'm not fragile. Not in the least."

Darian restrained himself from inquiring into the nature of a "plane," and focused on Emily. Despite her relaxed manner, she was the most guarded woman he'd ever met. He knew the reason now—her husband had mistreated her. All the more reason to teach her, gently, to trust again. "I knew, of course, that your sometimes belligerent nature could be attributed to a romantic heartache in your past."

Her face tightened, her lips formed a small 'o.' "You are judging me against women of your own time, Captain. My 'heartache' did nothing but teach me caution."

Darian adopted a ponderous expression, gazing thoughtfully at the bar mirror. From this angle, he could watch Emily's reaction without her knowing he was watching.

Emily sat looking tense beside him. Waiting for him to reassure her, to tell her that her guard was foolproof. "You are correct, Miss Morgan. You do differ somewhat from women of my time."

He watched her from the corner of his eye. Her former self-assurance returned, but he knew it wasn't deep or heartfelt. She nodded. "I am very different." She paused. "In what way?"

"You are more fragile, and more vulnerable."

Her eyes widened. "I am not!"

"And unlike the women of my time, you are afraid of your tender femininity."

She puffed a furious breath, looked at him in horror—revealing all the traits he had just mentioned—then hopped up from her stool. She was too offended to speak. But not offended—terrified. As she marched back up the stairs to her room, Darian knew why. She was afraid of him—because he could look inside her and see her true self.

Darian felt manly. Strong. Filled with power. He eyed the stairs, then caught MacLeod watching him, one brow elevated. Darian rose, carefully and slowly, from his stool and stretched, casually. "I fear I have offended the lady. I must, as a gentleman ought, seek her out and apologize at once."

He aimed for the stairs, but he heard MacLeod's low chuckle as Herring passed the sergeant a drink. "Apology is the last thing our young captain has on his mind."

Darian Woodward was a fiend. Worse than an outlaw, worse than any kind of marauder. He was Attila the Hun masquerading as Prince Albert. A fiend.

Emily sat on the edge of her bed, furious. Her heart sped in uneven pulses, and occasionally, she shuddered. Yes, he was a good kisser. He was eccentric, with the added charm of not realizing how far off the beaten track he was. And he was beautiful to look at, but that wasn't a good quality, given her experience with Ian.

A fiend.

It was time she killed off the last of her romantic longings, and accepted that femininity led to trouble, and nothing else. He wanted her feminine because he wanted her weak.

Fiend.

Someone knocked on her bedroom door. Evenly, with precision. She knew who it was. Emily sat frozen, glaring at the door. She hadn't locked it, but she knew Darian. He wouldn't enter without an invitation. She had no intention of giving one.

The door opened and Darian walked in, then closed it behind him. Emily's eyes widened as he locked it— from the inside. She opened her mouth to object, but he turned around, and the smile on his lips stopped her cold.

The fiend had turned seductive. It had been a long time, but she recognized that look. Her pulse raced until she felt dizzy. He walked across the room to her—feline grace much belying the stiff Victorian she had believed him to be.

"If you've come to apologize, you're wasting your time." Her voice came high and rushed, and Darian's brow angled, indicating that he had no intention of apologizing. Emily crossed her arms over her chest, tried to cross her legs, but entangled them in her long burgundy skirt instead.

Darian stood in front of her, saying nothing, just looking at her. Very slowly, as if mesmerized, he reached to touch her face. He had gentle hands and a sweet touch, capable of sending shivers along her nerves, distracting her from her resistance.

"Miss Morgan, I am deeply, passionately sorry for the pain and fear you feel." His voice had turned lower, more seductive. Not a direct apology, but still. . . . His fingers moved on her skin, as if feeling her softness. Emily bit her lip, hard, to remind herself of what he had done. How he had insulted her and made her feel weak.

She pushed his hand away, but her own hands were shaking. "Well, good. You can leave now."

His smile deepened. He had dimples. Emily closed her eyes, but she felt him sit down beside her. Close. She peeked at him through one eye. "What are you doing?"

He touched her hair, and his fingers grazed her neck. A small shudder tore through her. She hoped he didn't notice. "I am, Miss Morgan, reminding you of what you are."

She exhaled, then realized she had been holding her breath. "You have no idea 'what I am.' " She started to get up, but he caught her arm and drew her back.

She refused to look at him, but he cupped her chin in his hand and gently forced her to face him. "I do not know you fully, Emily, but my heart tells me I will."

"It's not your *heart* you're hearing, Captain!"

She expected him to revert to his former indignation

and gentlemanly dignity. Instead, Darian chuckled. "The heart speaks in many ways, does it not?"

"Many stupid ways."

He kept touching her, softly, his long fingers grazing her skin—there was no way that this man was a virgin. Every touch sent shivers to her feminine core, and he knew it. He had to know. "I have noticed, Emmy, that when you kiss, your fear dissipates."

"Have you, indeed?" She stopped and stared at him. "What did you call me?"

He hesitated, as if he wasn't sure. Emily grabbed his arm and pinched hard. "You called me 'Emmy.' "

A faint smile curved his sensual lips. "It is an endearing name."

"*He* called me that. No one else ever. . . ."

Darian exhaled an irritated breath, stopped touching her, and glared. "You will not compare me to that man again." He paused, his bright blue eyes glittering with challenge. When angry, the color of those eyes frosted to a blue river frozen beneath a sheet of ice. "*Emmy.*"

"Dar—*Ian.*"

He considered this, making the first connection between the two names. "Well, well. It seems you cannot resist me in any form."

This was not the reaction she expected. The ice gave way to a warm blue, a darkening blue of desire. He clasped her face in his hands and leaned close, lips not quite touching hers. "You say we were lovers—you have the advantage between us. You remember me. I do not remember you."

She wanted to comment, but he held her mesmerized. She did remember. She remembered her heart aching with love, opening her body for him, because she loved him. But Ian had been a shy, polite college student. Darian was a desperado. A different kind of desperado, but an outlaw nonetheless.

With one thing on his mind.

His lips brushed over hers and she closed her eyes. *I will not be weak.* He pulled her closer into his arms and deepened the kiss. His lips moved sensuously, he tasted, he teased. His kiss was more than desire—it was filled with emotion and appreciation of her as a woman.

His hands wandered uncertainly, as if he wasn't sure how to proceed. Maybe he really was a virgin, after all. Emily sat back, caught her breath, and looked into blue eyes on fire. Desire warred with fear and uncertainty— she cared for him. More than just desire, she found herself wanting to be close to him. And she knew how dangerous that could be.

Maybe, if she could separate romantic emotion from simple lust, it would be all right. If she didn't allow herself to imagine too much, to hope for too much. Better to skip the romance and seize what she could from passion. She was a woman, after all, with womanly needs and desires. And soon, she would be gone, once she had saved him from hanging. It wasn't as if she could plan for their future.

She had now, and that was all.

She placed her hands on his shoulders and felt the taut muscle. He seemed hesitant, uncertain but eager. Emily fought her own nervousness. "Darian. . . . I want you to touch me."

He gulped. "I am touching you."

She shook her head, then took his hands and placed them on her breast. His eyes widened, then closed as his palm covered her fullness. Maybe she had gone too far. Her invitation couldn't be deemed "romantic," in any case. But Darian didn't pull away as she expected. Instead, his hands moved slowly, feeling her, shuddering as desire tore through him.

He felt every portion of her skin as if it were the most erotic part of her. So slowly that she ached with tension, he slid his hands over her snug bodice, feeling the contour of her breast.

"You are weak from your injury." His voice came like a groan. "You've been through too much." He hesitated, fighting himself. "I should not. . . ."

"I am weak because I want you. Didn't you know?"

He shook his head, but he fingered the edge of her bodice, then toyed beneath the rim. Emily trembled. Never had she felt desire this way. Unexpected, and so strong. Her pulse raged, centering in her woman's core, filling with need. She didn't expect to make love with him, but neither had she expected to feel this way about a man again.

He explored the shape of her breast with wonder, just grazing the nipple, then again more firmly. It hardened to his touch, visible even through the thick velvet, and he murmured with pleasure. He tried again, more deliberate this time, and Emily moaned.

"This. . . ." His voice caught as his thumb circled the taut peak. "This is pleasurable. For you, too?"

She nodded. "For me, too."

"I have never touched a woman this way before."

"You do it very well." Too well. Darian Woodward learned fast. Hesitancy disappeared. He unlaced the velvet bodice, exposing more of her flesh. Emily trembled as if it were she who was the virgin, not Darian. As if she had no idea what she would do in his arms. As if he controlled her, and she had no choice but to succumb to whatever bliss he chose.

He edged her corset beneath her breasts, freeing them

to his touch. The sight of her nipples seemed to inflame him—his reaction inflamed her. He cupped both breasts in his hands, teasing the nipples with his thumbs as he watched her face for her reaction. When she moaned, when she gasped, he tried again, learning more, creating more desire than she'd ever experienced in her life.

Her skin flushed with heat and she pressed herself forward to kiss his neck. He started to speak, failed, then kissed her, long past restraint. He began to lower her to the bed—her whole body swarmed with need. *I can't do it—I can't make love with him and not love him, too.*

"Darian, I can't do this." He didn't seem to hear her. He kissed her face, her throat. He would kiss her breast soon, and she would lose all thought of her fate, of what their union would do to her. . . . Emily squirmed from beneath him and tried to cover her breasts with her disheveled bodice. Her hands shook too much. Darian sat back, staring as if in shock. He said nothing, but he gently tied her laces, then stood up from the bed.

"Miss Morgan. . . ." His voice held a strange, rich timbre, deep with emotion. "I do not know what came over me. It is not my way. Please forgive me."

She was shaking, but she met his gaze evenly. "It's not your fault, Captain. I wanted you." A shudder ran through her. "I want you now. But . . . I'm scared. I want you too much, and I don't see any way for this to work."

He watched her without speaking for a long while, as her heart throbbed in her chest, as her breaths came heavy. "You intend to return to the future?" She nodded. Darian nodded, too. "I have no right to ask you to stay, not with so much uncertain."

Had he considered it, asking her to stay? Her heart took a quick leap, hope surged inside her. But Darian walked to the door and unlocked it before he looked back at her. "Then you are right, Miss Morgan. From this moment forward, we must restrain our wayward passions and keep our eyes fixed on our duty. There is no other way."

Chapter Seven

Four days passed, and Darian held to his word. It hadn't been easy. Sexual images filled his dreams at night, fanned by Emily's presence during the day. Neither had mentioned their encounter. Emily seemed friendly enough, but she was avoiding him. She smiled, but she never quite met his eyes.

He told himself it was for the best, but instead, he found himself seeking her out, asking her advice as to how best to restructure Tucson. At her suggestion, he had placed Ping in charge of communications, lest any message be sent out without Darian's approval. The sheriff had been released, but the consumption of liquor had been regulated. This wasn't Emily's suggestion—actually, she had disagreed with his attempts to control the citizenry, but he had still consulted her.

He was running out of things to discuss. He sat at the bar, watching as Herring arranged bottles according to size. Darian checked a glass for spots, but found nothing. He looked around the saloon. Everything was neat and tidy. Even Agatha had donned a more proper gown, since he had confiscated her revealing dresses, and Marita had her lush black hair done up in an orderly bun.

. He turned his attention back to the bar. Minus the saucy portrait, the wall behind the bar looked empty and had left a spot lighter than the rest. The gold-framed mirror required another wall hanging for balance. Perhaps Emily would have a suggestion there. After he had complained about the haphazard color matching of the bedroom linen, she had gone upstairs to correct the problem. He hadn't meant for Emily to take on the task, but he suspected she wanted to place distance between them.

She came down the stairs, trailing her fingers on the banister. She met his gaze, swallowed, then looked quickly for something to distract her.

"Miss Morgan, if you please. . . ." He gestured for her to join him, which she did with obvious reluctance.

"The sheets are as coordinated as they're going to get."

"Welcome news." He tapped the seat, indicating that she should sit.

She sat down beside him, sighed, then sighed again. "What is it now? Would you like the saloon moved a little to the left?"

Darian gestured at the wall beside the mirror. "The wall decoration is lacking."

"Is it?"

"Yes. See, there. . . . Where that putrid insult to art once hung, there is an unpleasant spot. It offends the eye."

Her lips curled to one side, her eyes narrowed. "So?"

"Something must be done—to return a balanced

look." He sounded demanding, even to himself. "I thought you might have a suggestion."

"Well, Penelope paints. You could put up one of her pictures. She'd like that."

"What does she paint?" Darian didn't want to commit himself to anything potentially worse than the revealing tart, such as Agatha in the nude.

"She paints desert landscapes. They're quite good, actually."

"Very well. It will be done." That was too easy, too quick. Emily started to leave, probably to commission Penelope for a suitable picture. Darian wanted her to stay. "There is also the matter of . . . of. . . ." *Of what?*

She peered at him over her shoulder, eyes narrowed to slits. "Of what?"

"Proper towels beside each wash basin. As it is arranged now, the saloon patrons are drying their hands on articles of clothing."

She sat back on the stool, lowered her head to the bar counter and groaned. "I want to kill you myself." She took a deep breath, then looked up at him. "What is *with* you? I mean, you were persnickety before, but this is really over the top. You've had Marita and Penelope cleaning under the tables. Wetherspoon is cleaning the stables fit for a banquet. Everyone has washed every article of clothing, dirty or not, that they possess. Now . . . proper towels? What is going on?"

"Cleanliness is a virtue." He had no idea what motivated his recent directions. Frustration. Tension. He liked giving commands. He liked order. He ached inside.

He was twenty-five years old, and he had known a man's pent-up desire before. But it had never dominated him this way. He had cared for women before, been infatuated. But those feelings never outweighed his better judgment. Why now?

129

There was something different about Emily. Everything she said and did was a surprise to him. She never treated him with womanly deference. The women he had known in the past had feigned vulnerability and a fragile nature to make themselves more appealing, when inside they had been stronger and more realistic than the men who had marched off to war.

Emily pretended to be strong, when her heart was a delicate as a butterfly. Could the future be so different as to praise women for strength, so that they pretended power when inside they were terrified? And was that any different, truly, then when they pretended to be frail? Perhaps, in any age, people saw what society deemed they should be, then tried their damnedest to fit that mold.

Was he any different for trying to maintain chivalry when his body ached for passion? He drummed his fingers on the bar counter. He didn't like these flashes of intuition, but he never stopped having them. He had them during the charge at Gettysburg, wondering if honor had led ten thousand brave men to death. Wondering if each side had justified the war with their "cause" without ever seeing another way.

Something preyed on his thoughts, something troubled him. He wasn't sure, exactly, what it was. "So, I take it that in the future, men and women engage in conjugal bliss without the benefit of marriage?"

Herring dropped the bottle he was sorting. Everyone in the bar gasped at once, so that the sound was far louder than from a single utterance. Darian gasped, too, shocked that he had spoken aloud. *I have lost my mind.*

Apparently, Emily agreed. "Captain, you have lost your mind."

Darian closed his eyes tight, but his face felt warm. Hot, even. Even his neck felt warm. He could see absolutely no way to extract himself from his comment.

No one would question what he had on his mind.

Emily constructed a forced laugh. "That's what the book said." She spoke in a clear voice, so that everyone could hear. "Isn't that silly? Can you imagine? It was shocking—I almost fainted when I read it. Of course, it was scandalous and was banned from my school. . . ." She pinched Darian's arm, hard. Under her breath, she added, "Will you pipe down? Don't you have enough trouble without bursting out about sex, and the future?"

Clever girl. True, Herring eyed them with misgivings, but the soldier knew Emily's origin. The others went back to their duties, no doubt assuming the outlaw's woman had strange taste in reading material. Darian breathed a sigh of relief. "Thank you."

"You and I need to have a talk. In private." She took his arm, stood up, and tugged him after her.

"I see no need. . . ." If they were alone together, he would kiss her. He would find a way to touch her breasts again, he would probably kiss her there. . . . His whole body grew taut, aroused. He was a man possessed.

Emily made for the stairs, glanced at him, and probably saw the lust written on his face. Her eyes narrowed, and she turned in the direction of the saloon doors, instead. Darian followed, but he couldn't help the pull of regret as she led him outside into the street.

She looked left and right, making sure no one could overhear. The town minister and his wife walked by, so Emily directed Darian into the middle of the street.

"You. . . ." She sputtered, then poked him in the chest. "You need to stop thinking about sex!"

The minister tripped and his wife choked back a gasp. Darian cast his eyes heavenward. "Well, thank you for bringing me to 'privacy' to announce this."

Emily cringed, then cast an apologetic glance at the minister, who blanched and hurried away in the direction of the small church. "Sorry. I didn't mean to speak so loud."

Darian fidgeted. "I have no idea to what you are referring. . . ."

She cut him off with a huff. "Is that so? So it's never crossed your mind, has it?"

He swallowed. "No. Not once. Never in the smallest way have I dishonored you in such a fashion."

She glared, offended. He fought a smile. "Well, fine. I haven't thought of you that way, either."

He felt certain she had. "Your response to my kiss indicates otherwise."

"And I suppose you were thinking of the next stage-coach you plan to rob?"

"I was thinking. . . ." He was standing in the middle of a street, in a town he virtually commanded, and he had never been so hard, so potently male. "I was thinking. . . ." Darian grabbed her shoulders, pulled her close, and kissed her. Emily squeaked, struggled, then succumbed to the passion of his kiss. She wrapped her arms tight around his neck, pressed close to him, and . . . of all the sweet moments of bliss . . . sucked his lower lip.

She kissed his jaw, his neck, and he kissed her forehead. "I was thinking, my sweet, beautiful girl, of this . . . of taking you where you stand, of filling you, of loving you. . . ." He caught himself, stopped and stared. *"Of loving you."* Wonder filled him. Lust had never had such hold over him—he understood it as part of his animal nature. But with Emily, it went far beyond. *Because he loved her.*

She stared back at him. Doubt and hope filled her eyes. "You don't love me. You're confused."

He touched her cheek. "I have been confused for a very long time. All becomes clear in this moment. Miss Morgan, I want you to marry me."

"No!" She shook her head violently and stepped back from him. Darian just smiled.

He got down on one knee and held out his hand. "I will not take you as a harlot. Only as my wife."

"You are insane. You are the craziest man who ever lived. I will *not* marry you!"

Darian didn't withdraw his hand. His smile deepened. "Our time together is sacred. Let us treat it as such. Marry me."

"I said no! What don't you understand about 'no'? Never."

Darian glanced toward the saloon. Everyone, Herring, the saloon girls, Belle—all his men had come to watch them. Ping gaped, then moved closer to Penelope. Marita beamed. Bonner and Clyde came out of the bank and stood together like statues. MacLeod, wearing the sheriff's badge, stood with his arms folded over his chest, grinning. A shame Wetherspoon had to miss the event, but he was nowhere in sight.

"MacLeod, fetch back the minister, would you? I have need of him."

Emily glared. "What? You're going to force me to marry you? I don't think so!"

MacLeod took off after the minister. Darian heard loud protests when the sergeant caught his target, but the minister returned in tow. He turned his attention back to Emily. She was shaking. "I would never force you to do anything. I ask only that you look inside your heart, and answer me from there, not from your fear."

Her face blanched. "I can't marry you. We haven't known each other long enough. Marriage is one mistake I'm not going to make twice!" She glanced around, then lowered her voice. "In case you'd forgotten, I am from another time and I'm going back. You are destined to be hanged, and you're not doing much to change that."

"You are considering external factors. Consult your heart instead. Emmy, what do you see when you look at me? Do you want to be my wife?"

"I can't marry you just because you've got blue eyes!" She paused, unwillingly assessing him. "Or because you're incredibly handsome, and brave, and so peculiar. . . ." Her voice trailed, and her eyes filled with tears. "It can't be because you're so charming, though I know you don't mean to be, and you have no clue what you're doing, but you're so sure of yourself. I can't marry you just because . . . when you look at me this way. . . ." Her voice cracked, her tears fell. Emily came forward, placed her hand in his, then sank to her knees before him. "Yes."

Darian held her hand to his heart and kissed her forehead. "I knew you would."

She sniffed and peeked up at him. "This is crazy. It will never last."

"Marriage is forever." Darian motioned to the minister. "Sir, prepare to commence a proper service. I will marry this woman in one hour."

"Woodward, the only thing you'll be doing in an hour is lying face down in the dirt, choking up blood while you die." Darian froze. It was a man who spoke—a voice from the past. Darian rose to his feet slowly, instinctively edging Emily behind him. From behind the stable, a man in a ratty uniform stepped out, holding a gun to Wetherspoon's head.

Darian stared, shocked. It was the erstwhile Ranger called Tradman, General Davis's right-hand man—a violent, soulless criminal bent on destroying the Indian people of Arizona, a man who hated Darian as much as any Indian for defending them.

A man known as the best gunfighter between Texas and California.

"Release my soldier and face me, Tradman, or do you always hide behind another?"

Emily clutched Darian's shoulder. "Who is he? What are you doing?"

"Emily, get back with the others."

"No!" As his wife, could he ever expect obedience from her? Probably not. Darian didn't take his gaze from Tradman, but he nodded to MacLeod, who came to them and seized Emily. "If I should fall. . . ." He didn't want to die, not now. "See that she is taken to Tiotonawen."

"Darian!" MacLeod pulled Emily to the side. From the corner of his eye, he saw her struggle, and he knew she was crying. He wanted to reassure her, but every time he entered battle, a battle of any kind, he knew that he could die. He had seen too many men die to believe otherwise. A man does his best, and the outcome lies in God's hands.

Tradman chuckled, then spat. As always, a disgusting, mannerless devil. He cocked the revolver as if to shoot Wetherspoon. The soldier's eyes were wide with fear, but Darian saw the young man's trust. He allowed himself to smile. "You know better, Tradman. Pull that trigger, and my own bullet flies. You will not live to see the man you killed fall."

Tradman hesitated, then laughed again. "You're an arrogant bastard, Woodward. Showed that when you set Clem Davis up—but he set you back, didn't he?"

"I'm not surprised he didn't come for me himself. There is cowardice to hide behind a man like you."

Tradman's dirty lips formed a snarl. "You ain't worth his time. Figured he'd give me the pleasure of sending you to Kingdom Come, since you gave me so much trouble."

"Step out into the street, Tradman, and we will settle this, shall we?"

Tradman spat again. "I ain't no fool, Woodward. You got your men lining the street. I ain't getting pegged by one of them while you stand there looking pretty."

Darian nodded to his men. "Gentlemen, lay down your weapons."

Ping hesitated, but they all did as he asked. Darian moved to the center of the street, then bowed. "Is there anything else you require?"

Tradman looked around, then let go of Wetherspoon and swaggered out into the street. A dry breeze lifted the dust around their boots, echoing a far-off howl from the mountains beyond. An eerie, timeless feeling filled Darian. He was about to marry a woman from the future. This night, he would hold her in his arms and find all life's secrets in her eyes.

Or he would be dead, and she would be weeping over his grave.

Was he cheating fate to claim her as his own? To hope for a life of joy and good, when so many had fallen? When his own brother had fallen?

He breathed slowly and deeply, he felt his own power all through his body, into his limbs, extending beyond his physical body and into the area surrounding him. His fingers clenched, then relaxed. He felt his revolver in its holster as if connected beyond touch.

Tradman held his arms out slightly to the side, as a well-practiced gunfighter usually did. Confidence emanated from his dark soul. The man wore a uniform that was part Union, part Confederate. He had no idea what he was.

Darian was a Union officer who had watched his brother die. In all those years, in all the hell, and through all the unexpected defeats, all the surprises, he had never doubted his own soul.

He did not doubt it now.

Tradman's fingers twitched. Not as instinct, but . . . as a signal! Darian ducked, rolled, bounded to one knee and shot a man from the stable roof. He heard Emily scream, and his men swore at the treachery. Tradman's ally fell headfirst, still clutching his rifle. Tradman took aim, and Darian fired.

His shot splintered Tradman's arm, just as he intended. The gunfighter howled in pain, then stumbled back. Darian walked to him, calmly, then holstered his own gun. Fate had spared him yet again. He knew it would not always be so.

"I suggest you bind your arm, Tradman, and bind it tight. It may have to be amputated, but better men than yourself have endured worse."

Ping scurried out into the street and picked up Tradman's gun. "Aren't you going to kill him, Captain?" Ping paused, obviously disappointed. "I ain't never seen you miss before."

Darian glanced at the small soldier. "I didn't 'miss,' Ping."

"Well, he's still standing, sir. Sort of."

Darian pointed at Tradman's shattered arm. "I have put an end to the man's gunfighting career, but not to his life. I put no value on his life, but as a messenger, he will serve admirably."

Darian seized Tradman by the collar. "Know this. I could have killed you, and I may yet, one day. But for now, you serve me better alive than dead. Take this message to Davis, and take it with good speed, as I tire of waiting for his foolishness. I will face him, and no other. For it is at my door he will find justice. Do you understand?"

Tradman nodded, furious. Amazingly, he still had strength to spit. Darian grimaced. The man would die with spittle on his chin. "Clem ain't finished with you,

Woodward. He'll bring in the whole damned army, if that's what it takes."

"That would seem more logical than sending a sorry marksman like yourself." Darian paused, liking the dark fury in Tradman's eyes. "I find it odd he chose this route. Why, do you suppose? Because he fears what I might tell his commanders? Because my cause is just, and it is Clement Davis himself who has reason to fear?"

"He ain't got no reason to fear the likes of you." Tradman snorted, then winced with pain, clutching his arm as blood oozed through his shirt. "You're a mutinous devil, and the only thing you're headed for is a noose."

"Assuming one of Davis's hired guns doesn't get me first." Darian spoke lightly, but he remembered Emily's warning. Not shot, but hanged. Which meant that even in the telling of his mutiny and subsequent actions, the government would still believe Davis. His pleasure at defeating Tradman faded. "Go now—on foot." Darian motioned to Wetherspoon. "We will keep your horse. The walk will do you good."

Tradman backed away, staggering more from fury than from his wound. He nodded to Belle, whose eyes narrowed as if a silent communication had passed. It was possible that the wench had gotten a message past his men, though Darian had no idea how. Tradman's dark gaze fell on Emily, and he stopped.

A slow, evil smirk formed beneath his mustache as he eyed her, then glanced at Darian. "Got yourself a girl, have you, Woodward? And all set up to marry her. Ain't that sweet?" As was typical of his punctuation, Tradman paused to spit. "Enjoy your night, boy. But any girl that'll take you for a husband, she's got some explaining to do down at the fort. And if Clem has his way, she'll be 'explaining' all through the night—to me."

A foul threat, and one that would never come to pass.

But a wild heat spread through Darian, and he aimed his revolver at Tradman's back, this time to kill. He cocked the trigger, and Tradman didn't notice. His men saw his intention, and not a one would object. He was justified.

He saw Emily watching him, too. She had seen him shoot a gunman from the roof, she had seen him kill in battle. But he had never shot a man unawares, in the back. She deserved a better man than one who killed in anger.

Darian lowered his gun. Tradman glanced suspiciously over his shoulder. Darian smiled, and the dark glower in the man's eyes proved that a smile was far more frustrating than death could be to such a man. Darian's smile became a laugh. "Enjoy the walk, Tradman. I don't envy you having to report failure to Davis, but then, perhaps he will be merciful."

Tradman's face tensed, his eyes shifted to the side, but he didn't respond.

Darian snapped his fingers as if to jog his memory. "Ah, but then, mercy isn't one of Clement Davis's strong points, is it?"

Tradman staggered out of town, and Belle marched back into the saloon, almost as defeated as Darian's enemy. Darian took Emily's hand and kissed it, then turned to the minister. "Pastor, prepare your service." Darian checked his pocket watch. "You have approximately forty-five minutes, given the loss of time to the interruption. I don't want to be late for my wedding."

It was possible that she had bumped her head, very hard, probably when she was eavesdropping on Adrian and Cora. She had knocked herself out, and was now dreaming. She could not be on the verge of an impromptu wedding for the second time in her life. . . .

Marita pulled hard on Emily's corset, and Emily

coughed. It was no dream. "It isn't exactly white, but it has a lot of cream coloring in it." Marita held out Emily's gown, and Emily caught her breath.

"Marita! It's beautiful. It's the prettiest dress I've ever seen." Her eyes watered. It was prettier than the fifty-dollar gown she'd rented when she married Ian. Marita pulled the dress over her head, and Penelope brushed away tears.

"You look so lovely, Emily." Penelope squeezed Emily's arm. "I envy you."

Emily looked at her reflection in the mirror. She saw her own face, and in her eyes, she saw the girl she had been when she married Ian. Full of hope, trust, faith. But beyond that, now, she saw the doubt.

Emily sank onto her bed. "I can't do this. He has no idea what he's getting into. And he's crazy. There's no getting around that fact."

Marita looked at Penelope, then sat down beside Emily. "You're just getting cold feet. It happens to new brides all the time."

Penelope sat at her other side. "You do love him, don't you?"

Emily closed her eyes. "How could I not? But I loved someone else once, too. And he left me."

Marita patted Emily's hand. "Do you think Captain Woodward will leave you, too?"

"Yes. One way or another, he will."

Penelope bit her lip, then tapped her chin. "If that's true, then perhaps you shouldn't marry him."

Marita cast a sly glance at Penelope, then nodded. "I agree. You stay here, and one of us will go and tell him you've changed your mind. I'm sure he'll understand. He's downstairs now with his men. He has them all lined up, checking their uniforms to be sure they're spotless. He has asked Sergeant MacLeod to stand up for him, and Mr. Ping has secured a ring. Naturally, the first one Mr. Ping chose didn't fit the Captain's specifications. He can be very . . . exacting, can't he?"

Marita stood up and aimed for the door. She looked back at Emily and shook her head. "No, I don't know how you could live with a man like that. He'll have you polishing buttons, cleaning silverware twice because he can't see the reflection of the Northern Star in a spoon. . . . Don't worry. I'll tell him for you."

Tears dripped down Emily's cheeks. "Tell him. . . ." She sniffed and brushed the tears from her face, but more came. "Tell him I'll be right down."

The church was new, and very small. Yet as Herring led her through the door and down the aisle, the room felt ancient, as if she walked through the mists of time into the past. From the corner of her vision, she saw the rustic pews, the last rows empty. Then the guests—the townspeople, some smiling, some tense as if witnessing an outlaw's wedding might bring some curse upon them.

Marita and Penelope walked before her, new friends. She saw the magnificent seven, some seated in the first row, Ping as usher, and then MacLeod, faithful and sturdy standing beside Darian.

Not time, nor any twist of fate could change what she felt for him. He stood tall and proud, his uniform almost as neat as if it had just been made. The sun slanted through the high church windows and glinted on his blond hair, lighting his blue eyes with some strange, sacred light.

All the heartache of her past, all the doubt—these things lived inside her. And she was walking down the aisle to try again, hoping to seize something that always seemed to elude her. *Belonging*.

Another feeling haunted her. She had walked down

an aisle this way before, to stand beside another man, the same man. As she looked at Darian, tall and straight-backed, and so utterly sure of himself, she saw Ian like a ghost hovering above him.

Her footsteps faltered as she passed the last pew, her knees felt weak. Herring's grip on her arm tightened. She was trembling. Darian looked at her, tenderly, as if he understood her dilemma. He left MacLeod and came to her, but he didn't touch her. He wouldn't force her. If she turned around and ran, he would let her go, then come after her, he would talk to her until she again believed him.

A slow, gentle smile formed on his beautiful lips. He held out his hand. "Trust me."

Tears swamped her vision. She felt herself placing her hand in his. Darian's strong fingers wrapped around hers and he led her to the altar.

Their wedding went by like a dream passing, unstoppable, filled with mystery and hope, never quite removed from the fear. She heard herself as if from a great distance repeating the vows. She heard Darian, strong and sure, promising to love her forever, *'til death do us part.*

A death that, in her time, was already recorded. . . .

In every word he spoke, she heard the far-off echo of Ian Hallowell's soft voice, saying those same words.

"I now pronounce you man and wife."

Not the same words. . . .

If she'd had the presence of mind to arrange her own ceremony, she would have modernized it considerably to "husband and wife." As Darian bent to kiss her, she wondered if she'd promised to "obey," too. She'd never promised Ian that.

His lips touched hers, gently, with reverence. She looked into his blue eyes and saw tears shimmering there—tears still unshed. "Darian. . . ."

He smiled. "Emmy."

She stood as if enchanted as Darian turned to shake the minister's hand. The minister appeared somewhat pained, and Emily realized this must be the man Darian unwittingly once held up in his flight to justice. Darian was speaking. . . . "I hope the incident of a few months previous is forgotten, Pastor."

The minister swallowed hard, and nodded, too eagerly. Darian smiled as if all was well. With the evidence of peculiarity, reality made its way back to her senses. Darian, confident as always, faced a terrified victim, with no idea what he'd done to provoke such fear.

She reached to shake the minister's hand, too. He eyed her with grave misgivings, but allowed her offering. "So nice you two could meet again."

The minister nodded again, but seemed tense. "I wish you the utmost of good fortune as the result of your blessed nuptials." He paused, and his lip curled slightly. "Not that you'll need more than he took from the north-bound coach."

Darian obviously heard, but though his bright eyes narrowed, he made no comment. Probably didn't want to dampen the spirit of their wedding. Emily took his arm, feeling like a historic wife. "I am sure you will find all that gold returned, as soon as my husband has settled things here."

Darian patted her hand. "My wife is correct, of course. I assure you, Pastor, that the gold we unwittingly discovered is in safe keeping." He gestured at Bonner and Clyde, who looked even more like criminals than usual, dressed all in black standing in a white church. "Bonner and Clyde are men worthy of trust."

For the first time, Emily detected slight expression on the soldiers' faces. Pride. Darian's faith meant a great deal to them. She hoped it meant more to them than

143

gold. Emily looked around at his gang. They all congratulated him—Bonner and Clyde, wordlessly, with a slap to Darian's shoulder. Ping, filled with tearful emotion, stopped short of an emotional embrace but clearly was deeply moved by Darian's wedding. Herring watched Darian with quiet amusement and deeper affection. MacLeod, fatherly, was yet always respectful of his proud young commander.

How could Darian fail, with such friends? How could he fail with Emily at his side? A man who inspired such love and such loyalty could not end up hanged as a criminal. Emily wouldn't let it happen.

As Darian's men and the townspeople gathered around, Emily's thoughts turned to his fate. The history book hadn't revealed much—only that Darian was hanged, and that General Davis was remembered as a hero. Though Adrian had searched for more, nothing else was recorded, so Emily had no idea if the past's course had altered yet or not. She had to go on her best judgment, and what she knew of Darian Woodward.

Maybe, if she saw his first choices in each situation, she could sway them to something else, thus putting him off that dark path.

But nothing he had done so far seemed likely to save him from hanging. Except Emily. He had married her. She had distracted him from heaven knows what he might have inflicted on Tucson.

If she could keep him occupied, thoroughly distracted, she might convince him to give up his quest and save himself.

The setting sun sent a golden ray through the church, heralding a night of magic to come. Darian shifted his attention from his well-wishers to her. And in his glittering eyes, Emily saw the perfect way to distract her husband.

Chapter Eight

He hadn't expected to be this nervous. Darian sat on the edge of the large four-poster bed in the room he had confiscated from Belle, waiting for Emily to emerge from the dressing room. His heart pounded with furious leaps and bounds as he tried desperately to calm himself.

Their wedding had come off admirably, with the slight exception of realizing that the minister performing the ceremony had been the same man he'd held up by mistake. That might have been awkward, but Darian's good intentions had to be obvious to a man of the cloth.

They had enjoyed a rousing feast after the ceremony, thanks to Herring's abundant skills. Even the minister had loosened up after a few drinks, and began dancing with his wife. Darian had sat with Emily, feeling like a king. The king of Tucson. Maybe the power, the victories, his new love had all gone to his head.

It all came crashing down now as he sat fighting for

self-control, waiting for his wife to arrive.

Emily seemed to be taking an inordinate time dressing. Or undressing. Then again, he knew very little about a woman's private ministrations. She was fastidious with her person—he had learned that traveling with her, and it pleased him, since he was the same. She probably wasn't nervous, because she had been through this procedure before. A wedding night. Despite a certain amount of jealousy, Darian welcomed her experience, because he had no idea how to proceed from here.

If Emily were calm, he would be calm, too.

The dressing room door creaked open, slowly, and Emily emerged. Darian gulped and his pulse moved quicker still. There were ways a man could relieve his desire, in private, in the company of his own erotic thoughts—he wished he had utilized those means recently, so that his desire would be less demanding.

He tried to reassure himself. Emily would know what to do. It would all proceed smoothly.

She wore a long, white nightdress that seemed a little too large for her slender body. Across the room, their eyes met. Emily bit her lip, took a step toward him, and tripped on the hem of her nightdress.

Darian leapt up from the bed and steadied her. She peered up at him, her cheeks bright pink. Her breath came in small, swift puffs, and she was trembling.

She was as nervous as he was. They stared at each other, then looked away at the same time. No, she wasn't doing much to calm his fears.

Darian cleared his throat and adjusted his narrow tie. It felt awkward. He started to remove it, then realized this seemed suggestive, so instead, he tightened it too much. Emily eyed him doubtfully.

Darian forced a smile and took off his tie. Her hands were clasped at her waist. Even a virgin bride couldn't be this terrified. He wondered what she feared. As her husband, it was his duty to treat her tenderly, with care. Yet his primal instincts demanded something far wilder. He would have to contain them.

"Perhaps, my dear, we should sit."

Emily stole a quick glance at the bed, then seated herself on a small, stiff dressing stool. Darian sat in the other chair and looked at her, fighting for something to say to break the tension. "Well. Married. We're married."

She swallowed. "Yes. We are."

"I thought the service transpired pleasantly."

"It was very nice."

"The minister did a good rendition of the nuptials, I thought."

She looked a little weak. "Did he? Oh, yes. He did. I thought so, too." Their conversation wasn't doing much to ease her nervousness. His own was compounding with leaps and bounds.

"The church was well-constructed, for a Western town. Of course, in the East . . ." He forgot what he was going to say. "In the East, churches have steeples. . . ."

Emily's face changed. Her cheeks puffed, and she began to giggle. Her giggle became a laugh. She stood up from her stool and came to him. She touched the side of his face. "Darian. . . ."

"Yes?"

"Let's go to bed."

He placed his hand over hers, feeling the sweetness of her palm against his skin. "I think that's a good idea."

She walked to their bed, looked down at it as if it posed some unimagined threat, then straightened her shoulders and turned back to face him. Her breasts rose and fell beneath the nightdress. Her gaze followed his, and she saw what had captured his attention. Apparently, his expression revealed his soaring desire, because her lips curled into a seductive smile.

"Is there something, Captain, that interests you?"

Her mood had altered into something far more dangerous than nerves. Her green eyes slanted at the corners, her long, black eyelashes cast small shadows on her cheekbones. The lantern light warmed her skin and danced with tantalizing grace through her hair.

"All of you interests me, Emmy." He was grateful for the ability to speak when his throat was so tight, but she moved toward him, then dampened her soft lips with a deliberate, sensual touch of her tongue.

"Is that so?" Her little fingers toyed with the string at her collar, loosening it, then edging it open. Darian's pulse hammered in his head, filling him with need, but he stood immobile, frozen as she drew near.

She stopped, then gathered the skirt of her nightdress in her hands. "All of me?" She closed her eyes, and with a quick motion, pulled the nightdress over her head.

He expected more underpinnings. Perhaps several layers. Instead, bare flesh met his gaze. Soft curves, compelling shapes. Pure womanhood, inciting pure desire.

Darian couldn't move. He couldn't breathe. From the top of her head, where her dark hair parted and fell in lustrous waves over her shoulders, over one breast, and down her back; to her long throat, smooth shoulders, rounded breasts . . . a taut, soft stomach; even flare of slender hips; a trim dark triangle of curly hair at the apex of her thighs. Long, shapely legs to bare feet.

His.

She ran her hand over her arm, then down her side. "Do I interest you still?" She sounded nervous, but seductive. He felt as if he'd been brought before a goddess to make some holy offering, and received the gift instead.

No longer did lust settle just in his loins, but throughout his whole body. Every portion of him seemed designed to revel in this moment, to be this man who was her husband.

And Darian had no idea where to begin.

Emily watched him, her head tilted to one side. "I haven't felt this way in a very long time. I thought I never would again, but tonight, I feel feminine, and I feel romantic." She moved to him, standing right in front of him, naked. She placed her hand over his chest, where surely she could feel every throb of his heart. "Because of you, Darian Woodward."

He wanted to please her, to show her how much a woman she was. "I don't. . . ." His voice came like a croak. "I don't know what to do."

She smiled. "That's never stopped you before."

He smiled, too. It hadn't. He hadn't known how to fight, but he survived the bloodiest war in American history. He hadn't known how to lead other men, but they followed him anyway. He hadn't known how to negotiate with the local tribes, but they became his ally.

He could be a husband tonight.

Emily led him to the bed. She fiddled with the lantern. He expected her to douse it, but instead, she lowered it only a little, so that every portion of her remained visible to his sight. It would have been easier to control his lust without seeing her. He considered dousing it himself, but he caught a glimpse of her breast as she bent, then viewed her rounded bottom.

Not all the heavens could compare to the temptation of a woman's firm, round backside. A shame they wore cumbersome skirts, disguising the pert shape. He shifted his weight to ease the pressure on his manhood, but nothing dulled the ache.

Emily turned to him, and he felt her fingers toying

149

with the buttons of his shirt. He couldn't look away from her face, but he felt her hands against his bare chest. Very slowly, her touch spread over his chest, then down to his stomach as she loosened his shirt and then pushed it off his shoulders.

She stood back to look at him. She caught her lower lip between her teeth as if the sight of him stirred her, just as looking at her stirred him. Darian glanced down at his chest. It was well-formed, broad, the muscles defined, lean and hard.

Emily fiddled with his waistband. Darian caught her hand lest she discover just how much her presence affected him. She peeked up at him. "You've seen all of me. I want to see all of you."

"Not that!" Darian's brow furrowed. "You can't see *that.*" How would she react to him, this way? How could he hide how vulnerable she made him, how hard, and how weak?

"Darian. I was married, you know. I've seen 'that' before."

He frowned. "I don't want to shock you." He liked to be in control of how Emily thought of him. Maybe, of how everyone thought of him. His behavior was perfectly reasonable, at all times, his desire well-contained. Now, on his wedding night, he had every intention of expressing it tenderly, with utmost chivalry. True, their kisses had pressed the bounds of his control, and seeing her naked would again make restraint difficult, but at least, he could hide the evidence.

Somehow.

Darian reached for the lantern, but she laughed and seized his hand. "What are you doing? I can't see you in the dark."

Darian fought to compose himself. "It is . . . proper for the conjugal night to transpire in darkness."

A soft, adoring smile formed on her lips. "You're shy. I'm standing here naked, and you're shy. Darian. . . ."

"I am not shy."

She toyed with his waistband, teasing him. "But you are beautiful here." As she spoke, her eyelids lowered, her expression softened. Darian's resistance faltered.

"How do you know? You have never seen me . . . in a state of complete and utter undress."

"Almost."

Had she been spying on him during their travels? Darian considered this. Despite himself, he liked the thought. "In what manner?"

"While you were sleeping in the desert, I saw you." The light in her eyes danced, but he pretended not to know what she meant. "I think you were dreaming." She moved closer to him, so that her naked body touched his. His nerve endings quivered when her bare flesh met his, lightly. Control. He could not lose control.

"Men dream. It is natural to dream." His voice sounded odd. Hoarse.

She placed her hand on his chest, and he felt his heart throb against her palm. "And what do you dream of, Darian Woodward? Do you dream 'proper' dreams? Are you good, upstanding, and virtuous in those dreams?" She moved closer still, so that her breasts pressed against his chest. He felt as if an ocean of fire pressed against a fragile dam of ice. . . . "Or do you have outlaw dreams, do you dream of taking me, of doing all those things you forbid yourself while you wake?"

"Yes!" It burst out of him before he could stop himself. Wild dreams, reckless abandon. In his dreams, he was as violent and primal as legend made him. Darian was shaking. He caught her shoulders to steady himself, but the touch of her soft flesh beneath his hands stirred his inner demons to wild life. He knew himself perfectly.

He knew he had demons inside, and maybe those demons were wilder and more dangerous than other men's, but he was strong enough to hold them at bay.

Until now. Until his wife's small hands ran down his chest and slipped beneath his waistband. The clasp came loose. He had know idea how she did it, but now her fingers toyed inside his drawers. He wasn't afraid of shocking her—he was afraid of what he would do unleashed and uncontained.

"Emmy, please. I don't know. . . . I don't know what I'm capable of."

For a reason that eluded him, she seemed to like this thought. "We'll find out together, then." No, she obviously didn't understand how dangerous an outlaw could be. He felt his trousers lowered. If only he'd kept on his boots, it would have slowed her progress, but instead, his pants fell around his ankles. He felt foolish, so he stepped out of them.

She looked up at him and she seemed almost mesmerized, as if she, too, were feeling some strange, primal power. Feminine power. Maybe she was as dangerous as he. *Outlaw's woman.* "You have such a perfect veneer, Captain. So beautiful and cool and strong. But when I touch you, I feel fire within." She placed one hand on his chest again. "Here." She smiled, and her eyes never wavered from his as her hand moved down along his chest, over the tightened muscle of his stomach, and down.

She almost touched him there, but stopped just before touching his manhood. He ached, he wanted, and he couldn't stop her, nor ask her to continue.

He'd imagined that a woman would touch him there, where he was most fully male, but he hadn't thought she would actually do it. He'd felt certain it was disrespectful to even imagine it, and he wanted to treat his wife like a queen.

Very slowly, as his breaths moved in and out, as his heart beat, Emily slipped her hand lower, then closed her fingers around his rigid staff. His breaths stopped. His heart sped. Emily leaned to him and kissed his neck, whispering softly against his skin. "Fire."

He caught her face in his hands and he kissed her mouth. No thoughts formed in his brain, only wild images of lust and emotion swirled as her fingers played against him, teasing and caressing until his whole body went tight. She had pulled off his drawers and he was naked. He had no idea how she did it, but he couldn't stop kissing her.

"Darian. . . ." She sounded breathless. He stopped her words with another kiss. He tasted her lips, her tongue, but she pulled back and moved away. He stood naked before her, his erection poised and hard, standing rigid from his body. Emily was trembling, uncertain, as if she truly hadn't expected the full force of his reaction. He saw her swallow and move farther back until she bumped into the bed.

He watched as her vision lowered. A small squeak erupted from her throat. "Oh."

She never failed to amaze him, even now. First, she asserted herself as experienced and calm, then tripped into their wedding chamber. Then she reminded him of her first marriage, seduced him, stripped herself and him naked. . . . until she panicked at the sight of him.

In everything she did, Emily was filled with sweet contradictions. He had been nervous. Seeing her peculiar vulnerability calmed his fear and Darian felt strong again. "If you faint, my dear, I will catch you and place you on the bed. But when you wake. . . ." His voice trailed and he took a step toward her. "When you wake, I will have you."

She squeaked again. It occurred to Darian that he, too, had become a study in contrast. Hero and outlaw, protector and threat, husband and lover. He held out his hand. "You and I, my love, are many things, but together. . . ." Her hand was shaking, but she placed it in his. He drew it to his lips and kissed her fingers. "Together, we are one."

Tears formed in her green eyes, sparkling in the lantern light. "I am scared." Her vulnerability pierced his heart, and he drew her into his arms. Inconveniently, his erection refused to abate, and he felt it pulse against her stomach. He intended to reassure her, but his body made that difficult.

"I won't hurt you, Emily. Yes, my desire has reached. . . ." He stopped to gather himself. "Somewhat of a fury in its potency. . . ." Those weren't the most reassuring words, but she still leaned against him as if seeking protection. "But though my body does command a bestial force, which is directed at you. . . ."

She chuckled. He'd half expected her to scream. Generally, he was better at word selection, but he was so distracted by lust that nothing came out as he'd intended. She wrapped her arms tight around his waist and looked up at him. "It's not your body that scares me."

"Isn't it?" He paused. She was lying to salvage his pride. "My body is formidable in this condition. Your reaction indicates that your feminine delicacy has been shaken."

"Your body is beautiful. All that you are is beautiful. And so perfectly *you*. You have this amazing face, perfect bone structure, perfect features, and then over it all, Darian expressions. Pride and arrogance, and kindness and nobility. But most of all, when you look at me this

154

way, when you look so incredibly sensual, I just seem to melt."

"That sounds . . . good." Very good. The wedding night should commence. Darian closed his arms tighter around her, relishing the feel of his erection against her slender body.

"It is good."

"Then why are you afraid?"

"I'm scared of losing you."

"Tonight?" No, he wasn't thinking clearly. "You mean, at some point, you fear I will leave you?"

She nodded, then rested her cheek against his chest. "Maybe you won't walk out on me. I can't imagine you doing that, but you're not doing much to save yourself, either."

From hanging. Darian disliked the reminder, but she was right. He now had a wife to think of, a woman to protect. His choices involved her. But neither could he imagine making her the wife of a permanent renegade. "I will do my utmost to ensure a satisfactory outcome."

She looked up at him. He sensed that his words hadn't exactly reassured her, but she accepted him. "I know you will. I do love you, Darian. I've been so empty, and I had no idea how lonely I was until I found you."

Darian smiled, then kissed her cheek. "You will never be lonely again."

She slipped out of his arms and climbed onto the bed, to the far side leaving space for him. She puffed a quick breath, then lay back against the pillows, exposing her lush body to his sight. Darian stood by the bed looking down at her. He realized his mouth was open, so he closed it, but he couldn't take his eyes from her.

Her curly, black hair spread out around her shoulders, and she positioned one arm so that it curved over her head. Her little fingers curled. Her bright eyes gleamed with anticipation.

Round and full, tapering to rosy peaks—he would never see enough, nor have enough time to spend lavishing attention on her breasts. Darian knelt on the bed, then lowered himself beside her. He knew what to do, in theory, but in practice, he wasn't sure how to start. He considered his options.

The basic goal must be not to harm her, to make the procedure as pleasant as possible, given that he must sate that bestial force within himself. He knew that women possessed tender hearts, rich with emotion and love, so they tolerated a man's darker, more primal nature, then gifted him with children. In return, he would protect her, treat her with utmost respect—he would have to replace the mule with a woman's palfrey—and she would tolerate these marital encounters.

That is what he'd been raised to understand about marriage.

But how to begin? Women liked kissing. Emily especially enjoyed it. She liked touching, too. She had touched his most fervent maleness, which indicated she would accept the ultimate, bestial encounter.

Darian looked down at her while she waited. It was important to have a plan. He always had a plan, and such foresight generally yielded the best results. He would start with something she liked. Kissing. Then he would proceed to touching, and when the time seemed right, he would quickly enter her body, find release, and apologize profusely afterwards.

Her brow quirked and she looked at him strangely. "What are you doing?"

"What do you mean?"

"Your lips were moving."

Darian felt uneasy. He had been planning aloud? "I was considering how best to proceed."

"I thought you might be saying a prayer." A smile played on her lips. "You have the same expression now that you do before battle, or before you do when you're planning something really weird. I'm surprised you haven't checked your revolver."

She was teasing him, now, when he was doing his utmost to frame a perfect encounter between them. "It is important to know one's path."

Her face formed a serious expression, but he still detected a smile. "I understand. Well, I wouldn't want to interfere with that. What have you planned first?"

Darian propped himself on one elbow to study her face. He edged a wayward strand of curly hair off her cheek. "I thought I would kiss you."

She closed her eyes and dampened her lips. "Okay."

He bent and pressed his mouth against hers. Soft and sweet, he kissed her. He would restrain his earlier, raging impulses and do this right, if it killed him. She seemed to like the gentle kiss. He deepened it, subtly, and ran his tongue along the edge of her lips. She liked that, too, because he felt her quickened breaths against his face.

Her lips parted beneath his, and he slid his tongue between. Her tongue met his, and they engaged in a teasing, sensual dance. He liked it too much. His heart throbbed, his erection pressed hot and hard against the mattress. Darian pulled back, feeling flushed.

Emily didn't move. She just gazed up at him, trusting and in love. "Step one completed, I take it?" He nodded, took a breath, then eyed her body. She smiled. "What's next?"

"I thought . . . touching."

"That sounds good. Do I touch you, or do you want to touch me?"

He couldn't allow her to touch him. Her touch earlier threatened to bring him to his knees. He couldn't spill himself in her hand, as that would truly shock her and go beyond the accepted bounds of matrimony.

"I touch you."

"Okay." She folded her arms up behind her head and waited. This posture had the effect of raising her breasts and elongating her slender stomach. A beautiful sight. Darian ran his hand along her side, then to the soft swell of her breast.

"There was a time when men worshipped naked goddesses." He'd seen Grecian statues when his family took him to Europe when he was a boy. His mother had tried to whisk him by, but his brother and he snuck back and gaped at the glorious objects. The vision had fueled many a secret fantasy since then. He felt the contour of Emily's skin, circling her breast with a light touch. A goddess. "You are softer than I'd imagined."

Softer than marble, and far warmer. He felt fortunate that she didn't know his inner comparison to a statue. He cupped her fullness, then trailed his finger over the peak. It grew taut and he repressed a groan. Emily liked it, too. Her eyes closed.

No, a statue couldn't emulate the intricacies of real feminine flesh. He'd had no idea. He teased the little peak until Emily uttered soft moans. He watched her face. She more than liked his attention. If he hadn't been taught better, he would imagine that she was experiencing the same primal lust as he. But no, he was mistaking feminine emotion for the more animalistic, male need. He had to restrain the impulse to gauge her reactions through the veil of his own.

Still, he liked her response. Darian bent to brush his

lips over her nipple. She liked this, too. His tongue swept out to taste her and her moan became a whimper. It sounded like lust. He tried sucking, gently, and heard a muffled cry. He stopped and looked at her. Her head was tipped back, her white teeth clasping her lower lip. Maybe he had gone too far.

"Emmy?"

Her eyes opened. She seemed to be almost . . . gasping. The look in her eyes indicated strong, even fierce emotion. "I like the touching part very much, Darian. You do it really well."

He smiled. *"Really?"*

"Really."

He had gotten carried away with touching her breasts. "Perhaps I should try another spot."

Her eyes widened. "As you wish."

He liked her words, but he couldn't allow himself to take advantage of his wife's trust. He forced his attention from her tempting, round breasts, and ran his hand down her stomach. Her muscle tensed as if in anticipation. He touched her hip, then her thigh. Such soft skin, so tantalizing! He moved his hand to her inner thigh and found it softer still.

Emily seemed to be quivering. Maybe he had come too close to her feminine core. He started to move his hand away, but instead, brushed the satin curls between her legs. He meant to apologize, but Emily murmured, and the sound was decidedly encouraging.

Darian hesitated. Breasts were a well-known and common point of male attention, often used to tantalize a man beneath suggestive bodices such as the less attractive Agatha wore. He had imagined Emily in this garb, but hadn't dared suggest it. The space between her legs was more private, however. He would place himself there, quickly, causing her discomfort, though less so

159

than had she been a virgin. He had already formulated his apology for the aftermath.

But Emily seemed to want him to touch her there, too. He liked the teasing feel of her curls against his fingertips. He tried a little more, grazing his fingers over the soft triangle. She offered no objection, so he tried again. He progressed lower, against her inner thigh, and found the curls there damp.

A woman's body prepares itself, making the male invasion easier. Yet there was something more. A delicate, womanly fragrance to her skin, a warmth beneath her flesh—all this lured him closer. With infinite care, he slid one finger inward, beneath the curls to the softest, most inviting flesh he'd ever imagined.

A mistake. A hideous mistake. All he could imagine was his own thick, aching staff pressed hard against this satin skin, driving inward. . . . Darian fought the image, but Emily reached down and touched his hair. "Darian. . . ." Her voice sounded dreamy, sensual. "Don't stop."

He froze. *She liked it.* A lot. Darian gulped, then ran his finger along her damp cleft. He found the opening that his own raging body longed to invade. He explored it with Herculean restraint. So tender, so pure and soft. . . . He circled the area, then found a tiny, firm bud at its apex. When he touched that, Emily moaned and squirmed.

There was no mistaking her reaction. This was lust. He teased the little bud and it hardened still more. That enchanting fragrance compelled him, luring him like a mystic siren's song. He had found some ancient core of womanhood in his new wife, a tiny, potent secret of femininity. How many men had failed to discover this, and missed forever his woman's haunting moan?

The more he teased, the more she reacted. He loved

Thrill to the most sensual, adventure-filled Romances on the market today...

FROM  LOVE SPELL BOOKS

As a home subscriber to the Love Spell Romance Book Club, you'll enjoy the best in today's BRAND-NEW Time Travel, Futuristic, Legendary Lovers, Perfect Heroes and other genre romance fiction. For five years, Love Spell has brought you the award-winning, high-quality authors you know and love to read. Each Love Spell romance will sweep you away to a world of high adventure...and intimate romance. Discover for yourself all the passion and excitement millions of readers thrill to each and every month.

Save $5.00 Each Time You Buy!

Every other month, the Love Spell Romance Book Club brings you four brand-new titles from Love Spell Books. EACH PACKAGE WILL SAVE YOU AT LEAST $5.00 FROM THE BOOKSTORE PRICE! And you'll never miss a new title with our convenient home delivery service.

Here's how we do it: Each package will carry a FREE 10-DAY EXAMINATION privilege. At the end of that time, if you decide to keep your books, simply pay the low invoice price of $17.96, no shipping or handling charges added. HOME DELIVERY IS ALWAYS FREE. With today's top romance novels selling for $5.99 and higher, our price SAVES YOU AT LEAST $5.00 with each shipment.

AND YOUR FIRST TWO-BOOK SHIPMENT IS TOTALLY FREE!

IT'S A BARGAIN YOU CANT BEAT! A SUPER $11.48 Value!

Love Spell ⊕ A Division of Dorchester Publishing Co., Inc.

Get Two Books Totally
FREE —
An $11.48 Value!

▼ Tear Here and Mail Your FREE Book Card Today! ▼

PLEASE RUSH
MY TWO FREE
BOOKS TO ME
RIGHT AWAY!

Love Spell Romance Book Club
P.O. Box 6613
Edison, NJ 08818-6613

AFFIX
STAMP
HERE

it. It fueled him beyond his own need, until he felt filled with masculine power. He wanted more. He wanted to taste her, and own her, and hear her moan become a wanton demand. Without thinking, beyond planning, Darian bent and flicked his tongue over the little bud.

He heard the echo of every goddess in her cry of pleasure. He had found a god inside himself. He licked again, then tried sucking. She squirmed, her hips moved. Her fingers entwined in his hair and she gasped his name. He found a sweet, mesmerizing rhythm to his godlike ministrations—he teased her and lavished her until her whole body quivered, until her back arched and her toes curled.

Something wild, primal, and exquisitely female seemed to shatter in Emily. She seemed as wild as he had feared to be. He recognized her reaction—he had experienced it himself in private. He had never known a woman could feel it, too. But his wife wanted more. She clasped his hair, feverishly, and called to him.

"Darian. Come here. Now." She sounded breathless, demanding. He had no idea what she wanted, but she pulled him up above her body. He looked down into her eyes and her passion astounded him. "Now."

He wasn't sure what she wanted, but she squirmed beneath him, and wrapped her legs over his. Now he knew. Her damp curls teased his erection, and he knew. He had found her passion, and now she was welcoming his. A more than fair trade.

In pleasuring her, he had almost forgotten himself, but the need returned with such force. . . . His erection burned, filled beyond endurance from witnessing his wife's secret desire. He had no choice. He needed her, too. Emily reached between their bodies and clasped his length in her hand. She understood.

She guided him to her opening, and he felt that perfect

flesh against him, even better than he'd imagined. He hesitated, then edged himself inward. She felt warm, even hot, inside. Warm and wet, and snug around the tip of him. Emily wrapped her arms around him and whispered soft words. He didn't hear what she said, but she wasn't asking him to stop.

His body quivered with restraint. She adjusted her hips and took him deeper inside. Her inner walls closed tight around him, and she moved. Darian groaned, but he could hold himself back no longer. He arched and drove himself inside her, then again. Over and over, he thrust inside her, deeper, wilder until he lost all thought of control.

She rose to meet him, moaning and twisting, increasing his pleasure, driving him to an ecstasy beyond anything he'd known. Nothing in his secret fantasies came close, and the release he experienced surpassed all dreams. It poured from him, ripped from his core, in pounding waves that seemed unending until at last it abated and left him deep and embedded inside her.

He couldn't move, not even to withdraw from her body. His eyes were closed, but he felt her heart pounding, he heard her breaths as she lay beneath him. Darian didn't dare meet her eyes. What would she think of him now? He had crept like a thief into her most secret places, then unleashed himself like a raging hurricane inside her.

He had never lost control of himself before. And now, here in the most tender encounter of his life, in his wife's arms, he had erupted like a heathen's volcano. . . . Loving every second of it, relishing it like a war god.

He knew, because he was an honest man and honorable, that every time he lay with her would be the same. He tried to recall the apology he'd planned. *My dearest wife, allow me to apologize for venting my animalistic passions upon you.* . . . It didn't seem sufficient. Maybe he should thank her for accepting him with such fervent emotion. Or for the way she had moved her hips in tandem with his.

The thought stirred his blood unexpectedly, and he grew hard again inside her. He was an animal. A beast incapable of truly subduing his impulses. . . .

With utmost care, he withdrew from her body. His eyes were still closed for fear of seeing the shock surely written on her face. He drew a shuddering breath of shame and perfect satiation, then opened his eyes.

She stared up at him as though he were a god.

Chapter Nine

"I am the luckiest woman in the world." Emily lay on her back, happier than she'd ever been in her life. Darian gaped at her as if she'd said something truly unexpected, something he didn't quite dare believe.

His eyes shifted to one side, then back to her. "Really?"

"Really."

He considered this a moment, his expression serious. "My invasion of your person has not disturbed you substantially?"

She loved him because he was crazy. Emily reached to touch his hair. When damp, it curled slightly, making him look young and innocent. "I felt it in my toes." She paused. "Twice."

He appeared confused, but she detected a flicker of pride. "Felt what?"

"Climax. What you felt. . . ." His brow furrowed, he

appeared disbelieving, as if she'd said she'd sprouted wings and could fly. "You know, what happened . . . at the end."

His blue eyes widened so that she could see the lantern reflected like the moon on the ocean. "You felt that, too?"

"Yeah."

"Exactly?"

"Well, sort of. I suppose yours is like a volcano, and mine like an earthquake, but it's still . . . cataclysmic."

Darian moved to lie beside her, then propped himself up on one elbow and stared, astonished. Emily laughed. "Couldn't you tell?"

He thought about it for awhile, and she watched as a small smile grew on his lips, as that beloved self-assurance returned. "Yes. I could." He lay back and edged her into his arms. Emily rested her cheek on his shoulder, more content than she'd ever been in her life.

Darian was still thinking. "I was led to believe a woman endures this act, tolerates it because she loves her husband. Not that she enjoys it."

"I suppose it depends on the woman. And on the man. But you, Darian Woodward, are very, very good at making love."

"Am I?" He seemed pleased, but surprised.

"Yes." She peered up at his face, liking the obvious satiation there. "I wondered if Adrian was wrong about you."

"In what way?"

"He said you were a virgin."

Darian uttered a miserable groan. "That man had no sense of privacy."

Emily waited, but nothing more was forthcoming. "Well?"

"Well, what?"

"Are you a virgin?"

Darian smiled, then kissed her forehead. "Not any more."

"Why did you wait? Is it some Victorian thing?"

"I'm not sure what you mean by a 'Victorian thing,' but my reasons from abstaining from the . . . bestial embrace before marriage. . . . I had no idea how truly wonderful the bestial embrace could be. . . ." His voice trailed and Emily tapped his arm.

"Your reasons?"

"Ah, yes. Well, it is not uncommon for a young man to seek out a lady of the night, especially during war. My brother and I did so, not long after Bull Run. We both had sweethearts at home, but neither of us looked favorably upon dying as a virgin."

"What stopped you?"

Darian huffed. "The sight of the strumpet I was to bed. Her teeth were black, she reeked of liquor, and we were standing in line outside her hut for two hours."

"That is disgusting."

"I thought so myself."

"What about your brother?"

"He went in first, spent fifteen minutes, and came out. He told me afterwards that it was not worth the expense."

"So you didn't go in?"

"I went in. My brother had done so, and I couldn't look unmanly beside him."

"Of course." Emily's heart moved and she kissed his shoulder. "But you didn't . . . didn't. . . ."

"The sight of her diminished any desire I had accumulated, which hadn't been substantial in the first place." He paused. "She was disappointed because she considered me handsome, and offered to reduce her fee if I would kiss her."

"Did you?"

"No. That's when I noticed her teeth. I paid her, in full, for her time, then left."

Emily laughed and hugged him. "What did you tell your brother?"

"I told him I had become a man, but it didn't seem worth going back a second time. He agreed." A faraway look crossed his face. "I had never lied to my brother before. The next time we went into battle, the guilt overwhelmed me, and I told him the truth."

"What did he say?"

Darian closed his eyes. "That he had lied too, paid the woman extra, and left without touching her."

Tears clouded Emily's vision. "How sweet! He must have been very dear."

"Yes."

Darian said nothing further. He carried his brother's death deeply, and as Emily watched him, she knew the guilt he felt hadn't subsided over time. Maybe this explained his subconscious march toward death, his determination to avenge wrong no matter what the cost. "Your brother would have wanted you to live."

He didn't respond, confirming her fears.

"You know that, Darian."

"I know."

"He wouldn't blame you for what happened to him."

"I know that, too."

"But you blame yourself, don't you?"

"It is over now."

"Darian, until you forgive yourself, it will never be over, and you know it."

Despite her satiation and happiness, Emily slept fitfully. She felt sure she hadn't reached Darian about his brother. He blamed himself. He was a stubborn man, and it would take more than her word to convince him otherwise.

Her restlessness hadn't troubled Darian. He slept like a baby beside her, contented, with a smile on his lips all through the night. No matter what else had happened, she had made him happy. He had certainly done the same for her.

She hadn't thought of Ian, not once. Darian's passion obliterated her memories, and far surpassed anything she had known before. Ian had been shy—he had never dared to explore her body the way Darian did, nor did he take her with the reckless abandon she found in Darian. She hadn't climaxed during her first brief marriage, but assumed that when he relaxed, it would happen. Her desire had been there, and he had certainly been beautiful.

She felt certain that in some way, Ian and Darian were the same person. Yet Ian seemed . . . less. Somehow, she felt reincarnation should be progressive, like the rings of a tree as it becomes greater—the same, yet more. But Darian seemed *more* than Ian. Adrian had told her that his father, the Apache chief who commanded the whirlwind in time, believed that Darian's fate was altered by his brush with time travel.

So what happened to Ian when Darian's fate changed? What would happen to him now that she was his lover in another time?

It seemed an impossible quandary, one she wasn't equipped to answer. She lay on her back, studying the woodwork on the ceiling as the first rays of sun slanted into their bedroom. Darian stirred in his sleep, then murmured low and sensual. He rolled onto his back, and the covers tented over his groin.

Emily's thoughts bounded from philosophical ponderings to renewed desire. She wanted time to explore him, now that he knew her body and felt comfortable in the "bestial embrace." Morning seemed the perfect time to awaken his desire once more.

She trailed her finger over the covers to his rigid length. She took it in her hand, and he woke with a groan of pure masculine pleasure. She kissed his face, then intensified her caress. "Emmy. . . ." His voice was cut short by another moan, and his hips arched as she stroked him.

"Good morning, Captain."

"Mmm."

She looked into his sleepy eyes and saw both fire and joy. She moved to kiss his mouth, and he reached to hold her.

"Captain!"

Emily and Darian flopped back and groaned in unison. "Ping."

Ping rapped vigorously on their door and Darian snarled. Ping rapped again. "Captain! They're coming, they're coming! Captain!"

Emily's heart clenched, her pulse raced to dizzying speeds. She hopped out of bed and searched desperately for her clothes. Darian issued a low growl, stretched, then rose and went to the door. "Ping. What is it? Speak plainer, if possible. Who is coming?"

"Indians, sir! Lots of them. Thousands!"

Darian glanced at Emily. "Ten, at most. Ping tends to exaggerate."

Emily buttoned her bodice with shaking hands. "Would they be associated with that general?"

"Unlikely. Ping, are any of Davis's men among them?"

"Don't know, sir. Didn't stick out on picket duty long enough to find out. I saw them riding down out of the eastern hills. Riding fast, sir."

"Not as fast as yourself, I'm sure." Darian yawned and Emily stared at him in amazement.

"What do we do?"

Darian buttoned his uniform, then glanced into the mirror. "I have noticed that you utilize a toothbrush. Since we are now one, married of body and soul, I wondered if I might. . . ."

"You're brushing your teeth? During an Indian raid?" Emily fought hysteria as he brushed his teeth, carefully, but it wasn't easy.

Darian finished dressing, then opened the door. Ping looked him up and down, then blushed. "Good night, sir?"

"That would be none of your concern, Ping."

"Right, sir." He cast a fond glance at Emily. She tried to smile, but she was shaking. "Good morning, Miss. Sorry. Mrs. Woodward."

My new name. She liked the sound. "Good morning, Ping."

He turned cheerfully back to Darian. "About the Indian raid. . . ."

"Indians don't 'raid' during the morning hours. If they meant harm to this town, they would attack at night, and there would be no warning. Gather the men, and be sure the townspeople are inside the saloon. Not a shot is to be fired without my word. Do you understand?"

"Yes, sir." Ping sounded disappointed, but agreeable as always. He skittered away and sped down the stairs shouting orders that Emily felt sure no one obeyed. Darian sighed, then took her hand and kissed it.

"I am sorry our first morning has to be interrupted by something so trivial. I will handle this matter, and then perhaps we might breakfast together."

"Breakfast? Darian. . . ." There was no use arguing with him. His self-confidence had returned in full, perhaps even more than it had been. "An Indian raid might take at least until lunch."

"Be that as it may, you will remain here until I have ascertained the danger."

Emily cocked her head to one side. "Surely you know me better than that."

"I do, and that is why I tell you to stay here."

She crossed her arms over her chest and shook her head. "I want to be with you."

His blue eyes glinted. "I could tie you to the bed."

Emily smiled. "Later, Darian. After you've handled the 'little matter' of marauding Indians. . . ." She seized his hand and pulled him to the door. "Let's go."

The townspeople of Tucson were in a predictable panic. Darian surveyed the room with disgust. Belle screamed and hid in a closet. The former sheriff hid in a corner with the former barkeep, fighting over a half-empty bottle of bourbon. The three saloon girls held themselves with more dignity, but their faces were uniformly white, and Penelope whispered quiet prayers for their lives.

Darian's men took position by the door, with Ping as lookout at the window. "They're coming, sir. Whole mass of 'em heading up the street."

Despite his experience in battle, Ping's voice betrayed more fear than usual. Strange that a man could face an army of thousands during the Civil War, attend his duty as a soldier, yet become white with fear faced with a few Indian warriors. Darian himself had experienced the same reaction when he came west with the cavalry, during his first forays against warriors painted, shouting war cries.

Until he saw the first dead Indian, and knew all men died the same. Then, held captive among them, he realized that they went about their day no different from white men. Children played, women bickered and laughed, men played sports and prepared weapons. Young lovers found occasion to escape from the others to be alone.

He listened as the horses came closer. He glanced at Ping, who nodded. Emily stood close behind him, defying the first command of their marriage, but there was nothing he could do about that now.

Darian opened the door and stepped out, shading his eyes against the morning sun. Nine warriors formed a semicircle outside the saloon. *Not even ten. . . .* They held weapons, but none were aimed. Darian assessed them calmly and, as he expected, found a familiar face.

"Haastin, I believe. What brings you to Tucson?"

A lean young man met his gaze and smiled. "You have made a name for yourself we didn't expect, Captain."

"Have I?" Even the Apache had heard of his deeds? He found that fact curiously satisfying. "What name?"

"Outlaw."

Not quite what he'd hoped. Darian frowned. "That name isn't warranted."

"The white general believes otherwise." Haastin leaned his arm on his saddle and lowered his voice. "He is bringing men from the fort, forty soldiers, to come for you here. Tiotonawen sent us to warn you, and to offer you safety among us."

Darian hesitated. Forty. That might be more than his small group could handle. "It is my intention to meet General Davis, and bring him to justice."

"He does not come with justice in mind. He comes with a rope."

For hanging. Darian heard a sharp squeal, and realized Emily stood behind him. Danger moved in around him. He had to get her to safety, and Tiotonawen was

172

the only person who could send her back to her time, if the need arose.

Haastin eyed Emily, then raised his brow in surprise. "Another one?"

He must be referring to Cora, another woman from the future. How odd that the Apache recognized this, accepted it, and said nothing! "Another one." Darian paused. "This one is mine."

Haastin huffed, then shook his head. "The men of times to come lack much, to send their women to us."

Emily stepped forward, annoyed. "That is not the case at all. And I wasn't 'sent.' I chose to come back to help Darian."

Haastin remained unimpressed. "The son of the whirlwind sent you."

She frowned. "If you mean Adrian, yes. He helped. But I did it myself."

"The son of the whirlwind sent you to help his white brother. You were sent."

"Because I wanted to be!"

Haastin looked at Darian, who shrugged. "She was sent."

Emily sputtered, then turned her attention to Darian. "Well? What do we do? Even you can't hope to fight forty soldiers."

"Davis's aggression indicates fear of my plan. I will meet him on my terms, not his own. We will go to Tiotonawen."

At Darian's word, his men emerged. Wetherspoon collected the horses, and MacLeod reluctantly returned his badge to the sheriff. "Liked that, I did. Be wearing it again when I come back." The sheriff didn't argue, and pinned the badge to his shirt with shaking hands.

Herring pulled off his apron and tossed it to the former bartender. Ping took Penelope's hand and gazed adoringly into her eyes. Bonner and Clyde emerged from the bank, glared uniformly at their predecessor, then mounted their horses. Emily hugged Marita, then Penelope, as Darian lined up the horses.

Emily looked around. "Where's my mule?"

Darian led a small brown and white mare to her and smiled. "My wife requires a better mount."

Emily patted the mare's nose. The mare pushed her as if requesting a treat of some sort. "Did you have to pick the fattest one, Darian?"

"She is a gentle mount fit for a lady."

"Couldn't I have that black one?" She gestured at a sleek horse that stomped its hoof in restive energy. It snorted at a bird, and Emily turned back to her mare. "Never mind. This mare will do fine."

Emily climbed into the saddle, and Darian mounted his gray. He turned to the townspeople and tipped his hat. "I must leave you now, though I think you will agree that the town is in better shape now than when I first came." He paused. No one answered, though Belle snorted derisively. Agatha was already tugging her bodice lower, but Marita and Penelope looked sad.

Marita turned to the others. "Everything is much cleaner since Captain Woodward arrived."

No one argued, but the others didn't seem as pleased with this development as the two young women.

Obviously, the people of Tucson had no idea what was best for them. Well, he'd done his part. Darian nodded to Belle. "You, madam, will relay this message to General Davis for me. Justice is in my hands, and I will see it to its rightful end. When he least expects me, then I shall appear, and no sooner."

"You're turning tail and running, outlaw. That's what I'm telling Clem!"

Darian smiled, infuriating her. "If you choose to ig-

nore my warning, so be it. But a warning it remains."
He paid the woman no further heed. "Gentlemen, our
journey takes a new turn. Unexpected, yes, but always
to the same end. Every step we take leads us closer to
justice."

His men appreciated his words. As always, they had
ultimate faith in his leadership. But as they started out
of town, he caught the look in Emily's eyes. *Every step
closer to your hanging. . . .*

The Apache led Darian's gang into the western hills,
following a path only they seemed to see. They spoke
among themselves, quietly, and Darian's men rode
along, silent, too. The men of two races didn't interact
much, but Emily detected a certain humor in the Apache,
not unlike what she herself felt amidst Darian's peculiar
group. Yet they had risked themselves for Darian—he
must have garnered their respect somehow.

Ping seemed nervous of the Indians, as did the others,
though Bonner and Clyde remained as impassive and
expressionless as always. It occurred to Emily that the
Apache had best watch their valuables around those two.
She had noticed that their saddlebags appeared suspiciously full when they emerged from the bank.

Only Darian conversed with the Apache, and seemed
to know their leader. He treated them no differently than
anyone else in his path—by nightfall, he would have
corrected their English to perfection, and directed them
in proper saddle upkeep and in better ways to shoe their
horses.

Emily loved him. He treated everyone with the same
dignity and respect, with a slightly world-weary edge to
everything he did. He knew what to expect from people,
yet he trusted, still. She rode along beside him. Unlike
the mule, her mare proved to have a surprisingly speedy

gait—smooth, but determined to keep up. Like herself, perhaps.

She reached over to tap Darian's knee as they rounded a corner of juniper bushes, heading farther into the Catalina mountains. "Where are we going? Do you know?"

Darian smiled at her, reassuring. "I have no idea. But it is right that you should meet Tiotonawen, in the chance that you shall need him to return you to your time."

Here was something they hadn't discussed. The subject of her return, her plans for the future, had been the elephant in the room during their conversations, unspoken, but always there. Did she even want to go back? She had assumed she would, she hadn't considered staying in the past. But she hadn't planned on marrying a Civil War hero, either.

Who would miss her if she never returned? Her parents had been killed in a car accident when she was seventeen. She had no siblings, and what remained of her family was so distant as to not notice her disappearance. Cora and Adrian would wonder, but would probably guess it had been her choice. Maybe she could send them a message of some sort.

"I want to stay with you."

The look on Darian's face told her the issue had been preying on his thoughts, too, and that her decision gave him great relief and happiness. He reached for her hand and squeezed it. "I would not ask that you do so, if you wished otherwise. But I am pleased at your choice."

He glanced back over his shoulders, at the fading plains of the desert, and his expression changed. "No outcome is assured, my dear. If the need should arise, you may wish to return to your time, after all."

"You mean, if you fail and are hanged?" Emily's heart beat slower, and a shiver tore through her. "Darian, can't you make peace with this general somehow?"

She saw sympathy in his eyes, but no yielding. "Emmy, do you see these people we ride with? These are the people, and thousands like them, that General Davis is bent on destroying. Not because they have done him any harm, but because they exist. Because since the war ended, the Indian people are the only ones he can battle with impunity, and consider himself a hero. Do you understand? When we were at war, North against South, he sought the blood of rebel soldiers. Now we have peace, and he looks elsewhere."

"He sounds like a psychopath."

"If you mean he likes to kill, then, yes. If he could brand Swedish people enemies, he would pursue them with the same bloodlust. I stopped him once. I will stop him again, and this time, for good."

"But Darian, what if he stops you?"

Again, she saw no yielding, but she saw doubt. "I cannot let that happen."

"There has to be a way. . . ." Emily chewed her lip. "Maybe this Tiotonawen can help. He must be a wise man."

"As I recall, the Apache leader was a grumpy old man. In fact, he reminded me of my grandfather on my mother's side. Stubborn, illogical, with a single-minded dedication to his people."

Emily slanted her brow. "Gee. Who does *that* sound like?"

Darian nodded. "I know. Sergeant MacLeod shares many of those same qualities."

Emily groaned, but Darian's eyes twinkled. He knew she meant him. He would always be this way. She could picture him as an old man, aligning items in the refrigerator to his own specifications, socks according to color, spices by alphabetical order. . . . She stopped herself, surprised that she was imagining him not in his own time, but in hers. Was it possible? Could this Apache chief send both her and Darian to the future?

Her eyes widened and she caught her breath. The perfect solution presented itself. Darian could save himself not by fleeing to Mexico, but to the future. She opened her mouth to explain, then caught the determined set of his jaw. He wouldn't agree, not yet. Maybe, when the situation had become irreversible, then he would relent. When he could see it was in everyone's best interest, he might yield, after all.

Emily fell silent, her own determination taking shape. It would be her duty to show Darian this was just the course he should take.

Haastin led the group on a zigzag course up into the hills, careful to leave no sign of their passing. Darian paid attention to their path, however, and knew he could find his way back. He had a gift for geography—it had served him well during the war, and afterwards, when tracking.

Emily said nothing as she rode beside him, but he could tell from her thoughtful expression that she was planning something. Probably something to save him. He understood her fears. There was nothing he could do to allay them.

They rode until sunset, then came to the edge of a small, makeshift Indian village. Darian dismounted, then turned to watch the sun setting over the desert. Gold and orange and rays of purple arched over the sand, glinting on the cactus that dotted the landscape, receding into forever. A beautiful sight, and it moved Darian's heart with its strange permanence.

He loved the desert, though he was far from his original home, far from his own people. He felt more at home here than he ever had in the East. He loved the desert because it was raw and untamed, its permanence beyond civilization. He had tried to be a good man, a civilized man, yet as he entered an Apache village, he felt more alive, more himself, than he had anywhere else.

Emily stood beside him, and he took her hand. "Tell me, is the desert much changed in your time?"

She looked out at the magnificent sight and sighed. "In some places, I suppose it would shock you. The roads and the homes, the city. But here, where we're standing, it's not all that different from now."

"I expect the population will have more than doubled in your day."

Emily's brow slanted. "Darian. There are almost four million people living in Arizona now . . . then."

Darian laughed, saw that she was serious, then gaped in disbelief. "That isn't possible. Four million people wouldn't fit."

"They fit okay. In a way."

Darian considered the implications of such a vast number. "Do they get along?"

"Pretty much."

"Are we still at war with the Indians?"

"No. Everybody's kind of mixed together."

This sounded more promising. He had many questions, like a child reading a fantasy novel. He wanted to know the end result of what he did today. He found himself wanting to see this future world, to see people living in a different world.

Maybe, when they lay together at night, after sex, he would have Emily tell him more. But for now, he had to face the Indian chief, face his own dark future, and somehow, find a way to make it work out right.

Haastin rode ahead, then returned to call Darian forward. He walked into the village with Emily beside him. As he walked among the Apache, he recognized familiar faces. A young mother, Laurencita, who had befriended Cora Talmadge, then adopted an orphaned white boy. He remembered that she was Haastin's wife. He saw an elderly woman who, he recalled, had a tendency to swat people rather than speaking, and he made a wide berth around her. Emily smiled at her, and she frowned.

Tiotonawen sat on a rock whittling a stick. He looked the same as Darian remembered him from their previous campsite near Fort McDowell. Old and withered, yet handsome and venerable, too. As soon as he spotted Darian, the old man sighed and shook his head. With the help of two older women, Tiotonawen rose to greet Darian.

Darian doffed his cap and bowed. "Tiotonawen, it gives me great honor to return to you this day. . . ."

Tiotonawen snorted and shook his head again. "You, young onion, make trouble wherever you go."

Emily choked back a laugh. " 'Onion?' "

Tiotonawen glanced at her, assessed her origin, then nodded. "Many layers hide the center."

She coughed. "That much is certain." She pressed her lips together.

Darian glared. He was attempting formality, to be at his utmost polite, and that old man treated him with overt disrespect. *Onion, indeed!* He had no "layers." He was as straightforward, direct, purposeful as . . . a carrot.

Tiotonawen brandished a wooden cane, then tapped Darian's chest. Darian resisted the urge to brandish his revolver, and a saber, too, but it wasn't easy. "So, the white general hunts you down?" The chief asked. "What you started when you rode among my people goes far off the path."

Darian would have liked to argue, but Tiotonawen had

180

summed up his situation with fair accuracy. "That will not last."

The chief appeared skeptical, but turned his bright gaze on Emily. "My son sent a woman as his messenger?"

Emily frowned, then stepped forward. She slung her pack off her back and rummaged through it, then drew out the pictures. "Adrian and his wife gave me these pictures to give to you."

Tiotonawen eyed her suspiciously, but he took the paper. He stared at each sheet for a long time, and his face softened. "This, this small speck with black hair and a feather . . . this is my seed?"

Emily glanced at Darian and shrugged. "It's your grandson." A small smile crossed her lips. "His name is Darian."

Darian's mouth dropped open. His heart simultaneously warmed and constricted, and he snatched the picture out of the chief's hand. "They named him for me?"

"I told you they liked you."

He was deeply moved as he stared down at the baby's image. Somewhere in the future, a child bore his name. They would tell that child of his great deeds, of what a good man he was. *I cannot let my name go down as outlaw.*

Emily touched his arm. "Are you pleased?"

"I am honored."

He looked at her. If he lived, they would have children. He would name his first son after his brother, Oliver. A daughter, perhaps for Cora, for bringing him together with Emily. Another son, for Adrian, because though infuriating, the Indian was a man of honor.

"We will have many children, Emmy."

Tiotonawen snapped him with his cane, bringing Darian's thoughts back to the present. "You will have no children unless you alter your path now."

Yes, he remembered that the old Apache had a way of making dire predictions—predictions that often came true. "My path is dictated by honor, and the pursuit of justice."

Tiotonawen huffed. "Your path is marked by stubbornness, and will lead to your death."

I don't want to die. Not now. Not yet. Darian met the old man's steady gaze. He felt vulnerable, yet locked by what he had to do. "I know no other way."

"There is always another way. Haven't you seen that around you? My son returns from the future, then goes back with a wife. In turn, he sends a wife to you. Was that expected, Captain? Did you plan it? You did not. Yet it came, of its own accord. There is always another way."

"So you would have me abandon my quest, and do what? Head to Mexico? Bring my wife, my men, all to be outlaws forever, away from their own land? Would you have me leave General Davis in a command he does not deserve? A command that may lead to the destruction of your own people?"

Tiotonawen placed his cane in front of him and rested both hands upon it. "You must defeat Davis for that end in itself. But that is not the reason that drives you. It is the past that sends you forward, not the now." He leaned closer, bright eyes glittering. "There is something you hold too dear, and unless you can surrender what you hold too dear, you will fail."

Darian hesitated. What did he hold dear? Emily, most of all. His men. Justice. How could a man hold those things too dear? "My honor is important."

"The honor within, or that which is spoken by other men?"

"Both. I will not be remembered as an outlaw."

Tiotonawen sighed heavily, then turned to walk away. "If that matters most to you, Captain, you will die."

Chapter Ten

Emily lay awake beside Darian, staring at the ceiling of the Apache hut. He slept fitfully beside her, dreaming. More than once, she heard his brother's name. The Apache chief's words haunted her. Though Darian had said no more about the old man's predictions, Emily felt sure they held truth. She didn't fully understand the old man's meaning, but she suspected Darian did.

They had made love, once Darian was sure the Apache were asleep and there was no chance of anyone walking by their hut. He made love to her as if it might be the last time, as if every moment were precious. But Emily wanted more. She wanted a lifetime at his side, in the future or the past, but she wanted her life spent with Darian.

He was a wonderful lover. When passion overtook him, all his reserve disappeared, yet he had already learned to use his natural restraint to intensify her pleasure as well as his own. When she told him afterwards how wonderful he was, he beamed, then began to explain why he, of all men, was best suited to being her husband.

Emily sighed. She would never tire of Darian's peculiar ways. She wanted to see him react to everything. He would learn fast, then proceed to give directions to everyone he met. If he ever had the chance to travel by airplane, he would make his way to the cockpit and begin lecturing the pilots on steadier flight patterns.

Ian hadn't possessed the confidence to advise others. He was easily led, living his life as if afraid it might catch up with him and devour him. Part of his appeal had been his vulnerability, and Emily's confidence that she would be the one to save him.

Maybe Darian's resemblance to Ian Hallowell was coincidence, after all. Beyond looks, they had little in common. It would take more than Darian's own death to shake him that deeply. Emily pondered this as the morning sun lightened the stick walls of their hut. What could devastate Darian beyond his death, even into a new life?

Not his death. . . . Outside their hut, she heard Ping greeting MacLeod, his voice lowered. The sounds of their voices warmed her. Good men, unique and charming. She loved them like family. And if she loved them after so short a time, Darian loved them more.

Her heart constricted. She knew what would destroy him now. Not his own death, but the deaths of his men. The dishonor of his men, which he would consider his fault. Adrian's history book recorded the hanging of a Civil War hero turned desperado, but it would have left out the less interesting executions of his gang. That didn't mean it hadn't happened, and in all probability, Emily guessed that his men must have died with him, or before.

Tears puddled in her eyes. Maybe this was why Ian left her. When she became his wife, it must have triggered the deep anguish of Darian's soul over the deaths of his men. When Ian viewed her as a responsibility, he cracked and left her—all because of a responsibility he had failed a lifetime ago as Darian Woodward.

Dark, horrible images flooded her mind: Darian forced to watch as his men were killed, torn apart by their cries, maybe shattered by a word of blame from one of them. She started to cry. The image in her head tormented her. She was sure it was true.

Not only did she have to save Darian, but the men who followed him, too.

Emily sat up. Tears ran down her cheeks and she sniffed. Darian stirred beside her and she held her breath. She didn't want to wake him. She didn't want him to see her cry, then have to explain why. Under no circumstances could he know what she had foreseen.

Quietly, Emily rose and dressed. Darian's breath deepened and slowed as he sank deeper into sleep. His expression was peaceful now. She looked down at him for awhile, loving him, determined to save him. She had failed with Ian, but then it had been too late. It was Darian who needed her, before the "onion" was stripped down too far and destroyed.

Emily walked around the village trying to gather her thoughts. She spotted Darian's men seated together looking uncomfortable among the Apache, who ignored them. Ping in particular appeared pale and uncertain. He noticed her, then rose hurriedly to his feet. Even fear of Indians couldn't keep Ping from his enthusiastically polite manners.

She smiled and joined them. The others rose, too, and greeted her. Neither Bonner nor Clyde spoke, but they nodded, and she had come to accept that greeting like a hug. She sat on a rock between MacLeod and Ping, quiet while they conversed. She felt safe among them, because they protected Darian and cared for him. Because they loved him, too.

After a while, MacLeod took note of her silence and he laid his broad hand on her shoulder. "Are you fretting about your 'young onion,' girl?"

She smiled, but tears still felt perilously close. "A bit." She wanted MacLeod to reassure her. After all, he knew Darian better than Tiotonawen did. "Do you think he'll be all right?"

MacLeod hesitated, and she knew that the comfort she desired wouldn't be forthcoming. MacLeod scratched his nose, then shifted his weight on the rock. The other men waited, too. Darian's fate mattered to them almost as much as to Emily, and at last, comfort trickled back into her.

MacLeod crossed one leg over the other and rubbed his ankle. "Now, don't you be worrying. The Captain, he's a good shot. He thinks quicker than any man I've ever known in a battle, and I seen about every one that mattered."

"Were you with him at Gettysburg?"

MacLeod nodded. "The boy got made lieutenant of my company just before Antietam."

"You must have admired him very much."

MacLeod snorted, surprising her, then he laughed. "Hell, no! What soldier wants an eighteen-year-old boy leading him, calling the shots when he's got a rain of hellfire pouring down on his head? Especially not a boy with a white shirt and even whiter teeth. . . . Hell, no! We thought we'd be seeing Kingdom Come before our time when that blue-eyed child stepped up."

Emily could see Darian as a young officer, and yes,

he would have a very white shirt.... "You weren't mean to him, were you?"

"Gave him hell, we did."

"Oh, no!"

MacLeod chuckled at the memory. "Only Ping here liked him, and that's because Ping was the only one younger."

"Poor Darian. How could you?"

"Well, it were easy. Started off, he did, by lining us up, holding a regulations code book, which he kept checking.... Thought him a damned fool. Then he reprimanded more than half of us for the condition of our uniforms."

Emily couldn't restrain a smile. "That does sound like Darian."

"Figured we'd kill him first chance we got."

"What? Kill him?"

MacLeod patted her shoulder. "Nah—figured a boy wet behind the ears like that would get himself killed when the guns started firing, if he didn't run off scared first."

"He had been promoted, after all, Sergeant. He must have done something right."

"Sad to say, that weren't always the case. Not a few of them officers got upped in rank because their families had the money to put them there."

"Oh." Emily sighed. "That does seem to be a certain trend in American culture. Okay, in human culture.... But I can't believe that was true of Darian."

"His parents had enough money to swim in."

"Really?" She'd never asked about this facet of his history. Another thing he shared in common with Ian. "Still, I can't believe that's why he was promoted." She paused. "What happened in battle?"

MacLeod didn't answer at once. He gazed up at the

188

morning sky, and she knew he saw another world entirely. "We thought we had it bad, but it got worse. Our company got sent in first, into the worst damned bloodbath a man's ever seen. Saw men mowed down like wheat before a scythe. Never saw anything so bad, not before or since, as what we saw at Antietam Creek."

Emily's skin went cold. She had vague memories of watching the PBS Civil War series, memories of huge numbers of dead men, graying pictures of devastated battlefields. Now she sat among a group of men who had walked among them. Now she was married to their leader. "Darian. . . . What happened?"

"We got sent out first of ten—frontliners. I remember someone saying we got picked because one of the higher-ups must be trying to get rid of Woodward."

Herring cleared his throat. "Think that was me, Sarge."

MacLeod nodded. "Didn't want to finger you, Herring, but so it was."

Emily glared at Herring, who looked uncomfortable. Her voice hardened. "What happened?"

"Ten companies went out. One came back." He paused for effect. "Ours."

Emily sighed with relief, though their survival was obvious in retrospect. "You were lucky, then."

MacLeod shook his head. "We weren't lucky. We caught more fire than any other. We got through that hellfire for one reason, and for one reason only." Emily's eyes filled with tears and dripped to her cheeks. "Your husband."

She dried her cheek and saw tears in the sergeant's eyes, too. "What did he do?"

"Can't say as I recollect fully now. All went by in a blur. Never been so damned scared in all my days, and I can speak for the rest of us there, too." The other men

189

nodded, and Ping appeared deeply moved.

Ping sniffed, then patted Emily's knee. "It was my first battle. I'd written a letter to my mother, figuring I wouldn't make it, but when I saw the bodies lying everywhere, I knew there'd be so many that no one would think to search mine for a letter. Captain Woodward, he took my letter himself, because they always search the officers, no matter what."

Emily choked back a sob, and she shivered despite the heat. "He is wonderful."

"Then he told me I'd misspelled the name of my hometown, and my penmanship needed work, too."

She couldn't help crying. She knew him. He hadn't just been trying to correct Ping's spelling. He had been reassuring a terrified boy that there was life ahead. A life that mattered. *Darian. . . .*

MacLeod uncrossed his legs. "I don't remember that battle too well. Only thing I see when I look back—and girl, I don't look back often—is that blue-eyed boy up ahead of us, straight back, white shirt and all, giving orders just as clear and sure, when so many bullets were flying that I couldn't see him straight. Everything he did made sense. Let me tell you, after that, when he said 'drop,' we'd drop. When he said 'fire,' we'd shoot. Not a man questioned his orders after that day."

"How does he stay so calm?"

MacLeod shrugged. "Who knows? The Captain, he just goes where he's pointed, and he's got the brain to get him there. But there's more to him than a good brain. He's not looking for any old path. He's looking for the right path. He don't think just about himself. He thinks about us, and he puts himself out there to be sure every one of us comes out alive. When he's on a battlefield, he sees it all. If there's a path through hell, he'll find it."

"What if . . . what if there is no path?"

MacLeod didn't answer for a long while, and no one spoke. After a time, he heaved a deep sigh then looked at her. "Then we'll lose him."

"You think that day is coming, don't you?"

He didn't answer. She hadn't expected him to. The burly sergeant who had followed Darian through hell just looked at his feet and sighed again. Emily took his hand and squeezed it tight.

"I will not let him die, Sergeant. I can't have come back through time just to watch him die. There has to be a purpose."

"I'm hoping that's true." The sergeant didn't sound convinced. "But I've seen a lot in this world, so that even having you drop out of the sky don't seem all that surprising. And when the dust clears, and you're looking at an endless field of blue, bloated bodies, you come out thinking maybe there is no purpose, after all."

She couldn't argue, but something deep inside her re-belled against this philosophy. There has to be a meaning, a point to it all. There has to be a god looking down, a Great Spirit, something so that it all made sense. And if she acted in accord with her heart, her most true heart's desire, with love as her guide, then she would be in line with that spirit.

Darian did that. Now that she'd heard MacLeod's story, she knew he'd done it all along. She remembered Tiotonawen's word, in contrast. The old man implied that Darian wasn't motivated solely by love or a higher purpose now. Yet he also said Darian must face Davis. So that could only mean he had to win against his corrupt former commander. . . .

It didn't make sense, but Emily felt sure there was a meaning behind it all, a path they could follow to reach a higher ground, freedom, and safety. If only she could find it. And she had to find it, because somehow Darian was off the trail, confused. It was up to her, but she also knew it wasn't her choice to make. Ultimately, it would be Darian's.

Something was blocking him. But what? The men sat silently around her; thinking of the man who had led them through the endless, nightmarish days of war. She couldn't make his choice for him, but she could help him get past whatever inner obstacle stood in his way.

"Did you know his brother, too?"

"Young Oliver, aye. I did. Good young fellow. Not quite so straight and neat as our captain, but damned close. Got handed another company same time as his brother, but he weren't sent in that first day like we were. I saw him—broke command to come out and talk to the Captain, he did, so I liked him. Weren't emotional, not on the outside, but you could see they were close. When we got back, beat up, half-dead, young Oliver were waiting. Didn't say much, those two. Just looked at each other. Oliver put his hand on the captain's head. Just stood there. . . ."

"He meant so much to Darian." Emily could barely talk. Her throat felt swollen for the tears welling inside. "But when Darian speaks of him, it's as if from a distance. I've never seen him cry."

Maybe Victorian men didn't cry. Maybe his men wouldn't understand her concern, but MacLeod drew a long breath. "He cried the day his brother died. Held him in his arms and sobbed like a child. We stood around him. Not a one of us knew what to say. We'd stayed with him, when he fought with the surgeons to get them to take care of his brother, when Oliver's leg turned green and we all knew what was coming. I'd seen the captain perform some heroic acts, and I thought I'd never seen a man so brave. But that day, when he took that saw and cut off his brother's leg—that day, I knew I was seeing a man that was one in ten million."

Emily bowed her head into her hands and cried. "What am I going to do? He can't end up hanged. He can't. He deserves to be happy, to find peace. He doesn't have it now, but he can, someday."

MacLeod cleared his throat and looked thoughtful. "Well, now. As I'm seeing it, there's not much you can do. Captain's got to follow his own path, so to speak. But you've done more than any of us ever thought possible."

She peeked up at him. "Have I? What?"

"You've gotten past his high collar and polished buttons."

Emily's face burned. "We are married, you know."

MacLeod paled with embarrassment. "I was meaning it in a figurative sense, you understand. Not to be mentioning . . . well . . . those times that are the rights of married persons. . . ."

Emily held up her hand. "I understand, sergeant. Figuratively. Yes."

"What I'm meaning to say is that you've made the young man happy, no matter what comes his way in the future. You've got him thinking of something else besides what's right, and maybe what he thinks he done wrong in the past. You've given him a reason to keep living."

"I hope it's enough. Did his brother say anything before he died, any final request that would make Darian feel guilty?"

MacLeod shook his head. "Nope, weren't nothing like that. Oliver just thanked the captain for trying, and then he died. Weren't nothing he said, that's for sure."

"Then, what?"

MacLeod didn't answer. His brow furrowed as if he

truly had no idea. Emily's brow assumed the same posture, but Ping peered up at the sun, squinting. "Think I know, ma'am."

MacLeod and Emily looked at Ping, both doubtful as to the value of Ping's input. But it was worth a try. "What do you think is motivating Darian, Mr. Ping?"

"It ain't too complicated, ma'am." It was like Ping to drag out his explanation, now that he had everyone's full attention. "Figuring it happens all the time, 'specially with brothers."

"What?" Emily's voice had taken on a growlish quality, which she tried to soften with a stiff smile. "Go on." No wonder Darian got so exasperated with Ping!

"One lives, one dies. I'm thinking Captain Woodward would have done most anything to trade places with his brother. Sometimes, it hurts more to see someone close in pain than it does to feel it yourself. The captain's thinking it ain't fair that he's the one who lived. He's thinking he don't deserve it, underneath. No matter how hard he tries, he can't quite prove otherwise to himself. Now you've come along, and you're so pretty and nice—and right from the beginning, you were falling over your feet in love with him. . . ."

Emily braced. "I was not! I was slightly attracted, true, but it was gradual." Ping's skeptical gaze was matched by the other men, so she surrendered her argument. "Continue, Ping. What's the danger in me loving him?"

"You'd think nothing. But now he's got a wife, he's got more than he dreamed he'd have after the war, 'specially out west here. He left New York because of the accolades he got, everyone treating him like a hero. He couldn't handle it, when inside he was thinking he didn't deserve it."

Emily's heart chilled. Ping was right. "When inside,

he thinks it was he who should have died, not his brother."

Ping nodded, and they all fell silent. Emily understood now what motivated her determined husband. She understood why he felt no fear. Yet something had changed him, something surprised him. He had fallen in love. Despite all his doubts, his heart came forward and claimed the woman he wanted.

For that reason, there was hope. But Darian was standing on the edge of a precipice, still. And what he chose was up to him. Emily couldn't help him until she understood the nature of his choice, so she would have to keep a close watch on him. She would consult with the Apache chief, and maybe he could offer advice. Despite his gruffness, he obviously cared for Darian.

There was still time. But Darian's past was thick with concealed emotion. Like his love, his passion was deep and well-hidden, but strong. If it could be used for him, he would win. If it worked against him, Emily feared there was nothing she could do now to change his fate.

Darian woke to find himself alone in an Apache hut. For a moment, he wondered if his life since his capture was real. Maybe Emily, his mutiny, all of it, had been a dream. He rolled to his side, then noticed a pleasant, sated feeling in his groin. Emily, at least, was no dream.

He lay for a moment wondering where she was, and if she would soon return so that they might repeat their night's revels. One day, they would have a house of their own, with privacy to engage in all manners of lovemaking. He wasn't sure what variations there might be, but of late, his imagination ran wild.

They would have to have a home, preferably here in the West. And naturally, he would have to have facilities nearby for his men. Perhaps they, too, might have residences on his property. Together, they would reform Tucson, turn it into a town to rival those in the East.

Darian sat up and pushed his hair from his eyes. He remembered Emily running her fingers through it, telling him it was soft and beautiful, and then whispering that she loved him while he moved slowly in and out of her body. Darian hardened at the memory. Where was the woman?

He waited awhile longer, but when he heard the Apache outside, he knew he'd have to wait for the next night to return to erotic bliss with his wife. Darian rose and dressed, feeling irritable at missing a prime chance as a husband. He peered out of the tent and saw Emily sitting with his men. None of them were talking. In fact, they all appeared pensive and even sad. Even from a distance, he could see that Emily had been crying.

Disquiet replaced desire. Had something happened to cause her pain? And what troubled his men? Himself, he knew. Probably the old chief's dire prediction from yesterday. It wasn't the hint of a dark fate that bothered Darian, but the suggestion that he was acting from something other than pure justice. Well, Tiotonawen didn't know him. And Darian had no idea what the man meant. First he said Darian was wrong, then insisted he must face Davis, and win. . . . There was no pleasing some people.

Darian emerged from the hut, yawned and stretched. Emily noticed and hurried to him. She appeared concerned, hesitant, yet hopeful. "Did you rest well, Darian? I mean, are you all right?"

Darian's brow furrowed. "What have they been telling you?"

She looked guilty. "Nothing. We were just talking."

"About me?"

"About all sorts of things." Yes, she averted her eyes and looked around at nothing.

"About me."

She puffed an impatient breath. "Well, why shouldn't we talk about you? I don't know you that well. You sped me into marriage before I even knew your birthday."

"October twenty-sixth."

"So you're a Scorpio. . . ."

"A what?"

She shook her head. "Never mind. Something tells me you're a nonbeliever."

Just as she spoke, he heard a whoop, and Haastin galloped into the village. The Apache gathered around, but Haastin raced into Tiotonawen's hut. Darian nodded to his men, and they rose to gather their gear. "Trouble, it seems."

Emily groaned. "Not again?"

Darian checked his revolver, and his men prepared their horses. "I suggest you gather your gear, Emmy. Be ready to move."

"What's going on?"

"I have no idea, but we'll find out soon enough."

Haastin came from the chief's tent with Tiotonawen beside him. Both appeared worried. The old man motioned to Darian. "Captain, trouble follows you."

"In what way?"

Haastin fingered his rifle, ready for battle. "The white soldiers ride from the town, they ride toward these hills. They look for you."

"Many?"

"Enough. I do not think we can fight them and win."

Darian pondered their situation, not liking it. "You are outnumbered, even with the addition of my men. But

197

they cannot wage a frontal assault against this position. We can hold them off for a time."

Tiotonawen huffed. "That is why I chose this position, onion. Here, we can defend ourselves."

"They will not give up. It's only a matter of time." Darian paused, frustrated. "If only we had a more secure hiding place, to bide our time and attack when Davis is apart from the rest!"

Haastin spoke to Tiotonawen in their language, then shook his head. "We have not lived in this area long enough to know of such a place. We came here to escape the soldiers at Fort McDowell, only to find more danger here."

Tiotonawen looked north and sighed. "We will return to our natural home soon. Let trouble not follow us. We will meet it on our own ground."

Darian glanced at the surrounding hills. "Be that as it may, we will have to drive them off before they discover your village. I suggest we ride now and do what we can to stop them."

Haastin readied his rifle, but Tiotonawen touched Darian's shoulder. "Ever quick to battle, are you, Captain? You are right, for today, but tomorrow, you might better choose the other path."

Darian grit his teeth, but for now, he knew his course. He turned to Haastin. "My men and I will ride with you. We must make them fear the Tonto Apache in these hills. That will give you time to move your people again, preferably back where you came from."

Tiotonawen liked the suggestion. "We will leave them the memory of fear, and we will return to our home. Yes."

Darian fingered his revolver. "You are outnumbered, so we cannot meet them on the field. In such circumstances, ambush often works best, but if we fail, we all will die."

A sharp squeal cut him off—one he recognized from the last time he made such an announcement. Emily came up beside him, her face white. "You are not going into battle! Darian! You have to get out of here."

He motioned to the Apache. "What? And leave them to face an enemy I brought upon them?"

"They can run, too!"

He paused as if considering the best argument. "If you are correct about my fate as written in your historical text, I do not meet my ending in battle."

She gritted her teeth and looked fierce. "That is one possible ending, Darian. If I thought there were no other way, I wouldn't be here, would I?"

"No. I suppose not."

"Right. And if there's a chance of you surviving your hanging, there's also a chance of you getting shot before you ever get that far!"

Her argument was hard to argue against. A change of subject seemed in order.

Darian took Emily's hand. "We can drive them back, Emmy. Don't worry. I know what I'm doing."

"Then I'm coming with you."

She really meant it. And she'd disobeyed him before. He couldn't ride into battle fearing she might come after him. Darian called to Laurencita, the young mother who had befriended Cora Talmadge. She came to him, calm despite the impending attack.

"Captain, it is good to see you again. We have heard much of you. Much of it strange."

He didn't want to know what she'd heard. "I need your help."

"I will do what I can."

"My wife has a propensity for following me into dangerous situations. I need to be certain she stays in this village while I'm gone. I must leave her with you, tied up if necessary, to keep her from following me."

Laurencita looked uncomfortable as Emily fumed beside him. No, this gentle young woman didn't stand a chance against his sputtering wife. "Perhaps you could suggest someone less kind-hearted than yourself for the task."

Laurencita looked around, then fixed her gaze on the old woman Darian remembered from his captivity before. The old woman who swatted people. Darian liked the idea. "She will do admirably." He hesitated. Emily might never forgive him. Well, it was in her own best interest. "Would you relay to her my request, please?"

Laurencita sighed, cast an apologetic look at Emily, then spoke to the woman. As she spoke, the woman's dark eyes glittered, and her face changed into an expression revealing the glee of power. Perfect.

"Toklanni will take your wife into her care. She says she will teach her that a husband's word is to be obeyed." Laurencita appeared very guilty at this, then lowered her voice. "Her own husband, before he died, might have said she did not learn that lesson well herself. . . ."

Emily backed away. "You cannot leave me with that woman! I won't stay. I will follow you wherever you go. Darian!"

He sighed. "If you follow me, you'll get lost, and how will I find you?"

"I will not 'get lost.' You forget, I've lived in Tucson all my life. I know my way around."

"You know another Tucson . . . not this one." It was no use arguing. From the moment he met her, Emily's confidence had far outweighed her abilities.

Darian caught her by the hand, then led her to Toklanni. He smiled graciously, then bowed, which Toklanni seemed to appreciate. He sensed that she favored men heavily over women, especially strong young men, and that he would have no trouble with Emily's defiance now.

He turned to Emily. "I do this for your own good, and because I love you." Before she could speak, he bound her hands with the rope in his pack, then passed her to the old Apache woman. Emily appeared too shocked and furious to speak. Toklanni took the rope and spoke to Laurencita.

"Toklanni says that you may ride in peace, as a warrior should, and know that your woman is safe until your return."

Emily opened her mouth to speak, but no words came. She just stared, aghast. Darian went to her and kissed her cheek. "I know your fear. Emmy, I will do my best to return. If I fail, Tiotonawen will return you to your time."

At last, sounds came from her lips. Sputtering, furious growls. "Oh, that's very comforting! Lucky me! How dare you? Darian Woodward, I am your wife, not your slave. You may not leave me here, under no circumstances. How am I supposed to protect you?"

Darian took his horse from a young warrior, mounted, then looked down at her. He loved the fury in her eyes, the indignation, the determination to follow him and protect him. He loved her. "You can't protect me. You are a gentle, delicate woman." He smiled at her abject horror. "It is your duty to obey."

"I don't think so! What if something happens to you?"

"Then at least I will have escaped my hanging."

"Wonderful! That makes me feel so much better. Darian. . . ."

"Emmy, I love you."

Tears welled in her eyes. "I love you, too."

Darian turned his horse and rode away.

Chapter Eleven

If the old woman struck her hand one more time, Emily would fling her whole body at her, knock her to the ground, and be done with her forever. What hell! "I cannot believe you won't listen to me. This is so primitive. We are both women. . . ." Toklanni didn't speak English. This was getting nowhere. Emily eyed Laurencita. She seemed pleasant, though she had deferred to Darian about binding Emily.

Emily smiled at her, though the expression felt forced. "You speak English. Could you translate a few things to this woman for me?"

Laurencita looked uncomfortable. "It will do no good."

"This is ridiculous. Darian doesn't own me."

"You are his wife."

"Yeah? Well, he's my husband. And if I owned him, he'd be the one tied up, not me! Look, do you really feel as if a husband owns his wife? Does Toklanni feel women are inferior?"

Laurencita fiddled with her long hair, then glanced at Toklanni. "No. . . . I can speak to Toklanni for you, but unless you have a reason better than the one the captain gave, she will not hear you."

"I have a much better reason!" She stopped. What reason would convince the Apache woman to release her? "I have to protect him. He needs me."

Laurencita appeared skeptical, but relayed the message to Emily's captor, who responded with a brief grunt. "She says that is no reason, and that you are not capable of protecting a warrior."

"She said that with one grunt?"

"That is what she meant."

"Oh." Emily considered her predicament, and nothing came to mind.

Toklanni grunted again and Emily eyed her suspiciously. Laurencita listened, then turned back to Emily. "She says that you speak from your heart—emotion rules you. You do not think. You cannot help your husband."

"I can, too!" She was responding emotionally. Toklanni was right. Tears puddled in Emily's eyes, and she sank to her knees, her hands bound before her. A sharp tug yanked her back to her feet. Toklanni glared down at her and issued a long series of unintelligible words.

"Toklanni says that you are small and weak and cry when you should be thinking. She does not know why the captain picked so weak a wife."

"How mean!" Emily tried to stop crying, but suddenly, she didn't know why Darian picked her, either. Laurencita appeared sympathetic and she briefly touched Emily's arm.

"Toklanni speaks harshly to all young women. I am

sure you are very brave, and a good wife to the captain."

Emily shrugged, miserable. "I don't think so. I don't know why he picked me. I just dropped here out of the future, because Adrian said I had to, and instead of saving Darian as I promised, I fell in love with him, and he's done every crazy thing I've told him not to. . . . If Adrian had picked someone better, things might be different."

"The son of the whirlwind picked you for a reason, I'm sure."

"I can't think why. I was just the only one crazy enough to do it."

Laurencita paused. "That is a reason."

Emily used the back of her bound hands to dry her cheeks, but more tears came. "I really don't know why he loves me. I've spent so much time loving him and pretending I didn't that I hadn't thought about it, but now I don't know. It's obvious why I love him. He's heroic and wonderful, and he's funny when he doesn't mean to be, and he cares about people."

Laurencita studied Emily's face, probably wondering why Darian loved her, too. Emily would have sunk to the ground in misery, but Toklanni wouldn't let her. "You have a a a pretty face, and pretty hair," Laurencita said. "Your body has not yet turned to fat."

Emily glared at her. "Those aren't very good reasons. I meant something . . . not superficial. And I don't intend to 'turn to fat.' "

"If you are married, you will soon be fat with child."

Emily's mouth dropped. She hadn't considered pregnancy. Not once. But Darian certainly hadn't used protection, and she'd had no reason to be on the pill for years. "You're right! I could be pregnant." She hoped she was, desperately. To hold a baby, Darian's baby, seemed a dream beyond belief. It would be a persnickety child, very precise, with bright blue eyes, and Darian would be the best father in the world.

If he lived.

Emily struggled against her ties. "I have to get out of here! I have to make sure my baby has a father." She glared at Toklanni. "Let me go, or you'll be very sorry." She gestured at Laurencita. "Tell her!"

Laurencita obeyed, but Toklanni snorted. Laurencita sighed. "She says that she is sorry now, because she has more important tasks besides watching over you."

Emily deflated. "I hate her."

"She sometimes affects young women that way."

"I don't doubt it." She fixed a threatening stare upon Toklanni, who paid no attention. "I would like to smack her, just once. . . ."

For a reason Emily didn't understand, her threat seemed to illuminate something for Laurencita. "I believe that the captain loves you because you are brave. Because you have no idea what you're getting yourself into, but you go anyway. Otherwise, you would not have come back in time, and you would not want to head out after him now. And you would certainly not threaten Toklanni."

"In other words, he loves me because I'm crazy."

Laurencita hesitated. "Yes."

"Wonderful."

"Maybe 'crazy' appeals to the captain more than you realize, Emily. He seems very . . . rigid. But you come from a world he doesn't know, and he doesn't know what to expect from you. Underneath, you are more the same than you know."

"In what way?"

"You both care for others. You are not selfish. You put others first. Today, he rides with my people, to protect them. All he has done has been for others. You came back in time for him."

"I suppose that's true." Emily peered at Toklanni. "I don't get the feeling she admires my better qualities, though."

"Toklanni admires strength, and a sharp mind."

"I'm not stupid."

"She says you are emotional first, and if you have a sharp mind, it is hidden inside your heart. She says that inside you are answers, but you cannot see them, because you don't think."

"How does she know? She doesn't know me at all." Emily burned with resentment, mostly because she couldn't think of anything to counter the claim.

"I'm not sure how she knows. It may be because she saw you try to follow your husband into battle, to help him, when you had no idea how to help him."

Another good point. Emily frowned. "I would think of something." She paused. "Maybe if I knew the situation better."

"We do not know about battles much. Tiotonawen knows."

"Where is he?"

"He is in prayer, in his hut. When he comes out, you can ask him."

"I will do that." Emily tried to force patience, but it wasn't easy. Somewhere, Darian was riding into battle, and she couldn't help him unless she could "think." Despite her anger, she knew this was the only way she could make a difference now.

Darian had fought against Indians, but never beside them. It was a new experience, and one he quickly appreciated. They hid themselves silently along the canyons, positioned to best advantage for the ambush Darian had planned. Haastin proved a fine lieutenant, and Darian wished he'd had a soldier as level-headed during the war.

The horses were hidden nearby, of no use for the strategy they'd planned. The only weakness he foresaw was the aftermath. If they defeated Davis's soldiers, they would need a place to retreat to—a place more secure than Tiotonawen's village. But the Apache didn't know this landscape the way they knew the northern hills, and no one had a good suggestion as to where they could go.

Still, he could foresee a temporary victory, if all went well. If he acted swiftly, if not a shot went astray. . . . Darian checked his revolver, then went over his men's positions. They knew what to do, but they always looked to him for confirmation. He had never let them down before. He couldn't fail them now.

Time moved slowly but steadily forward as Darian waited for Davis's men to come into view. No sound came but the wind through the hills, dry and haunting. Then, so faint as to be mistaken for imagination, he heard the distant thunder of horses galloping. Horses across the desert.

He saw the dust first, a cloud around them, then the blue uniforms of the cavalry he once served. Served still, in his heart, upholding justice, but the world wouldn't understand that. History wouldn't understand either, if Emily's history book was accurate.

The dust cloud grew larger as the soldiers approached. One by one, the horses came into view, then slowed as they reached the narrower access into the hills. They possessed none of the Apache stealth, but what they lacked in skill, they made up for in weaponry and in numbers.

Suddenly, Darian liked his position among the Indian warriors. Outnumbered, outgunned, yet defending their own ground. It seemed more honorable than invading. Still, those were his peers riding toward him. Union soldiers, many of them. He hesitated. Then, at the rear, surrounded by guards, he saw Clement Davis.

Darian's blood chilled when he spotted the gunfighter Tradman among them. Not Union soldiers—these were Davis's mercenaries, men off duty no doubt engaged by the corrupt general to do his work before the army could be officially involved. Darian's sympathy turned to ice. These men weren't content to let justice unfold along its proper course. Their loyalties could be purchased by the likes of Davis.

Any doubt he harbored vanished, and Darian aimed his revolver. Here, at last, he would meet his true adversary. First, he would defeat the mercenaries, then challenge Davis, here in the desert. His heart palpitated with anticipation of a long-imagined confrontation. Inside him surged a brief pang of regret that Emily wouldn't witness his victory.

Davis's group closed in, their horses clattering on the desert rock as they moved up along the valley where Darian's force lay in wait.

Ping motioned to Wetherspoon, who nodded to Darian. The first rider was in line with Ping's position. Darian waited until the rider reached the first Apache position, then aimed. He didn't aim to kill—but his first shot disabled the rider, who fell to the ground. Horses snorted and screamed, the soldiers shouted, and shots rang blindly against Darian's invisible position.

Rather than riding forward as a true leader would, Davis remained behind, out of the gunfire, still protected by his personal guard. *Coward.* One by one, then together, the Apache fired. Most used muskets, some bows, but every shot found its mark. The positioning Darian had chosen had the effect of making their targets feel overwhelmed, as if the ambushers were far greater in numbers than they actually were.

Like the rise to a crescendo of an Italian opera, the battle reached its culmination. The soldiers tried desperately to return fire, but their shots shattered boulders and split rocks, hitting no one. The whole event was easier than he had imagined. Darian relaxed, slightly, harboring his energy for the more important confrontation to come.

The soldiers retreated toward Davis, and Darian motioned for his force to edge after them. He expected Davis to flee, to gather a more impressive force, but instead, the general rode forward, yet still protected by his men, still beyond the range of fire.

"Woodward! We know your bloody hide is up there in the rocks! Surrender, and we might spare your bloodthirsty red friends."

Darian smiled. "Surrender, General, is an option you might better consider yourself. Your men, it seems, weren't paid enough to complete your attack." Even from a distance, he saw Clement Davis's mustache twitch, or maybe he just imagined the furious expression. He liked the image, anyway. "This fight is between you and me, Davis. For once, meet me yourself rather than sending others in your place."

"Your life ain't worth squat, Woodward!" It was Tradman the gunfighter who spoke, articulating with his usual flair. Darian rolled his eyes.

"You, Tradman, I am done with. Unless your shooting arm is much improved from the last time we met."

Tradman snarled, but since Darian had utterly ruined his shooting arm, the conversation ended.

Davis spoke quietly to his grim ally, then again faced Darian in the hills. "As it happens, I have not come for you today, but to make an offer to those deluded soldiers you bribed into mutiny. Surely by now they know what a mistake was made, and that their lives are worthless as long as they stay with you."

Darian sighed. A weak tactic, if ever there was one. He glanced at MacLeod, who rolled his eyes. Even Ping shook his head. Wetherspoon, however, fidgeted in anger. Darian gestured to MacLeod, who spoke quietly to Wetherspoon. The young man's dark glower did not leave, but he took no action.

"General, I fear you follow the wrong path, and not for the first time. My men are with me of their own accord, preferring the honor we uphold to serving a corrupt and foolish man like yourself."

Tradman spat, but Davis laughed. "Honor, is it? Was it 'honor' that won the war, boy? I was there, when you were back East playing hero. I saw how it was—it was blood that won for the North. More men, more power."

"If what you believe is true, then we won for nothing. But it is true for you only, General."

"Let's see, shall we, whether your men prefer 'honor' or power?" Davis rose in his stirrups, a showy gesture, then waved toward the hills. "Listen to me, MacLeod, Wetherspoon, the rest of you. . . . We know you're out there, riding with Woodward. He's brought you all damned low, riding alongside red men. You men are as wanted as he, considered nothing but outlaws yourself. That can be changed, should you come to your senses and again return to the government you once served. This is my offer: Bring me Woodward, and your crimes will be pardoned. Not only that, but you will be handsomely rewarded."

Darian sighed. Bribery, and not a very plausible promise, seemed all Davis had up his sleeve this day. "Do you have nothing more, General? Cannot you not promise Ping, at least, the rule of a small country? He might favor Switzerland."

His men laughed, and even the Apache who understood English chuckled. But Davis refused to relent. "I have here the promise, in writing, of the commander of Fort Lowell. Send down a man, Woodward, and look at it yourself. Then mock my offer!"

Wetherspoon gestured down at the general. "Let me, Captain. We'll find out what he's up to. He ain't gonna shoot—let me go."

Darian looked at Wetherspoon carefully. His fist was clenched, but he appeared calm. Yet in the man's eyes, he saw the same dark anger he'd detected before. But anger at Davis, or Darian himself?

He didn't want to endanger his men, but Wetherspoon rose as if accepting a command Darian hadn't given. If, somewhere in the man's heart, he feared a life as an outlaw, he deserved at least this chance.

Darian nodded. "Go."

Wetherspoon scrambled down out of the hills, then made his way to the general. Davis laughed, then had Tradman deliver the paper to Wetherspoon. Wetherspoon ignored the paper, then turned to Davis.

With a sick flash, Darian knew what his soldier intended. He rose as if slowed by time, shouting as Wetherspoon aimed his gun. "No!" At close range, gun in his left hand, Tradman fired and Darian's soldier fell lifeless to the ground.

All time held. Darian's pulse moved like ice. He should have known what Wetherspoon intended, and stopped him. Darian's senses blurred. Nothing mattered now but vengeance.

Dimly, he heard Davis shouting at him, accusing him of sending a soldier on a suicide mission. He heard the general threatening his other soldiers with the same fate if they refused his offer.

Wild rage burned in Darian's heart. He heard nothing

more, but the fire in his soul moved him to battle. He moved like a panther down the rocks, hidden from sight, yet ever closer. Behind him, the Apache followed, and his men joined in.

Darian aimed with icy precision, and the guard beside Davis fell dead. Davis whirled his horse backwards, evading the fire, and Tradman galloped away. Guns blazed as one. Soldiers fell, and men shouted. No other of Darian's force besides Wetherspoon was hit.

Davis sounded a retreat, his horse reared. He turned in his saddle, fueled by hatred that Darian felt like a whip even in the hills. "I'll be back, Woodward! Next time, I'll bring the whole damned army down upon you, and those red bastards you've got with you. Hide in these rocks, if you dare, but you'll never get out. Mark my words, it'll be your own men who bring you down. And then I'll have you hanging by a noose until the crows pick your bones clean!"

Davis galloped away, racing ahead of his men in retreat. Darian stood amidst the rocks as the dust cloud faded across the desert, but Ping stumbled down to where Wetherspoon lay. Darian watched as if from a great distance as Ping cradled his friend's head in his lap, crying, and he remembered when he had done the same.

With his soldiers, Darian came down out of the hills and they gathered silently around Wetherspoon's body while Ping cried. Darian knew he should say something, but no words came. He had seen men die, many times, men he knew well and cared for. He had seen his own brother die.

Oliver had gone into the field at Gettysburg because of Darian. Today, Wetherspoon had done the same. Frozen with emotion, Darian stood like a statue staring down at the man's lifeless body. *What were you thinking? I am not worth this kind of sacrifice.*

He felt stunned, because Wetherspoon's act surprised him, and he should have expected it. Wetherspoon had followed him when Darian mutinied. He never asked questions, he just trusted that Darian was following the right path. He never philosophized about justice or honor, he just followed because Darian had been his commander during the war—because he trusted, even when Darian made the whole group outlaws.

The dry wind offered a low, haunting whistle through the hills, broken only by Ping's quiet sobs. Darian felt MacLeod watching him, but he couldn't meet the sergeant's eyes. He felt accusation, blame, though it was probably in his imagination. Or maybe it was in his own heart. Certainly, there.

Wetherspoon lay dead, and Darian would go back into the hills with his beautiful wife who loved him. She would forgive him for this failure, she would comfort him. But Wetherspoon lay dead, because Darian hadn't been quick enough to stop an emotional man's rash action.

Emotional actions . . . such as Emily herself employed daily. Would he be quick enough to save her? The thought burned inside him, and he banished it, but the fear hung over him like a low torment.

MacLeod knelt beside Ping, then laid his broad hand on Wetherspoon's forehead. "He's free now, Ping. There ain't nothing you, nor anyone, could have done to change this. Wetherspoon, he made his choice. It weren't a good one, but he was free to make it. Let us remember him for his bravery and his loyalty, and that he died trying to set things right."

Darian sensed that MacLeod's words were meant for him as well as Ping, but the words sounded hollow because Darian knew better. As their leader, sanctioned by the army or not, he was responsible for his soldiers' actions. If he had forbade it, Wetherspoon would not have gone and attempted assassination.

MacLeod patted Ping's shoulder. "Come on, now, lad. It's over. We've got to lay him to his rest and move on."

Ping nodded, but he didn't look at Darian when he rose. Darian still found no words, but he bent and lifted Wetherspoon from the ground. Without a word, he carried the body back up into the hills to the horses, then strapped it on Wetherspoon's horse. With the horse's reins in his hand, he mounted his gray, then headed back to the Apache village.

"You have to leave these mountains, Tiotonawen, now. There's nothing you can do when Davis comes back."

Emily stood watching as Darian tried to convince the Apache chief to escape now, while he had the chance. Tiotonawen looked stubborn, but he didn't argue. They had buried Wetherspoon beneath the shadow of the hills, and now the sun had faded into night. Emily had cried, his men had cried, but Darian had just stood there, staring while they lowered his soldier's body into the ground.

She knew he blamed himself. But they hadn't been alone long enough to talk. He needed her, and instead, stood there alone, his face grim and set.

Tiotonawen sighed heavily, then tapped his cane by Darian's feet. "This is not the ground of my ancestors, and I will do as you say. I cannot help you now, Captain. But a time may come, if you choose the path ahead wisely, when I can help you once more. If that time comes, and I do not say it will, then come to me where we met before."

Darian looked at Emily. She saw his heart in his eyes,

all his pain and doubt and guilt, and she saw his love.
"Emmy, you must go with them."

"What?" She hadn't expected this. "Darian, I will
not."

He took her hands and squeezed tight. "It is the only
way. If I succeed, I will come to you there. If not, Tiotonawen will send you back to your rightful time."

Desperation closed in around her and she started to
cry. Nearby, Toklanni grunted and shook her head. "You
can't send me away! Please." More tears came, and Toklanni appeared even more disgusted.

Think. I must think.

"Emmy, it's best. You know that."

"I know no such thing! You need me, Darian Woodward."

He smiled. "In what way?"

"To protect you!" Her mind raced. What did she have
that he lacked, that all his men, and the Indians, too,
lacked? She had lived in Tucson all her life. She'd taken
school field trips into the hills, knew its history, its land-
marks. . . .

And then, she knew. "I am the only person who
knows the perfect hiding place for your gang."

Darian looked confused, and suspicious. "What are
you talking about? And why didn't you mention it
sooner?"

She glanced at Toklanni, and saw the first glimmer of
respect as Laurencita translated the conversation. "Because, Captain Woodward, I wasn't thinking. I was feeling."

He shifted his weight. "What hiding place?"

Emily felt triumphant. "The Colossal Caves! They're
not far from here. Bandits used to hide out there—it's
perfect for you. Huge caverns. . . . Of course, when I was
there, it was lit, had handrails, and a coffee shop, but I

should remember my way around pretty well. I used to think it was a fascinating place. I have several books on the caves in my shop."

Darian's eyes narrowed. "It sounds like what we need, true. Tell me how to get there."

She put her hands on her hips and her mouth curled to one side. "Not a chance. I take you there myself, or you're not going."

Beside her, Laurencita beamed with pride. "Toklanni says you think well. Your husband has now the wife he deserves."

Darian looked between the women. "What's going on? Did you plan this?"

Emily rolled her eyes. "Right! Like I plan *anything.* No, it just came to me. I was thinking about what I have to offer you, and what I have is knowledge of the secret caves. Are you accepting my offer to guide you, or not?" She paused, fearing he would still refuse. "Of course, if you refuse, I will break free from these guys somehow and come after you. You know that."

He gazed into her eyes for a long while, then smiled. "Yes. I suppose I do." Darian sighed, but he was still smiling. "Very well. You may escort us to the caves. Maybe this would be a better place for the Apache to hide, too."

Tiotonawen grimaced at the suggestion. "Men do not enter holes like rats. We will not go into caves."

Emily looked around at his people. "That's probably wise. There are many caverns, and it's not safe for children without handrails."

Obviously, the chief had no idea what "handrails" were, but he seemed content to accept her excuse. He touched Emily with his cane and looked into her eyes. She hadn't realized how closely he resembled Adrian, but he had that same ageless wisdom as she'd seen in his son—when he shoved her out of an airplane. "We will meet again, young woman. Your onion has added another layer today. Those layers stand before life."

She didn't fully understand Tiotonawen's words, but she nodded. Yes, Wetherspoon's death would weigh on Darian, and now nothing would stop him from pursuing Davis. "I know."

Tiotonawen fixed his attention on Darian, who looked impatient as if expecting another mystic lecture. "I have nothing to say to you, young onion, that you don't know already." Darian interrupted with a sigh of relief, and Emily smiled. "Except this: Sometimes to win, a man must fall before his enemy, and only then is his victory complete."

Darian's frown tightened, but the old man appeared pleased with himself. "Mark my words, onion. You will need them one day. One day soon."

"I'll keep that in mind."

Tiotonawen's smile grew. "You will try not to, but you will." He tapped Darian with his cane, then headed off to direct his people in tearing down their huts.

The Apache busied themselves gathering their belongings for the move north. They would take the slower passage through the mountains rather than the swift way through the desert. What Emily considered an hour's drive was a journey of days. Somehow, she would have to pry Darian from his quest, and follow them.

Darian watched Tiotonawen giving orders, a dark glower on his face. "I do not like his references to onions."

"Not onions, Darian. Onion. Just one. You."

His glower intensified. "That old man doesn't understand the nature of my quest."

"I wonder. . . . Maybe he understands it better than you do." Emily placed her hand on Darian's back. He was strong and lean, his muscles hard. Yet beneath, she felt his vulnerability as if it had grown since he rode out with the Apache. "We need to talk."

He turned to her, smiling but distant. "As you so wisely pointed out, we need to ride. To these caves of yours, my dear."

As she feared, he didn't want to talk. He was trying to shut her out, deny his need for comfort and for love. He needed time. She knew that, but how much? She hadn't been very successful in her first marriage. She'd had no idea of Ian's inner demons. She had just flung herself in and tried her hardest to please him. And she'd failed. She couldn't fail now.

Emily found her brown and white mare and saddled it before any of Darian's men could help her. Wetherspoon had generally saddled the horses, liking the task, and tears filled her eyes when she saw his well-cared-for horse standing alone. She went to the horse and patted it, because if Henry Wetherspoon hovered anywhere, it would be with the horses.

Darian came to her and stroked the horse's shoulder. "I offered this horse to Ping, but he said the Apache would take better care of it. Less chance of getting hit in battle."

Emily took Darian's hand. "Ping will be all right, Darian. He is a very sensible man. He just needs to go through his emotions first. Actually, he's quite healthy in that regard."

Darian didn't comment on her psychological insight, but he eyed her doubtfully. " 'Sensible' is not a word I would apply to Ping."

"He's young, and rather high-strung. But I bet he'll make a good name for himself someday."

Darian's expression darkened. "If he lives that long."

"Every man, every person, chooses their own actions,

no matter what the rest of us do. Wetherspoon kept a lot inside, Darian. Ping doesn't, not one bit. If he heads out to shoot someone, you'll know about it beforehand."

Why did Darian insist on blaming himself? But there was no use arguing now. Maybe the little things she said would eke their way into his consciousness and take hold. Maybe not. She started to speak again, to try again to convince him, then stopped herself. She wasn't taking her own advice. She could offer advice, but she couldn't change Darian Woodward.

No matter how much she wanted to.

Darian's gang mounted their horses and waited for Darian. Emily made sure her parachute pack was affixed to her saddle, then mounted too. Darian seemed hesitant, though she wasn't sure why. Without speaking, he went to Wetherspoon's fresh grave and stood a moment.

Though she couldn't hear his words, she saw him mouth, "I'm sorry," and her heart ached with pity.

Darian went to his tall gray horse and mounted. He seemed weary, older than she'd seen him before, touched by an ancient, tragic beauty as he gazed around at the Apache taking down their village. She loved him, yet he seemed unreachable, distant like some figure out of myth, out of time. A hero on a journey inside himself where she couldn't follow.

And then Emily realized she was on that journey too.

Chapter Twelve

"So, dear leader, where's the entrance to these grand caverns of yours?"

"I have no idea." Emily marched up and down in the spot where she distinctly remembered a coffee and gift shop, which had been very near to the Colossal Caves entry point. They had hidden the horses a mile behind, then trekked their way to where Emily hoped she remembered the tourist attraction. "Damn! I don't remember what the tour guide said. I was fifteen."

"Not paying attention, I fear." Darian clicked his tongue, but the others waited patiently. It occurred to her that his men were beginning to trust her, too. She had to prove herself worthy, and soon, or lose all this hard-won respect.

Something moved in the juniper bushes behind her and Ping went to investigate. A bobcat snarled, then bounded from the bush to dart away. Ping whistled.

"Weren't that a beauty, Captain? You don't see fellows like that back East!"

Darian looked pained. "This is not a nature expedition, Ping. And we have bobcats in the East."

Ping appeared utterly crestfallen. "Oh. Don't see 'em much in the city, though."

Emily repressed a smile, then returned to her excavation. "You know, I don't think the entrance is quite the same as in my day...."

Darian's brow angled. "Apparently not." He looked around, dramatically. "In particular, the 'coffee shop' you mentioned appears lacking."

Emily glared at him, but at least he was cheerful enough to tease. The sun was setting rapidly, and she wished she had the extra hours of sunlight provided by summer. "I remember that bandits hid out here, and they had a secret entrance, so when the cops came, they'd sneak out back and leave them all . . . confounded."

Darian glanced at his men. "Cops?"

"Policemen." She was tired, hungry, and getting odd. "Ya know, pardner—them thar shiriffs and depitties."

Darian closed his eyes, his brow tight as if he, too, guessed she'd cracked. Emily giggled from weariness and failure. "Sorry."

He nodded, but said nothing.

"I think . . . the thing is . . . do we have ropes, by the way?"

"We are amply supplied with ropes."

"Good. Because I think we'll have to lower ourselves in through that hole." Emily pointed at a small opening, beside a juniper bush, that she had hoped they wouldn't have to use, and Darian's expression of horror reached its pinnacle.

"Madame, this was all a ruse to stay at my side, wasn't it?" He paused, collecting himself. "Emmy, I know you want to be a loyal wife, but I am not squeezing myself into a hole that harbors . . . God knows what." His voice grew more shrill as he spoke. Emily winced.

"There are bats. I remember that part. That was really neat, actually. They use their, um, excrement—*guano*—for cosmetics, mascara and stuff."

Darian's men shuffled around, moving farther from the cavern entrance. Darian gazed heavenward and sighed. "Useful information, my dearest."

Emily shifted her weight from foot to foot. "Well, since we're here, we could gather some up and stuff it in our packs, then sell it when we get back to the future."

He looked aghast until she burst out laughing, then shook his head. "Since nightfall approaches, I suppose we must do as you say."

Ping stepped forward. "I'm the smallest, sir. Let me drop in first. Then if I fall into some bottomless pit. . . ."

Darian glared. "I will go in first." Emily sensed he didn't like enclosed spaces, and wondered if he suffered from claustrophobia. Just her luck. "We should fashion torches first, to see our way around."

All dubious, his men proceeded to make torches out of branches while Emily waited. Maybe this wasn't such a great idea, after all, but it had sounded good at the time. They made a stack of the torches, then tied all but one to a rope. With a deep sigh, Darian tied a rope around his waist, then went to the hole. He cast a dark, forlorn glance at Emily, squeezed himself in, wriggled around to drop foot first, then waited for his men to lower him.

MacLeod passed him a torch, and seemed to like the sight of Darian hanging there, dark and dutiful.

Emily tried to smile. "It will be fine. Not a far drop

at all, I'm sure. I remember a very nice walkway. Rather steep."

The men lowered Darian, and he glared until he was out of sight. They lowered him to the end of the rope, and he was still hanging. Emily leaned in, could see nothing, then called to him. "Darian? Are you all right?"

"My legs have been scratched several times by oddly shaped rocks, and I bumped my head."

MacLeod glanced at Emily, then shrugged. "He's all right."

Emily peeked in again, utilizing her most comforting, soothing voice. "We're almost at the end of the rope. . . ."

She heard him from the darkness. "That makes two of us."

She loved him when he grumbled. "Well, what do we do? Can you set foot anywhere?"

A long pause followed. Then, "Drop me."

"No!"

Before Emily could act further, MacLeod dropped the rope. Emily held her breath. A long series of curses wafted upward from the dark, then further grumbling. "Darian! What happened? Did you break anything?"

"Bats."

"Bats? You broke a bat? Be more careful! Bats are sensitive and useful creatures."

"Bats! I suggest you all move. . . ."

A whirring rush sounded, the rush of wings. Before Emily could move, a breeze brushed her face and a bat zipped over her head. She squealed in surprise, fell back, and watched as hundreds, maybe thousands of bats emerged from the hole, darting into the darkening sky.

She waited a while, then peeked down again. "You might have warned me sooner." He didn't respond, so she guessed his act was deliberate.

MacLeod looked in beside her. "Well, now, Captain. What about the torch?"

Darian fumbled below in the dark, then lit his torch. Emily saw the light on his blond hair, on his face, and then the look of wonder as he looked around. "Magnificent! Wondrous!" Without further explanation, he ventured off, leaving the others stunned.

When he didn't return, Emily began to fidget. "Sergeant, lower me down there, too."

"Now, you just wait a bit, girl. The Captain will tell us when it's safe to head after him."

"What if he's fallen into a pit, or gotten lost? Put me in there!"

When his men failed to assist, Emily seized the rope and began pulling it up to tie it around herself. MacLeod grabbed her arm and held her back. "Hold on there!"

As he spoke, a glimmer of light returned in the cave, and Darian appeared below. He waved enthusiastically. "This place is amazing! It must go on for miles! Emily, this suggestion was brilliant. If only we'd thought to put that gold we found in here, for safekeeping."

Emily caught a furtive glance between Bonner and Clyde. She forced her attention back to Darian. She didn't want to know.

"Well, can we come down with you?"

Darian looked around. "I don't see any reason why not. You come first, and I should be able to reach you when the rope reaches its full extension. And send those torches down too. I'd like to see this place fully lit."

His men did as he asked, and sent the batch of torches in after him. Emily looked into the hole, then at the long skirt she wore. "I can't go down there in this." She fished around in her pack, found her shorts and T-shirt, then went behind a bush to change. The men paid no attention when she emerged in her old clothes. Apparently, they'd gotten used to the bare flesh of women from the future.

Emily tied the rope around herself and climbed through the hole. They lowered her with ease, and Darian's lit torch kept her from banging herself on the rocks that had assailed him.

Darian caught her by the waist and lowered her to the ground. He assessed her new attire, and seemed embarrassed. His men paid no attention, but Darian took one look at her bare legs and blushed. Emily frowned. "You've seen me wearing less, you know."

Darian cleared his throat and applied a false smile. "I was simply surprised to see that you had changed your wardrobe so quickly."

"Uh-huh." Emily looked around. The caves looked somewhat more forbidding without electric lighting, without a path and handrails. "Now what?"

He cast her a skeptical glance. "This was your idea. What do you suggest?"

She hesitated, chewing her lip. "Well, I guess once the guys are down, we should move inward a bit, so there's no chance of our light being seen. Then we make camp like a good bunch of bandits would. What do we have for food?"

"We have adequate supplies. Dried meat that old Apache woman gave me, some kind of stew preparation, a form of tea they make . . . and what we took from Tucson, of course."

Emily felt comfortable, pleased with her success as the others lowered themselves into the hole. "What about the last one?"

"The last what?"

"Man."

Darian looked up as Bonner and Clyde, followed by Herring and Ping, joined them in the caverns. Darian looked up and MacLeod looked down. "Not to worry, Sergeant. Now that the rest of us are down, and the torches are lit, it should be possible for you to bring the rope with you, and see well enough to climb down."

MacLeod appeared extremely dubious, but with a great sigh, he wedged himself into the hole. He was a big man. Emily thought of Pooh caught in Rabbit's doorway, and held her breath.

With painstaking care, MacLeod made his way down over the rocks and limestone. He hitched the rope around a stalactite, lowered a bit, then pulled it after him. Darian watched the process with approval, offering bits of advice that Emily felt sure MacLeod resented.

The sergeant reached the bottom, waited obviously for Darian to comment on his skill, then frowned when Darian turned cheerfully back to examining their new surroundings. Emily's pleasure faded toward doubt. Had Wetherspoon's death stirred up some kind of latent discontent toward their leader? Would they resent him for leading them on a mutiny, when surely to remain behind would have been the safer route?

No. She remembered MacLeod's tale of Darian's heroism. They loved him. Love had to be deeper than self-interest. And Darian had never done anything deliberately to hurt them. He certainly hadn't asked them to mutiny alongside him. She knew that much without asking.

Darian and his men prowled like bandits along the mystic corridors, issuing gasps of awe and speculation that would have thrilled a modern-day tour leader. Even children couldn't have displayed the wonder that Darian's gang exuded as they examined the ancient cavern.

Bonner and Clyde separated from the others. Emily watched them, certain they were looking for places to stash large quantities of gold. They seemed happy, so she couldn't bring herself to comment. After a while, Ping and Herring set about making camp, and Herring prepared a dinner with their provisions. The group gathered in a circle to eat, and MacLeod recited a prayer as always. He spoke of their good fortune, then of Wetherspoon's bravery and heroism. They held a moment of silence, then turned to their meals without further comment.

Emily ate too, listening quietly to their conversation. For the first time in her life, she truly belonged. She had been lonely for so long. Her parents had been killed in a car crash when she was nineteen, during her first week at college, leaving her shattered. She had met Ian Hallowell that same week, when he found her crying outside her dorm, alone.

He had comforted her, as if in her loneliness and misery he recognized himself. She fell in love with him, utterly, and they had been inseparable ever after—until he abandoned her just as completely. She had been too dependent on him, no question. Maybe she had asked too much. Somehow, Darian allowed her to maintain her autonomy, nor did he ever place his own emotional needs upon her. Sometimes, she wished he would.

Like tonight. Darian sat beside her, but he didn't reach out or draw her into the conversation. She wanted to talk to him, about Wetherspoon, about what he intended next, but first she had to get him alone. She waited until the meal ended, then helped clean up afterwards, biding her time for the right moment.

As Herring and the others laid out their sleeping gear, Emily caught Darian's arm. He smiled at her, but he seemed tense. "What is it, my dear? Surely you need rest. Your search for these caverns must have worn you out." He paused. "It certainly wore me out."

He was teasing her, but he was also suggesting that a

good night's sleep might behoove them better than engaging in bliss. Her chest tightened. She was losing him, slowly. He had seen something that frightened him, as Ian had, and he was pulling away.

Her grip on his arm tightened, until she realized what she was doing. Emily released him and stood back. Her gaze fixed on his, she seized a torch. "As it happens, I'm not tired at all. In fact, I intend to take a walk around these caverns and find a nice, secluded spot where I can sleep comfortably without hearing Herring snore." She didn't invite him to join her. She just smiled, then headed off, refusing to look back.

He hesitated behind her. She felt his suspicious expression without looking. She heard his quick steps as he pursued her. He caught up with her and took the torch. Emily glanced at him. "I thought you were 'worn out.' "

His full mouth quirked upwards at one corner. "I am. By a wife I cannot predict in any way."

Emily climbed up an incline, balanced herself on a great hanging stalactite, then slid down the other side. "And I am exhausted by a stubborn husband who keeps too much to himself."

Darian followed her, bumped himself on the stalactite, cursed, then slid after her. The torchlight glinted on limestone that looked like a waterfall frozen in time.

Emily pretended not to await an answer, and Darian walked behind her down a narrow passageway. Though she walked upright just below the hanging rock, Darian kept bumping his head. She peeked back. "Haven't you learned when to duck yet?"

He glared. "I was distracted."

Her brow furrowed. "By what?" His expression appeared tense and he shrugged. She detected a flare of pink in his cheeks. "By what?"

He puffed an impatient breath. "Nothing. Move on."

Emily shrugged, then walked on ahead. She bent low to avoid a massive rock, and Darian issued a muted groan. She looked at him doubtfully. "What is the matter with you?"

He appeared very tense now, but he offered her a formal nod. "Nothing at all. Proceed."

Emily twisted left to avoid the rock icicles, then left to avoid another patch. She heard Darian's harshly in-taken breath, then glanced back. He looked quickly at the ceiling of the cave, as if he found it of unsurpassable interest, but he seemed to be breathing quickly.

Emily studied his expression. "Are you all right? We'll find a place to sleep soon, I'm sure. Maybe over there—on that flat rock." Not quite what she was hoping for, but they would fit together, anyway.

This promise seemed to unnerve him. He looked around, nervously, and shook his head. "Nothing here appears adequate for resting. Move on."

They walked a long while without taking. Walls hung like sheets of rain, mystic and eternal. Tiny droplets of condensed water sounded like music. Emily spotted a long, flat area, covered by a low overhanging ceiling, decorated with smaller clusters of stalactites. A small stream flowed underground, cascading over the rocks and splashing into a dark pool before it disappeared.

She pointed. "There! Isn't it beautiful? Let's sleep there."

Darian eyed the spot, his face knit into a frown as if searching for some reason not to stop there. He hesitated, then sighed as if faced with the inevitable. "Very well. It appears adequate."

They climbed over a jagged ridge of rock and lime-stone, then laid out two bedrolls side by side. Darian took an inordinate time arranging their bedding. Emily went to the water, then looked back at Darian.

"Do you suppose it's safe to drink?"

Darian cupped water in his hands, sniffed, then tasted it. He grimaced, then shook his head. "Let's stick with our canteens. It tastes of limestone."

"Is it clean enough to wash in?"

"I suppose so. . . ." He sounded suspicious, as if he dreaded something.

Emily stuck her hand beneath the falling water. It was cool, but not icy. Not warm enough for a lengthy encounter as she'd hoped, but enough to wash themselves. Darian was watching her as if wondering what she intended. Her pulse quickened. She hadn't been daring in her marriage—she'd never felt quite confident enough to seduce her husband, nor entice him.

But Darian was resisting her, and more than that, she liked seeing his face when he wanted her. She liked knowing that no other woman affected him this way. Emily licked her lips, subtly, then splashed water on her face. She splashed herself. The water felt good, cool after a long day in the sun.

"There's no need to get my boots wet." She pretended to talk just to herself, as she bent to remove her hiking boots, but she knew Darian watched her intently. She set them aside and noticed that his eyes were closed. If the sight of her bent over affected him this strongly, she had made progress.

She smiled, a small smile, then moved closer to the water. The spray soaked her shirt until it clung to her skin, refreshing, yet so erotic because he was watching her. Her heart pounded, and her nipples tightened into hard peaks beneath the wet cloth, not from the chill but from Darian's presence. She wanted to look at him, to see his reaction, but her mind whispered, *not yet*.

The falling water formed a pool on a ledge near the

level of her knees. Emily bent to gather some in her palm. Normally, when she moved or acted, it was without forethought. Before this moment, she had washed herself to get clean, to cool off. When she bent over, it was to pick something up.

But each muscle in her body came alive with acute awareness as she moved, now. She knew if she bent just so, slowly, that the womanliness of her body would be highlighted, drawn to his attention. She had never thought this way before, but the realization flooded her now with power—and desire.

She ran her hands through the small pool, dabbling her fingers. All the while, she felt the spray gently soaking her, trickling down over her shorts, down her thighs. She straightened and stretched, a sensual, feline act, then ran her damp fingers through her hair.

The water dampened her hair so that it coiled into long curls. It ran over her breasts, tightening them still more, then down her stomach and between her thighs.

Darian groaned as if tortured, and her body swamped with fiery pleasure. She looked, slowly, over her shoulders, her eyelids lowered not for effect, but because sensuality had overcome her and filled her with its delicious weight.

"Is there something you want, outlaw?"

His blue eyes flashed in the torchlight, his sweet face altered with a flush of primal male lust. He didn't answer. He didn't look capable of answering, but he tore off his uniform jacket and flung it aside. He didn't look to see where it fell. This proved how far gone he was— Darian always folded his clothes, with care. Now he ripped away his white shirt and it landed near the jacket.

Emily waited, unable to look away as he pulled off his black riding boots, then his trousers. Her heart throbbed in her chest. He stood naked before her, and he didn't look young, nor safe, nor did any vestiges of the cautious Victorian yuppie remain. Instead, in Darian Woodward, she saw something far more ancient, like a Viking enraged with lust, or a Saxon warrior pillaging his Celtic neighbors.

She trembled at the look in his bright eyes, but her own power remained. She allowed herself another smile, though her hands were shaking. She held her breath and turned away from him, then spotted massive rock hanging in front of her, a stalactite that was decidedly . . . phallic.

I have lost my mind. Or maybe, not. *Men like visuals. Especially subliminal, erotic ones.* Emily reached to touch the rock, and found the surface hard and grainy. She slid her hand down, then up again, then laughed softly when she heard Darian's low, tortured groan. He caught her waist from behind and kissed the back of her neck, licking and nipping like a man possessed with desire.

Emily leaned back against him, her eyes closed. He ran his hands up over her stomach to cup her breasts beneath the wet shirt. Less gently than during their first encounter, but wilder, a man driven beyond thought of restraint. He teased her hard nipples until her every breath was a gasp, then circled her breasts with his palm, playing with the small buds, never hurting, yet bringing her to more erotic awareness than she'd ever imagined possible.

His erection felt hard against her backside, and she pressed back against him. His hands shook as he tore her shirt up and pulled it over her head. He threw it aside, then fumbled with her shorts. Somehow, those came off too, and she stepped out of them. She started to turn, but he caught her shoulders and held her facing away from him.

233

"Do you know what you're doing to me?" His voice came ragged, hoarse with lust. She had never heard him sound quite this way before. The man behind was half a stranger, half dangerous, half outlaw. She peeked over her shoulder and smiled.

"Show me."

A low growl rumbled in his throat, his eyes burned. "Every time I look at that. . . ." He glanced down at her bottom, and his expression grew more fiery still. "That perfect, firm, exquisite backside. . . . My mind, Emmy, goes to such lengths, so that I think at the dawn of time, when a man first looked at a woman, he took her this way."

He sounded almost hypnotic, as if he had fallen under a spell, then drew her in, too. She had never imagined herself as sexually adventurous, and Darian seemed the least likely person to take her to new realms, but she found herself turned back to the wall, gripping the rock she had used to tease him. Darian gripped her hips in his strong hands. He bent her forward, gently, but irresistibly, then guided his length between her thighs.

Emily held her breath against an onslaught of desire so beyond her, so wild, and so deep that she wondered if she would float from her body and disappear. He slid back and forth along her damp cleft until she writhed with need, until the warm heat of her soaked him, begging. She had teased him, lured him, seduced him, and now he claimed all of her. She had created a monster. A beautiful, erotic creature that would take her and make her a monster, too.

Darian drove suddenly, unexpectedly up inside her, lifting her to her toes with the power of his entry. She cried out with the shock of pleasure, and he thrust again. Over and over, he moved inside her, until she seemed to spin without bearings, turned into some wild creature herself. Like him.

Just when she thought she could stand no more without shattering into fiery bits of energy, he stopped and withdrew. Emily sputtered, aching without him, needing him to finish what he had started inside her. "You can't stop now!" Her words came in a rushed breath, and she heard Darian's low chuckle behind her.

"I have no intention of stopping."

He turned her to face him, and the man she saw before her was surely a god. His eyes burned like a conqueror, his lips curled into a smile that said he knew she longed for his victory.

She expected him to take her again, but instead he kissed her, sensually. While her body throbbed with savage passion, he awoke tiny threads of sweet pleasure, so that the two, savage and exquisite, rose side by side to send her where she had never been before.

She whispered his name, and he murmured against her neck as he kissed her throat. The spray of the water cooled them, and sent fire through them, and Emily reached down to touch him. She touched his erection, her fingers chilled from the water. He gasped and moaned with pleasure. She massaged him firmly, until his hips bucked, until he drove himself with desperate need against her palm.

Emily wrapped her leg around his, higher to draw him closer to her core. Darian cupped her face in his hands and kissed her passionately, and she guided his staff into her opening. A low growl sounded in his throat as he edged between the soft folds.

She squeezed tight around him and he shuddered, then drove himself deeper, up inside her. Darian's arms closed around her and he gripped her bottom, then lifted her. He held her like a doll while he made love to her, thrusting deeper and deeper into her. Her head tipped back as he filled her, as the thick base of him rubbed rhythmically against her small woman's bud.

Her climax erupted unexpectedly, shocking her as she clung to his broad shoulders, reveling in the waves of pleasure. He recognized her pinnacle, and his own joined hers. His beautiful head tipped back and she licked his neck, then sucked as his muscles strained in his rapture. He poured himself inside her, then stilled. He seemed surprised as he lowered her gently to her feet.

He touched the side of her face, still breathing hard, eyes wide. "Did I displease you, Emmy? I . . . did my manly duty rather sooner than I expected."

Emily gaped at him. He had taken her to heights she felt sure no woman had ever known, and he was apologizing. "Darian. . . . My knees are weak. I feel like I've found all the universe inside myself."

He considered this, then led her farther from the water. "In the aftermath of this glory, icy water on the flesh is not pleasant."

"It's not icy, Darian. Not even cold, really."

He smiled and kissed her hand. "Your small and delicate body was so fiery with passion that you didn't notice."

"Did you?"

"My body also attained a degree of heat." He paused. "Your fingers touching me in . . . that particular spot of innate maleness . . . were cold."

Emily smiled. He could make love to her like a barbarian warrior, and still use the most abstract euphemisms. "I'm sorry."

His brow angled. "I liked it." He paused again. "Very much."

Emily rose to her tiptoes and kissed his cheek. "I liked it, too."

Darian looked thoughtful as they picked up their clothes, then walked barefoot, carefully, to their bedding. "I have noticed that you like our unions a great deal." He held the torch lower to illuminate the ground before them. "I find that witnessing your reaction gives me a pleasure equal to my own."

"I find that, too." They looked at each other and smiled, and Emily felt suddenly what they really were. Newlyweds, in the old-fashioned sense, exploring each other, getting to know each other. And feeling love in a way neither had quite expected. If it could last. . . . But was something so perfect possible, could it withstand all the dark forces in the world against them?

She banished the fear as they went to their bedding. Darian folded their clothes, then set them in a neat pile. He was certainly back to his old self. He set their boots side by side, adjusted them again, then set the torch in a rock. "This will burn for awhile, and I have another for when we wake."

"You always think ahead."

He glanced at her. "Most of the time."

"And you always seem to know what to expect."

Darian gestured at the falling water. "Not always."

Emily smiled and patted the bedding beside her. "Come to me."

He lay down beside her as if he felt safe. Too safe. His erection had subsided. He looked sated and happy. Darian closed his eyes and breathed deeply, satisfied. Emily snuggled closer beside him. She ran her hand over his hard chest, feeling his strong heartbeat within. She felt his stomach, which tightened as she moved her hand across it.

She was fully sated. So why was desire stirring in her again? There was just something about him, something she had to hold, to touch, to join with. Emily's hand moved lower.

Darian's eyes popped open when she grazed the tip of his satisfied penis. "What are you doing?"

Emily kissed his shoulder. "I like the feel of you."

He cleared his throat as she ran small circles around the tip. It hardened and grew against her touch. She drew her finger from the tip to the base, and back again, then circled the ridge. Darian's body grew taut. "Emmy. . . ."

"Just playing."

"Ah." He sounded hoarse. "You like the feel of me. I understand."

She peeked up at him. "I think I might like the taste of you, too."

His blue eyes widened. "Taste?" Good. His voice sounded weak, as if he couldn't believe what she intended.

Emily sat up, then maneuvered herself to the level of his waist while Darian watched, aghast. Her hair fell loose and damp around her face and over her shoulders. She took him in her hand again, stroking him slowly, without pressure. "You smell good, you feel good. I wonder if you taste the same?"

Chapter Thirteen

Darian stared down at her, shocked, but he couldn't say a word. After all, he had done the same to her in a fit of passion during their first night. Still, he had never imagined that she would return the favor.

With her eyes focused on his, Emily bent and kissed his hard tip. There was something about her looking at him this way. He had been fully satisfied, but now his blood raged again. Darian fell back in pleasure, then propped himself up on his elbows so that he could see what she was doing.

She licked and circled the tip, then trailed her tongue to his base, cupping his tight sack in one hand. She played and teased until he quivered, then took just the tip into her mouth. She bobbed her head up and down, then took him deeper, sucking gently, then with more force. As he gave in to her power, she stopped, then began the slow path again.

It was bliss. A different bliss from the one he'd experienced when watching her bathe, when bending her forward and taking her like some . . . barbarian. Now, he was helpless in her hands, in her mouth. And he loved it.

She pulled away slightly, gazing up at him beneath lowered eyelids. "Do you like this, outlaw? I would not think of doing something that offended you."

He had to smile. "Since when?"

She drew back, a look of feigned innocence and surprise on her beautiful face. "When have I ever . . . ?" A quick dart of her tongue reminded him of the throbbing, sweet pleasure she ignited within him. "If you wish me to stop, just ask it."

"I ask. . . ." She licked him again. Darian leaned back, his eyes closed as pleasure swarmed his senses. "I ask that you never stop."

She smiled, then pressed her lips against his hot, slick flesh. "Never, my love. Never."

For a long, agonizingly intense while, he thought she'd taken his command literally. Emily brought him repeatedly to the verge of release, while he groaned her name, as he clasped his fingers in her hair, as he writhed in perfect bliss, just short of satisfaction. She teased him until he thought he could endure no more, yet nothing could make him hurry her, for each second brought a pleasure he'd never imagined before.

A bead of moisture formed at the tip of him, and she brushed her lips back and forth over it. Darian cried out a shuddering moan, shocked by the passionate echo of his voice. A sudden image of Ping charging through the caverns thinking they'd been attacked flashed in his mind, and he bit his lip hard to stop himself from shouting again.

He ached so much that he thought it would never

abate. As she held him back from release, he knew she tormented herself with desire, too, because her breaths came ragged and swift against his skin, telling him she utilized painful restraint, too.

She gasped as if she could take no more, then climbed on top of him, straddling his hips as he pressed against her soft cleft. She gripped his length in her hands, positioning him for entry, but instead of taking him inside her as he longed for her to do, she moved along him until his breath came in hoarse gasps. She laughed, and circled his tip, but Darian grabbed her hips, held her firmly, and thrust upward.

He entered her deepest center, filling her. She braced herself on his shoulders and made love to him, moving with wild, passionate abandon as he thrust up to meet her. He felt her climax approach, but she fought against it, prolonging the sweet waves of its onslaught.

He experienced his own as if it came upward from his toes, swirling through his body and overtaking even his soul in its paradise. Emily whimpered his name as her body writhed above him, and Darian drove himself hard up into her. It shattered her restraint, and he watched as her own rapture exploded in unison with his.

The waves abated, leaving Emily shaking and weak. She collapsed to his chest, gasping to catch her breath. Darian felt her heart pounding against him, met by the powerful throbs of his own. He wrapped his arms around her, holding her safe and protected against his body, and he loved her.

He stroked her hair, then kissed her head. "You, my beloved wife, are a treasure worth waiting for."

Emily's pulse slowed to a more even beat, and she squirmed to lie beside him. Darian rolled over and tucked her close, adjusting the blankets to keep her warm. "I am worth living for, too."

He kissed her again. "I have every intention of living, Emmy."

She looked up at him, and he saw the doubt in her eyes. "Do you? I sometimes wonder."

He didn't want to talk, not now. For a few blissful moments, he had forgotten all that assailed him, and had been only a man. Her man.

Emily wrapped her arm around his waist and pressed her face close to his neck. "Darian, I don't want to lose you. Not now. I've lost everything that mattered to me. But nothing has mattered the way you do."

"You won't lose me. Our situation, at least, proves that death is no true ending."

She hugged him tighter. "That is true. Not for me and you, and not for your brother, or Wetherspoon, too."

Darian's jaw tightened. *Not now. Please.*

She must have sensed what he was feeling. "You are not responsible for their deaths, Darian. I know you feel you are, but you're not."

Why couldn't she see the obvious? "They both died trying to protect me."

"Yes. Because they loved you. You would have done the same for them."

He frowned. "I never got the chance."

Emily propped herself up to look into his eyes. "Darian, you're worth loving. You're worth dying for."

Dying for. What made people so dear think this way? "You are not to say that. You are not to die for me." He sat up, surprising her. "Do you understand?" He clutched her shoulders, hard. "Emily, don't you do anything to put yourself at risk for me. This is *my* battle. The one thing I can't lose is you."

"Okay." Emily paused. The fervor of his reaction had surprised her. It had surprised him, too. "I won't do anything stupid, I promise."

She couldn't know, not fully, what it would mean to him to lose her. She couldn't understand. "Swear it."

She nodded. "I swear. But why do you think. . . ?"

He lay his finger to her lips. "You can't know what it means to lose someone this way, when you know they lie dying because they loved you. Because they put my worthless life before their own. Emily, I loved my brother. I love him still. But I've never loved anything the way I love you. I can't lose you, especially not in some foolish act you might take to protect me."

Emily's eyes filled with tears. "Darian, we love each other. How can you think your life is worthless? You are the best man I've ever known."

He looked away, his head bowed. "I accept your love, because I can't resist it. But I can't let you sacrifice yourself for me."

"Yet you intend to risk yourself, don't you?"

"I must defeat Davis. He is a scourge upon this land."

Emily's brow puckered, but she lay back again. She held out her arms to him, and he lowered himself beside her. She hugged him and kissed him, and he relaxed, but his fear didn't fully abate. "Tiotonawen implied you are doing this for yourself, somehow. I think, Darian Woodward, that you're doing it because you don't know how much you're worth."

Love is clearly blind. "I'm doing it because it is the only way, Emmy. Because I have no choice. But nothing I do must hurt you. Whatever happens, I must know you're safe. If it's in the future, so be it, but you must be safe."

"No one's after me, Darian. You're the one in danger."

Darian got up and doused the torch. "Not here, Emmy. Not tonight. Tonight, we are safe, and we have all that we need."

243

He lay back beside her in the utter darkness and held her small body close to his. She kissed his neck and whispered, "Each other."

Emily woke to darkness, but she felt well-rested and content. She wished her watch had a glow-in-the-dark capacity. Darian stirred beside her, then yawned. He rolled to his side, then took her sleepily into his arms.

"A night spent with you, even in a pit, seems a night spent within castle walls, my dear." He kissed her and she snuggled closer. When she felt Darian's erection press against her, repeating their night's activities seemed promising.

"Captain!" Ping's voice echoed with extraordinary force in the caverns. Emily wondered if every morning of her marriage would be spent with Ping's cheerful but untimely alarm.

Darian issued a long groan, and winced as the light from Ping's torch appeared along a far wall of the cave. "Ping, if you come any closer, I will draw my revolver and shoot you."

The light stopped. Ping maintained silence for several seconds. "Sir?"

"I am naked, Ping. My wife is naked. One step closer, and you'll be buried in these caves."

Ping coughed and cleared his throat, shifted from foot to foot, then backed up the corridor again. "Sorry, sir." He paused, message still burning for delivery.

Darian sighed, but Emily saw his veiled smile. "What is it, Ping?"

Ping straightened. "It's morning, sir. Wondered what you wanted done about the horses. Can't just leave them out there. Figured I might take them to that stream we passed for water, then hide them again."

"That sounds good. See to it, Ping."

Darian found his own torch before the light from Ping's faded up the cavern, and it glowed to dancing life. Emily still lay on her back, feeling peaceful as she gazed at the intricate patterns on the low limestone ceiling just above her. Swirling, dancing, mesmerizing . . . the shapes took form and her imagination wandered. Some even appeared carved by human hand.

She saw human shapes, bent as if gathering harvest, some seated as if working pottery. One was clearly leading a horse. One stood like a young king, a king with long, black hair, taller than all the rest. Behind him, like a sacred image, was a whirlwind.

Emily sat up and bumped her head. "Darian! There are pictures here!"

Darian glanced at her as he pulled on his clothing and boots. "Fairies dancing? Lovers entwined?"

She shook her head. "No, truly. Real carvings. Pass me that torch!"

He gave her the torch and she held it up to examine the pictures. "I'm right! These are cave drawings . . . very old ones. I know quite a bit about this sort of thing, as it happens. They must have been done by the Hohokam Indians. They were here from at least 900 A.D."

"Never heard of them." Darian bent to look at the pictures, too. "But you're right. These pictures are done by men."

She frowned. "Or women." She pointed out the whirlwind behind the tall man. "Isn't this ironic? A whirlwind. I wonder if the Hohokam had something to do with this time travel thing Tiotonawen uses."

"I have no idea how it originated. Did Adrian say anything?"

"No. I don't think he had any idea. We will have to ask Tiotonawen." Emily examined the pictures closer. "I wonder who he was?" Even in the dim carving, the man depicted seemed larger than life, broad-shouldered, strong and, more than anything else, proud. His hair reached halfway down his back, depicted with great care. "That's odd."

"What?"

"Look." She gestured at the man's feet. "What he's wearing."

Darian looked at the area and shrugged. "What of it?"

"Well, he's the only one whose feet the artist bothered to show. As if they were important, or unusual."

"Maybe he was a swift runner. . . . Emmy, we should rejoin the others. I can waste no time studying the distant past when our own future lies at stake."

Emily started to agree, to leave the images for another time. The man's feet caught her eye again, and she knew. "He's wearing hiking boots!"

Darian eyed her doubtfully. "What are those?"

"What I'm wearing—Timberlands."

"I had no idea the history of your peculiar, less-than-feminine footwear was so long and so proud."

"It's not. The Hohokam certainly didn't invent them. What is this guy doing wearing hiking boots?"

Darian rolled his eyes. "Emmy, it's dark in here. These images aren't all that clear. It's probably some odd footwear worn by their people that resembles your . . . less-than-feminine footwear."

She glared at him. "Do you have something against my boots?"

"Nothing."

Emily left the image, and retrieved her clothing to dress. "Except that you consider them 'less-than-feminine.' "

Darian's blue eyes widened. "Where did you ever get that idea?"

*   *   *

Darian and his gang milled about uneasily in the cavern near the entrance, waiting for Ping. Emily felt worried, too. She kept checking her watch, then mentally timing the distance from the horses to the stream.

"Maybe one of them got loose." Maybe. Emily chewed her lip and Darian looked at her as if trying to draw hope, and failing.

"I don't like it. Ping, though high-strung, is no fool. He wouldn't be gone this long. By the look of it through this tiny shaft you chose as a foyer, I'd say it's high noon."

Emily didn't like the sound of 'high noon.' It reminded her of some kind of judgment day moment. "Maybe we should go look for him."

Darian drew his revolver and checked it. "We should. You stay here."

There was no use arguing, so Emily smiled obediently and seated herself on a rock while the others arranged ropes over stalactites and climbed out, one by one. Darian waited for the gang to reach the open air, then placed his hands on her shoulders. She met his bright gaze innocently, but it wasn't easy.

"I mean it, Emmy. You wait for us here."

"Of course."

His eyes narrowed into dire suspicion. "Marriage involves trust."

"Marriage involves each person acting on the truth and intuition of her—or his—own heart, and with love as her guide."

"I don't like the sound of that."

Emily frowned. "You don't? I thought it quite beautiful. Poetic, even."

"Emily. . . ."

"I'll stay behind and let you go on ahead without me."

"Good." He hesitated, still unsure. "Good."

247

Emily watched Darian leave. She waited a few moments, staying behind while they went on without her. Then she climbed the rope, straining for speed, and squinted up into the bright sun of high noon. She put on her sunglasses and went carefully after Darian.

She caught up with them near the place where they'd left the horses, but she was careful not to let the gang see her. Ping was nowhere in sight, and the horses apparently hadn't been moved. Darian directed his men with stealth around the area, so Emily hid behind a juniper bush, with a prickly pear cactus perilously close to her backside.

MacLeod spoke to Darian, and Darian shook his head. Emily heard a rustle, and apparently, Darian's men did, too. They dropped silently behind boulders, disappearing in seconds. He was good, she had to admit. Not a man likely to be caught unaware.

She heard a sound like a muffled scream, pained, as if struggling, and her heart held its beat.

From a position across from hers, facing Darian, a man emerged with Ping clutched before him. Ping appeared badly bruised, bleeding at his lip, one eye swollen shut. Rage swelled in Emily's heart and her fists clenched. Ping struggled, but it was obvious he had been overwhelmed by his attacker.

The attacker spat, a trait probably learned from the noxious Tradman, and kept Ping in front of himself lest Darian shoot. "Woodward! Got something for you!"

Emily closed her eyes. What could they want now? Why hadn't they shot Darian when he was out in the open, why hadn't they killed Ping?

She heard Darian from his position behind a boulder. "Release my soldier, fool. You are surrounded."

Ping's captor looked around and laughed. "Well, be damned! So it seems." He laughed again as three more soldiers appeared behind him. "We're outnumbered, sure, but we didn't come here to fight you, Woodward. General Davis wants you in Tucson, but he ain't fool enough to think a few of us can bring you in." He jabbed his revolver under Ping's chin, but the small soldier appeared too weak to care. "Was thinking of a trade— hoped to get your woman, but this here boy will do fine instead. Unless you want to see his little head blown off? Figured you're used to that from the war and all, but it won't look too pretty to them other scoundrels with you. They'll be thinking maybe they're next, huh?"

They had come for her, and taken Ping instead. Emily closed her eyes. She knew Darian. He wouldn't let Ping die. But if Ping was shot, there would be nothing to save Darian from his dark fate.

Darian motioned to his men, and Bonner started to move. Apparently, Ping's attackers had a lookout. "Hold there! All of you, out in the open!"

She waited, knowing Darian had no other choice. Slowly, one by one, the men emerged. The captor laughed, but he sounded nervous. "Drop your weapons."

Darian did so, but his revolver fell very close to his feet.

"I ain't no fool, Woodward. You can pick that gun up in a flash. But as I said, we ain't here to fight you. Give yourself up, and we'll let your man go."

He would do it. She knew him too well. He would be hanged by sunset, and she couldn't save him. Ping's captor cocked his revolver and Ping closed his eyes. Ping, kind and trusting and so enthusiastic—Darian couldn't save him now. But Emily could.

She felt herself rise from beneath the juniper bush. At first, she wasn't sure what she intended. She just knew Ping's fate, and Darian's, was in her hands. As the men, both good and evil, turned in surprise, her thoughts coalesced into reason: Davis's men had wanted to capture her, to lure Darian to Tucson. She was the prisoner they were really after, not Ping.

She heard Darian's sharp breath, but she couldn't look at him. She faced Ping's captor, removed her sunglasses, and forced herself to smile. "Do you really think you will get away with my husband, or his soldier? Surely your general could think of a better plan than that. I can assure you, sir, that you won't reach the desert below with his men following you."

The man spat. She didn't recall men of the future spitting so much, then remembered baseball players. Odd that in the most dangerous moment of her life, she should think of something so foul.

"Emily, no . . ."

The captor looked between Darian and Emily, and his small eyes narrowed. She watched as his unspectacular brain worked. She knew he'd feel safer dragging a woman back to Tucson than the outlaw Darian Woodward. And she would probably be considered a prize, even without Darian's capture, which would earn the general's praise.

"Get over here, girl."

"Not until you release Mr. Ping."

Darian moved from the boulder. He would stop her, and in doing so, get himself shot. Emily hurried to Ping's captor, and faced Darian. "You know this is the best way. It gives you time, Darian. Time."

He shook his head, his expression stunned, and terrified. "Emily, please. . . ."

"Nothing will happen to me. I swear it. I can take care of myself." She saw his pain, and knew he believed another person he loved was sacrificing life for him. "I am not doing this for you. I'm doing it for Ping."

Ping's head lolled in her direction, and the tiniest

smile formed on his bloodied lip. "Thank you, Miss Mrs." He paused and coughed as if it might be his last breath.

Please, don't let him die.

"When you get to town, please tell Penny that I share her feelings, and love her dearly to the fullest capacity of my heart. Ask her to remember me, and tell her that I would not give away the captain's hideout, no matter what they did to me. Tell her that I died a brave man."

For a man on the verge of death, Ping had much to say. "I will tell her, Ping. But you won't die. I promise."

Ping's captor shoved Ping to the ground and seized Emily, but Darian had his own revolver in a flash. He aimed, but the grubby soldier held Emily before him like a human shield. "Don't try anything, Woodward, or your girl here gets it. General Davis wants you in Tucson where he can get the fort commander to witness your hanging, all right and proper."

Darian held his revolver still aimed, looking for any angle to shoot. If he saw one, he would fire, and she would be free. But for how long? Emily's mind worked feverishly. She had acted on the impulse of her heart in giving herself up for Ping, but she hadn't abandoned all thought in doing so. There had to be evidence somehow to prove Davis's corrupt nature. And the only place she would find that was Tucson.

The captor backed away, dragging Emily before him. "High noon tomorrow, Woodward. Got the noose all ready for you."

Darian's bright eyes never wavered, his hand remained steady. "Tell Davis I will be there. But before I enter that town, I want my wife sent out to my men, and I want her safe. If she is harmed in any way, I will come to Tucson, but not a man will be left alive when I leave."

He meant it, and in his blue-eyed fury, he could do

it. But it would kill him. Emily cranked her head to look back at Darian. "Don't worry about me." She paused, wondering what she could say to ease his fear. "I have a plan." She spoke triumphantly, hoping it was true.

He met her eyes and she saw tears. She saw his poignant vulnerability as he watched her go, but she smiled, and it came from deep inside her. *I have a plan.* "Nothing can truly separate us. You know that. I am not afraid. Don't you be."

His revolver never lowered as his enemies pulled her away.

"I'm going now. Tonight. I will hear no further argument, MacLeod."

Darian sat with his men inside the cave hideout, his gaze fixed on the flickering torchlight. His men remained adamant against his plan to sneak into Tucson and free Emily, but he had no choice. He couldn't leave her in Davis's clutches.

The sergeant placed his large hand on Darian's shoulder. "Captain, I know Davis has your wife, but you can't go in there half-cocked. You'll get yourself and all of us killed."

"I am not asking that you men accompany me. But I am going to save my wife, and that is my final word. I need your help to do it."

MacLeod released Darian's shoulder and bowed his head. Ping lay beside them, breathing heavily, but awake and still alert. A thorough check of his condition had revealed that though Ping was badly bruised, he had no broken bones nor had he been seriously damaged. Ping proved a more resilient man than anyone had guessed, but he still lay dramatically with his hand to his forehead.

"Captain, you can't go. The sergeant is right." Ping

sounded weak, but the effect seemed forced.

Darian hesitated, surprised by their reaction. His men had never defied him before, nor had he ever sensed resentment from them. True, when he was first given command of their company, they had defied him at every turn, but that was long ago—before he had proven himself worthy.

"My wife is in danger, gentlemen. I will thank you to remember that fact."

MacLeod didn't appear convinced. "That girl is as strong as any one of us. She ain't going to fall apart because you're not there looking after her. She said she has a plan. Maybe it's time you trusted her."

Darian frowned, deeply annoyed. "This is not a matter of trust, Sergeant."

MacLeod raised his heavy brow. "Isn't it? It were trust that kept us all at your side when you mutinied. Trust that had us following Indians, whom some say we should rightfully be fighting. Captain, it's been trust all along—the trust others put in you. There'll come a time when it's you who must do the trusting. Maybe that time's come now."

Dark anger flamed in Darian's heart and he stood up, then went to the cavern entrance. "Fine words, Sergeant. Words that say only I can expect no help from you."

Ping started to rise, and Darian's anger faded. They would help him, even if they doubted. Their loyalty had never failed him. Surely now, with Emily's life at stake, they would stick by his side.

Bonner and Clyde sat silently, waiting, but Herring laid his hand on Ping's shoulder, preventing him from getting up and following Darian.

MacLeod stood up, but he made no motion to gather his gear. "Captain, you're taking a wrong step here. We've followed you to hell and back, but this thing

you're doing, it's just foolhardy. You're thinking with
your heart, and I ain't never seen you do that before."
The sergeant fell silent, his dark eyes fixed on Darian's
as if contemplating the man they had all respected, and
sacrificed everything for.

Darian stood defiant before them. He considered giving an order, then realized it was no good. They were
outlaws, all of them. No longer could they call themselves Union soldiers, but men who had taken the law,
and life, into their own hands. He would go on alone.

"Gentlemen, I am no longer your commander. Do as
you wish."

Darian seized the rope, half-expecting them to relent
and accompany him. He glanced back, but no one
moved. "Very well." His heart beat slow knowing he
had lost the one thing he'd considered unchanging—the
support of his men. But Emily needed him, and she mattered more than life, than loyalty, than anything. Darian
climbed the rope and went out into the darkness alone.

Darian found his horse tethered with the others. With
each twilight sound, he expected to see his men appear-
ing to join him. Nothing came but desert hares, startled
by his presence as they returned to secret burrows. Darian saddled his gray and mounted.

Why had they lost faith in him? He had never failed
them. Maybe it was Wetherspoon's death, but though he
bore guilt over that loss, his men had placed no blame.
He hadn't ordered Wetherspoon to act, after all. Had he
followed Darian's orders, Wetherspoon would still be
alive. Perhaps the resentment had been stirring for a long
while. Maybe they resented that Darian had become distracted with his new wife. Maybe they thought love
clouded his judgment.

But what man would leave his wife in his enemy's

clutches, without riding forth to save her? He didn't understand their reluctance to help him. They liked Emily, all of them. MacLeod asked him to "trust" her. Surely they knew she had sacrificed herself to save him. Plan, indeed! What plan could she have formed in so short a time? Emily had no experience in battle. She was trusting and innocent. She probably thought she could befriend Davis and convince him to pardon Darian.

The woman had too much confidence. This, more than anything, made Darian ride out into the night, urging his horse to a gallop as he crossed the desert plains. She wore confidence as a shield, but the vulnerability within could pierce his heart. She needed him. He could not fail her now.

As he rode, images of the past assailed him. He saw his brother, Oliver, leading his company in a charge toward death, because Darian's company was under desperate fire. He saw Oliver ahead of the rest, and he saw his brother fall in a spray of blood and gunfire. He saw Wetherspoon aiming a gun with no hope of survival. . . .

He saw Emily give herself up because she had known Darian would not let Ping die. Darian's horse galloped, leaping forward over rocks and cactus with great strides, its sides heaving with the exertion. Its hoofbeats thundered across the desert. He would have to stop and hide the horse before they reached Tucson, but the time covered now could make the difference between life and death for Emily.

He heard Tiotonawen's warning in his mind. *"Surrender what you hold too dear."* What if the old man had meant Emily? He would give up everything to save her, no matter the cost. Was it possible to love too much?

No. No one would expect him to surrender his wife.

Stobie Piel

Yet he knew the Apache chief had wisdom, and there was meaning behind those words. If he could find it, he might save his wife. If not, he would lose far more and far worse than his own life.

Chapter Fourteen

"So you're the bandit's whore. . . ." Clement Davis sat back in his seat, Belle standing close behind him. They made no attempt to deny their intimacy. She massaged his shoulders like a doting wife as he interrogated Emily.

Soldiers stood on guard outside the saloon doors, and Emily was tied to a chair near the bar. She understood her own vulnerability, and the fear of captivity with a man who hated her husband had grown toward terror when she arrived back in Tucson. She met his impenetrable, dark eyes without wavering, not for her own sake, but for Darian's—his wife would not be remembered as a coward.

"As a matter of fact, I recently became Darian's bride." She glanced at Belle. "A whore refers to a woman who places a low value on her self and her sexuality, who gives herself indiscriminately to any man. . . ." She eyed Davis and shook her head. "However silly and unattractive he might be."

Belle read her meaning and glared, but Davis gave her a low-lidded smirk. He reminded her of a pompous businessman who attended a Confidence Betterment seminar she had once tried in Phoenix, when she was trying to free herself from the self-doubt that haunted her after Ian divorced her. The businessman had "shared" his supposed life secrets at every opportunity, while Emily had checked her watch and wondered if she was any better yet.

Davis had the same look, one of confidence and superiority that covered a weak mind and a weaker heart. Both men were a little too thin in the shoulders, their mustaches a little too big and too well groomed, indicating too much time spent looking into a mirror. Their hair curled into tight waves, just a little too even, and a smirk never quite left their faces.

Sitting quietly during the seminar, Emily had formed a lasting impression of that man, because many of his confessions centered around the affairs he'd had at his office, trying to find a woman advanced enough to understand him—until he mentioned finally casually that his *wife* "just didn't get it."

Emily watched now as Davis offered Belle a patronizing slap to her backside. "I think you get reincarnated, General."

He eyed her suspiciously. "What are you talking about, pretty lady?"

Emily groaned. "Yep. That's just what he called me, too."

Belle intensified her ministrations upon Davis's shoulders. "Don't let her get talking, Clem. She's a devil, she is, just as bad as Woodward himself."

Emily felt proud. "Thank you. It's true, Darian and I

have more in common than I thought when I first met him." She had met the man of her dreams, fallen in love, and married—all without a friend to share her joy. She thought of Cora, and wondered how she and Adrian would feel about the romantic turn of her quest back in time. Maybe they expected it. Or maybe they'd feel that her love for Darian had clouded her ability to save him.

She fought a peculiar desire to prattle on about Darian to his enemies, and remembered her true task. Belle wore a large golden locket around her neck, well made and expensive-looking. Despite her tacky nature, she was always well-dressed. "That's a pretty necklace, Belle. I have to say, as repugnant as I find you, that I do admire your taste."

Belle missed the insult entirely. She patted Davis's shoulder and said, "Clem keeps his woman in fine style, girl. Don't expect your outlaw husband to give you anything like this! He may have robbed a coach of gold, but he ain't half smart enough to keep his neck out of a noose."

Davis's eyes narrowed as if he didn't like Belle's loose tongue, but, like the businessman at the seminar, he forced a broad smile when he was nervous. "Woodward is an outlaw and a traitor to his country; his honor is forfeit. He *will* find justice, because I am committed as a man of true honor to that end."

"A pat speech." Emily tried to cross her legs, but remembered that her ankles were tied. She rolled her eyes, and attempted a casual expression despite her bonds. "I had no idea officers were paid so much as to drop expensive baubles in their mistress's lap."

Davis's eyes narrowed still more, until they formed lizard-like slits. "It was a family heirloom, given to Belle in thanks for her loyalty to our country."

Emily snorted and arched her brows. "If that's what you call it. . . ."

Belle tossed her head. "I serve my country real well."

Emily peered toward the ceiling as if searching her memory. "I think I've heard this one before. You're 'just friends,' right?"

Davis looked smug, but Belle wasn't smiling. "I know where to give my friendship, girl!"

Emily turned to Davis. "And what about your wife? Does she approve of this dear 'friendship'?" His dark eyes flashed in true surprise. Emily smiled. "I had a hunch you were married. So where is she? Back east?"

A quick glance told her Belle was aware of Davis's marriage. A shame, because Emily had hoped the news would inspire Belle to reveal some of Davis's darker secrets. "Clem don't have no use for that skinny baggage."

Emily nodded. "So she's not rich, then?"

"She weren't rich or nothing," Belle said. Davis shot her a warning glance, as if he guessed where Emily's line of questions was heading, but Belle didn't notice. "He married her before he got the chance for something better. . . ."

Emily nodded again. "She was pregnant, I guess."

"She claimed to be, but she turned out to be barren."

"Barren and poor. So your current situation isn't based on your wife's money, either."

Davis appeared tense, and his smile grew harder, more forced. "My 'situation' is nothing unusual, Mrs. Woodward. One gift to a friend is hardly an indication of great wealth."

Emily assessed Belle's gold damask gown and arched her brow meaningfully. "*One* gift? That woman has more gowns than Queen Victoria, and just as many jewels. I don't think she got them herself. But maybe she has more 'friends' than just yourself."

It was the perfect gibe. Before Davis could stop her, Belle surged forward and shook her fist at Emily, rattling the heavy golden bracelets around her wrist. "You hush your mouth now, impudent girl! Everything I got, I got from Clem! I ain't dallying with no other man!"

Emily turned to Davis, whose smirk had finally faded to a dark frown. "Isn't that interesting? Those bracelets she's wearing must cost a year's salary alone. And the dress. . . . Hmmm."

Davis rose abruptly from his chair. "Tradman!" He paused. "Where the hell is he?"

Belle tapped his shoulder. "Bill's upstairs with Agatha. She's showing him a real fine time."

Emily grimaced. "Gross. I don't need to hear this."

"A lot you know about men, girl, what with that baby-faced, blue-eyed husband of yours. Bet he don't know nothing about pleasuring a woman."

Davis seemed to like this implication and his smirk returned. "I know Woodward. He'd spend the night quoting poetry."

Emily considered arguing on Darian's behalf, but she didn't want to go overboard. "Darian knows every verse Shakespeare ever wrote." She had no idea if he knew a single word, but knowing Darian, it didn't seem impossible. "He's very romantic."

Davis scoffed. "Romantic! Woodward wouldn't know the first thing about a woman."

"He knows better than to purchase her with trinkets while married to another." It was crazy of her to defy him, and she knew it, but Emily had taken enough. "But then, he hasn't robbed quite enough coaches of gold yet to be able to afford the kind of gifts I see on Belle."

Davis's income was obviously a topic of secrecy, but

how would she prove it had something to do with his condemnation of Darian? Emily sensed this was the angle she had to pursue if she was to prove Darian's innocence, but she had so little time. "So where did you find that lovely dress, General? Marita didn't sew it—she told me that you provide all Belle's gowns."

He knew where she was heading, and he was too smart to fall for it. "Let's talk about something more interesting, shall we? Such as where your blue-eyed husband is hiding."

"Right! Like I'm going to tell you that!"

Davis caught her chin in his hand, a patronizing gesture. Emily met his mocking gaze straight-on, showing no fear. "It doesn't matter. Woodward will have his red friends at his side, and I'm not fool enough to walk into another ambush. No, I've got the trump card now. I've got *you*."

"Darian knows I can take care of myself."

"And leave his wife, a lady, in my grasp? I know your husband better than that. He made a damned fool of himself fawning over that cursed Indian's woman. If he doesn't show up tonight to rescue you, I'll be surprised."

It was like Darian to try to rescue her. . . . "What Indian's woman?"

"Tiotonawen's son and the white wench he had captive." Davis's eyes glinted as if hoping to find a sore spot. "Didn't know about that, did you? Your pretty husband was falling all over his feet to take her for himself."

Emily didn't respond. Had Darian been in love with Cora? It wasn't hard to imagine. Cora was all the things Emily could never be, sweet and feminine, yet still elegant and brave. The contrast between herself, rather small and dark, against Cora, tall and willowy and blond, seemed, marked.

"Cora and Adrian are married and very happy. Darian was happy for them."

Belle looked at Davis in surprise. "I thought you said that Indian was dead."

Davis's jaw set to one side. "It seems I was mistaken. So you know of them, do you? It would heighten my victory if I could bring in that damned Indian to hang beside your husband."

"I'm afraid that's impossible, general. . . ." Emily stopped herself. She couldn't alert him to the true nature of her presence in that past. Giving Clement Davis the knowledge of time-travel might truly pose some danger to the world. "But give it your best shot. I think you'll find them living happily in the Andes mountains in Peru."

Davis hesitated, then apparently decided Peru was too far to go—even to bring Adrian de Vargas to justice. "He's out of the country. That's good enough."

"Then maybe you'd consider exiling Darian instead. Killing him would truly be a blot against your soul."

"A blot against my soul?" Davis leaned closer to her, so that she could feel his breath. "My dear Mrs. Woodward, your husband's death will see my way into heaven, and there is nothing, nothing that can stop me from seeing him crumple from the scaffold into his coffin, and dropped into the ground."

Tucson slept uneasily. Darian crept like a ghost into the quiet town, but he felt the eyes that watched for him. No moon lit the sky, and distant clouds hid the stars. Fate protected him, this night.

He concealed himself in the blacksmith's shed and surveyed the main street ahead. Two men staggered drunkenly from the saloon. Darian recognized the sheriff and one of the bankers. Apparently, the progress he'd established in Tucson wasn't as lasting as he'd hoped.

The men ambled in the other direction, and Darian saw no soldiers near them. The jailhouse was dark, but he detected the light of a dim lantern within. Someone was being watched, and not by the sheriff.

Darian moved silently from the blacksmith's shed nearer to the jailhouse. Two soldiers stood guard outside the entrance. Dark shapes moved to and fro behind the barred window. One reached for a bottle, then set it down as if ordered not to drink. The prisoner they guarded was either very dangerous—or Emily.

Darian made his way to the rear wall of the jailhouse. He stopped to listen, but though he heard muffled voices within, he couldn't make out the words spoken. He moved close along the side wall, until the dim light slanted from the nearest window.

He had to risk a quick glance, lest he break into the jail for nothing. He moved closer, then looked in the window. The gunfighter, Tradman, sat in a chair, his boots on the sheriff's desk while a young soldier stood on guard by the first cell. Darian couldn't see beyond the bars, but he knew Emily sat within. If they were guarding her, she was alive, and she was well enough to be a threat.

Darian sank back into the darkness to plan his assault, but something about the young guard bothered him. The boy was tall, with pale blond hair, a straight, proud stance, and a clean uniform. Darian scratched his neck, wondering why those traits should give him pause. But he knew instinctively that the boy was doing his duty, trusting in his commander's judgment, as Darian himself had done during his first months in the Western territory.

If Darian was to break Emily out of this jail and get away with her before being seen, there would likely be gunfire. He had no qualms about shooting Tradman, but that young soldier. . . . Darian closed his eyes. Emily's life hung in the balance. He would do what he had to do.

Darian checked his revolver, then went to the front door. He tested it, shoved it open, then backed away into the darkness. He heard Tradman's chair overturn as the gunfighter leapt up, he heard orders shouted.

"What the hell was that? Forbes!"

"Do you think it's Woodward, sir?" The soldier sounded young, too, but Darian detected no fear. "I have the key on my belt. He'll have to get through me to reach his wife."

For a reason Darian didn't understand, the young man's vow triggered an unfamiliar ache in his own heart, as if he heard himself speak from a great distance. The distance of time.

Darian steeled himself against doubt and waited. He saw Tradman's shadow emerge from the jailhouse door. Darian pitched a rock across the square, and Tradman dropped to one knee, aiming. With a keen eye, Darian aimed another rock at the blacksmith's anvil, then let it fly. The anvil twanged and Tradman growled an order to the guards. "Over there. Get the others, and we'll have him surrounded."

Darian rolled his eyes at the ease of it all. He waited, hidden in darkness as the soldiers assembled under Tradman's dubious orders. They spread out, taking position around the blacksmith's shed. Darian hesitated, then threw another, smaller rock so that it knocked the blacksmith's pinchers from the wall hanging. He smiled when the soldiers reacted.

Darian left the shadows and circled the jailhouse on the far side, then went to the entrance, his revolver drawn and ready. He kicked the door open and stepped into the light. Blue eyes met blue eyes as the young soldier startled. For a moment, they stared at each other. He found a startling resemblance in the young soldier's face—not to himself, but to his brother.

Darian swallowed, but the soldier aimed his revolver to kill. Darian hesitated. He had never hesitated here, at the brink of life, before. He saw the trigger drawn, and his instincts took over. He dropped, rolled to one side, then bounded up. He moved like a predator, an animal intent on killing to survive. He caught the boy soldier and held his gun against the boy's head.

He had to shoot or the kid would call out, bringing the whole damned lot down on the jail. But he couldn't. . . . "Forbes, you listen and you listen well. I'm here for my wife. Nothing else. I don't want to shoot you, but I've got to get her out of here."

For an instant, held interminably as Darian waited, Forbes hesitated as if warring between duty and instinct. Then, with the force of a young man doing what he feels is right, the soldier shouted. "Woodward, in here! Woodward!"

Before Darian's finger could clench the trigger something came down hard and strong on Forbes's head. A metal plate. Darian jerked in surprise. He looked up and saw Emily with tears running down her cheeks.

"He's so much like you. . . ."

Darian stood, shocked beyond fear and beyond life. She had saved him, more truly than had she cut the noose around his neck. "Emmy. . . ."

"Darian, get the keys. They're coming!"

Darian yanked the keys from the soldier's belt and unlocked Emily's cell. He shoved the dazed Forbes inside. He grabbed Emily's hand and pulled her to the door. Men ran everywhere, racing to cut him off before he could break free, but Darian couldn't stop now. He had her. Now he had to get her out of Tucson to safety.

Darian took shelter behind the door and pushed Emily behind him. "Emmy, I'm going to have to fight our way out of here. I can do it, but it won't be easy. For once in your life, you're going to have to do exactly what I tell you. Run when I say run. . . . Do you understand?"

She nodded, but though he saw fear in her eyes, he also saw something else. Courage. Emily retrieved Forbes's fallen revolver and Darian watched amazed as she checked it the way he always did himself. "Shoot when you say shoot. I understand."

He didn't think of arguing. "Just shoot straight."

She smiled. "I always do."

Darian nodded, signaling her the way he had always communicated to his men. Apparently, Emily had picked up a lot during their journey. She obeyed without question. They ran from the jailhouse, heading to the buildings on the east side of the road. Emily took the right, and Darian the left. Their action surprised the soldiers, and guns fired wildly, hitting no mark but the side of the wall.

Emily fired, and a man staggered back gripping his arm. Darian smiled. He should have known she could shoot. Darian fired again, and another man fell. For an instant, he thought beyond hope they might win and escape, but Tradman spotted Emily and moved in to kill.

Darian leapt into the street and fired. The gunfighter fell forward, clutching his gut. He grimaced as death swarmed over him, but the gunfighter didn't drop his gun. Emily moved back as Darian signaled, but her sudden scream startled him. Darian whirled to see a soldier aiming at his head. Emily jumped forward, running toward Darian. She stopped, aimed, and fired.

The shot knocked the man to his knees. Darian ran through the gunfire to her, but as she turned to run with him, running to freedom, Tradman fired his last shot.

The bullet grazed Emily's head and knocked her against a wall. Darian fired, and Tradman sank dead to the ground.

Darian ran as if the wind carried him to Emily. He bent to pick her up, but from the corner of his eye, he saw the young guard, Forbes, aiming at Darian's head. This boy wouldn't miss. He had the keen, bright eyes of a man who hits his target. *My eyes.* And Darian saw his own death before him, unavoidable. . . .

He closed his eyes, and he saw his brother, Oliver. *Please, let me save her. I love her so. . . .*

A second flashed by, and Darian lived. He opened his eyes and met the soldier's steady gaze. For a moment only, the boy hesitated, and Darian saw the war raging within between what is deemed right, against what is truly good. With the slightest motion, the boy nodded.

Darian lifted Emily into his arms, but she didn't move. He heard Forbes's shot, gone purposefully awry, but he didn't look back. Darkness swallowed them as Darian carried Emily out into the desert into the starless night. Bullets flew over his head, but he paid them no heed. Nothing mattered but the woman in his arms. He ran while his lungs ached, while his body screamed inside as if on fire. He stumbled, and his vision blurred.

Rain fell. In Arizona, in a dark night so dry that no water could form. But rain obscured his vision and he ran blind through it, as it stung his face and coursed into his hair. He didn't know where he was going, but the pursuit faltered behind him. Tradman's death had thrown off the soldiers and left them uncertain, giving Darian time to escape.

Darian carried Emily to a mound of boulders and laid her gently behind the shelter. They wouldn't be found before morning.

He knelt beside her, and still the mist fell to his face.

His hands shook as he checked for her pulse. When it met his fingertips, soft but steady, he heard a sharp cry of relief, then realized it came from himself. She was alive. She lay in his arms, her head cradled against his chest, and she breathed. She was alive.

Darian buried his face against her neck and sobbed.

Emily tried to open her eyes, but she couldn't move. She wondered if she was dead, after all, but Darian held her close. She felt his arms tight around her, his face against her neck. A strange sound rumbled from deep inside him.

Her neck was wet.

Suddenly, with shock and with force, Emily recognized the sound. Darian was crying. Not a gentle flow of tears, but deep, anguished sobs poured from the deep well of his heart.

Into her mind came an image of the Apache chief, and he was smiling. *The onion is down to his core.* Emily didn't try to stop him. She moved her hand to touch his head and she stroked his hair gently, letting him cry, and the softest, most wonderful feeling she had ever known surrounded her. The heart of the man she loved had opened wide at last, and all he was inside was giving itself to her.

When he felt her touch, he tried to contain himself, but Emily kissed his head, then rested her cheek against his hair. "We're all right. Darian, it's all right now. You saved me."

At last, his tears abated, and he gathered her up into his arms. "Forgive me."

Emily touched the side of his face. He had become so dear, beyond heroism, beyond desire—a spirit so dear that nothing could ever surpass what they found together. "Forgive you? For what?"

Darian held her against his body, rocking her like a child. "For ever risking your life, for letting you go."

"I don't remember giving you a choice."

"I should have stopped you."

Emily sank closer into his arms. "I keep telling myself that about you, you know."

Darian drew back to look at her. "Telling yourself what?"

"That I should have saved you before now. That's what I came here to do, after all. Adrian didn't send me back in time to seduce you. He thought I could save you."

Darian smiled. "It seems neither of us is too agreeable to being saved."

"No, it seems we're not. But we did all right tonight."

Darian kissed her cheek, and Emily's soul filled with happiness. "You, especially, my dear. I had no idea women of the future were so proficient with the revolver. How did you learn?"

"Well, not in the future, that's for sure. I'd never touched a gun before tonight."

"Then how did you learn?"

"From watching you, of course."

Darian looked amazed and impressed, and Emily felt satisfied. "You learn quickly."

"I thought the same of you on our wedding night."

She knew he blushed, though it was too dark to tell. "My learning was the more interesting, I fear."

Emily leaned to kiss him. Their lips met softly, a gentle union heralding a love that would never be broken. She wrapped her arms around his neck and held him. "What now? Do we head back to the caves?"

Darian hesitated. "I'm not sure exactly how to progress at this point. My horse is nearby, but I don't think we can reach the caves by morning. Considering the pursuit Davis is likely to engage, it seems unwise to move during the day hours. This spot I've found offers shelter, and you must rest."

"I'm all right. I think we should at least move into the hills, if we can."

"Are you sure, Emmy? Are you well enough?"

Emily paused to consider the state of her body. "My head hurts, but it's not bad. The shot went past me, but I hit the wall pretty hard."

"I thought you'd been shot." Darian's voice sounded small.

"I'm fine."

Darian appeared convinced. He rose and looked around. "What happened to the rain?"

"What rain? I don't remember any rain." Emily paused. "Darian, we're in Arizona."

"I felt it distinctly when I was running, carrying you. Rain on my face."

Emily's heart ached with love as she reached to touch his damp face. "Darian. . . . You were crying. Didn't you know?"

His blue eyes widened with shock, then misted with another veil of soft, beautiful tears. "I have not cried in a very long time."

"Since your brother's death."

He nodded. "I thought I could never lose anything again so dear, but Emmy, if I had lost you, I would have welcomed my hanging, for life would hold no meaning."

Emily wrapped her arms around his neck and hugged him, then kissed his face. "Life happens to us, and most of the time, it's so unexpected. I have thought for most of my life that the only person I can rely on is myself. Since I met you, I've learned that if you love me, if you let me love you, then nothing that happens can touch me."

He held her close against his strong body, so that she heard the beat of his heart and felt his warmth. "Emmy, I never expected you. I never imagined I could deserve the heart of a woman like you. I never knew there *was* a woman like you. I don't know if I deserve you now, but it doesn't matter. You are the gift to my life, and I am grateful, for you came from a higher place where there is no question of deserving or not, but only on the one thing that matters where all else fails."

His voice trailed, his blue eyes shining, and Emily felt the full force of life flying inside her, as if now finally life was perfect, trust was perfect. "On love."

He smiled. "On love."

Chapter Fifteen

They lay together as the sun peeked over the eastern hills, as it turned the saguaro cactus from dark, mystic shapes back to green. Neither spoke. Darian watched the sky change color as it crowned the desert. The purple hills, the golden sand—these things had become dear to him since he rode west. His wife had slept in his arms, and he knew they were truly home.

Now he glanced down to see if she was awake, not wanting to disturb her, but needing her also. She looked up at him with a slow, sensual smile, her eyelids lowered in that way he had come to know, to dream of, to need to the depth of his soul.

Marriage was so much more than he ever imagined. No venting of lust, no chivalrous speeches. Just this deep connection between two souls who wanted more than anything else to be together. Once, when Adrian de Vargas first brought Cora back in time, Darian had imagined himself in love with her. Maybe it was because she seemed a lot like himself, or because she was the kind of woman he'd always pictured himself marrying. But now he knew he would never find true happiness with any woman but Emily.

In all the world, in all time, only Emily belonged to him. Only he belonged to her. They were one thing, two halves of a whole, joined at last.

Mating between them took on a far vaster meaning, and yielded far greater satisfaction because he sensed this bond between them had been forever, and would never end. Not only his body, but his soul, too, found perfect bliss in her arms.

She was still watching him, a bemused expression on her face. She reached to touch his cheek. "What are you thinking?"

Darian propped himself up on one elbow and looked down into her eyes. "I was thinking that you and I are truly one thing, so that when I take you in conjugal bliss, our pleasure is far exalted from what it might have been with anyone else."

Her smile widened. "I've noticed that."

He hesitated, then brushed an errant curl from her cheek. "Was it thus with my counterpart?" Why was it so hard to say her former husband's name? Why did the thought of Ian Hallowell trouble him so, when he only half believed her claim of them being the same man?

Emily's smile faded and she sighed. "I loved Ian, so I gave him all myself. But was it like this? No. He always seemed to hold something of himself from me, as if he was afraid to give fully. Our fears and our doubts drove us apart, I suppose. You give yourself with all your heart, and you're not afraid to take all of me."

Darian's brow angled. "I don't fear that anymore, it's

true." He paused. "But if you're in pain, from your injury."

"I had a bump on the head. It's not bad."

"I wouldn't want to put any demands on you when you are in a recuperative state."

"I am completely recovered, my love." Her lips curled with womanly invitation and he touched her mouth. She kissed his fingertips, and a hot shiver coursed through him, centering mercilessly in his groin.

Darian bent to kiss her, feeling the softness of her lips against his. He slid his tongue between her lips and she engaged him in a sensual dance until his need spread throughout his body. He unbuttoned her blouse and slipped his hand beneath the sheer fabric.

Emily murmured and ran her hands over his shoulders and down his back. She seemed to like his strength, and her appreciation fueled his own pleasure simply at being a man. Darian drew back to pull off his uniform jacket, then his shirt. She dampened her lips eagerly as his chest was revealed, and Darian smiled. He had never truly known the thrill of being desired this way, of knowing he could pleasure her with a touch, with a kiss.

His body was a tool for her pleasure, and he would learn every aspect that delighted her. Darian sat back and let her look at him. Her fingers grazed his chest with a soft touch, then slid down over his stomach. Darian removed his trousers and set them by his cast-off boots, then placed his hand over her heart. He felt the quick intake of her breaths, and saw the wild pulse at the base of her throat.

"Do you want me, here, Emmy? Here in the desert, would you have me love you?"

Her eyelids drifted shut and her breath came like a sigh of joy. "I would."

He wanted to wait, to take hours to make love to her,

but Emily seemed eager. She squirmed free of her dress, awkwardly because she wasn't familiar with the garments of his time. He noticed that she had abandoned her corset somewhere along the line, as well as the petticoat beneath.

She tossed her dress aside, then lay back naked before him. Her shapely, beautiful legs bent at the knees, and her feet looked even smaller than he remembered. So small, and yet so sure of herself. She held out her arms, and he lowered himself above her.

He wanted to make love to her perfectly, but something stronger burned between them. As she reached for him, he knew what he wanted. He wanted her now, he wanted to be deep inside her, where she was truly his. He wanted to know he would never lose her again.

Darian positioned his length between her legs, then hesitated. She deserved more, the tender kisses and touch of her loving husband, not the desperate passion of a man who feared he might never hold her again. But Emily slipped her hands between their bodies and gripped his staff in her small hands. As he watched spellbound, she guided his erection back and forth over her woman's mound, letting her soft curls tease his heated flesh.

As her gaze fixed seductively on his, she guided him lower until he met the slippery flesh that welcomed him and lured him beyond resistance. He hesitated, still unsure, but her fingers wrapped tight around his base while she arched beneath him. It was too much—he could stand no more. Darian drove himself deep inside her. He watched the look of surprise on her face, followed by the intoxicating pleasure of his entry.

She gripped him still, her fingers heightening the wild pleasure of being inside her body. Darian moved, and she followed him. Fire coursed through his veins, seizing control of his actions and driving him wild as it escalated, spiraling tighter and tighter as their bodies strove together.

Emily's eyes closed and she bit her lip. Her hips arched to increase the friction between them. She freed her hands from between them, and clutched his shoulders tight to steady herself. They made love with all the fury of passion, defying all that stood against them, and all that threatened to deny them each other. They rode long, slow waves to their pinnacle, prolonging each moment until neither could resist the fever. Their climax came at once, together, as if it had been one thing, as if *they* were one thing.

Waves and waves of pleasure spilled through him, pouring from him into her. For a moment, they were beyond time and beyond fear, and nothing could separate them. Darian felt as if together, they touched eternity, and it would linger forever no matter what followed.

The spasms of ecstasy slowed, then faded, leaving tiny shocks twitching through his body in the aftermath. For a long while, Darian stayed inside her, holding her close. Then he withdrew and gathered her into his arms. They lay silent together once more as the morning sun made its way over the purple hills. When it formed a golden crown over the highest peak, he turned to her and took her hand.

"Emmy, no matter what happens, no matter where we end up, we have this love between us."

Emily smiled up at him, true contentment in her eyes. "I know."

Emily lay with her head against Darian's chest, but though he drifted toward sleep, a sense of urgency grew inside her. *We have to get out of here.*

She prodded his shoulder. "Darian, it's time to go. We have to get back to the caves."

Darian sighed heavily. "It's still early yet, love. The sun is barely topped the horizon."

Emily poked him again, more fiercely. "It's well up over the hills. Get up."

Darian yawned. "Perhaps it's the moon you see." He closed his eyes. "It's the nightingale, love."

"This is no time for Shakespeare!" She paused. "Well, I told Davis right about one thing. You can quote Shakespeare."

Darian smiled, his eyes still closed. "Every verse."

Emily seized his shoulders and shook him. Darian opened one eye. "I am well sated, Emmy, but if you request it. . . ."

"There's no time for sex!" She paused again. He was so good at it. Manly and passionate, and tender at once. "You are a wonderful lover."

"I know."

Emily grabbed his clothes and placed them on top of him. "Please, get dressed. We have to get out of here."

He opened his other eye, too. "Why?"

"I don't know. Call it woman's intuition, but I have a feeling we're in danger."

Darian sighed. "We're always in danger, but if it will make you feel better. . . ." He rose with obvious reluctance and gathered their gear, then held out his hand for her.

They stood face to face, and as she gazed up at him, she saw the blue Arizona sky mirrored in his eyes. "Darian Woodward, you are so beautiful."

He smiled and laid his hand gently against her cheek. "My dear wife, I can never behold more beauty than I see in you. Not just for the perfection of your face, or the way your hair falls around your shoulders, nor even for the feminine delicacy of your body. . . ." As he spoke, his gaze shifted to her body, and those blue eyes darkened. "Although those attributes are much welcomed, and cherished by me."

She'd never truly felt beautiful, but she did today. "I see that."

He bent to kiss her and he looked a little shy. "Last night, when I saw you there beside me, I realized I wasn't looking at a fragile woman who needs my protection. I was looking at a woman with all the courage I strive for myself, because you act from your heart."

Emily liked this praise even better than the compliments directed at her physical self. "I have never felt brave. I've felt like I was fighting all my life just to catch up."

He kissed her forehead. "Then you need fight no longer, my love. You won that battle long ago."

Emily didn't respond, but she knew the only battle worth fighting was the one for Darian's life.

He untethered his horse and helped Emily into the saddle. He got on behind her, and they headed for the eastern hills that harbored the bandits' secret hideout. They rode for an hour, taking the longer trek through a path with foliage for concealment. When they reached the shelter of the foothills, Darian relaxed.

"We should be out of danger for the time being, my dear. No one, even one of Davis's Indian scouts, can track us here."

Emily looked back over her shoulder. There was no sign of pursuit, but her uneasiness refused to yield. She felt as if the danger wasn't behind them, in pursuit, but ahead, as yet unnamed.

She knew where they were going—to the Colossal Caves where Darian's men waited. Why hadn't they accompanied him? Maybe Darian hadn't wanted to risk their lives, but her uneasiness grew.

Darian turned his gray horse southward and they began the climb up into the hills. The horse startled, then snorted as if calling an alarm. Emily looked up at Darian as he drew his revolver. Her heart throbbed with uncertain fear. "What is it?"

Darian shaded his bright eyes against the new morning sun. "There."

Emily looked in the direction he indicated. Three men on horseback stood silhouetted against the sun, dark shapes she couldn't make out well enough to identify. Her heart held its beat, she didn't breathe. "Who are they?"

Two more riders appeared on the horizon. The sun glinted on the black and white coat of a stout pinto, and Emily gasped a breath of relief. "Ping. It's your men. Thank God!"

Darian relaxed, too, and holstered his revolver. He guided his horse up the hill. As they climbed, the sun released its shadow, illuminating the five men who waited on the hilltop. MacLeod was at the center, but between MacLeod and Herring, the men had left a spot for their leader. For Darian.

Emily's uneasiness disappeared. They were home.

Darian held up his hand in a wave, smiling. Emily glanced at him, and saw both love and a sense of forgiveness in his eyes. Maybe his men had refused to accompany him, but he understood and wouldn't hold it against them.

Emily waved, too.

Darian ascended the hill to take his place again with his men. But as he reached the summit, MacLeod moved his horse to the side, and another man rode up from the far side of the hill.

Clement Davis sat atop an immense black horse, one hand on his hip in a posture of utter assurance. Emily stared in disbelief. Darien reined his horse back, but he seemed too stunned by his enemy's presence among his men to react. Slowly, he drew his revolver and aimed, but he didn't pull the trigger.

"Woodward. . . . We meet at last, face to face." Even the general's tone was smug. Emily's heart filled with hatred. What had he done to Darian's men? What horrible threat had he levied over them? At least, they were all present, so no one was dead.

Darian glanced at his men, and for the first time, Emily noticed their expressions. Not smiling, but hard, they looked more like enemies than the general himself.

It's not possible. . . .

Darian kept his gaze fixed on the general, but he nodded to Emily. "Emmy, get down, and get under cover."

Emily refused to move, but the general held up his hand. "Your wife is in no danger. In fact, she can ride free among us."

Darian hesitated. "Us?"

MacLeod slumped like a man possessed not of his usual solid dignity, but arrogance instead. "Got tired of following you, *'Captain.'* You promised us a hell of a lot more than hiding out like a bunch of stinking rats. Ruin your own name. From now on, we're back on the side of the law."

Darian's mouth opened, but he didn't seem quite willing to believe his soldiers had betrayed him. Emily felt certain they hadn't. It had to be a ploy, a ruse of some kind. They must have a plan of some sort.

General Davis smiled, gloating, more arrogant than Emily had yet seen him. She wished she could summon a laugh to remind him of his personal failings, but her power felt gone, her hope shattered. "It seems your men

281

have had a change of heart. Fortuitous for the side of 'right,' isn't it? My men couldn't bring you in . . . but your own? Who among them will you shoot first?"

Darian's fingers clenched around his revolver. Tears blurred Emily's eyes. "Darian, shoot him. It's the only way."

Davis recoiled, then puffed in arrogance again. "Dare you shoot me, Woodward? Can you be sure of your pretty wife's fate? In this, before your men and my own . . ." Davis gestured behind the hill. "You didn't think I came alone, did you?" He paused to laugh. "In this matter, you have my word. Your wife will go unharmed, and no charges will be brought against her. She did no more than accompany you as your whore, after all. A woman can't be blamed for staying at the side of a man worth a coach-load of gold."

Emily's hands clenched into fists. "Well, you should know! It must take more than a 'coachload of gold' to keep Belle at your side, that's for sure!"

Davis's smirk disappeared, but Emily met his challenging stare defiantly. They had nothing left to lose. "You won't be harmed, pretty lady. It's against the custom of the United States Cavalry to hang a woman for her own foolishness. As it happens, I have enlisted the commanding officer of Fort Lowell to witness your husband's hanging. Nothing will be handled out of its due course."

Emily looked up at Darian. "What do we do? Can we run?"

He shook his head. "There is only one thing we can do, Emmy." He paused and closed his eyes. His head tipped back so that the morning sun fell fully on his beautiful golden-tanned skin. "Surrender."

Emily seized his hand. "No, Darian. The only thing we can do now is trust."

* * *

Trust came harder than Emily had imagined. She expected secret signals between Darian and at least MacLeod. She expected a reassuring look from Ping. Surely, Ping couldn't keep a secret this well. But as they rode back to Tucson, nothing revealed itself.

Emily rode Darian's gray horse, while Darian himself walked behind Davis's horse, his hands bound behind his back. Emily kept looking back to see if he was all right, but Darian revealed no hardship. He simply walked along, straight-backed and proud, his head high despite the dirt and dust kicked up by Davis's oversized mount.

She knew he expected retribution. He expected justice to turn in his favor, because he was in the right. Darian had always believed right would prevail, somehow. Emily wanted desperately to speak with his men, separately if possible. She couldn't risk any plan they might have concocted by talking to them now, but surely, alone, they would reassure her and fill her in on their scheme.

It had to be a scheme. But as they reached the outskirts of Tucson, her doubts grew stronger. What if Darian's fate as Ian wasn't brought about by the deaths of his loyal followers as she'd imagined earlier? What if, instead, he had been completely devastated by their unexpected betrayal? No wonder their executions weren't recorded alongside Darian's—not a one had died. All those men, Herring, Ping, MacLeod, even Bonner and Clyde, had turned against him to save themselves.

She had no idea what she was up against, but somehow she would have to turn them back to Darian's side. Emily fought against panic. It wasn't impossible. She would remind them of their days in the war. Ping had wept at the memory of Darian's heroism and courage, and even more, because of his compassion. MacLeod thought of him like a son, and respected him like a king.

She had no idea what Bonner and Clyde thought, but they had followed him this far. He never questioned their activities, even when Emily felt sure that a good portion of the bank's proceeds had left Tucson in Bonner and Clyde's pockets. Darian had respected their honor. Surely, they would respect his.

As they rode into town, Emily's resolve hardened. She would convince Darian's men to save him, one way or another. It was possible that Davis had confused them, so it was up to her to find proof that Davis himself was corrupt.

Everyone in Tucson waited at the end of the street, gathered to see the outlaw Darian Woodward at last brought to justice. Marita stood with Penelope, and both women appeared confused. Agatha stood close beside a soldier, so Emily guessed Tradman's death hadn't affected her adversely. The bib Darian had fitted over her ample cleavage had long since been tossed aside.

Clement Davis rode into town like a conquering hero, a pompous king returned from the crusades, finally victorious against unspeakable barbarism. He held up his hand and the crowd cheered. Emily cast a quick glance at Darian's men. Here, she would see their true loyalties emerge. But instead of the barely concealed anger she'd expected and hoped for, MacLeod smiled like a hero himself. Ping waved at Penelope, beaming, and Herring doffed his hat to the ladies as they rode past. Bonner and Clyde revealed no emotion, but neither did the scene unfolding seem to disturb them.

Emily met Penelope's sorrowful gaze and saw pity, but no reassurance. Clearly, Ping's beloved had no idea of any daring scheme on Darian's behalf. Her disquiet soared when Marita brushed away tears. The fort soldiers called out congratulations to MacLeod, while hurtling angry insults at Darian. Only one soldier stood quiet and apart from the rest. Emily recognized her young jailer, Forbes. His brow furrowed as if he warred inwardly.

But against what? The likeness to Darian gave Emily hope. Maybe she could convince the young man to listen, and even to help her. Maybe he suspected something about Davis. It was a long shot, but if she couldn't count on Darian's men, it might be the only hope she had left.

Davis's guards seized the rope that bound Darian, then led him toward the jailhouse. He offered no resistance and Davis frowned. A guard took his commander's hint and yanked Darian forward to his knees.

Davis laughed, too loudly. "You see, ladies and gentleman. Our blue-eyed outlaw is already on his knees!"

The crowd erupted in laughter. Even Ping pointed as if at a clown's antics.

Darian revealed no emotion. His face remained utterly impassive, showing nothing of humiliation or fear or hurt. He simply regained his footing, stood up and waited until they tugged him forward. Davis laughed again, and Emily's heart throbbed with fury and hatred.

Davis gestured at Darian. "Already as gentle as a lamb! I've brought the boy to heel at last."

The guard hauled Darian forward. The crowd laughed again, but with less enthusiasm. Darian's innate dignity remained untarnished. If they'd dragged him behind a horse across the desert, leaving his body broken, he would retain the same nobility of spirit, and not a man or woman watching him could doubt it.

Emily's eyes flooded with tears as she watched him. *I love you so.* She saw his youth and his deep heroism and his ageless pride, and he would never be broken. Not this way.

Apparently, Davis recognized the subtle defeat. "Lock

him up. I want twenty guards posted at all times."

Emily cast him a knowing look. "For such a 'lamb,' that seems extreme. I wonder what beast is so wimpy within to fear a lamb, anyway? A worm, perhaps?"

The general started to frown, then noticed the admiring crowd, and replaced his anger with an exaggerated smile. "I have enjoyed the assistance of this outlaw's men, but I'm no fool."

Emily offered a brief laugh. "You keep saying that. I'm still waiting for any evidence to the contrary."

He ignored her, but his eyes darkened. "I'll be watching every one of them until the noose has choked the life out of Darian Woodward for good."

MacLeod urged his horse forward beside Davis's overly large black mount. For an instant, Emily hoped the sergeant would at last prove his true loyalties and save Darian, somehow. "You ain't got to worry about any of us, General. We know a good thing when we see it, and your offer of clemency, it were more than fair." He paused, looking sly, and again Emily's hopes raised. "Not quite so pretty, though, as your offer of . . . well, our positions. . . ."

Emily had no idea what MacLeod referred to, but it sounded as if the men had accepted some kind of bribe. Her brow furrowed. "What positions?"

Davis smiled, forced, probably nervous that the fort commander might hear of impropriety when he arrived tomorrow. "I felt, given MacLeod's former record of good service in the U.S. cavalry, under my command. . . ."

Emily huffed. "You mean, Darian's."

The general ignored her. "I felt that MacLeod might resume the role he adopted briefly as sheriff of Tucson. As it happens, the current sheriff has proven somewhat less than adequate."

286

MacLeod smiled, dismounted, and seized the sheriff's badge without ceremony as Emily watched in disbelief. She turned indignantly to Davis. "What did you promise the others?"

Davis nodded to Darian's waiting soldiers. "Nothing extraordinary. Herring will take over as bartender at Belle's saloon. Several of her customers have expressed a preference for his concoctions. Bonner and Clyde will become proprietors of the bank."

Emily sighed. "It figures." She paused. "What about Ping?"

Ping dismounted and took Penelope's hand in his, tenderly. "I have gained the greatest treasure of all. Miss Penelope and I will marry, and be granted ownership of a small plot of land just outside of town. As long as I have the woman I love by my side, I have everything I need."

"A shame you had to sell your own soul to do it." Emily looked at Ping in disgust, but nothing in Ping's stance indicated any shame or doubt at all.

Ping offered a pert, hopeful smile, ignoring Emily. "Dearest love, will you agree to marry me?"

Penelope hesitated, and for a moment, Emily prayed the girl would slap her sentimental suitor for his disloyalty. But Ping leaned to kiss her cheek and whisper sweet nothings into her ear, and a shy smile grew on her face. "I have long dreamed of becoming the wife of a good man. Yes, I will be honored to marry you, Mr. Ping."

Ping made a face, wincing as if some unpleasant business had yet to be taken care of. "We'll wait until this matter has passed. We can't hold our wedding ceremonies on the same day as a hanging, after all. Bad luck."

Penelope nodded. "How about the day after?"

"That would be perfect. I'll talk to the minister at once."

Emily listened in disbelief as they planned their marriage, practically standing on Darian's grave. Bonner and Clyde had dismounted and were headed for the bank. Herring fiddled with his gear and already had his well-worn apron in hand. MacLeod stood polishing his badge with great care.

"Stop right there!" Emily got off Darian's horse and faced them. Her chin quivered with emotion, but she didn't cry. "You men are making the biggest mistake of your lives."

They all looked at her innocently, as if they had no idea what she meant. MacLeod went to her and placed his broad hand fondly on her shoulder, like a father. "It's hard on you, I know, girl. But you're a pretty young woman. You won't have any trouble finding a new husband."

Emily smacked his hand from her shoulder and backed away, trembling with fury and hurt. "What is the matter with you people? Darian has done everything for you. He's saved your lives countless times. You told me so yourself!"

MacLeod shrugged. "The boy did well for himself during the war, that's the truth. But as for saving our lives, I'd say he'd put us in the pot so as we needed saving."

If he dared mention Wetherspoon's death, she would seize the sergeant's gun and shoot him herself. Perhaps the look in her eyes told MacLeod as much, because he said no more on the subject. Emily glared at him a moment, then the others. "You all disgust me. You betrayed a good man, a man who loves you."

Not a man revealed the slightest flicker of shame or doubt. Emily's stomach tightened with a wave of nausea.

288

"No matter what happens to Darian, I pity you most of all." She closed her eyes, then looked at them all again, one by one. "I hope you'll be happy with your new positions. You've earned them by treachery and faithlessness. I'm sure they'll bring you great joy."

General Davis dismounted and handed his reins to a guard. He went to the steps of Belle's saloon and turned to address the crowd. "You good people have nothing to fear from this outlaw now. I have ensured your safety, and you may sleep easy in your beds tonight."

Emily went to Darian's side. "I will accompany my husband to the jail now."

Davis appeared suspicious. "Thinking of breaking him out yourself, little lady? I don't think you'll have much chance, but for the sake of the good citizens of Tucson, I'm not taking any risks. You will stay in the saloon." He nodded to Darian's guards. "The outlaw's wife may walk free in Tucson—let it not be said I behaved in an ungentlemanly fashion toward one whose naïveté must account for her confused loyalties. But she is not to visit her husband without my approval. Is that understood?"

The young soldier, Forbes, stepped forward. "It is usual for a wife to be allowed time with her husband prior to execution, General."

The general's eyes narrowed. Perhaps he, too, saw the likeness between Forbes and Darian. "Lieutenant Forbes, isn't it?"

The young man nodded. "Yes, sir."

"You're the fort commander's nephew, aren't you?"

"I am, sir."

Emily saw the flash of dislike in Davis's eyes, but also the recognition that this boy shouldn't be ill-treated. "I'll put you in charge of their visitations, Forbes. When your uncle arrives tomorrow, I'm certain he will be pleased that this matter was handled with utmost propriety."

"I'm sure he will, sir."

Forbes didn't like Davis, either. Here was her one hope, this boy who looked like Darian.

Davis motioned to the guards. "Lock him up, men. See that he's well-treated." Emily hated his patronizing tone, the way he made himself seem benevolent and kind when inside she knew he seethed with dark energy, with evil. "It will be Woodward's last night, after all."

Davis cast a dark smirk Emily's way, then waved at the onlookers. The guards led Darian to the jail, but as he waited for them to open the door, he looked back to Emily and smiled in gentle reassurance. She knew he had no reason for hope, only that he wanted to comfort her. She met his eyes and whispered, "I will not let you die."

Davis went into the saloon with Belle. Emily waited for the others to disperse, then went to Forbes and placed her hand on his arm. "I thank you, Lieutenant." She paused. "You seem a good man." She paused again. "Like my husband."

"I know no good of your husband, Mrs. Woodward. He has betrayed the United States government, and the cavalry he once served."

Emily met his gaze and saw doubt beneath the sure words. "Is that true, do you think? Or has it betrayed him?" This young man was her only hope. She had to make him understand.

"Your husband took the law into his own hands."

"What if that were the only way to see right prevail?"

Forbes hesitated. "There had to be a better way."

"Is that so? And what would you do, Lieutenant, if you discovered that your commander was corrupt, that he was making war on people who had done him no harm?"

Forbes gave no answer. She was making headway. "What would you do if you knew he was about to kill an innocent man?"

He looked at her, his blue eyes bright. "I don't know that, madam."

"Yes, but you feel it, don't you?"

He looked away, at his feet. "Feelings aren't enough to go on."

He had a point. "If I found you proof, would you act?"

He glanced at her. "It would have to be very good proof."

Emily straightened, determined. "It will be."

Chapter Sixteen

Darian sat in his cell and stared at the wall. Outside, he heard MacLeod talking to his guards. He wasn't sure what they said, but he heard the men laugh. There hadn't been a chance to talk privately since the general appeared on the hilltop. Darian felt sure his men were up to something, but they hadn't told him what yet. He understood the difficulty. As soon as they had a chance, one of them would alert him to their intentions.

Whatever their plan was, they certainly hadn't told Emily. Perhaps that was for the best—her fury and grief would convince the general that their betrayal of Darian was sincere, but he hated to see her suffer this way. Worse still, he feared she might act rashly in an effort to save him. If his men had found a better way, they would have to tell her before she risked herself unnecessarily.

MacLeod entered the jail, leading the former sheriff

by the collar. As usual, the man was inebriated and barely able to stand. MacLeod shoved the former sheriff into the cell beside Darian's, then huffed in disgust. "You, lad, had better find another pastime soon."

Yes, MacLeod would make an admirable sheriff. A shame that his efforts on Darian's behalf would make that career impossible. Yet if somehow, still, they could set things right, perhaps the sergeant's heroism would be lauded, and many such positions open to him.

Darian watched with approval as MacLeod seated himself at the sheriff's desk, then put his feet up comfortably. Already at home. He would have liked to ask what his men had planned, but he remembered Emily's words. *Trust.* For just the space of a second, when Davis had emerged on that hilltop, Darian had doubted. But his deeper faith in the men he had marched beside, fought beside, held sway. He trusted.

The jail wasn't well furnished, nor were the prisoners treated with any extraordinary comforts. A hard, narrow bench with one tattered sheet had been provided, and an empty metal cup. Though Darian had revealed nothing of his discomfort, the walk through the desert had created a powerful thirst.

"Sergeant, if you please. . . ." He held up his cup, careful not to seem too friendly, yet still unable to muster much feigned anger.

MacLeod cocked his head in Darian's direction and slanted him a well-done, unfriendly glare. "What are you after now, Woodward?"

Darian hesitated. He wasn't used to the sergeant speaking to him in any way short of polite. Teasing, perhaps, but never rude. All part of the act. Darian smiled to himself. "I'm thirsty."

MacLeod adopted a very convincing sneer. "Is that so?"

Darian nodded, hoping Davis's guards had taken note of MacLeod's adversarial posture. Not a one besides young Forbes seemed to be paying any attention, but best not to take chances. "I worked up quite a thirst in the desert."

MacLeod rose slowly from his chair, then swaggered to the cell door. "Forbes, get the boy some water."

Forbes hesitated. "From the saloon, sir?"

"The horse's trough will do."

MacLeod was clearly overacting. Darian frowned, but he said nothing. The young lieutenant hurried outside to the trough, ladled water into the cup, then returned to the jail. Darian waited for MacLeod to catch his eye, to exchange some kind of favorable signal, but nothing was forthcoming.

Forbes passed the cup to MacLeod and Darian reached through the bars. Thirst became a hurting inside, his throat was dry and tight until it ached. MacLeod twirled the cup with his large fingers. "Thirsty, are you?"

"I am." Something felt wrong. Deeply wrong. Forbes stood beside MacLeod, looking uncomfortable. Darian held out his hand. "Please."

"Begging are you, 'Captain'? Ain't like you."

Darian said nothing. Forbes chewed his lip and glanced between Darian and the sergeant. MacLeod held up the cup as if to pass it, but when Darian reached for it, the sergeant snatched it back. A look of dark anger, cruel hatred, crossed his face and he tossed the water into Darian's face.

Darian stood as the water dripped down his face, and he knew he had been betrayed. No reassurance would be forthcoming now. He stared a moment into Mac-Leod's eyes, and he saw nothing of the man he once trusted. MacLeod's purpose was veiled to him now, but he wasn't ready to believe that he had been betrayed.

He would trust his men until the end. He had to.

Darian turned away and returned to his bench. MacLeod laughed like a stranger, then left the jailhouse to stand outside conversing with the other guards. Darian sat staring at the barred window as the sunlight faded toward night. If he was wrong about his men's true purpose, at this time tomorrow, he would be hanged.

He closed his eyes and he saw Emily, her beautiful face lit with love and trust. Tomorrow, she would watch him hang, and her heart would break. Why hadn't he listened to her? Why hadn't he taken her and run away, to the future, if that's what she wanted?

He had stayed for honor and justice, and he had stayed to clear his name and restore his pride. He had stayed for the honor of the men who followed him, men he believed he knew like brothers. How could he have been so wrong and so blind?

Darian lay back on the bench, one arm behind his head, his eyes closed. For the first time in his life, he questioned the nature of his existence, of who he truly was. He had won the heart of a beautiful, strong, vulnerable woman, and tomorrow he would be executed as a criminal. He had led men to the best of his ability, and they had betrayed him.

He lay in the darkening cell, and he had no idea who he was at all. He heard Emily's voice in his mind, "*I used to think hanging was the worst thing that could happen to you, but now I know it isn't. You will go on, because souls never die, but you will have lost something of yourself.*"

He'd had no idea what she meant at the time, but he knew now. How could he go on, even to some other life in the future, when he had lost the core of himself? He loved her, and he had no idea how to spare her the horror of his death. If his men had truly betrayed him, then he couldn't hope for a reprieve, he couldn't maneuver a daring escape, nor ever bring Clement Davis to justice.

"Sir. . . ."

Darian startled and sat up. Forbes stood outside his cell holding a cup. Darian rolled his eyes. "I've fallen for that once already, Lieutenant. I need a drink, not a bath."

Forbes didn't withdraw his offer. "I was not raised to watch any man suffer of thirst, even an outlaw such as yourself."

Darian looked up, weary and feeling older than he ever had in his life. Something in the young man's eyes reminded him of who he had been, and the part of himself he had lost. He stood up, slowly, as if the weight of years had crushed him, suddenly, making him an old man. He reached through the bars, not caring if Forbes tossed the cup into his face.

He took the cup from sure hands and he drank until his parched throat eased, until the desperation of an animal dissipated from his veins. "I thank you."

Forbes nodded. "More, sir?"

Darian shook his head. "There's no need."

Forbes started to turn away, then looked back. "I am sorry, sir. They say you were once a great man, during the war. I wasn't old enough to serve at that time, but I hold those who did in high esteem."

"Thank you." Never had he felt so old. Darian studied the boy's face. There was nothing Darian could do to save himself now, but for Emily. . . . He had to know she would be protected. Somehow, he had to spare Emily the sight of his death, and be sure she would be returned to the future. He couldn't rely on his men to look after her or send her to Tiotonawen.

"Lieutenant, you have met my wife."

"Yes, sir. A lovely woman, sir. Very brave, I thought."

"She saved your life, you know. I was going to shoot you, and she stopped me."

"I know."

Darian looked around and lowered his voice lest he be overheard and place Forbes in jeopardy. "You allowed me to save her yesterday. Come tomorrow, I won't be able to help her."

Forbes hesitated. "No."

"You won't understand what I'm about to ask, and I can't explain. I can't let my wife see my execution."

"I understand that, sir."

"Good, then maybe you will accept my word in what is to follow. There is one true safety for Emily, and one only. Upon my death—before, if you're able—she must be taken to an Apache chief called Tiotonawen. His tribe is heading north now to their village near Camp McDowell. Take her there, and she will be safe."

Forbes appeared confused, but Darian reached through the bars and clasped his arm. "Please. I ask it as a dying man, upon my own soul. Do as I ask you, and let no one stop you."

The jailhouse door opened, and MacLeod entered. His eyes narrowed suspiciously at their conversation, but Darian refused to release Forbes's arm. "Save my wife."

Forbes nodded once, then backed away. Darian returned to his bench and knew he had to do the one thing that seemed impossible.

Trust.

General Davis must have felt his victory was complete already, because he used very little precautions that might prevent Emily from saving Darian. Maybe he didn't feel she had a chance, but Emily felt certain she would find a crack in the armor of the general's plans. There had to be something that would prove Darian's innocence.

Emily sat in the bedroom she now shared with Marita and Penelope, considering how best to proceed. She had twenty-four hours, and not a moment could be wasted in sleep, nor in fear. Toklanni told her to think, not become lost in the reactions of her emotions. Emily thought. Each time fear rose in her heart, she turned her focus away from it and fixed on her goal of saving her husband.

Penelope entered the room, carrying her bag of nighttime toiletries. She seemed uneasy, but she smiled at Emily. "Shouldn't you be getting ready for bed, Emily? It's late, and you need your sleep."

Emily glared. "My husband, betrayed by your betrothed, is to be hanged tomorrow. What possible good can a night's sleep do me now?"

Marita joined them and sat beside Emily. "I don't know what you can do for him at this point."

Penelope hesitated, then sat on Emily's other side. "We know you're worried about your husband. But there's nothing you can do now."

Emily's lips tightened as anger filled her chest. "Like hell. I don't have time to sleep because I am going to find evidence against that bastard Davis, and I am going to save my husband. I know he's up to something, or Belle wouldn't be dripping in jewels and pretty dresses."

Marita considered this, then nodded. "I wouldn't be surprised. But how are you going to prove anything before they kill your husband?"

"You're going to help me." Emily paused. "You're both going to help me." Penelope started to shake her head, but Emily pinched her arm, hard. "You're going to help me, because if you don't, your marriage to that snake Ping will be cursed forever."

Penelope seemed unmoved, even amused, by Emily's threat, but Emily pinned her hardest, most dangerous stare upon her. Penelope's smile faded and she patted Emily's arm. "What do you want us to do?"

"Help me break into Belle's room. I need you as lookout."

Penelope eyed Marita, then shrugged. "We can do that, but all you'll find are oversized corsets and strong perfume."

Emily stood up. "We'll see. Belle is downstairs in the saloon with Davis. I should have time to get a look around and see what she's hiding."

Marita stood up, too, eager. "Penny will go down and keep an eye on them. I'll stay in the hall and warn you if they're coming."

"Thank you, Marita. I knew I could count on you."

They went to the door, and Marita looked out. She chewed her lip, then glanced at Emily. "What did you think of him?"

"Who? The general? I thought he was a sleazy jerk. What else?"

"No. . . ." Marita hesitated and looked shy, not a customary mood for the beautiful and vivacious girl. "Lieutenant Forbes."

"Forbes? He's nice, I guess. I mean, he looks something like Darian, and I don't think he cares much for Davis, but. . . ."

Marita looked at her feet, but her eyes were shining. "He doesn't."

Emily's eyes narrowed. "You have a crush on him." Easy enough to see why. Forbes was handsome and had that same peculiar restraint Darian possessed, with the suggestion of an inner nobility carried deep within. Emily felt tempted to slap Marita. "So, he's cute. Big deal! My husband is about to be hanged. I can't believe you people. Ping is planning his wedding, you're giggling over a blue-eyed boy. . . . Get a grip!"

Marita appeared shamed and she nodded. "I'm sorry. I just wanted to know if you liked him. You have good sense about men."

Emily rolled her eyes. "Right. It's certainly been a strong point of my life so far."

Penelope touched Emily's arm, gently. "Don't discount what you know about people just because they've acted in a way you don't understand. Sometimes that knowing is more true than what you see with your own eyes."

"Well, I would never have expected Ping to betray Darian, that's for sure."

Penelope didn't comment, dashing hopes that a secret plan was in the works. Emily's shoulders slumped, but her determination didn't alter. She eyed Marita and her brain wrapped around a new angle. "How well do you know Forbes, anyway?"

Marita blushed. "He asked me to dance at a fair earlier in the fall, and he was very polite."

Emily sighed. It didn't sound like an affair, nor a close enough relationship so that she could enlist Marita to convince Forbes to help them. "Do you think he'd help me if you asked him?"

Marita shook her head. "I am not sure he even remembers me. I am not of his class. I don't even know who my real father was."

How incredibly irrelevant! Emily had almost forgotten the time period she now occupied. "If he's a good man, he will only care about who you are as a person."

"He didn't make any advances. Men usually do." Marita's back straightened and her dark eyes glimmered with pride. "I have turned every one of them down, and made sure they never dared ask again."

"How did you do that? Did you hit them?"

Marita's brow rose. "No. . . . That doesn't work very well. They see it as a challenge."

"Then what did you do?"

Marita smiled. "I laughed. Have you ever seen anything work so well as laughing at a man?"

Emily smiled, too. "Come to think of it, no, I haven't."

"They deflate admirably."

"Maybe cornered women should use that tactic more often."

Penelope looked between them. "I have put off unwanted advances by reciting a list of what I expect in a husband, and by telling them how many children I expect to have."

Emily's heart lightened. She was among friends, though she couldn't fully understand their actions. The energy surrounding her felt good, no matter how it seemed on the outside. Buoyed by this truth, she would find a way to save Darian, and by tomorrow evening, all would again be right with the world.

Belle's room was a cornucopia of gaudy trinkets, some valuable, some hideously tacky. Emily fingered a perfume bottle, then sniffed it. She winced, then sneezed at its overwhelming fragrance. "Maybe if she'd just bathe once in a while. . . ." She set the bottle aside, and began rummaging through Belle's drawers.

Nothing immediately condemning revealed itself. Emily found an expensive-looking gold bracelet engraved, *"to my doll."* This proved Clement Davis had money to spare on gifts for his mistress, but that in itself wasn't condemning. Though she felt sure his money came from unscrupulous means, she had no idea how to prove it.

She rifled through drawers, checked shelves, opened pockets and small bags, and even looked under Belle's mattress. Nothing. Fear returned, in force. If she found nothing, then where would she look? And truly, what did she hope to find anyway? What if Davis had committed no major crime other than being a dark soul with a hatred for Indians, and a lust for power?

Emily closed her eyes. No. Darian believed Davis had done more wrong than that, and it was up to her to prove it. A fat, golden pocket watch on the bedstand caught Emily's eye. Probably nothing, but she went to examine it. As she reached for the watch, Marita rapped on the door, startling her.

"Emily! They're coming. Hurry up!"

Emily's hands shook, but she fingered the watch and it popped open, surprising her. A small golden key dropped to the floor. Emily hesitated, then picked it up and stuffed it in her pocket. Marita knocked again, and Emily hurried to the door.

She opened it, peeked out, and saw Marita motioning her feverishly to the far end of the corridor. Emily scurried from Belle's door and positioned herself beside Marita just as Davis and Belle ascended the stairs. They eyed her suspiciously, but Emily maintained an impassive expression.

Davis smirked at her, his perpetual expression. "A shame you girls missed the celebration downstairs. Many a toast has been made tonight, for Ping's upcoming nuptials, and of course, to myself for capturing your renegade husband."

Emily tilted her head to one side, thoughtfully. "Isn't there some saying about toasting yourself too soon, before the victory?"

His smirk deepened, creating creases in his cheeks.

He walked to her and caught her chin in his hand. "My victory is already won, pretty lady. I've taken everything from Woodward—his men, his pride, his renown—all squandered because he dared defy me. Your husband is worse than dead, and he knows it."

"There's something worse than death, and that's a life without honor, and without love. Nothing that can happen to Darian will ever bring him as low as you yourself have sunk."

Davis laughed. "I can't bring any vengeance upon you, Mrs. Woodward. Not yet, not with the commander's spoiled nephew hovering at attention." Davis reached out and flicked her cheek as Emily quivered with hatred. "But afterwards, when this ugly matter has settled, I'll be sure you are left in my care. And then I'll show you, for hours on end, how big a mistake you've made."

She knew what he meant, and it scared her, but Emily managed a sarcastic expression nonetheless. "I don't know if I can take hours of laughter, General, but . . . you know best."

His eyes flashed with anger, but the smirk remained. "You won't have the strength to smile when I'm through with you."

"All the vomiting will have worn me out." She kept her voice steady, lest it reveal the quaver of fear, and the general backed away. This man, with his loathsome efforts at power, could not cause Darian's death. Surely, heaven wouldn't allow it.

With that faith rising in her heart, Emily brushed past Davis and Belle and went down the stairs. She spotted Lieutenant Forbes standing awkwardly near the door, as if being in a saloon both offended and confused him. *Like Darian.* She went to him, and he seemed relieved to see her.

"Lieutenant, I would like to visit my husband now. Will you take me to him?"

Forbes seemed even more relieved to have a reason to vacate the saloon. He took her arm like a gentleman and led her to the jail. As they walked along the street, Emily saw Bonner and Clyde through the bank window, playing cards. Probably placing bets with the money stored there. MacLeod sat outside the jail with his feet up on the porch railing, talking to Ping. Both men rose and tipped their caps when she approached, but she ignored them.

Emily turned her back to Darian's betrayers and faced Forbes. "I would like to be alone with my husband for a short while. Is that possible, Lieutenant?"

Forbes glanced at MacLeod for approval, and the sergeant hesitated. "Just be sure you don't try anything foolish, girl."

Emily cast a disparaging, disdainful look at MacLeod. "Something heroic, you mean. The sort of thing you would do if you were a better, more honorable man yourself."

MacLeod came to her and place his large hand firmly on her shoulder. Still paternal, no matter how evilly he had treated her husband. "I mean it, girl. You can go in and talk to your husband, but don't you try anything that's going to get you killed."

Emily drew a calming breath, shoved his hand from her shoulder, and went to the door. "That would be a shame, wouldn't it? If I got killed now. . . . Well, if my husband dies, then my reason for living goes, too."

For the first time, MacLeod revealed discomfort, even fear, at her words. Maybe he feared what she would do. "You stay away from the hanging tomorrow."

She looked at him in disgust. "Do you really think I would abandon him at such a time? But if I have my say, that time won't come, and you will all be very sorry for what you have done, and the wrong you have caused."

His nervousness increased. "What do you mean?"

"Should my husband die, then there will be nothing for me to live for, no reason to stay safe. I will do whatever I must to see that the wrong he sought to correct is made right."

MacLeod rolled his eyes and groaned. Ping practically hopped from foot to foot in agitation. "If I must, I'll keep you locked up, young woman."

"For what crime? I will do nothing . . . amiss . . . until the time comes. . . ."

MacLeod clenched his fist, then shot a dark glance at Forbes. "You keep an eye on this one, boy."

Forbes took Emily's arm protectively. "It is desperation you hear, sergeant. Surely you understand a young wife's desire to save her husband."

MacLeod huffed. "I understand it too damned well. That's why I tell you, don't let her out of your sight tomorrow." He looked like he wanted to say more, but couldn't. MacLeod sighed heavily, then seated himself again on the porch bench. "Let her in, Ping."

Ping held open the door, still cheerful, still polite. Emily walked past him without meeting his eyes.

MacLeod called after her. "You remember, we're right outside this door. You say your piece to the captain, then get back to the saloon."

Emily didn't look back. "My 'piece,' Sergeant, will take all night, so you'd best be prepared for a fight if you try to pull me away. Is that understood?"

"Too damned well." He sighed, but he didn't try to stop her.

Emily entered the jail and saw Darian standing at his cell door. She opened her mouth to speak, but a wave of emotion crashed over her and no words came. Darian held out his hand for her, and she went to him, tears flooding down her cheeks.

She placed her hand in his and his fingers closed around hers, tight. "Emmy, I heard you out there, and you are not to attempt anything in an effort to save me. Do you understand?"

Emily squeezed his hand. "Do you truly expect me to do nothing, just to let you hang?"

"The mistakes that have been made were mine, love. Not yours. You tried your best to turn me from this path. I refused to hear you. Now I must face the results of my stubbornness and pride."

Emily pressed her cheek against his hand, then kissed it. "I won't let them hang you."

"If you attempt anything—it terrifies me to think what you might do—but know this. . . ." He touched her face and waited until she looked into his eyes. "Know this, my love. The regret of my death, of watching my men turn against me, yes, even my brother's death—those things would pale in the shadow of knowing you were killed for trying to defend me."

She knew he was right, but she also believed she could make some difference that could turn the tide of a dark night to come. "There has to be another way. I promise you that I won't do anything foolish, but there's still time to expose Davis for the treacherous fiend that he is."

Darian appeared doubtful. "How?"

She hesitated. "I don't know. I searched Belle's room. . . ."

Darian's gasp cut her off. "You *what*? Emily! What if you'd been caught?" He paused to groan, then clasped his hand to his forehead.

"I had no intention of being caught." It occurred to

her suddenly that her self-assurance had neared his own. "Marita and Penelope helped me as lookouts."

"That brings me very little comfort." He paused. "What did you expect to find in Belle's room, other than vulgar garments and pink upholstery?"

"I expected, hoped, to find some sort of evidence proving what General Davis is up to. I know there's something. He gives Belle expensive gifts. She doesn't mean that much to him—he's just throwing his money and power around."

"I wasn't aware that Davis was a wealthy man. His salary wouldn't be enough to make a man so free with his money."

"I know. But he's getting it from somewhere."

"I have suspected as much, but I have no idea what source."

"That's why I searched her room."

Darian smiled, but he looked wistful. "Emmy, it was a good try, but finding evidence now, at this late hour, seems unlikely."

"I found this." Emily fished in her pocket and pulled out the small key she'd found in Belle's room. "This key was hidden in a pocket watch by Belle's bed. I figured it belongs to Davis."

Darian took the key and examined it. "I would say . . . it would go to a personal safe, probably in the bank."

Emily brightened. "Oh! A lock box, just like in the future. I'll have to check it out."

Darian seized both her hands. "You will do no such thing. I will not have you breaking into a bank, not for any reason."

"Bonner and Clyde are busy playing cards. I won't have any trouble at all."

Darian groaned and gripped her hands tight. "Emmy,

Bonner and Clyde have a tendency to shoot first, ask questions later."

"I've never heard either one of them speak, let alone ask questions."

"My point is made. Emmy, as your husband, I command you. . . ."

She huffed. "Well, it's a good thing you're in jail, isn't it?"

She struggled to free herself from his grasp, but he was stronger and he held her fast. "No. Do you understand me, wife? No! I forbid it."

Emily smiled sweetly, relaxed, and bowed her head. His grip loosened, almost imperceptibly. Emily yanked free and hopped back beyond his reach. She held up the key so that it reflected the evening light. "I'll wait until midnight, sneak in, and see where this fits." She paused while Darian shook his head and tried to reach her through the bars. "I'll need help. I can't ask Penelope, not now that she's engaged to Ping. She's a nice person, but I can't trust her. That leaves Marita. She's more sensible anyway."

Darian issued a series of indistinguishable curses. "More sensible? Emmy, that young woman has no more sense than yourself. You're both likely to get yourselves killed."

"We'll be fine." Emily paused, gazing at Darian. "I want to kiss you, but I know you'll grab me to keep me from going, and I can't risk that. I know you—it's not beyond you to hold me here all night, or turn me over to MacLeod."

"A fine idea. . . ." He started to shout, but Emily squealed.

"Can you trust him not to turn me in?"

Darian stopped, then bowed his head. "No."

"Then let *me* go."

He drew a long breath, then met her eyes. "Be careful, my love. If not for your own sake, then for mine. If I lose you now. . . ."

"You won't lose me, Darian. I know what I'm doing. I handled Davis fine when I was captured, after all."

"Only because he needed you to lure me. Emmy, he has me now. There's no reason for him to spare you."

"I don't think he's going to try anything now, not with Lieutenant Forbes here to report any impropriety back to the commander."

Darian hesitated. "That is true. Despite occasionally being an irritant, Forbes's sense of correct behavior is a blessing. . . ."

Emily laughed. "Do you, of all people, think so? Darian Woodward, you have changed."

Darian ran his hands along the bars and smiled, self-mocking and sweet. "Mrs. Woodward, I cannot argue with that."

Chapter Seventeen

"Are you sure we need these masks?"

Emily glanced back and saw Marita tugging at the black hair net she'd carefully placed over the girl's face. "Stop that! And yes, we do need them. Our faces reflect light. Criminals know what they're doing."

Marita didn't appear wholly convinced, but she left the black mask in place as ordered. Emily turned her attention back to the bank looming before her. She fingered the key in her pocket to be certain it hadn't fallen out. Inside that bank lay her hopes and possibly Darian's life. She had to get in without being seen, and she had to find Davis's secret safe.

Both she and Marita wore dresses in dark fabric. Emily would have preferred jeans or her shorts, but if someone spotted them outside, they would have to look natural. The masks could be torn off and stuffed in their bodices, so the clothes had to be normal, too.

Emily inched her way to the nearest window and peeked in. Bonner and Clyde had stopped playing cards and now lay on bunks near the far wall. If only she could trust them! But that hope was gone. The door was locked, but the window nearest to the vaults looked easy to open. It was a hot night—no doubt Bonner and Clyde felt safe enough leaving the window ajar. The bank didn't harbor that much money, anyway—especially since Bonner and Clyde's last tenure.

With Marita's help, Emily edged the window open. Bonner startled in his sleep, and she held herself motionless until he sank back into a deeper sleep. Emily motioned to Marita. "Here, help me up, then stand guard. Whistle if anyone suspicious comes by."

"I hope they don't shoot you." Marita formed her hands like a stirrup, giving Emily a leg up, and Emily crawled through the window.

"I hope so, too."

She sank silently from the window to the floor, then eased herself behind an old desk. Neither Bonner nor Clyde stirred. Bonner in particular lay like a dead man, while Clyde lay sprawled on his cot, snoring.

Emily eyed the vault. Far less elaborate than modern banks, yet with the same principle of security applied. The vaults appeared to be behind an iron gate. A locked iron gate. Emily drew a long breath. *Of course. It had to be locked.*

She looked around and spotted a large ring of keys affixed to a chain protruding from Bonner's black coat. She had no choice. She tiptoed across the bank to his bedside, then held her breath as she took the key ring. It jingled slightly when she picked it up and she froze. She waited motionless as minutes ticked by, but neither Bonner nor Clyde reacted in any way. Odd, because in times of crisis, when Darian's gang was threatened even

311

in the smallest way, it had always been these two men to react first, to jump up and be on the task.

Apparently, their subconscious wariness didn't extend to considering Emily a threat.

She allowed herself to breathe, then crept back to the vault. She tried three keys, and then the fourth one fit. Not bad, considering there were at least ten keys on the ring. She opened the gate and it opened with a loud creak.

Emily cringed and prepared to bolt for the window, but Bonner and Clyde slept through her invasion without the slightest awareness of her presence. Emily relaxed and seized a dim lantern from the wall. She made her way into the vaults, opened the inner door, then closed it so the light wouldn't be seen. Inside, she found a row of safes not unlike a modern bank's collection of safe deposit boxes.

Emily felt strong. She felt more sure of herself than she ever had in her life. Tonight, everything worked as she planned. She took out the key and tried it in the first box. It didn't fit, but it appeared to be the right size, so she felt sure it would fit one of the boxes.

She tried the next, and the next. With each failure, her hope dwindled, and her fear returned. As she reached the last, she hesitated. Her heart beat heavily and tears threatened. She closed her eyes tight. *Please, I need this evidence to prove General Davis's true nature. Nothing else can save Darian. Please, let this box be the one.*

She stuck the key into the hole. For a moment, she didn't dare try. Then she wedged it inward, and it fit. Emily offered a silent prayer of thanks, then opened the safe door.

There wasn't much inside. A wad of money, but not enough to prove Davis corrupt. Emily set it back inside, then picked up a large envelope. She opened it carefully and pulled out the papers inside. At first, she didn't understand what she read. It seemed garbled, almost like hints for a computer game. It appeared to be written in General Davis's hand, but much had been written by someone else, and much was written in Spanish.

She could read Spanish, but those words, too, seemed garbled. Until she realized they were messages revealing army secrets—number of troops at various forts, weaknesses at certain posts, even the best times of day for attack. But not attack—these messages revealed an interest not only in one country spying on another, but detailed accounts of gold shipments, of officer's salaries, and where in transit that money could be most easily stolen.

General Davis was playing the oldest game since tribes had first set themselves up against each other, and since power and money had begun to mean more to people than love. As she read on, she realized his crime was much worse. Not only was he giving secrets to the bandits, but he was actually the leader of their activities.

Emily stared at her prize in amazement. She'd expected to find something, but never this. Never something so utterly condemning.

No wonder he disapproved of Darian's activities. Probably afraid the "Blue-Eyed Bandit" would be better at it than he was!

Emily clenched her fist around the papers. "I've got you now!" She would have to be careful, wait for exactly the right moment. . . . Then, when there was no chance he could escape or kill her before she could reveal her find, she would expose Davis as the worst bandit leader the Wild West had ever known, and Darian would return to the hero status he deserved.

Satisfied, Emily locked the box again, stuffed the envelope into her dress, then slipped back out of the vault.

Stobie Piel

She checked Bonner and Clyde, but though Clyde had
rolled over to one side, Bonner still lay flat on his back,
motionless and stone-faced.

She went to the window, crawled out, and jumped
down to where Marita stood biting her nails in worry.
Marita clutched Emily's arm. "What happened? Did you
find anything?"

Emily held up the envelope, aglow with happiness. "I
found everything and more." She motioned Marita from
the bank, and after a safe distance, they removed their
masks.

"What are you going to do with what you found?"

Emily hesitated, considering her best assault on Darian's enemy. "I'll wait until tomorrow, when the fort
commander arrives. If I act sooner, Davis might find a
way to stop me. Then I'll talk to Sergeant MacLeod.
He'll have to believe me now."

Marita breathed a deep sigh of relief. "That was fun.
I can see why bandits take these risks. It's incredibly
exhilarating!"

"I hope, my dear, that it's not a role you will take to
permanently." A man's voice came from the darkness
behind the saloon, and both Emily and Marita jumped
and squealed in terrified unison.

With shaking hands, Emily drew the pistol she'd stolen from Lieutenant Forbes during her breakout, and she
aimed into the shadows.

A tall man emerged, his face still concealed in darkness. "Will you add murder to your many crimes, Mrs.
Woodward?"

She recognized his voice now. "Forbes!" Despite the
fact he'd caught them, Emily puffed a breath of relief.
"It's you. I thought we were in for it."

Forbes stepped forward so that light illuminated his
young face. "What makes you think you're not?"

Marita issued a strange, small squeak, but Emily felt sure she could trust him. "Don't worry. I didn't steal anything important, really."

Forbes took the envelope from her hands. "Let me guess. Bribery funds?"

Emily snatched it back. "Certainly not! And it's none of your business."

Emily wanted to trust him, but she couldn't risk placing Darian's fate in another's hands. "You'll just have to trust me, Lieutenant."

Forbes hesitated. "If you have placed yourself in danger. . . ."

"I haven't, I swear. Please, don't tell anyone about this. It's my only chance of saving Darian. Please."

He drew a long sigh, then nodded. "I will do as you ask, and I hope you have found what you were looking for. But know that I gave your husband my word of honor to protect you. I would not betray that now."

"You're a good man, and I thank you. Please, forget you saw us here and go about your business."

"I will ask no further questions, but forget. . . ?" He glanced at Marita and his expression softened. "There is more to you than beauty, I see. I had imagined you capable of much, Miss Sanchez, but bank robbery? Never."

He was flirting. For someone as stiff and upright as Lieutenant Forbes, it seemed impossible. But then, no man was as upright as Darian Woodward, and he was a lion in love. Emily beamed. "Marita can do many things. She is an excellent seamstress, a beautiful dancer, and a very good friend."

Forbes smiled. "I see that." He took Marita's hand and kissed it. "A woman like yourself must have many suitors. . . . Older and more acclaimed than myself, perhaps. I wonder if you might allow me to be counted

315

among them?" He seemed nervous, but Marita placed her hand over his.

"Lieutenant Forbes, I thought you'd never ask."

Emily watched as he led Marita back to the saloon. She sighed, seeing herself with Darian, free and happy. It was a close call, but she had found the evidence Darian needed to win justice. She considered heading to the jail to tell him, but that might arouse suspicions.

Now that she'd found proof against Davis, she could relax. Her whole body ached from the tension of fear. She needed sleep. The battle was almost won, and tomorrow, she would be ready for the final assault.

Emily woke to bright sunlight. She felt rested and happy, ready to witness her husband's redemption, and the fall of a dark and evil man. She yawned and stretched, feeling the light of the sun warm her soul. "A beautiful morning."

She rose and dressed in the most beautiful gown Marita had provided, then stuffed her shorts and T-shirt in her backpack. She fingered the folded parachute and smiled. *Soon, we'll be going home. Today, my mission has succeeded.*

Emily brushed her hair and her teeth, then went downstairs. The saloon was empty except for Belle, but Emily was happy enough to smile at the bitter wench. Though Belle's eyes narrowed to slits, she made no mention of the watch, so Emily guessed the theft of Davis's key hadn't been noticed.

Belle eyed Emily's gown and sneered. "Looking pretty for your outlaw's hanging? But maybe you're happy to see him go."

Emily looked into Belle's unpleasant eyes and arched her brow dangerously. "I am happy about many things, Belle. Today will see justice, that much is certain. But whose, I wonder? The person who is truly guilty at heart will pay. I think, at last, we can all be sure of that."

Belle went to the saloon door and held it open. "Seems a lot of folk agree with you. Clem put your outlaw's boys to work early this morning."

Emily glanced out the door and saw Bonner, Clyde, and Herring heading out of town carrying gear that looked like a landscaper's tools. "What are they doing?"

Belle smirked. "Why, they're heading out to dig your husband's grave, that's what."

Emily's happiness faded. It wouldn't happen. It couldn't, not now—but that Darian's men would do such an evil deed. . . .

Emily walked out the door. The morning sun that had warmed her when she woke now stung her eyes. She shaded her eyes against the sun, and a new construction loomed in the town center.

She recognized the structure from movies. A scaffold, hastily constructed. An open coffin of light wood had been set beneath the trap door in the platform. Ping worked on the upper board, banging nails while he whistled. MacLeod stood below giving orders. He looked over and saw her. For an instant, his expression revealed sympathy.

Emily felt dizzy, in shock, and her legs moved like they were formed of cement as she walked toward the scaffold.

She stared up at the structure, shaking her head slowly. "What are you doing? Why would you do this? To betray him is horrible enough, but to help with this? What kind of men are you?"

Ping stopped hammering, and MacLeod started to speak, but Emily backed away. Tears obscured her vision, then fell to her cheeks. She wanted to shout at them, to pour her fury like a killer tidal wave over them, but no words would come. She turned, crying, and ran to the jail.

Emily stopped outside the door. Darian couldn't see her like this. She had to show him her strength, so that he felt her confidence. Emily reached for the door, but her hands were shaking. *I can't let him see me this way.* She turned and walked from the town, her head down, barely noticing where she was going.

As she passed the blacksmith's shop, she noticed Bonner and Clyde toiling on a small hillside. Herring seemed to be giving directions. Emily's chin firmed and she marched toward them. Herring noticed her arrival and motioned a quick signal to the diggers.

Dark fury boiling inside her, Emily reached the site of the hole they were digging. She looked in. Without warning, her legs went weak. A hot wave of nausea flooded through her, so strong that she sank to her knees. A harsh sob wracked her body, so fiercely that it hurt. She heard herself as if from a distance, "No, no. . . ."

She looked up. Bonner and Clyde had stopped digging and glanced at each other, then Herring, who appeared awkward. He shifted his weight from foot to foot, then cleared his throat twice. "Mrs. Woodward, I don't think this is the place for you this morning."

He sounded so calm, reasonable. Emily forced herself up, but she trembled with emotion. "Please, tell me you are going to save him."

None of the men answered. Emily looked at the hole again. It was already deep, deeper than a usual grave and seemed to extend overlong in one narrow passage. It was as if they enjoyed their craft and had made it elaborate for sport's sake.

"It's his grave. . . ." She closed her eyes, terrified. There had to be a reason, some plan. But no one said anything to comfort her. "How could you?"

She didn't expect an answer, and the men offered no explanation. All three looked pained, as if they wanted to comment, but couldn't. Emily looked from one to the other, then back at the hole. She pointed, her hand still shaking, at the dry, gaping sand. "He will never be here. No matter what you do, no matter what anyone does, I will stop this."

Without waiting for their comments, Emily turned and marched back to town. Her tears dried, but the vision of that grave burned into her mind. *I won't let it happen.* She shoved her hand into her dress pocket and fingered the pistol she'd stolen from Forbes. He hadn't taken it from her last night—an oversight on his part, but fate was with her in this, at least.

The fort commander hadn't arrived yet, so she would have to wait. She had expected him earlier. But what if he arrived just prior to Darian's scheduled hanging? She would have to be prepared to use her pistol, anything she had, to make him hear her.

She wanted desperately to talk to Darian, to ask his advice. But if he was guarded, there would be no opportunity. She headed back to the jail, fighting fear and anger for his sake. She gathered her courage, then opened the door. She'd hoped to see Forbes, but two new guards stood by Darian's cell. She couldn't risk telling him about her find in front of them, but she could give him some hope, still.

Darian saw her, and he rose, smiling. His courage astounded her, and the calmness inside him. She went to him and he took her hands through the bars. "Emmy, I've missed you."

She tried to smile. He couldn't know that she'd be crying. "I had a good night's sleep, Darian." She had to alert him to her success somehow, but the guards were paying too close attention. Probably instructed to report anything she said to Davis. "It was a very good night."

He appeared suspicious, but he understood her meaning. "I see that you remain unharmed, so I assume your good night did no damage."

She glanced at the guards who watched her intently. "No damage to me or to you, but. . . ." She stopped and cleared her throat. "It might be damaging to some." She gave him a look that screamed hope and victory. Darian smiled, but she didn't see the hope or confidence she'd wanted to create. Instead, he looked sad and resigned.

She had seen that expression before, but not on Darian's face. She had seen it on Ian Hallowell. Emily closed her eyes. *No. I can prevent this. It will not happen.*

Darian squeezed her hands. "Emmy, whatever happens, I want you to promise me that you'll take no risks." He paused as if broaching an uncomfortable subject. "There is one other thing."

"What?"

"When the time comes, this evening, at sunset. . . ."

Her throat tightened, but she fought her tears. "It will not happen."

He smiled, but she saw tears in his eyes, too. "If it does. . . . I don't want you there. Do you understand? I don't want you to see me that way."

The tears came, and she couldn't stop them. "How could I leave you at a time like that?"

Darian's tears fell, too. "I don't want you to see. Please, let your last memory of me be sweet, not horrible."

She nodded, but she would be there, even if he couldn't see her. They sank to the floor together, holding each other through the bars. He kissed her gently and they sat as close as they could get.

An old clock ticked slowly, in a haunting rhythm of

the past, on the jailhouse wall. All they wanted to say to each other passed unspoken, but heard fully, as Emily waited for the fort commander to arrive and stop a fate too horrible to endure.

Darian held Emily through the bars of his cell. He stroked her soft hair, and remembered the first time he had touched her this way. He thought of his brother, and the hours before Oliver's death. Now he faced his own. He had seen so much death during his lifetime that he had imagined his own could carry no particular terror, but as the hours ticked by, he knew he was wrong.

He wasn't afraid of pain, nor of humiliation or the loss of his once-impenetrable pride. He was afraid of losing Emily, of knowing that his death would shatter her. No longer did he care about vanquishing Clem Davis. As the day wore on, he began to see the general as just a small soul, perhaps spinning like a clock going backwards, negative, and bringing more negativity with him.

Maybe that's what all villains were. Not a huge force, just a human energy gone awry. Suddenly, Davis's fate didn't concern Darian. It was his own and Emily's that mattered. It was their love that meant everything now. He had been a foolish man. Justice and good would go on without him. Nothing Davis or any villain could do would truly alter that. Forever, there would be the battle between dark and light, and perhaps, after all, the dark served the light by allowing good to define itself. Perhaps in every action he'd taken, he had defined himself.

For that, however strange, he had his enemies to thank.

As the afternoon sun passed the window heralding sunset to come, a strange calm permeated Darian's soul. *I have done what I thought was right. I have loved oth-*

321

ers, and served them. And when the woman I loved most came into my life, not one of my fears or the scars of my soul stood in our way or prevented us from being together. I have joined with her, and become whole. Nothing they can do to me now will change that.

Emily had fallen asleep in his arms, her head half against his shoulder, and half against the cold steel bar of his jail cell. Despite what she'd told him, he knew she hadn't slept well. He knew the horrible toll this day had wrought upon her.

From outside the jailhouse, he heard riders. The fort commander had arrived. Now, within one hour, he would face death. For just a moment longer, he let her sleep. He looked down and saw the softness of her expression, the comfort she took in his presence. Gently, with all the love of his heart, he kissed her forehead.

She stirred in his arms, and for a moment, he saw that she had forgotten where they were, and what was to come. She smiled softly as if expecting him to take her in his arms and make love to her. Then with a wrench of pain, he saw her awareness flood back. He saw her terror when she heard the soldiers outside.

Her hands shook as she bolted upright. "Darian, they're here."

He smiled, gently, and nodded. "I know."

Her small body trembled and her eyes grew wide and round. "I have so little time."

"Emmy, there's nothing you can do now. Just love me, and know I love you."

She shook her head as if madness threatened to overcome her. "Like hell! I won't let anyone hurt you. You are the best man in the world. I will protect you."

"Emmy, no. . . . Please."

She kissed him, crying, then stood up. "Darian, I will not let you die." She cast a quick glance at his guards.

"I wish I could explain, to comfort you, but I can't. Just trust me."

"Don't do anything foolish. Promise me."

"I won't." She started to leave, then returned and held his hand once more. "I have to go. There's something I have to do, but I'll come back. We will be together again."

She started to pull away, but he drew her back and waited until she met his eyes. "If we are prevented from another farewell, know this: I have loved you since I first saw you lying tangled in that peculiar kite of yours. From that moment, you gave life to my heart, a heart that had nothing but pride for so long that I can't remember it otherwise. You have brought joy and warmth into my life, and I love you. I can't say that I don't long for a life spent at your side, but if this is all the time we have, it has been worth a thousand lifetimes."

She was crying, but she kissed his hand. "There is no parting between us. I will not let you go."

He watched her leave, but when she opened the door, he saw Davis and the fort commander shaking hands, smiling as if a victory had been won. And then he knew that their parting had already arrived.

"I need to speak with you, sir." Emily shoved her way between the guards and approached the fort commander. He was a tall man, stoic in appearance, but he didn't look cruel. She had been hoping for someone with Lieutenant Forbes's gentleness and warmth, but this man appeared logical, rational. Sometimes, she knew, those qualities were the most dangerous of all.

Davis smirked at her and turned to the commander. "It seems our outlaw officer took a bride during his rampage. Pretty little thing, but somewhat high-strung." He motioned to the guards. "Bring the prisoner, gentlemen. His hour is at hand."

Emily shook her fist. "It's your hour that's come, General."

Davis didn't appear nervous. "She's a troublemaker. MacLeod, keep this girl out of our way. Shall we take our places, sir?"

The commander nodded and went toward the gallows with Davis, chatting as if nothing more than an award's ceremony lay ahead. Emily tried to follow them, but MacLeod stepped forward and took her arm, preventing her.

"You watch yourself, girl." MacLeod spoke low, but sternly and his grip on her arm tightened. "For once, let the day unfold without interfering."

"I will not!" She tried to break free, but he held her fast. "I have proof that Davis is the one. . . ."

MacLeod's eyes narrowed. "What proof?"

She hesitated, then drew out the envelope. "I robbed the bank last night, and found this." Maybe if she could convince MacLeod that Darian had truly been wronged, he would come to his senses and do the right thing, after all.

"What is it?"

"Absolute proof that General Davis was the one directing those bandits who repeatedly robbed military funds. What do you think of that?"

A slow smile grew on MacLeod's face. At his expression, Emily's heart soared. "You do care, don't you?"

"It seems this day is going even better than I imagined. So it was Davis all along, was it?"

Emily bit her lip. His reaction made no sense. "It was Davis. It should be enough to prove him guilty . . . and Darian innocent."

MacLeod looked over the notes. "It certainly proves

Davis guilty. As for. . . ." He stopped and looked thoughtful. His expression altered again.

"Will you help him?"

He hesitated. "I'll do what needs to be done. You can be sure of that, my dear."

He sounded kind, as always before this nightmare began, but an element of doubt still floated inside Emily. "I will take the evidence to the commander. Now."

He nodded, slowly. "They won't let you anywhere near him. I'll handle this, don't you worry."

She hesitated. The sergeant was right—with Davis at his side, the commander wasn't likely to even let her speak. But MacLeod could do it easily.

She held tight to one side of the papers as MacLeod held the other side. He met her eyes, and she saw the old MacLeod, the faithful sergeant who loved Darian almost as much as she did. He smiled like a father, gentle and kind, and he whispered a quiet word, "Trust."

His word reached into her heart and gave hope to her soul. Emily released the papers. "Save him."

As she spoke, the guards led Darian from the jail. He walked straight and tall as always, his hands tied behind his back. He looked at her and smiled. She saw no fear in his eyes.

A crowd gathered around the gallows, chatting amiably. Even Penelope stood among them. Marita stood near Lieutenant Forbes and appeared to be crying. She spotted Emily and came to her.

"I will be here with you, Emily, if you want me to, but I think that it would be better to go inside until it's over." Her voice broke and she was trembling.

"Go inside, Marita. I'm all right."

Marita hugged her, then nodded. "I'm sorry, but I just can't watch this. If you need me, later, I'll be in my room. I'm sorry." Marita burst into tears, then ran back into the saloon.

The guards led Darian up the scaffold steps. Ping took his place near the noose, and to Emily's horror, she realized it was he, the young and faithful Ping, who would place the noose around Darian's neck. Even now, he smiled out at the crowd as if awaiting a summertime picnic at a festival.

MacLeod maneuvered himself to the seats set up for the general and the fort commander. Emily's heart held its beat as the sergeant took his place beside them. She waited, holding her breath, for him to reveal the general's crime, for the tables to turn on his villainy.

As the dark moment moved forward, she realized the sergeant was saying nothing other than pleasantries. He even laughed. She felt so sick she could barely see, barely breathe, but she forced herself to move. It couldn't be true. Despite their actions, she had trusted Darian's men, hadn't truly believed they would let him die. She had believed that somehow they were acting to save him.

Forbes must have noticed her expression, because he followed her as she stumbled forward through the crowd. As she reached the front of the gathered onlookers, Davis rose and went to the scaffold platform. He looked like the keynote speaker at a businessman's luncheon.

"Welcome, ladies and gentlemen, and honored guests. We are privileged to have General Forbes himself among us, as we witness the ending of this abominable threat to Tucson's peace and safety. This year, since Captain Darian Woodward mutinied against my own command in Camp McDowell, allying himself with the red men who terrorize the good people of Tucson almost daily, we have suffered much loss and hardship. Today, we will see an end to that threat, and a cessation to the bandit attacks led by Woodward since he turned traitor."

Emily flung herself forward. "*What?* Darian had nothing to do with those robberies. You did!"

For an instant only, the general's dark eyes flashed. A smile replaced his surprise, and then he laughed. The crowd joined him, and the laughter came like a rain of hellfire to her ears.

"I have proof!"

Emily shoved a guard aside and tried to reach the commander, but MacLeod caught her arm and held her back. She struggled like a wild animal. "What are you doing? You know! I gave you the evidence. Damn you, Sergeant! Tell them! Tell them the truth!"

Like the worst, unreal moment of a nightmare, MacLeod, too, laughed. He nodded to Ping. "I'd say we'd best get this over with before this little lady gets herself in more trouble."

He spoke lightly. Emily fought a violent wave of nausea. She fought, she bit, and she kicked. Nothing reached her, no one could stop her.

"Emmy. . . ."

Darian's voice came like the voice of heaven and she froze. She looked up and met his gaze. Tears shimmered in his eyes, but he smiled. "Don't fight them, love. There's no need." She stared up at him, amazed by his calm. "You and I will never be truly parted, because our love is true and forever. We are one thing. I will not truly leave you, because we are part of each other. Do you understand?"

The crowd fell silent, like ghosts themselves around her. She looked up at Darian and knew he was the strongest man who ever lived. And he was part of her. She nodded, then whispered, "I love you so."

Davis's harsh laugh broke the eternal magic. "A sweet

farewell. I'm sure the ladies in the audience are deeply moved and have taken out their handkerchiefs." He turned to Darian. "Have you any last words, Woodward, or was your tender farewell to your wife enough?"

Darian met Davis's mocking gaze and held it for a long while. Davis squirmed, dark and suspicious, twitching with nervousness. The red setting sun sent a golden light that glinted on Darian's hair, shining on him like a god. Never in all the time Emily had known him had he looked more beautiful than he did right then.

"I have only this to say, General, and nothing more." Darian paused and Emily waited for the condemnation that Clement Davis surely deserved, for a speech from Darian that would prove to all that he was an innocent man, and Davis worse than a demon.

His gaze still on the squirming Davis, Darian smiled. It wasn't the mocking smile Davis deserved, but a gentle smile. "I forgive you."

Davis reeled as if he'd been struck. Dark anger glittered in his eyes, but Emily stared at Darian in disbelief. He hadn't spoken in mockery, or in sarcasm. He truly meant it. In his face, she saw peace and wisdom. It was as if she had seen his spirit elevate and ascend to something she had never seen before.

She looked at Ping, sure there would be a reaction in the men who had followed him so long and so well until this nightmare began. But Ping was looking at MacLeod as if waiting for a signal.

The signal for Darian's hanging.

You can't die.

Emily turned to MacLeod. "Please, tell them. Show them the. . . ." Herring leapt forward and clamped his hand over her mouth to stop her from speaking the nature of her evidence.

Davis eyed MacLeod and Herring suspiciously, but

he nodded his approval at their method of silencing Emily, then returned to his seat. "MacLeod, you may give the order at will."

Emily watched, horrified but frozen in shock and grief so overwhelming that she couldn't breath or move. Ping spoke quietly to Darian. He placed a black blindfold over Darian's eyes, and Darian didn't resist. He even paused to adjust Darian's uniform so that the buttons matched evenly.

As Herring held Emily, MacLeod stepped forward. "It will be my pleasure, General Davis. But this method, this hanging. . . . It seems a mite too easy, a bit too . . . impersonal for my tastes."

Davis eyed him doubtfully. "What are you talking about, Sergeant?"

"This young scoundrel has been a torment since he was first given command of our company back at Antietam Creek. I've been waiting for this moment for years. Stuck at his side just so as one day, I'd get a chance to do this."

Davis started to rise as MacLeod drew his revolver. "Sergeant, what are you . . . ?"

MacLeod aimed his revolver at Darian's heart, and a dark, evil smile crossed Davis's face before he replaced it with concern. Emily tried to scream, but Herring held her fast. A wall of terror closed in around her.

"Boy, hanging's too good for you. It's gonna be my bullet that stops your traitorous heart." Emily's scream drowned in her throat as MacLeod pulled the trigger of his gun.

Everything happened in a sick flash. The shot rang out, Ping pulled the platform lever, and Darian dropped through the trap door. He fell into the open coffin beneath with a dull thud and Ping jumped down beside him. He reached to check Darian's pulse.

"Good shot, Sarge! He's deader than a doornail!"

Emily's senses blurred and she swayed back against Herring. The crowd swarmed forward toward Darian's coffin, and the guards shoved them back. Davis made his way beneath the scaffold, bowing low to get beneath the railings and platform. He looked down at Darian's body and he smiled.

"A good shot, indeed, MacLeod. Went right through his heart." Like a monstrous barbarian, possessed by his own evil, Davis reached down and dabbed Darian's blood on his fingers. He held it up and sniffed, then laughed.

"A dead man's blood, for certain!" He turned to the onlookers. "MacLeod, I give you and your men the honor of removing Woodward's body. Take him and bury him, and let his grave be a monument to warn others of the dangers of walking the dark path."

Herring loosened his grip on Emily and joined the others. She struggled to reach Darian, but the guards formed a wall between them. Hatred filled her. Grief overwhelmed her. Nothing mattered but the fire inside.

Time moved in slow motion as the crowd milled about, commenting on MacLeod's dramatic victory. As if she watched herself from a distance, Emily drew Forbes's stolen pistol. The crowd parted so that all she saw was Darian's enemy as he stood gloating, laughing with the stoic commander.

She aimed her gun and found the trigger. Lieutenant Forbes caught her from behind and the shot went wild, firing toward heaven instead, and her true target lived on. For a moment, Davis appeared shocked, as if surprised at his own foolishness for not having checked her for weapons. Then, realizing he was truly safe at last, he laughed long and hearty.

Forbes held her body close and whispered in her ears.

"He would not have wanted this, Mrs. Woodward. Grant him this dignity, to know that you are safe. He bade me promise to protect you, and protect you, I will."

She heard Darian's voice in her mind—*Promise me*. With all the pain of her shattered heart, she collapsed against Forbes and sobbed.

Chapter Eighteen

Darian's men nailed his coffin shut. With each thud of their hammers, Emily's heart died yet again. MacLeod had refused to let her see her husband "this way," speaking like a father to a much-loved daughter. She had been too grief-stricken to fight.

The crowd dispersed. Marita had come back out of the saloon, and she and Forbes stayed beside Emily while the general chatted with the fort commander. Penelope stood not far away, but clearly not daring to speak either. It didn't matter. Nothing mattered now.

Davis placed his hand on the commander's shoulder. "Well, sir, would you come into Belle's saloon and have a drink before you ride back to the fort? Maybe make a night of it. Woodward's demise is surely worth an army celebration."

The commander appeared appalled by the suggestion

and started to shake his head, but MacLeod stepped forward, looking thoughtful.

"You know, sir, there's a lot to celebrate this day. But there's one little wrinkle in this suit that needs pressing."

He sounded like the old MacLeod, Darian's friend. He had shot Darian in cold blood, for some vengeance Emily couldn't begin to comprehend. And now he talked in his warm familiar voice. *Impossible.*

Davis turned to him, mildly annoyed by the interruption, but too swollen with his victory to object. "What is it, MacLeod? You want praise? You'll get it. We'll be toasting your heroism all night long. A reward? It's coming to you."

"Well, now, General, I am wanting something, and that's for damned sure. But it ain't a reward. More, *retribution,* so to speak."

Davis appeared impatient. "What more do you want, Sergeant? Perhaps you'd like to take this up with us later, after we've all had a drink or two."

"Thinking it has to be now, sir."

Davis rolled his eyes. "Well, on with it, then."

Slowly, as Emily watched amazed, MacLeod drew the envelope she had given him out of his coat, then held it up to the last rays of sunlight. "Found something damned strange, we did."

Davis eyed the envelope, not quite recognizing it. "What the hell is that?"

MacLeod shrugged, then turned his attention to the fort commander. "Here's the thing—the piece of the puzzle that just doesn't fit. Captain Woodward, he were a fine criminal. He could shoot with the best of them, and put a hole in a pigeon's eye at a thousand paces if need be. When he held up a coach, like magic, it would

333

be filled with gold. That boy was bred for crime, as I see it."

Davis scoffed. "We are all aware of Woodward's 'virtues,' Sergeant. What of it?"

MacLeod moved a little closer, and Darian's men formed a subtle circle around the general. "Thing is, there were one thing he wouldn't do, and that's rob a fellow officer."

Davis looked around, confused. "Your claim is not substantiated by the facts, Sergeant. Several trains and coaches bearing army funds have been robbed, at a great loss to our country and men at arms."

"I know that, and that's a fact, sir. No mistake there."

"Then, what?" Davis growled the question, but MacLeod seemed in no hurry to reveal his intentions.

"We six men who followed Woodward—that would include the late Wetherspoon as well—we were with him all through, until just these past few days when we saw the light and changed sides, so to speak. We've proven our honor beyond a shadow of a doubt." He paused to glance at the commander, who nodded his agreement. MacLeod crossed his arms over his chest, still waving the envelope.

"What is your point, Sergeant, if you have one?"

"My point, General, is that young Woodward, bad as he were, never held up a one of those parcels, excepting the one we got by mistake, and that's . . . accounted for already. Some say, General, that those bars were being sent to you."

Davis paled. "There's no truth in that. I know nothing about the gold you stole."

"Is that so?" MacLeod unfolded his arms, tore open the envelope, then passed the notes to the commander. "Think this straightens out who was behind them robberies, sir."

334

Davis took one look at the papers and reeled backwards. He fumbled for his gun, but Forbes leapt forward and knocked it from his hand. Without orders, the guards surrounded Davis and pinned him to the dry earth.

The commander read the evidence, then turned in astonishment to MacLeod. "Sergeant, I am astounded by this discovery. Clem Davis has been no favorite of mine, but I never dreamed he was capable of such treachery."

MacLeod beamed. "It ain't that much of a shock to me, sir."

"This may be worth a promotion, Sergeant. You have served your country well this day."

MacLeod shrugged. "If it's all the same to you, sir, I'm liking where I am now. Think I'll stay on as sheriff."

"As you wish, Sergeant. See that Woodward is buried. We will take Davis with us. I can assure you his punishment will be in line with his crimes."

Davis struggled beneath the guards, but they held him pinned to the ground. Belle came out of the saloon and screamed. "Clem! What is going on?"

Emily watched spellbound as Davis's mistress assessed his current position. Belle's gaze darted from MacLeod to the commander, then back to Davis. "I didn't know nothing about his dealings! All those gifts he gave me, I didn't know where they came from."

"Loyal to the end." Marita spoke beside Emily, but Emily was too numb to care. Marita tapped Lieutenant Forbes's shoulder. "Emily found the key to his safe in Belle's room, hidden in a pocket watch. She knew what he was up to."

Forbes spoke to the commander, who motioned to Belle. "It seems you, madam, are possessed of more information concerning General Davis's treacherous activities than you claim. Your own fate might be equally dark. . . ."

Belle's face paled and her gaze shot between the officers. "All right, he told me some of it. But he threatened to kill me if I said anything."

Marita's brow angled. "He gave you expensive gifts. He even paid for the saloon. I'd say he didn't need to threaten you. You were bought and paid for."

Belle glared at Marita. "I don't want this cursed saloon!"

Herring stepped forward, looking hopeful. "I'll take it off your hands. Give you two hundred for it."

Belle hesitated, but apparently realized her options were limited. "Done."

The fort commander motioned to a guard, who took Belle into custody. "If you're willing to give evidence against Davis, I'm sure your fate will be much easier."

She cast a quick glance, devoid of affection, at Davis. "I'll do whatever you want. But I don't want to give back any of them presents. I put up with plenty to earn them."

Marita cringed. "I'm sure you did."

Emily watched in disbelief as Herring seized the keys to the saloon and fixed them to his belt. They all looked so happy, except for Davis.

The guards hauled Davis to his feet and bound his hands tight behind his back. His dark eyes flitted like a trapped animal, then fixed on Emily. "You bitch! You damned bitch! You're responsible for this. You've ruined me!"

Emily felt nothing. All she saw was Darian's face, his perfect calm. She spoke in a small voice which sounded far-off and strange to her ears. "General Davis, you are the luckiest man in the world."

The onlookers turned to her, drawn by her far-off voice. Marita touched her arm. "Why, Emily?"

Emily looked at her, then Davis again. "Don't you

know? You were forgiven by an angel, and now the angel is free."

Emily lay in her bed. As if heaven itself wept, a soft rain fell, pattering gently against her window. The raucous celebration in the saloon downstairs had died down, and now quiet filled the air. Forbes had promised to take her north to Tiotonawen, but Emily knew she would never leave the past now. Before dawn, she would rise, and she would walk out into the desert. She would sit by Darian's grave, then decide where to go next.

Maybe she would just walk forever until time itself swallowed her.

She hadn't cried since Darian fell into his coffin. As she lay in darkness, Emily knew she would never cry again. Like Darian.

Like Darian.

She closed her eyes and tried to feel him. *I will not truly leave you, because we are part of each other.* She expected to feel his spirit beside her, but instead, she just felt alone and so empty that she didn't feel real or human anymore.

The silence surrounded her, outside and within. Nothing or no one could enter it now.

She started to drift toward sleep, but footsteps woke her again. Someone was ascending the stairs, quietly.

Emily sat up in bed and stared at the door. It creaked open, and a large, dark man emerged. If he had come to kill her, she would welcome it. He crossed her room silently, and she made no move to flee.

Very little light came through her window because of the rain, so she couldn't see his face, even when he sat down on the bed beside her.

"It's not a night for strolling, but, Mrs. Woodward, will you take a walk with me now?"

She knew his voice. "MacLeod. . . ."

He took her hand and pressed it between his. "It's me."

She yanked her hand away. "How can you think. . . ? How can you imagine I would go anywhere with you? Davis, he was scum, a truly evil man, but Sergeant, you're worse."

In the darkness, he laid his hand on her shoulder—that old, paternal warmth was still evident in his touch. "Mrs. Woodward, I have only one thing to say, and I beg you to hear me."

She grit her teeth, hating him. "What is it?"

"Trust."

They rode out into the desert as the rain fell, Emily on her fat mare and MacLeod riding Darian's beautiful gray. MacLeod didn't speak, and Emily didn't ask questions. She hoped he intended to shoot her, but no explanation came for his odd behavior. As they rode on, the first light of the hour before dawn broke the black sky, grayed still by the veil of rain.

As she guessed, he led her to the site of Darian's grave. They dismounted, and in the dark mist over the desert, she saw a group of men standing shadowed against the gray sky.

She stopped, but MacLeod walked on ahead to join them. They stood in wedge formation, and MacLeod took his place beside the tallest.

The first light of morning dawned, casting a silver ray over the hills. It glinted on the tall man's hair, and silver turned to gold.

Emily fell to her knees and sobs tore through her like screams of pain and perfect hope.

Darian stepped forward, then knelt before her. He caught her in his arms and pulled her close, so close that she couldn't tell where she ended and he began.

"Emmy, my love. . . . My love."

She cried and cried, her body shaking with her sobs. He hugged her and kissed her and she knew he cried, too. "Darian, my angel. . . . You're alive. *Alive.* Oh, please tell me you're truly alive."

At last, she drew back to look at him. She touched his face to be sure he was real. His men gathered in around them, all smiling. All . . . *themselves.*

"I'm not a ghost, love. And we are together again, forever."

She looked around at his men, then at Darian. "What happened? I saw MacLeod shoot you."

"The sergeant is an excellent shot, my love. Good enough to miss by a hair's breadth."

"But I saw the blood." She checked his shirt, and saw that it was still streaked with red.

"Blood indeed, but not mine. I'm told it was chicken's blood, but I have not asked the details."

"Chicken's blood?" Emily was shaking so much that her teeth chattered, and Darian wrapped his arm around her to warm her. "You mean, it was all a ruse?"

"A very clever ruse." Darian glanced at his men and smiled. "So clever that I knew nothing about it until Ping went to wrap the blindfold around my eyes."

Emily gaped at Ping. "You told him all this in that short space of time?"

Ping nodded proudly, and Emily looked at Darian in amazement. "What did he say?"

Darian's smile grew. "Trust."

"But . . . but they buried you!"

Ping gestured at the opened grave behind them. "We buried him well and deep, and that's for sure. Thing is, though, Herring had the hole dug just perfect so that we could stick in one of the pipes from the blacksmith's

339

shop. The captain could breathe just fine until we could get back to dig him up again."

Emily cringed despite her relief. "Darian! Weren't you terrified?"

He kissed her cheek. "Today, I learned to trust beyond any doubt, my dear. I wasn't terrified, no. Uncomfortable, yes. But a man who has just been saved from execution can endure a little discomfort."

Emily stood up, and Darian stood with her, holding her hand tight in his. "It seems that word has found true meaning in both our hearts this day. You men have saved us both, and risked yourselves in the doing. I am forever grateful to you."

MacLeod looked embarrassed but proud. "It's a shame we couldn't think of a way to salvage your reputation, Captain. Tried our best, but we couldn't see a way to get around a few of your . . . well, your mistakes, if you will."

Darian laughed. "It seems I've made more than a few, but never in those I have loved. Never in you."

Emily's brow furrowed. "Is that why you didn't show my evidence before the hanging?"

MacLeod nodded. "That's right, girl. We had it planned to save your husband from the time he headed off like a madman to break you out of jail. We knew he wouldn't listen to us, so we put our heads together and came up with a way to save him whether he wanted us to or not. You finding that evidence was just icing on the cake."

Emily looked to Bonner and Clyde. "You knew! When I broke into the jail, you were awake. You knew what I was up to."

The two men nodded, slightly, offering nothing more, but MacLeod laughed. "Bonner and Clyde here figured they'd let you do your work, and they weren't going to turn you in, in any case. Said you made a damned fine burglar, too."

"Did they?" Emily beamed. Coming from those two, high praise indeed. She smiled at them. "Thank you!"

They nodded, but didn't speak.

Emily bit her lip. "I'm not sure I want to know this, but what really happened to the gold we stole?"

MacLeod shrugged. "Aw, it were just some of Davis's loot. Bonner and Clyde here put it into the bank. They've got good plans for it. Don't say much about it, but them two know numbers, I can promise you that."

Emily held up her hand. "Say no more. I don't want to know this. But what about the rest of you? What will you do now?"

"Well, thanks to old Davis, we're all set fine. Herring's got the saloon from Belle, I'm set up as the sheriff. Ping's going to marry Miss Penelope tomorrow morning. . . ."

Ping beamed happily. "I'm sorry you won't be there, Mrs. Woodward. I'd hoped more than anything to have the captain stand up for me, but it looks like that's impossible now."

Darian patted Ping's shoulder. "Ping, you have my blessing in your marriage. I know it will be a happy one. Penelope is a lucky woman."

"She's a good woman. I had to tell her we were up to something. She wanted me to tell you both that she loves you, and she'd have given anything to reassure Emily. But we couldn't take the risk of warning either of you."

Emily brushed away tears. "I understand, Ping. You saved Darian's life. You're the best friends anyone ever had. I love you all, and I will never forget you."

She turned slowly to Darian as the sun turned the gray

341

sky blue, and the rain faded to memory. "What about you?"

Darian smiled. "Don't you mean 'about us'?"

"That, too."

Darian looked to the sky. "There was a time when all that mattered to me was regaining my honor. But yesterday, when I found myself forgiving Davis, I knew that I had never lost it. He couldn't take it from me, because it was always within. I am willing to let my name go down as outlaw . . . as long as I have you by my side in life."

She hugged him and kissed his cheek. "Darian, you will have me at your side forever. But where? Here, or in the future?"

Darian looked around at his men. "All those who were in my care are now well-situated. There is no place for me in this world. But in yours? Perhaps I will find it there. There is something I have felt inside, from the time I lay in the coffin."

"What?"

"As if I'm looking for something. Or maybe someone's looking for me. Whatever the case, I believe that something lies in the future. We will go north to Tiotonawen, and there at last, I may find the answers I have searched for."

Emily hugged him, and he kissed her. "If you are with me, there is nothing we can't do."

Thundering hoofbeats shattered the silence of dawn. Someone galloped toward them, and for a horrible instant, Emily felt sure they had won the great battle only to lose, after all. As one, Darian's men drew their guns, and they formed a semicircle with Darian at their center.

Only one rider approached them. The faint morning sun glinted on blond hair, and Lieutenant Forbes leapt down from his horse. He stopped, shocked when he saw

Darian standing among his men. For a long while, he just stared openmouthed while Darian's soldiers aimed their guns.

Emily tugged at MacLeod's arm. "You can't shoot him! He saved me. He saved Darian."

Forbes looked between them, then at Darian, his young face revealing disbelief . . . and admiration. "How did you do it? To pull off something like this . . . it's unbelievable."

Darian smiled. "I am a fortunate man, Lieutenant."

"It's more than luck, sir. To have men that will follow you this way. . . . I envy you for that."

"Follow me? Yes, I suppose they followed me through hell and back, during the war, and after. But it takes more than loyalty, Lieutenant. It takes men who are willing to defy your orders and take matters into their own hands."

Forbes's brow creased at this military blasphemy. "That is not what we were taught at West Point, sir."

"No. You don't learn these things at a military academy, that's true." Darian sighed and looked up at the sky. "You learn them here, in the desert. You learn it in the mountains, and far out at sea. You learn them when what you truly love matters more than all the rules in the world."

Forbes touched the gun in its holster, his young face torn by doubt and confusion. "If I draw this, I know I will die, and perhaps take up residence in this grave you so recently vacated."

Darian glanced at his men. He said nothing, but he nodded a signal, and every man dropped their guns. Darian stepped forward, a pace away from Forbes. Their eyes met, blue on blue. Then Darian tossed aside his gun.

Forbes stared in astonishment. He cast his eyes heavenward, then drew his revolver and passed it to Darian. Emily breathed a shuddering sigh of relief as Darian passed it back to the lieutenant. "Keep it, Forbes. I am leaving now—my wife and I have a life to live far from this place. But this desert, it will see a flood of people coming west to call it home, and with them come greed and avarice, but also love. They will need all the help they can get to choose the right path. I will leave their protection in your hands."

Forbes seemed to like the higher task Darian appointed. He looked proud, and as Darian moved aside with Emily, the lieutenant took his place beside MacLeod. "I gave you my word to protect your wife. I can see that promise is no longer required."

Darian grinned. "My wife's protection is well in hand, I assure you."

Emily went to Forbes and hugged him. "I think you will have a wife of your own soon, Lieutenant. Marita is a very adventurous woman. She will need all the protection she can get."

Forbes blushed, but he was smiling. "I will do my best."

Darian looked pleased with the young officer's ascension to his former position as leader. "Then I know I leave my friends in the best of hands."

Darian turned one last time to face his men. One by one, he shook their hands, then hugged them. He stood back and they looked at each other, reliving an eternity at war, a love of peace, and a trust very few had ever shared.

"You men have been with me since my boyhood, when I came to serve you as a rash and proud officer. You gave me your trust, and in turn earned mine. You saved my life, and my soul. Wherever you go, whatever paths you choose, know that you have my blessing and my love. I will never forget you."

Ping led Darian's gray horse forward, along with Emily's fat mare. No one spoke as they mounted, though much passed between them. For a timeless while, they waited, speaking a silent farewell when no words would suffice. Then, as the sun at last broke through the gray clouds and turned the morning sky to blue, he faced his men one last time.

As one, the men saluted him.

He returned the salute and then, together, he and Emily rode away.

They rode north with more joy and peace than Darian had ever known in his life. No urgency drove them forward now. He realized he had lived every day for the last year as if it might be his last. Maybe he had lived that way since the Civil War began. But for the first time in his life, Darian felt free.

They rode at a leisurely pace, riding in the cooler hours of morning, stopping to eat and to lie together in the shade when the sun was high. They made love at every opportunity. Twice, sometimes four times a day. Each time, they learned something new. Sometimes, he took her slowly, building the tension between them until their cries of passion echoed across the desert. Sometimes, they would be riding together, look at each other, then stop and make love still standing, half dressed. He could never say which he liked better, and Emily encouraged each with equal fervor.

Sometimes, she directed their union—she would tease him, or go down on her knees before him to suckle him boldly beneath the sun. No one could see them—no one existed but them. If they passed water, they stopped to indulge themselves in its depths. When they found a space of soft sand, they made a bed for their love.

Darian had never known such bliss, and for the first time in his life, no doubt assailed him. He believed, no matter what, they would find a way to be together forever.

Their journey's end came sooner than he would have liked when they reached the foothills that concealed the secret path to Tiotonawen's village. They ascended the path and found the warrior, Haastin, waiting for them as if he expected their arrival.

Haastin smiled when Darian approached. "I see no rope around your neck, Captain, but word came to us that you had died."

Darian glanced at Emily. "You have heard of what happened in Tucson?"

Haastin cast them both a deliberately mysterious look. "The red man, he knows much."

Darian's brow rose. "The red man, he has a friend at the fort, I think."

Haastin's superior expression faded and he shrugged. "Come with me. The father of the whirlwind awaits you."

"So, young onion, you are now truly what you are." Tiotonawen stood assessing Darian, and then nodded thoughtfully. "I see the man I saw before, but much that he carried has gone. He has, I think, left his name behind him. He walks on nameless, but free."

Darian bowed. "If that is so, perhaps you will do me the favor of not calling me 'young onion' from this time forth."

"That is a fair request."

Emily stood beside him, hopping from foot to foot in agitation and excitement. "Never mind all this! We want to go back to the future. Can you send us now?"

"No."

She gaped, and Darian's heart skipped a beat. What if there were some glitch he hadn't foreseen? He closed his eyes. Had he so soon forgotten all he had learned. *Trust*. They would find a way.

Emily sputtered incoherently, then stomped her small foot. "No? What do you mean, 'no'? Adrian said you'd send me back when I was ready."

Tiotonawen fingered his cane. "That is true. I will send you back, because that is where you came from. But him. . . ." He pointed at Darian. "What makes you think he's not there already?"

Emily clenched her fist and punched the air. "Because he's here with me!"

"Are you not part of a whole already? Have you not always been so?"

She waved her fist fiercely at the chief, who stepped back despite her small stature. "Don't give me any of that double talk! I'm going back to the future, and Darian is coming with me. If you won't do it, then I'll . . . I'll fling myself into a whirlwind without your approval!"

Tiotonawen laughed despite himself. "That will get you bruised and dirty, but little else. Young woman, you will go where the father of the whirlwind directs you, and when he directs you."

She looked like she might actually attack. Darian seized her fist and eased her balled fingers apart as he took her hand in his. "Emmy, have you forgotten? *One thing*. That means trust."

She closed her eyes, then drew a breath. "I'm sorry, but it's so hard. I want to live. Do you understand? You and I have been fighting for the chance to love, and just to survive, since we met. Now I want to truly live. I want to see you in the morning, and take showers together, and go out to a restaurant for breakfast, and maybe go dancing at night. I want to teach you to drive a car, and take you to movies, and travel to interesting places with you. I want to go to a Caribbean island with you and lie in the sun, and snorkel and swim. I want to go into the mountains and teach you to ski. You'd love skiing. You're so . . . Nordic. More than anything else, I want to have children with you, and watch them grow, and see you adjust their small white shirts. . . ."

She turned to Tiotonawen. "Please, sir. We love each other so much. We've learned there's nothing more important. Now we want to live with the love that we've found. Please."

The chief looked between them. "I cannot send you now."

Darian's heart crashed, but he took her hand and kissed it. "We can live here, Emmy. It doesn't matter, as long as we're together."

She nodded, then smiled wistfully up at him. "I can live without those things, as long as I'm with you. We can still have children." She turned to the chief. "Well, thank you, anyway, sir. We'll be all right, I'm sure."

The old man puffed an impatient breath. "I said only that I cannot send you now. In a short while, I will do as you ask."

Emily looked at Darian and he shrugged. "Why in a short while?"

The chief straightened. "You will do us the honor of sitting with us for our evening meal, and you will tell us how you defeated the general who had the hardness of the earth's rock in his soul. You will tell us how you came to die, yet live. Then I will send you where you want to go."

Emily reached out and seized the surprised chief's

hand, then shook it vigorously. "Tiotonawen, it's a deal!"

Darian regaled the Apache with tales of their adventures in Tucson. Emily listened as he minimized certain parts that made him sound heroic, like his gunfight with Tradman, but what Darian failed to mention, she built up with momentous glory.

Darian continued their story, but when he told of Tradman's death, the Apache chief fell silent, then turned his proud face to the heaven's above.

"This man, Tradman, he killed my youngest son and my son's wife and baby daughter. While Tradman walked the earth, the earth suffered and groaned. Now it is lighter, and my son is free."

Emily nodded vigorously. "Tradman was a rotten man. But he didn't have the scope Davis possessed. Still, I can't help wishing that the general had met the same fate."

Darian patted her hand. "Trust me, my love. There was nothing worse for Clement Davis than seeing all that power he had built up around him crumble. There, at the end, when Belle turned on him to save herself— he knew his power had been built on nothing."

"So you heard all that, even nailed in your coffin?"

"I did, and what I missed, Ping filled me in on when they dug me up. Do you know, he chattered the whole time?"

"I'm not surprised." Emily kissed his shoulder. "You'll miss him."

"I'll miss them all. But I know they are happy, and now they can live their lives as they deserve. I believe that is what we were fighting for in the war. And I believe that is what my brother won when he died. The freedom to go on, knowing he had lived life to its fullest."

"You've forgiven yourself."

Darian looked up at the new stars in the dark blue sky. "I have. And I believe he is with me, and with you, because the bond between us was love, and for all that assailed us, love never dies."

Emily leaned against him and yawned. "We have to get up early tomorrow, according to the chief. Let us say good night to the others and go to bed. I am very sleepy."

Darian rose and took her hand, but he caught the bright glimmer in her eyes. "My love, we will do as you suggest. But I know you better than that, Emmy. The last thing you intend to do tonight is sleep."

Epilogue

Emily and Darian stood on the edge of a sharp cliff. Below them were huge boulders, then the endless desert glittering in the new morning light. Tiotonawen stood beside them, silent, his eyes closed as he summoned the whirlwinds from the bowl of the desert.

In the distance, Emily saw the wind and dust take shape, and many spirals formed to move toward them. Her brow furrowed as she contemplated the meaning and spiritual significance of the act.

"How come you can just call these things over the desert, yet Adrian had to fly up to ten thousand feet and drop me?"

Tiotonawen opened one eye, which twinkled devilishly. "My son is wise."

"Your son takes the hard way, I think."

"He puts you through the test."

"What test?"

"The test of courage, young woman. A woman who dares to drop out of the sky for the sake of a man she has never met—that woman is brave enough to save that man, and bring him with her to the future."

Emily puffed with pride. "That's true!" She hesitated. "Still, there is no chance of me *ever* skydiving again."

Darian glanced down at her. "The notion of flying appeals to me. Perhaps the Indian will teach me the art."

"No time soon!" She groaned, then clasped her hand to her forehead. "Just hang on to that parachute. It has to support us both, you know."

Darian kissed the top of her head. "I wouldn't let go for the world."

As he spoke, the whirlwinds drew near, then congealed into one giant spiral. It rose and the wind howled. Tiotonawen turned one last time to Darian and Emily. "Tell my son I will keep my grandson's image always, and that I expect many more grandchildren awaiting me when I reach the forever lodge."

Darian nodded. "I will do that, sir."

"Say farewell now to your fear, both of you. You take trust with you to the future, and the lessons you've learned can take their home in the past. Use it well, for each hour of your happiness lends hope to all. And, yes, to me as well. Live well. . . ."

Tiotonawen's voice trailed into the swirling wind, but Emily felt sure she heard the phrase "young onion" as it was blown back and driven into the past behind her.

The wind caught them and their parachute, and yanked them up and off their feet, spinning them together until Emily had no idea which end was up, or how far they had gone off the ground. Darian held tight to her, protectively, and she closed her eyes. They spun in endless circles, lifting and falling and jetting forward unexpectedly.

Without warning, the whirlwind jerked them backwards, then shot them free of its grasp. They slid onto a green surface, then fell facedown together on short, perfect, clipped grass.

Emily opened her eyes and looked around. "Oh, no!"

Darian struggled to free himself, but the parachute bound them together. "What's the matter, love? Are you injured?"

"We're on . . . I can't believe it . . . a golf course!"

Someone came running toward them, then stopped with a loud, defeated groan. "I knew it!"

Emily squirmed around to see Adrian de Vargas looking down at them. Darian unsnapped the parachute, dusted himself off, and sat up to greet Adrian. Darian's blue eyes twinkled and his lips curled in a satisfied smile. " '*Adorable,*' eh? Well, well, well. . . ."

Adrian winced and cast an accusatory glance at Emily. "I never said that."

He held out his hand and helped Darian up, yanking with slightly too much force. Darian slapped Adrian's shoulder fondly, yet a bit too hard. "It seems you missed me acutely, Indian. So much that you sent a lovely messenger to lure me forward to your time. I am honored."

"I did no such thing." Adrian paused. "It was all Cora's idea."

Emily looked between them. They greeted each other like old friends. Adversarial, competitive friends, but she could see their joy at reuniting. Cora hurried up behind Adrian, pushing a stroller in front of her.

"Captain Woodward! You're alive! Thank God!" She burst into tears, then hugged him. Cora turned to Emily, beaming with happiness. "I knew you could do it, Emily."

Emily smiled. "I had to do a lot more than I'd imagined, but yes, it worked out fine. He's alive, though I had to see him shot and buried to stop him from getting hanged."

Adrian's eyes narrowed suspiciously. "That isn't exactly what we'd hoped to hear."

Emily shrugged. "It's a long story."

Cora took her hand and examined her wedding ring. Her bright eyes glittered with understanding. "Will you have dinner with us, and tell us everything?" She fingered the ring. "This, in particular, must have a story behind it."

Emily bit her lip, then giggled despite her effort to remain dignified. "Do you suppose weddings performed in the past are still legal in the future?"

Cora twisted her lips to one side. "I think they bear repeating no matter what. We'll have to figure out what to do about identification for the captain, but we'll worry about it later."

Adrian nodded. "That could be a problem, but for now, we'll drive you back to Tucson and get you set up together. You've had a long day, and it's not yet eight o'clock in the morning."

Darian looked around in utter astonishment. He stared at the cars and seemed surprised by the level of noise in the air. Emily couldn't wait to show him her world, but a vague disquiet rose inside her. How would he get along, not knowing how to drive, or how anything worked? He had no money, no identification. . . . She banished the thought. They would find a way.

Cora glanced at the highway beyond the golf course where a long line of cars inched by, bottled up in the flow of traffic. She frowned. "Rush hour. We'll have to take the Ping Parkway to save time. It's a prettier drive, anyway."

Emily's brow furrowed tight. "I don't remember a Ping Parkway between Phoenix and Tucson."

Cora looked confused. "It's one of the most expensive, scenic highways in the country. The Ping water gardens along the way are amazing, too."

Adrian checked his watch. "We should have time to make a few stops. If you're interested, the Ping Desert Museum is worth a look."

Emily and Darian exchanged a glance. "A lot has changed since I left."

Adrian pointed across the golf course to where his Jeep was parked. "I've got to stop at the bank, but that will just take a minute. There's a branch just past the club house, right, Cora?"

She nodded. "There's a branch of the Bonner and Clyde Trust just about everywhere."

Emily gasped. "Bonner and Clyde Trust? You're kidding?" She looked at Darian. "This can't be a coincidence."

Cora drew out her checkbook and showed Emily the bank's address. Emily read the caption in amazement. " 'Bonner and Clyde Trust, the most trusted name in banking since 1870.' Dear God!"

Darian nodded his approval at his former soldiers' apparent fortune. "I don't know what you've got against Bonner and Clyde. They were very fond of gold, you know. It's only natural they'd make a name for themselves in banking."

Emily cast her hands up and then bowed to the inevitable. "Well, I guess we know what happened to the gold you stole, anyway."

Adrian slapped Darian's back. "So you turned out to be quite a bandit, did you, Captain? Terrorized the Southwest, made a name for yourself that will live in infamy ever after. . . ."

Darian glared. "I maintained polite behavior at all times."

Adrian winked at Emily, then gestured at her wedding ring. "Is that so? Then how did you manage to get this ring on her finger?"

Emily blushed. "His proposal was very polite and romantic." She paused, struggling with conscience. "Then, of course, he shot Tradman in a duel. . . ."

Adrian's brow rose. "A gentleman to the last."

Much had changed since Emily left the future. To Adrian and Cora, "Ping Parkway" was nothing strange. "I wonder what the history book you read says now?"

Cora tapped her lip. "As I remember, it said Captain Woodward was shot by a soldier just before he was to be hanged."

Adrian nodded. "The soldier . . . MacLeod, wasn't it? He was the one who turned Davis in, too. He's remembered as quite a hero."

Darian smiled. "Then the past is truly as it should have been."

Emily elbowed him. "Except for the 'Ping Parkway.' "

Adrian looked between them doubtfully. "So, are you two hungry? There's a great little diner not far from here. It's a chain, but the Herring Stops are about the best in Arizona."

Emily groaned. "*Herring* Stops? I guess we know what happened to Herring." She glanced at Darian, but he didn't react. Instead, he looked suddenly pale. Emily touched his arm. "Maybe we should eat. You look pale."

Darian shook his head as if to clear his senses. "It's nothing. I'm fine, Emmy. Yes, let us eat at Herring's new facility. I trust the place that bears his name will offer a meal as good as those he prepared himself."

Adrian motioned them forward, but Darian stumbled. Emily caught his arm. "Darian, what's the matter? Are you all right?"

He swayed. "I don't know. I'm dizzy. Emmy, something's wrong."

Emily turned desperately to Adrian. "What's wrong with him? Does it have something to do with time travel?"

Adrian took Darian's arm to steady him. "I don't know. Nothing like this happened to us."

Darian staggered forward, then dropped to his knees. Pain contorted his face. Emily knelt beside him and wrapped her arm around him tight. "Darian, what's the matter?"

He shook his head. "I don't know. . . ." He winced, but his pain seemed emotional rather than physical, as if he endured a great shock. "No . . . no."

Emily looked desperately to Adrian for help, but he looked as shocked as she was. "Can't we do something? What's happening to him?" She started to cry and she was shaking. *I can't lose you now. Please, don't leave me.*

Cora grabbed Adrian's arm. "We should get him to a hospital."

Adrian nodded and started away. "I'll get the Jeep."

"There's no need." Darian spoke clearly, and Adrian turned back.

Darian took Emily's hand and squeezed it. "Don't cry, Emmy. I'm all right." He stood up as if nothing had happened and drew her up with him.

She dried her cheeks and peered into his eyes. He had changed, but she wasn't sure how. "What happened to you?"

Darian touched her cheek. "Emmy, I'm sorry. Please forgive me."

He sounded different, too, but she wasn't sure how. "For what?"

"He was calling me. Since I met you, I've been troubled by dreams of someone calling me."

"Who was calling you?" Darian had obviously suffered some kind of trauma from time travel. But he looked healthy enough.

"Don't you know, Emmy? Haven't you guessed?"

"Know what? And who was calling you?"

"Ian Hallowell." He paused. "Myself."

Emily backed away. "Ian is gone. We changed the future, like Ping Parkway. Ian probably never happened."

Darian smiled. "Do you remember him?"

Tears welled in her eyes. "I will never forget."

"Then he happened." Darian placed his hand over his heart. "He is here."

The tears fell to her cheeks, but she had no idea why the emotion for Ian remained so strong. Darian had saved her from the heartache Ian had created, and she had saved Darian from becoming Ian. Hadn't she? "He left me."

"And you have never known why." Darian held her hand tight and looked deeply into her eyes. "Do you want to know why now?"

"No!" Emily bit her lip hard and looked at her feet. "Yes."

"He was dying, Emmy. Didn't you know? Somewhere in your heart, didn't you know that I would never have left you for any other reason?"

"That can't be. It can't." She fought her emotion. "How do you know?"

Darian closed his eyes, then looked at her again. In the deep blue, she saw a shadow of her former husband. "Ian's memories are within me now. He left you because the blood tests you took for your marriage license revealed a terminal heart condition. He could never have made love to you again, nor given you children. He . . . I . . . have been living at home alone with a personal nurse for seven years. I wonder what she'll say when she finds I'm gone."

Emily began to tremble as the full truth of her past came clear. "No . . . Why didn't he tell me? Why didn't his parents tell me?"

"They respected his wishes. Or were they my wishes? I'm not sure now. Ian believed you would find a life without him, but only if he destroyed your trust. Isn't that ironic? To save you, he thought he had to destroy the one thing you needed most—trust. I have learned better, but he knew no other way."

Emily stood with her head bowed. "What happened, then? Was it because your men betrayed you that he felt trust was an enemy?"

Darian stroked her hair gently from her face. "My men never betrayed me, not in the past we just lived, nor in any other. In the version which created Ian, they were killed alongside me. It was their trust in me that I blamed, the same trust Ian tried to destroy in you—because he thought it was a danger."

Emily looked up at him and saw him as she had never seen him before. This was her beloved Darian, but more, because he had accepted that part of him which reacted on fear, letting it obliterate love, and so, brought it home. Now he was whole, and he was hers.

Maybe he had been hers all along, but she had been too afraid to believe it.

Darian drew her into his arms and held her tight. He felt strong and powerful, truly alive. He stood back and turned to Adrian and Cora. "You mentioned breakfast, Indian. It seems I am hungry, after all."

Adrian held out his hand, and Darian shook it. "I am pleased to see you whole, Captain." Adrian paused, and his dark eyes twinkled. "I take it this 'Ian' version of yourself was also irritating."

Darian smiled, proud. "He was."

Adrian smiled, too. "Good. Wouldn't want it any other way."

They walked to Adrian's Jeep, but when Darian bent to get in, he stopped, then fumbled in his pocket. "That's odd. . . ." He drew out a wallet Emily didn't know he had and opened it. He pulled out a license and studied it intently, then read, "*Ian David Hallowell.*"

Emily took it. "There's an address . . . and you have credit cards." She felt strange looking at Darian, and knowing her young husband lived inside him, *was him.* "What do you remember of Ian's life?"

Darian hesitated, his brow furrowed. "It isn't clear." He closed his eyes, concentrating. "I have parents. My father is a history professor. Until I fell ill, I had joined him in that profession. He keeps a position open for me now, hoping against hope I will recover." A smile crossed Darian's face. "It is a good profession, and my thesis was on the Civil War. I shall better the teaching now, naturally. . . ."

Emily watched in amazement as Ian's memories returned to Darian. He opened his eyes and she saw the full light of his soul within. "There is one thing I remember more clearly than all else."

"What?"

He bent and kissed her forehead. "You, Emmy. Loving you. I never stopped."

Tears filled her eyes and she hugged him. "I never stopped loving you, either."

Adrian went to the driver's side door. "Well, Captain, it looks like you have a career all set for you. You've got two names to deal with, but I'm sure you'll manage that fine. Ian's sudden recovery will be considered a miracle, but I'm sure all his memories will come back to you in time."

Darian cast a devilish glance at Emily, then went around to the driver's side of the Jeep, too. Adrian paled and looked nervous, but Darian held out his hand for the key. "There's one other thing I remember. . . ."

Adrian's eyes narrowed to slits. "What's that?"

"How to drive."

Emily choked back a squeal. "I'd hoped to teach you that myself. Slowly, over time. . . . Darian, I don't think you should just start driving, especially not in rush hour."

Darian seated himself behind the wheel and waited for the others to get in. Cora whispered a silent prayer, then placed her baby in its carseat. She climbed in beside her son. Adrian hesitated, groaned, then got in beside Cora.

Emily stood outside the passenger's side. He could shoot, ride, hold up a coach and find a trunkload of gold, even die without dying. But drive. . . ?

Darian reached over to shove open her door. He smiled up at her, blue eyes twinkling with the pure joy of life, and the everlasting depth of love. Emily bit her lip. "Are you *sure* you can drive?"

His bright eyes glittered and he smiled. She waited for him to convince her, to offer proof that he knew what he was doing. But instead, he whispered one word, and that word was all she needed.

"Trust."

Emily climbed in beside him, and Darian Woodward drove them home.

AUTHOR'S NOTE

Dear Reader,

I hope you enjoyed *Blue-Eyed Bandit*. I had a lovely time wandering around Arizona hunting up sites for Darian to hide his gang, and came up with the delightful and fascinating Colossal Caves near Tucson. You can visit the caves in person, or online at http://www.colossalcave.com/.

I've loved the Southwest so much that I'm headed back for my next book. *Renegade* is a historical romance about a bold and daring hero in black. When he is captured and blamed for the murder of a cavalry officer, his loyal band of misfit followers hold up a train to free him, and end up capturing the officer's widow in the process . . . *Renegade* should arrive in bookstores in February of 2001.

You can write to me at: P.O. Box 1305, Suite 194, Brunswick, ME 04011, or e-mail stobie@midcoast.com. My new website contains updated information on upcoming books as well as other fun stuff, and can be found at: http://www.stobiepiel.com. I look forward to hearing from you!

—Stobie Piel

FREE FALLING
STOBIE PIEL

How did anyone talk her into jumping out of a plane strapped to a man? And why didn't anyone tell her that man was going to be her wildly handsome ex-boyfriend Adrian de Vargas? Cora Talmadge never thought she'd see him again, especially not at ten thousand feet—but their "chance" encounter turns out to be the least of her worries. When she and Adrian are sidetracked by a mysterious whirlwind and tossed into nineteenth-century Arizona, extraordinary measures are called for. Unfortunately, she isn't quite sure that she is the woman to perform them. Lost in a world without phones, cars, or even Scottsdale, Cora wonders if their renewed romance can truly weather the storm, or if their love is destined to vanish with the wind.

___52329-9 $5.50 US/$6.50 CAN

THE WHITE SUN

STOBIE PIEL

Sierra of Nirvahda has never known love. But with her long dark tresses and shining eyes she has inspired plenty of it, only to turn away with a tuneless heart. Yet when she finds herself hiding deep within a cavern on the red planet of Tseir, her heart begins to do strange things. For with her in the cave is Arnoth of Valenwood, the sound of his lyre reaching out to her through the dark and winding passageways. His song speaks to her of yearnings, an ache she will come to know when he holds her body close to his, with the rhythm of their hearts beating for the memory and melody of their souls.

___52292-6 $5.50 US/$6.50 CAN

Dorchester Publishing Co., Inc.
P.O. Box 6640
Wayne, PA 19087-8640

Please add $1.75 for shipping and handling for the first book and $.50 for each book thereafter. NY, NYC, and PA residents, please add appropriate sales tax. No cash, stamps, or C.O.D.s. All orders shipped within 6 weeks via postal service book rate. Canadian orders require $2.00 extra postage and must be paid in U.S. dollars through a U.S. banking facility.

Name_____
Address_____
City_____ State_____ Zip_____
I have enclosed $_____ in payment for the checked book(s).
Payment <u>must</u> accompany all orders. ❏ Please send a free catalog.
     CHECK OUT OUR WEBSITE! www.dorchesterpub.com

The Midnight Moon — Stobie Piel

Dane Calydon knows there is more to the mysterious Aiyana than meets the eye, but when he removes her protective wrappings, he is unprepared for what he uncovers: a woman beautiful beyond his wildest imaginings. Though she claimed to be an amphibious creature, he was seduced by her sweet voice, and now, with her standing before him, he is powerless to resist her perfect form. Yet he knows she is more than a mere enchantress, for he has glimpsed her healing, caring side. But as secrets from her past overshadow their happiness, Dane realizes he must lift the veil of darkness surrounding her before she can surrender both body and soul to his tender kisses.

___52268-3 $5.50 US/$6.50 CAN

Dorchester Publishing Co., Inc.
P.O. Box 6640
Wayne, PA 19087-8640

Please add $1.75 for shipping and handling for the first book and $.50 for each book thereafter. NY, NYC, and PA residents, please add appropriate sales tax. No cash, stamps, or C.O.D.s. All orders shipped within 6 weeks via postal service book rate. Canadian orders require $2.00 extra postage and must be paid in U.S. dollars through a U.S. banking facility.

Name_____

Address_____

City_____State_____Zip_____

I have enclosed $_____ in payment for the checked book(s).

Payment <u>must</u> accompany all orders. ❑ Please send a free catalog.

CHECK OUT OUR WEBSITE! www.dorchesterpub.com